NANCY KRESS

illustrations by jane walker

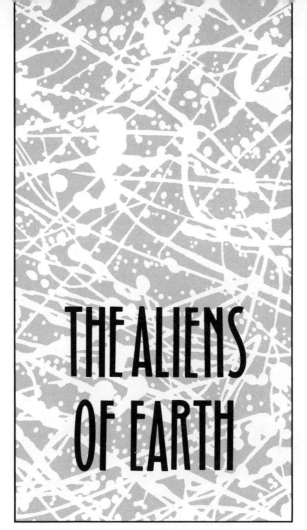

THE ALIENS OF EARTH

H

c.2

arkham house publishers, inc.

LIBRARY OF CONGRESS CATALOGING–IN–PUBLICATION DATA
Kress, Nancy.
    The aliens of Earth / Nancy Kress ; illustrations by Jane Walker.
 — 1st ed.
        p.   cm.
    ISBN 0-87054-166-8 (acid-free paper)
    1. Fantastic fiction, American.   I. Title.
PS3561.R46A64   1993
813'.54 — dc20   93-12450

FOR KEVIN AND BRIAN
WHO ARE THE FUTURE

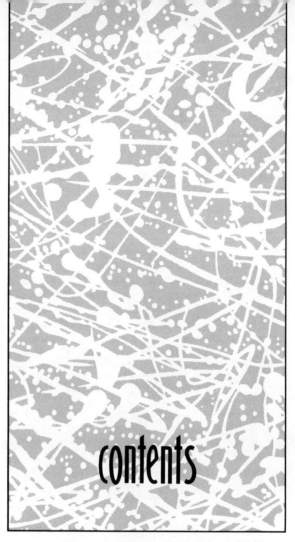

contents

CONTENTS

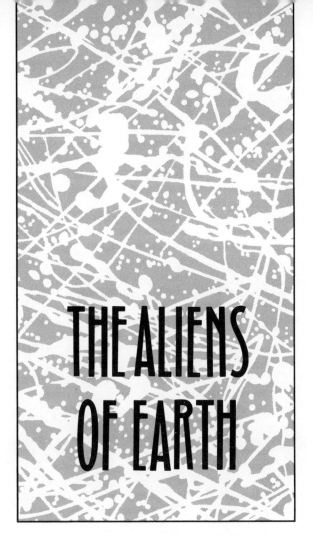

THE ALIENS
OF EARTH

the price of oranges

I'M WORRIED about my granddaughter," Harry Kramer said, passing half of his sandwich to Manny Feldman. Manny took it eagerly. The sandwich was huge, thick slices of beef and horseradish between fresh slabs of crusty bread. Pigeons watched the park bench hopefully.

"Jackie. The granddaughter who writes books," Manny said. Harry watched to see that Manny ate. You couldn't trust Manny to eat enough; he stayed too skinny. At least in Harry's opinion. Manny, Jackie—the world, Harry sometimes thought, had all grown too skinny when he somehow hadn't been looking. Skimpy. Stretch-feeling. Harry nodded to see horseradish spurt in a satisfying stream down Manny's scraggly beard.

"Jackie. Yes," Harry said.

"So what's wrong with her? She's sick?" Manny eyed Harry's strudel, cherry with real yeast bread. Harry passed it to him. "Harry, the whole thing? I couldn't."

"Take it, take it, I don't want it. You should eat. No, she's not sick. She's miserable." When Manny, his mouth full of strudel, didn't answer, Harry put a hand on Manny's arm. *"Miserable."*

Manny swallowed hastily. "How do you know? You saw her this week?"

"No. Next Tuesday. She's bringing me a book by a friend of hers. I know from this." He drew a magazine from an inner pocket of his coat. The coat was thick tweed, almost new, with wooden buttons. On the cover of the glossy magazine a woman smiled contemptuously. A woman with hollow starved-looking cheeks who obviously didn't get enough to eat either.

"That's not a book," Manny pointed out.

"So she writes stories, too. Listen to this. Just listen. 'I stood in my backyard, surrounded by the false bright toxin-fed green, and realized that the earth was dead. What else could it be, since we humans swarmed upon it like maggots on carrion, growing our hectic gleaming molds, leaving our slime trails across the senseless surface?' Does that sound like a happy woman?"

"Hoo boy," Manny said.

"It's all like that. 'Don't read my things, Popsy,' she says. 'You're not in the audience for my things.' Then she smiles without ever once showing her teeth." Harry flung both arms wide. "Who else should be in the audience but her own grandfather?"

Manny swallowed the last of the strudel. Pigeons fluttered angrily. "She never shows her teeth when she smiles? Never?"

"Never."

"Hoo boy," Manny said. "Did you want all of that orange?"

"No, I brought it for you, to take home. But did you finish that whole half a sandwich already?"

"I thought I'd take it home," Manny said humbly. He showed Harry the tip of the sandwich, wrapped in thick brown butcher paper, protruding from the pocket of his old coat.

Harry nodded approvingly. "Good, good. Take the orange, too. I brought it for you."

Manny took the orange. Three teenagers carrying huge shriek-ing radios sauntered past. Manny started to put his hands over his ears, received a look of dangerous contempt from the teenager with green hair, and put his hands on his lap. The kid tossed an empty beer bottle onto the pavement before their feet. It shattered. Harry scowled fiercely, but Manny stared straight ahead. When the cacophony had passed, Manny said, "Thank you for the orange. Fruit, it costs so much this time of year."

Harry still scowled. "Not in 1937."

"Don't start that again, Harry."

Harry said sadly, "Why won't you ever believe me? Could I af-ford to bring all this food if I got it at 1989 prices? Could I afford this coat? Have you seen buttons like this in 1989, on a new coat? Have you seen sandwiches wrapped in that kind of paper since we were young? Have you? Why won't you believe me?"

Manny slowly peeled his orange. The rind was pale, and the orange had seeds. "Harry. Don't start."

"But why won't you just come to my room and *see*?"

Manny sectioned the orange. "Your room. A cheap furnished room in a Social Security hotel. Why should I go? I know what will be there. What will be there is the same thing in my room. A bed, a chair, a table, a hot plate, some cans of food. Better I should meet you here in the park, get at least a little fresh air." He looked at Harry meekly, the orange clutched in one hand. "Don't misunder-stand. It's not from a lack of friendship I say this. You're good to me, you're the best friend I have. You bring me things from a great deli, you talk to me, you share with me the family I don't have. It's enough, Harry. It's *more* than enough. I don't need to see where you live like I live."

Harry gave it up. There were moods, times, when it was just impossible to budge Manny. He dug in, and in he stayed. "Eat your orange."

"It's a good orange. So tell me more about Jackie."

"Jackie." Harry shook his head. Two kids on bikes tore along the path. One of them swerved toward Manny and snatched the orange from his hand. "Aw riggghhhtttt!"

Harry scowled after the child. It had been a girl. Manny just wiped the orange juice off his fingers onto the knee of his pants. "Is everything she writes so depressing?"

"Everything," Harry said. "Listen to this one." He drew out another magazine, smaller, bound in rough paper with a stylized linen drawing of a woman's private parts on the cover. On the cover! Harry held the magazine with one palm spread wide over the drawing, which made it difficult to keep the pages open while he read. " 'She looked at her mother in the only way possible: with contempt, contempt for all the betrayal and compromises that had been her mother's life, for the sad soft lines of defeat around her mother's mouth, for the bright artificial dress too young for her wasted years, for even the leather handbag, Gucci of course, filled with blood money for having sold her life to a man who had long since ceased to want it.' "

"Hoo boy," Manny said. "About a *mother* she wrote that?"

"About everybody. All the time."

"And where is Barbara?"

"Reno again. Another divorce." How many had that been? After two, did anybody count? Harry didn't count. He imagined Barbara's life as a large roulette wheel like the ones on TV, little silver men bouncing in and out of red-and-black pockets. Why didn't she get dizzy?

Manny said slowly, "I always thought there was a lot of love in her."

"A lot of that she's got," Harry said dryly.

"Not Barbara—Jackie. A lot of . . . I don't know. Sweetness. Under the way she is."

"The way she is," Harry said gloomily. "Prickly. A cactus. But you're right, Manny, I know what you mean. She just needs someone to soften her up. Love her back, maybe. Although *I* love her."

The two old men looked at each other. Manny said, "Harry . . ."

"I know, I know. I'm only a grandfather, my love doesn't count, I'm just there. Like air. 'You're wonderful, Popsy,' she says, and still no teeth when she smiles. But you know, Manny—you are right!" Harry jumped up from the bench. "You are! What she needs is a young man to love her!"

Manny looked alarmed. "I didn't say—"

"I don't know why I didn't think of it before!"

"Harry—"

"And her stories, too! Full of ugly murders, ugly places, unhappy endings. What she needs is something to show her that writing could be about sweetness, too."

Manny was staring at him hard. Harry felt a rush of affection. That Manny should have the answer! Skinny wonderful Manny!

Manny said slowly, "Jackie said to me, 'I write about reality.' That's what she said, Harry."

"So there's no sweetness in reality? Put sweetness in her life, her writing will go sweet. She *needs* this, Manny. A really nice fellow!"

Two men in jogging suits ran past. One of their Reeboks came down on a shard of beer bottle. "Every fucking time!" he screamed, bending over to inspect his shoe. "Fucking park!"

"Well, what do you expect?" the other drawled, looking at Manny and Harry. "Although you'd think that if we could clean up Lake Erie. . . ."

"Fucking derelicts!" the other snarled. They jogged away.

"Of course," Harry said, "it might not be easy to find the sort of guy to convince Jackie."

"Harry, I think you should maybe think—"

"Not here," Harry said suddenly. "Not here. *There*. In 1937."

"*Harry* . . ."

"Yeah," Harry said, nodding several times. Excitement filled him like light, like electricity. What an idea! "It was different then."

Manny said nothing. When he stood up, the sleeve of his coat exposed the number tattooed on his wrist. He said quietly, "It was no paradise in 1937 either, Harry."

Harry seized Manny's hand. "I'm going to do it, Manny. Find someone for her there. Bring him here."

Manny sighed. "Tomorrow at the chess club, Harry? At one o'clock? It's Tuesday."

"I'll tell you then how I'm coming with this."

"Fine, Harry. Fine. All my wishes go with you. You know that."

Harry stood up too, still holding Manny's hand. A middle-aged man staggered to the bench and slumped onto it. The smell of whiskey rose from him in waves. He eyed Manny and Harry with scorn. "Fucking fags."

"Good night, Harry."

"Manny—if you'd only come . . . money goes so much farther there. . . ."

"Tomorrow at one. At the chess club."

Harry watched his friend walk away. Manny's foot dragged a little; the knee must be bothering him again. Harry wished Manny would see a doctor. Maybe a doctor would know why Manny stayed so skinny.

Harry walked back to his hotel. In the lobby, old men slumped in upholstery thin from wear, burned from cigarettes, shiny in the seat from long sitting. Sitting and sitting, Harry thought—

life measured by the seat of the pants. And now it was getting dark. No one would go out from here until the next daylight. Harry shook his head.

The elevator wasn't working again. He climbed the stairs to the third floor. Halfway there, he stopped, felt in his pocket, counted five quarters, six dimes, two nickels, and eight pennies. He returned to the lobby. "Could I have two dollar bills for this change, please? Maybe old bills?"

The clerk looked at him suspiciously. "Your rent paid up?"

"Certainly," Harry said. The woman grudgingly gave him the money.

"Thank you. You look very lovely today, Mrs. Raduski." Mrs. Raduski snorted.

In his room, Harry looked for his hat. He finally found it under his bed—how had it gotten under his bed? He dusted it off and put it on. It had cost him $3.25. He opened the closet door, parted the clothes hanging from their metal pole—like Moses parting the sea, he always thought, a Moses come again—and stepped to the back of the closet, remembering with his body rather than his mind the sharp little twist to the right just past the far gray sleeve of his good wool suit.

He stepped out into the bare corner of a warehouse. Cobwebs brushed his hat; he had stepped a little too far right. Harry crossed the empty concrete space to where the lumber stacks started, and threaded his way through them. The lumber, too, was covered with cobwebs; not much building going on. On his way out the warehouse door, Harry passed the night watchman coming on duty.

"Quiet all day, Harry?"

"As a church, Rudy," Harry said. Rudy laughed. He laughed a lot. He was also indisposed to question very much. The first time he had seen Harry coming out of the warehouse in a bemused daze, he must have assumed that Harry had been hired to work there. Peering at Rudy's round vacant face, Harry realized that he must hold this job because he was someone's uncle, someone's cousin, someone's something. Harry had felt a small glow of approval; families should take care of their own. He had told Rudy that he had lost his key and asked him for another.

Outside it was late afternoon. Harry began walking. Eventually there were people walking past him, beside him, across the street from him. Everybody wore hats. The women wore bits of velvet or wool with dotted veils across their noses and long graceful dresses in small prints. The men wore fedoras with suits as baggy as Harry's. When he reached the park there were children, girls in long black tights and hard shoes, boys in buttoned shirts. Everyone looked like it was Sunday morning.

Pushcarts and shops lined the sidewalks. Harry bought a pair of socks, thick gray wool, for eighty-nine cents. When the man took his dollar, Harry held his breath: each first time made a little pip in his stomach. But no one ever looked at the dates of old bills. He bought two oranges for five cents each, and then, thinking of Manny, bought a third. At a candy store he bought *G-8 and His Battle Aces* for fifteen cents. At The Collectors' Cozy in the other time they would gladly give him thirty dollars for it. Finally, he bought a cherry Coke for a nickel and headed toward the park.

"Oh, excuse me," said a young man who bumped into Harry on the sidewalk. "I'm so sorry!" Harry looked at him hard: but, no. Too young. Jackie was twenty-eight.

Some children ran past, making for the movie theater. Spencer Tracy in *Captains Courageous*. Harry sat down on a green-painted wooden bench under a pair of magnificent Dutch elms. On the bench lay a newsmagazine. Harry glanced at it to see when in September this was: the twenty-eighth. The cover pictured a young blond Nazi soldier standing at stiff salute. Harry thought again of Manny, frowned, and turned the magazine cover down.

For the next hour, people walked past. Harry studied them carefully. When it got too dark to see, he walked back to the warehouse, on the way buying an apple kuchen at a bakery with a curtain behind the counter looped back to reveal a man in his shirtsleeves eating a plate of stew at a table bathed in soft yellow lamplight. The kuchen cost thirty-two cents.

At the warehouse, Harry let himself in with his key, slipped past Rudy nodding over *Paris Nights,* and walked to his cobwebby corner. He emerged from his third-floor closet into his room. Beyond the window, sirens wailed and would not stop.

"So how's it going?" Manny asked. He dripped kuchen crumbs on the chessboard; Harry brushed them away. Manny had him down a knight.

"It's going to take time to find somebody that's right," Harry said. "I'd like to have someone by next Tuesday when I meet Jackie for dinner, but I don't know. It's not easy. There are requirements. He has to be young enough to be attractive, but old enough to understand Jackie. He has to be sweet-natured enough to do her some good, but strong enough not to panic at jumping over fifty-two years. Somebody educated. An educated man—he might be more curious than upset by my closet. Don't you think?"

"Better watch your queen," Manny said, moving his rook. "So how are you going to find him?"

"It takes time," Harry said. "I'm working on it."

Manny shook his head. "You have to get somebody here, you have to convince him he *is* here, you have to keep him from turning right around and running back in time through your shirts. . . . I don't know, Harry. I don't know. I've been thinking. This thing is not simple. What if you did something wrong? Took somebody important out of 1937?"

"I won't pick anybody important."

"What if you made a mistake and brought your own grandfather? And something happened to him here?"

"My grandfather was already dead in 1937."

"What if you brought me? I'm already here."

"You didn't live here in 1937."

"What if you brought *you?*"

"I didn't live here either."

"What if you. . . ."

"Manny," Harry said, "I'm not bringing somebody important. I'm not bringing somebody we know. I'm not bringing somebody for permanent. I'm just bringing a nice guy for Jackie to meet, go dancing, see a different kind of nature. A different view of what's possible. An innocence. I'm sure there are fellows here that would do it, but I don't know any, and I don't know how to bring any to her. From there I know. Is this so complicated? Is this so unpredictable?"

"Yes," Manny said. He had on his stubborn look again. How could somebody so skimpy look so stubborn? Harry sighed and moved his lone knight.

"I brought you some whole socks."

"Thank you. That knight, it's not going to help you much."

"Lectures. That's what there was there that there isn't here. Everybody went to lectures. No TV, movies cost money, they went to free lectures."

"I remember," Manny said. "I was a young man myself. Harry, this thing is not simple."

"Yes, it is," Harry said stubbornly.

"Nineteen thirty-seven was not simple."

"It will work, Manny."

"Check," Manny said.

That evening, Harry went back. This time it was the afternoon of September 16. On newsstands the *New York Times* announced that President Roosevelt and John L. Lewis had talked pleasantly at the White House. Cigarettes cost thirteen cents a pack. Women wore cotton stockings and clunky high-heeled shoes. Schrafft's best chocolates were sixty cents a pound. Small boys addressed Harry as "sir."

He attended six lectures in two days. A Madame Trefania lectured on theosophy to a hall full of badly dressed women with thin, pursed lips. A union organizer roused an audience to a pitch that made Harry leave after the first thirty minutes. A skinny, nervous missionary showed slides of religious outposts in China. An archaeologist back from a Mexican dig gave a dry impatient talk about temples to an audience of three people. A New Deal Democrat spoke passionately about aiding the poor, but afterward addressed all the women present as "Sister." Finally, just when Harry was starting to feel discouraged, he found it.

A museum offered a series of lectures on "Science of Today — and Tomorrow." Harry heard a slim young man with a reddish beard speak with idealistic passion about travel to the moon, the planets, the stars. It seemed to Harry that compared to stars, 1989 might seem reasonably close. The young man had warm hazel eyes and a sense of humor. When he spoke about life in a spaceship, he mentioned in passing that women would be freed from much domestic drudgery they now endured. Throughout the lecture, he smoked, lighting cigarettes with a masculine squinting of eyes and cupping of hands. He said that imagination was the human quality that would most help people adjust to the future. His shoes were polished.

But most of all, Harry thought, he had a *glow*. A fine golden Boy Scout glow that made Harry think of old covers for the *Saturday Evening Post*. Which here cost five cents.

After the lecture, Harry stayed in his chair in the front row, outwaiting even the girl with bright red lipstick who lingered around the lecturer, this Robert Gernshon. From time to time, Gernshon glanced over at Harry with quizzical interest. Finally the girl, red lips pouting, sashayed out of the hall.

"Hello," Harry said. "I'm Harry Kramer. I enjoyed your talk. I have something to show you that you would be very interested in."

The hazel eyes turned wary. "Oh, no, no," Harry said. "Something *scientific*. Here, look at this." He handed Gernshon a filtered Vantage Light.

"How long it is," Gernshon said. "What's this made of?"

"The filter? It's made of . . . a new filter material. Tastes milder and cuts down on the nicotine. Much better for you. Look at this." He gave Gernshon a Styrofoam cup from McDonald's. "It's made of a new material, too. Very cheap. Disposable."

Gernshon fingered the cup. "Who are you?" he said quietly.

"A scientist. I'm interested in the science of tomorrow, too. Like you. I'd like to invite you to see my laboratory, which is in my home."

"In your home?"

"Yes. In a small way. Just dabbling, you know." Harry could feel himself getting rattled; the young hazel eyes stared at him so steadily. *Jackie*, he thought. Dead earths. Maggots and carrion. Contempt for mothers. What would Gernshon say? When would Gernshon say *anything*?

"Thank you," Gernshon finally said. "When would be convenient?"

"Now?" Harry said. He tried to remember what time of day it was now. All he could picture was lecture halls.

Gernshon came. It was 9:30 in the evening of Friday, September 17. Harry walked Gernshon through the streets, trying to talk animatedly, trying to distract. He said that he himself was very interested in travel to the stars. He said it had always been his dream to stand on another planet and take in great gulps of completely unpolluted air. He said his great heroes were those biologists who made that twisty model of DNA. He said science had been his life. Gernshon walked more and more silently.

"Of course," Harry said hastily, "like most scientists, I'm mostly familiar with my own field. You know how it is."

"What is your field, Dr. Kramer?" Gernshon asked quietly.

"Electricity," Harry said, and hit him on the back of the head with a solid brass candlestick from the pocket of his coat. The candlestick had cost him three dollars at a pawnshop.

They had walked past the stores and pushcarts to a point where the locked business offices and warehouses began. There were no passersby, no muggers, no street dealers, no Guardian Angels, no punk gangs. Only him, hitting an unarmed man with a candlestick.

He was no better than the punks. But what else could he do? What else could he *do?* Nothing but hit him softly, so softly that Gernshon was struggling again almost before Harry got his hands and feet tied, well before he got on the blindfold and gag. "I'm sorry, I'm sorry," he kept saying to Gernshon. Gernshon did not look as if the apology made any difference. Harry dragged him into the warehouse.

Rudy was asleep over *Spicy Stories.* Breathing very hard, Harry pulled the young man—not more than 150 pounds, it was good Harry had looked for slim—to the far corner, through the gate, and into his closet.

"Listen," he said urgently to Gernshon after removing the gag. "Listen. I can call the Medicare Emergency Hotline. If your head feels broken. Are you feeling faint? Do you think you maybe might go into shock?"

Gernshon lay on Harry's rug, glaring at him, saying nothing.

"Listen, I know this is maybe a little startling to you. But I'm not a pervert, not a cop, not anything but a grandfather with a problem. My granddaughter. I need your help to solve it, but I won't take much of your time. You're now somewhere besides where you gave your lecture. A pretty long ways away. But you don't have to stay here long, I promise. Just two weeks, tops, and I'll send you back. I promise, on my mother's grave. And I'll make it worth your while. I promise."

"Untie me."

"Yes. Of course. Right away. Only you have to not attack me, because I'm the only one who can get you back from here." He had a sudden inspiration. "I'm like a foreign consul. You've maybe traveled abroad?"

Gernshon looked around the dingy room. "Untie me."

"I will. In two minutes. Five, tops. I just want to explain a little first."

"Where am I?"

"Nineteen eighty-nine."

Gernshon said nothing. Harry explained brokenly, talking as fast as he could, saying he could move from 1989 to September 1937 when he wanted to, but he could take Gernshon back too, no problem. He said he made the trip often, it was perfectly safe. He pointed out how much further a small Social Security check, no pension, could go at 1937 prices. He mentioned Manny's strudel. Only lightly did he touch on the problem of Jackie, figuring there would be a better time to share domestic difficulties, and his closet he didn't mention at all. It was hard to keep his eyes averted from the closet door. He did mention how bitter people could be in 1989, how lost, how weary from expecting so much that nothing was a delight, nothing a sweet surprise. He was just working up to a tirade on innocence when Gernshon said again, in a different tone, "Untie me."

"Of course," Harry said quickly, "I don't expect you to believe me. Why should you think you're in 1989? Go, see for yourself. Look at that light, it's still early morning. Just be careful out there, is all." He untied Gernshon and stood with his eyes squeezed shut, waiting.

When nothing hit him, Harry opened his eyes. Gernshon was at the door. "Wait!" Harry cried. "You'll need more money!" He dug into his pocket and pulled out a twenty-dollar bill, carefully saved for this, and all the change he had.

Gernshon examined the coins carefully, then looked up at Harry. He said nothing. He opened the door and Harry, still trembling, sat down in his chair to wait.

Gernshon came back three hours later, pale and sweating. "My God!"

"I know just what you mean," Harry said. "A zoo out there. Have a drink."

Gernshon took the mixture Harry had ready in his toothbrush glass and gulped it down. He caught sight of the bottle, which Harry had left on the dresser: Seagram's V.O., with the cluttered tiny-print label. He threw the glass across the room and covered his face with his hands.

"I'm sorry," Harry said apologetically. "But then it cost only three dollars thirty-seven cents the fifth."

Gernshon didn't move.

"I'm really sorry," Harry said. He raised both hands, palms up, and dropped them helplessly. "Would you . . . would you maybe like an orange?"

Gernshon recovered faster than Harry had dared hope. Within an hour he was sitting in Harry's worn chair, asking questions about the space shuttle; within two hours taking notes; within three become again the intelligent and captivating young man of the lecture hall. Harry, answering as much as he could as patiently as he could, was impressed by the boy's resilience. It couldn't have been easy. What if he, Harry, suddenly had to skip fifty-two more years? What if he found himself in 2041? Harry shuddered.

"Do you know that a movie now costs six dollars?"

Gernshon blinked. "We were talking about the moon landing."

"Not anymore we're not. I want to ask *you* some questions, Robert. Do you think the earth is dead, with people sliming all over it like on carrion? Is this a thought that crosses your mind?"

"I . . . no."

Harry nodded. "Good, good. Do you look at your mother with contempt?"

"Of course not. Harry—"

"No, it's my turn. Do you think a woman who marries a man, and maybe the marriage doesn't work out perfect, whose does, but they raise at least one healthy child—say a daughter—that that woman's life has been a defeat and a failure?"

"No. I—"

"What would you think if you saw a drawing of a woman's private parts on the cover of a magazine?"

Gernshon blushed. He looked as if the blush annoyed him, but also as if he couldn't help it.

"Better and better," Harry said. "Now, think carefully on this next one—take your time—no hurry. Does reality seem to you to have sweetness in it as well as ugliness? Take your time."

Gernshon peered at him. Harry realized they had talked right through lunch. "But not all the time in the world, Robert."

"Yes," Gernshon said. "I think reality has more sweetness than ugliness. And more strangeness than anything else. Very much more." He looked suddenly dazed. "I'm sorry, I just—all this has happened so—"

"Put your head between your knees," Harry suggested. "There—better now? Good. There's someone I want you to meet."

Manny sat in the park, on their late-afternoon bench. When he saw them coming, his face settled into long sorrowful ridges. "Harry. Where have you been for two days? I was worried, I went to your hotel—"

"Manny," Harry said, "this is Robert."

"So I see," Manny said. He didn't hold out his hand.

"*Him,*" Harry said.

"Harry. Oh, Harry."

"How do you do, sir," Gernshon said. He held out his hand. "I'm afraid I didn't get your full name. I'm Robert Gernshon."

Manny looked at him—at the outstretched hand, the baggy suit with wide tie, the deferential smile, the golden Baden-Powell glow. Manny's lips mouthed a silent word: *sir?*

"I have a lot to tell you," Harry said.

"You can tell all of us, then," Manny said. "Here comes Jackie now."

Harry looked up. Across the park a woman in jeans strode purposefully toward them. "Manny! It's only Monday!"

"I called her to come," Manny said. "You've been gone from your room two days, Harry, nobody at your hotel could say where—"

"But *Manny*," Harry said, while Gernshon looked, frowning, from one to the other and Jackie spotted them and waved.

She had lost more weight, Harry saw. Only two weeks, yet her cheeks had hollowed out and new, tiny lines touched her eyes. Skinny lines. They filled him with sadness. Jackie wore a blue T-shirt that said LIFE IS A BITCH—THEN YOU DIE. She carried a magazine and a small can of mace disguised as hair spray.

"Popsy! You're here! Manny said—"

"Manny was wrong," Harry said. "Jackie, sweetheart, you look— it's good to see you. Jackie, I'd like you to meet somebody, darling. This is Robert. My friend. My friend Robert. Jackie Snyder."

"Hi," Jackie said. She gave Harry a hug, and then Manny one. Harry saw Gernshon gazing at her very tight jeans.

"Robert's a . . . a scientist," Harry said.

It was the wrong thing to say; Harry knew the moment he said it that it was the wrong thing. Science—all science—was, for some reason not completely clear to him, a touchy subject with Jackie. She tossed her long hair back from her eyes. "Oh, yeah? Not *chemical*, I hope?"

"I'm not actually a scientist," Gernshon said winningly. "Just a dabbler. I popularize new scientific concepts, write about them to make them intelligible."

"Like what?" Jackie said.

Gernshon opened his mouth, closed it again. A boy suddenly flashed past on a skateboard, holding a boombox. Metallica blasted the air. Overhead, a jet droned. Gernshon smiled weakly. "It's hard to explain."

"I'm capable of understanding," Jackie said coldly. "Women *can* understand science, you know."

"Jackie, sweetheart," Harry said, "what have you got there? Is that your new book?"

"No," Jackie said, "this is the one I said I'd bring you, by my friend. It's brilliant. It's about a man whose business partner betrays him by selling out to organized crime and framing the man. In jail he meets a guy who has founded his own religion, the House of Divine Despair, and when they both get out they start a new business, Suicide Incorporated, that helps people kill themselves for a fee. The whole thing is just a brilliant denunciation of contemporary America."

Gernshon made a small sound.

"It's a comedy," Jackie added.

"It sounds . . . it sounds a little depressing," Gernshon said.

Jackie looked at him. Very distinctly, she said, "It's reality."

Harry saw Gernshon glance around the park. A man nodded on a bench, his hands slack on his knees. Newspapers and McDonald's wrappers stirred fitfully in the dirt. A trash container had been knocked over. From beside a scrawny tree enclosed shoulder-height by black wrought iron, a child watched them with old eyes.

"I brought you something else, too, Popsy," Jackie said. Harry hoped that Gernshon noticed how much gentler her voice was when she spoke to her grandfather. "A scarf. See, it's llama wool. Very warm."

Gernshon said, "My mother has a scarf like that. No, I guess hers is some kind of fur."

Jackie's face changed. "What kind?"

"I—I'm not sure."

"Not an endangered species, I hope."

"No. Not that. I'm sure not . . . that."

Jackie stared at him a moment longer. The child who had been watching strolled toward them. Harry saw Gernshon look at the boy with relief. About eleven years old, he wore a perfectly tailored suit and Italian shoes. Manny shifted to put himself between the boy and Gernshon. "Jackie, darling, it's so good to see you. . . ."

The boy brushed by Gernshon on the other side. He never looked up, and his voice stayed boyish and low, almost a whisper. "Crack . . ."

"Step on one and you break your mother's back," Gernshon said brightly. He smiled at Harry, a special conspiratorial smile to suggest that children, at least, didn't change in fifty years. The boy's head jerked up to look at Gernshon.

"You talking about my mama?"

Jackie groaned. "No," she said to the kid. "He doesn't mean anything. Beat it."

"I don't forget," the boy said. He backed away slowly.

Gernshon said, frowning, "I'm sorry. I'm not sure exactly what all that was, but I'm sorry."

"Are you for real?" Jackie said angrily. "What the fucking hell *was* all that? Don't you realize this park is the only place Manny and my grandfather can get some fresh air?"

"I didn't—"

"That punk runner meant it when he said he won't forget!"

"I don't like your tone," Gernshon said. "Or your language."

"My language!" The corners of Jackie's mouth tightened. Manny looked at Harry and put his hands over his face. The boy, twenty feet away, suddenly let out a noise like a strangled animal, so piercing all four of them spun around. Two burly teenagers were running toward him. The child's face crumpled; he looked suddenly much younger. He sprang away, stumbled, made the noise again, and hurled himself, all animal terror, toward the street behind the park bench.

"No!" Gernshon shouted. Harry turned toward the shout, but Gernshon already wasn't there. Harry saw the twelve-wheeler bearing down, heard Jackie's scream, saw Gernshon's wiry body barrel into the boy's. The truck shrieked past, its air brakes deafening.

Gernshon and the boy rose in the street on the other side.

Car horns blared. The boy bawled, "Leggo my suit! You tore my suit!" A red light flashed and a squad car pulled up. The two burly teenagers melted away, and then the boy somehow vanished as well.

"Never find him," the disgruntled cop told them over the clipboard on which he had written nothing. "Probably just as well." He went away.

"Are you hurt?" Manny said. It was the first time he had spoken. His face was ashen. Harry put a hand across his shoulders.

"No," Gernshon said. He gave Manny his sweet smile. "Just a little dirty."

"That took *guts*," Jackie said. She was staring at Gernshon with a frown between her eyebrows. "Why did you do it?"

"Pardon?"

"Why? I mean, given what that kid is, given—oh, all of it—" she gestured around the park, a helpless little wave of her strong young hands that tore at Harry's heart. "Why bother?"

Gernshon said gently, "What that kid is, is a kid."

Manny looked skeptical. Harry moved to stand in front of Manny's expression before anyone wanted to discuss it. "Listen,

I've got a wonderful idea, you two seem to have so much to talk about, about . . . bothering, and . . . everything. Why don't you have dinner together, on me? My treat." He pulled another twenty-dollar bill from his pocket. Behind him he could feel Manny start.

"Oh, I couldn't," Gernshon said, at the same moment that Jackie said warningly, "Popsy . . ."

Harry put his palms on both sides of her face. "Please. Do this for me, Jackie. Without the questions, without the female protests. Just this once. For me."

Jackie was silent a long moment before she grimaced, nodded, and turned with half-humorous appeal to Gernshon.

Gernshon cleared his throat. "Well, actually, it would probably be better if all four of us came. I'm embarrassed to say that prices are higher in this city than in . . . that is, I'm not able to . . . but if we went somewhere less expensive, the Automat maybe, I'm sure all four of us could eat together."

"No, no," Harry said. "We already ate." Manny looked at him.

Jackie began, offended, "I certainly don't want—just what do you think is going on here, buddy? This is just to please my grandfather. Are you afraid I might try to jump your bones?"

Harry saw Gernshon's quick involuntary glance at Jackie's tight jean. He saw, too, that Gernshon fiercely regretted the glance the instant he had made it. He saw that Manny saw, and that Jackie saw, and that Gernshon saw that they saw. Manny made a small noise. Jackie's face began to turn so black that Harry was astounded when Gernshon cut her off with a dignity no one had expected.

"No, of course not," he said quietly. "But I would prefer all of us to have dinner together for quite another reason. My wife is very dear to me, Miss Snyder, and I wouldn't do anything that might make her feel uncomfortable. That's probably irrational, but that's the way it is."

Harry stood arrested, his mouth open. Manny started to shake with what Harry thought savagely had better not be laughter. And Jackie, after staring at Gernshon a long while, broke into the most spontaneous smile Harry had seen from her in months.

"Hey," she said softly. "That's nice. That's really, genuinely, fucking nice."

The weather turned abruptly colder. Snow threatened but didn't fall. Each afternoon Harry and Manny took a quick walk in the park and then went inside, to the chess club or a coffee shop or the bus station or the library, where there was a table deep in the stacks on which they could eat lunch without detection. Harry brought Manny a poor boy with mayo, sixty-three cents, and a pair of imported wool gloves, one dollar on preseason sale.

"So where are they today?" Manny asked on Saturday, removing the gloves to peek at the inside of the poor boy. He sniffed appreciatively. "Horseradish. You remembered, Harry."

"The museum, I think," Harry said miserably.

"What museum?"

"How should I know? He says, 'The museum today, Harry,' and he's gone by eight o'clock in the morning, no more details than that."

Manny stopped chewing. "What museum opens at eight o'clock in the morning?"

Harry put down his sandwich, pastrami on rye, thirty-nine cents. He had lost weight the past week.

"Probably," Manny said hastily, "they just talk. You know, like young people do, just talk. . . ."

Harry eyed him balefully. "You mean like you and Leah did when you were young and left completely alone."

"You better talk to him soon, Harry. No, to her." He seemed to reconsider Jackie. "No, to *him.*"

"Talk isn't going to do it," Harry said. He looked pale and determined. "Gernshon has to be sent back."

"Be sent?"

"He's *married*, Manny! I wanted to help Jackie, show her life can hold some sweetness, not be all struggle. What kind of sweetness is she going to find if she falls in love with a married man? You know how that goes! Jackie—" Harry groaned. How had all this happened? He had intended only the best for Jackie. Why didn't that count more? "He has to go back, Manny."

"How?" Manny said practically. "You can't hit him again, Harry. You were just lucky last time that you didn't hurt him. You don't want that on your conscience. And if you show him your, uh . . . your—"

"My closet. Manny, if you'd only come see, for a dollar you could get—"

"—then he could just come back any time he wants. So how?"

A sudden noise startled them both. Someone was coming through the stacks. "Librarians!" Manny hissed. Both of them frantically swept the sandwiches, beer (fifteen cents), and strudel into shopping bags. Manny, panicking, threw in the wool gloves. Harry swept the table free of crumbs. When the intruder rounded the nearest bookshelf, Harry was bent over *Making Paper Flowers* and Manny over *Porcelain of the Yung Cheng Dynasty*. It was Robert Gernshon.

The young man dropped into a chair. His face was ashen. In one hand he clutched a sheaf of paper, the handwriting on the last one trailing off into shaky squiggles.

After a moment of silence, Manny said diplomatically, "So where are you coming from, Robert?"

"Where's Jackie?" Harry demanded.

"Jackie?" Gernshon said. His voice was thick; Harry realized with a sudden shock that he had been crying. "I haven't seen her for a few days."

"A few *days?*" Harry said.

"No. I've been . . . I've been. . . ."

Manny sat up straighter. He looked intently at Gernshon over *Porcelain of the Yung Cheng Dynasty* and then put the book down. He moved to the chair next to Gernshon's and gently took the papers from his hand. Gernshon leaned over the table and buried his head in his arms.

"I'm so awfully sorry, I'm being such a baby. . . ." His shoulders trembled. Manny separated the papers and spread them out on the library table. Among the hand-copied notes were two slim books, one bound between black covers and the other a pamphlet. *A Memoir of Auschwitz. Countdown to Hiroshima.*

For a long moment nobody spoke. Then Harry said, to no one in particular, "I thought he was going to science museums."

Manny laid his arm, almost casually, across Gernshon's shoulders. "So now you'll know not to be at either place. More people should have only known." Harry didn't recognize the expression on his friend's face, nor the voice with which Manny said to Harry, "You're right. He has to go back."

"But Jackie . . ."

"Can do without this 'sweetness,'" Manny said harshly. "So what's so terrible in her life anyway that she needs so much help? Is she dying? Is she poor? Is she ugly? Is anyone knocking on her door in the middle of the night? Let Jackie find her own sweetness. She'll survive."

Harry made a helpless gesture. Manny's stubborn face, carved wood under the harsh fluorescent light, did not change. "Even *him* . . . Manny, the things he knows now—"

"You should have thought of that earlier."

Gernshon looked up. "Don't, I—I'm sorry. It's just coming across it, I never thought human beings—"

"No," Manny said. "But they can. You been here, every day, at the library, reading it all?"

"Yes. That and museums. I saw you two come in earlier. I've been reading, I wanted to *know*—"

"So now you know," Manny said in that same surprisingly casual, tough voice. "You'll survive, too."

Harry said, "Does Jackie know what's going on? Why you've been doing all this . . . learning?"

"No."

"And you—what will you do with what you now know?"

Harry held his breath. What if Gernshon just refused to go back? Gernshon said slowly, "At first, I wanted to not return. At all. How can I watch it, World War II and the camps—I have *relatives* in Poland. And then later the bomb and Korea and the gulags and Vietnam and Cambodia and the terrorists and AIDS—"

"Didn't miss anything," Harry muttered.

"—and not be able to *do* anything, not be able to even hope, knowing that everything to come is already set into history—how could I watch all that without any hope that it isn't really as bad as it seems to be at the moment?"

"It all depends what you look at," Manny said, but Gernshon didn't seem to hear him.

"But neither can I stay, there's Susan and we're hoping for a baby . . . I need to think."

"No, you don't," Harry said. "You need to go *back*. This is all my mistake. I'm sorry. You need to go back, Gernshon."

"Lebanon," Gernshon said. "DDT. The Cultural Revolution. Nicaragua. Deforestation. Iran—"

"Penicillin," Manny said suddenly. His beard quivered. "Civil rights. Mahatma Gandhi. Polio vaccines. Washing machines." Harry stared at him, shocked. Could Manny once have worked in a hand laundry?

"Or," Manny said, more quietly, "Hitler. Auschwitz. Hoovervilles. The Dust Bowl. What you *look* at, Robert."

"I don't know," Gernshon said. "I need to think. There's so much . . . and then there's that girl."

Harry stiffened. "Jackie?"

"No, no. Someone she and I met a few days ago, at a coffee

shop. She just walked in. I couldn't believe it. I looked at her and just went into shock—and maybe she did too, for all I know. The girl looked exactly like me. And she *felt* like—I don't know. It's hard to explain. She felt like *me*. I said hello but I didn't tell her my name; I didn't dare." His voice fell to a whisper. "I think she's my granddaughter."

"Hoo boy," Manny said.

Gernshon stood. He made a move to gather up his papers and booklets, stopped, left them there. Harry stood, too, so abruptly that Gernshon shot him a sudden hard look across the library table. "Going to hit me again, Harry? Going to kill me?"

"Us?" Manny said. "Us, Robert?" His tone was gentle.

"In a way, you already have. I'm not who I was, certainly."

Manny shrugged. "So be somebody better."

"Damn it, I don't think you understand—"

"I don't think *you* do, Reuven, boychik. This is the way it *is*. That's all. Whatever you had back there, you have still. Tell me, in all that reading, did you find anything about yourself, anything personal? Are you in the history books, in the library papers?"

"The Office of Public Documents takes two weeks to do a search for birth and death certificates," Gernshon said, a little sulkily.

"So you lost nothing, because you really *know* nothing," Manny said. "Only history. History is cheap. Everybody gets some. You can have all the history you want. It's what you make of it that costs."

Gernshon didn't nod agreement. He looked a long time at Manny, and something moved behind the unhappy hazel eyes, something that made Harry finally let out a breath he didn't know he'd been holding. It suddenly seemed that Gernshon was the one that was old. And he *was*—with the fifty-two years he'd gained since last week, he was older than Harry had been in the 1937 of *Captains Courageous* and wide-brimmed fedoras and clean city parks. But that was the good time, the one that Gernshon was going back to, the one Harry himself would choose, if it weren't for Jackie and Manny . . . still, he couldn't watch as Gernshon walked out of the book stacks, parting the musty air as heavily as if it were water.

Gernshon paused. Over his shoulder he said, "I'll go back. Tonight. I will."

After he had left, Harry said, "This is my fault."

"Yes," Manny agreed.

"Will you come to my room when he goes? To . . . to help?"

"Yes, Harry."
Somehow, that only made it worse.

Gernshon agreed to a blindfold. Harry led him through the closet, the warehouse, the street. Neither of them seemed very good at this; they stumbled into each other, hesitated, tripped over nothing. In the warehouse Gernshon nearly walked into a pile of lumber, and in the sharp jerk Harry gave Gernshon's arm to deflect him, something twisted and gave way in Harry's back. He waited, bent over, behind a corner of a building while Gernshon removed his blindfold, blinked in the morning light, and walked slowly away.

Despite his back, Harry found that he couldn't return right away. Why not? He just couldn't. He waited until Gernshon had a large head start and then hobbled toward the park. A carousel turned, playing bright organ music: September 24. Two children he had never noticed before stood just beyond the carousel, watching it with hungry, hopeless eyes. Flowers grew in immaculate flower beds. A black man walked by, his eyes fixed on the sidewalk, his head bent. Two small girls jumping rope were watched by a smiling woman in a blue-and-white uniform. On the sidewalk, just beyond the carousel, someone had chalked a swastika. The black man shuffled over it. A Lincoln Zephyr V-12 drove by, $1090. There was no way it would fit through a closet.

When Harry returned, Manny was curled up on the white chenille bedspread that Harry had bought for $3.28, fast asleep.

"What did I accomplish, Manny? What?" Harry said bitterly. The day had dawned glorious and warm, unexpected Indian summer. Trees in the park showed bare branches against a bright blue sky. Manny wore an old red sweater, Harry a flannel workshirt. Harry shifted gingerly, grimacing, on his bench. Sunday strollers dropped ice-cream wrappers, cigarettes, newspapers, Diet Pepsi cans, used tissues, popcorn. Pigeons quarreled and children shrieked.

"Jackie's going to be just as hard as ever — and why not?" Harry continued. "She finally meets a nice fellow, he never calls her again. Me, I leave a young man miserable on a sidewalk. Before I leave him, I ruin his life. While I leave him, I ruin my back. *After* I leave him, I sit here guilty. There's no answer, Manny."

Manny didn't answer. He squinted down the curving path.

"I don't know, Manny. I just don't know."

Manny said suddenly, "Here comes Jackie."

Harry looked up. He squinted, blinked, tried to jump up. His back made sharp protest. He stayed where he was, and his eyes grew wide.

"Popsy!" Jackie cried. "I've been looking for you!"

She was radiant. All the lines were gone from around her eyes, all the sharpness from her face. Her very collarbones, Harry thought dazedly, looked softer. Happiness haloed her like light. She held the hand of a slim red-haired woman with strong features and direct hazel eyes.

"This is Ann," Jackie said. "I've been looking for you, Popsy, because . . . well, because I need to tell you something." She slid onto the bench next to Harry, on the other side from Manny, and put one arm around Harry's shoulders. The other hand kept a close grip on Ann, who smiled encouragement. Manny stared at Ann as at a ghost.

"You see, Popsy, for a while now I've been struggling with something, something really important. I know I've been snappy and difficult, but it hasn't been—everybody needs somebody to love, you've often told me that, and I know how happy you and Grammy were all those years. And I thought there would never be anything like that for me, and certain people were making everything all so hard. But now . . . well, now there's Ann. And I wanted you to know that."

Jackie's arm tightened. Her eyes pleaded. Ann watched Harry closely. He felt as if he were drowning.

"I know this must come as a shock to you," Jackie went on, "but I also know you've always wanted me to be happy. So I hope you'll come to love her the way I do."

Harry stared at the red-haired woman. He knew what was being asked of him, but he didn't believe in it, it wasn't real, in the same way weather going on in other countries wasn't really real. Hurricanes. Drought. Sunshine. When what you were looking at was a cold drizzle.

"I think that of all the people I've ever known, Ann is the most together. The most compassionate. And the most moral."

"Ummm," Harry said.

"Popsy?"

Jackie was looking right at him. The longer he was silent, the more her smile faded. It occurred to him that the smile had showed her teeth. They were very white, very even. Also very sharp.

"I . . . I . . . hello, Ann."

"Hello," Ann said.

"See, I told you he'd be great!" Jackie said to Ann. She let go of Harry and jumped up from the bench, all energy and lightness. "You're wonderful, Popsy! You, too, Manny! Oh, Ann, this is Popsy's best friend, Manny Feldman. Manny, Ann Davies."

"Happy to meet you," Ann said. She had a low rough voice and a sweet smile. Harry felt hurricanes, drought, sunshine.

Jackie said, "I know this is probably a little unexpected—"

Unexpected. "Well—" Harry said, and could say no more.

"It's just that it was time for me to come out of the closet."

Harry made a small noise. Manny managed to say, "So you live here, Ann?"

"Oh, yes. All my life. And my family, too, since forever."

"Has Jackie . . . has Jackie met any of them yet?"

"Not yet," Jackie said. "It might be a little . . . tricky, in the case of her parents." She smiled at Ann. "But we'll manage."

"I wish," Ann said to her, "that you could have met *my* grandfather. He would have been just as great as your Popsy here. He always was."

"Was?" Harry said faintly.

"He died a year ago. But he was just a wonderful man. Compassionate *and* intelligent."

"What . . . what did he do?"

"He taught history at the university. He was also active in lots of organizations—Amnesty International, the ACLU, things like that. During World War II he worked for the Jewish rescue leagues, getting people out of Germany."

Manny nodded. Harry watched Jackie's teeth.

"We'd like you both to come to dinner soon," Ann said. She smiled. "I'm a good cook."

Manny's eyes gleamed.

Jackie said, "I know this must be hard for you—" but Harry saw that she didn't really mean it. She didn't think it was hard. For her it was so real that it was natural weather, unexpected maybe, but not strange, not out of place, not out of time. In front of the bench, sunlight striped the pavement like bars.

Suddenly Jackie said, "Oh, Popsy, did I tell you that it was your friend Robert who introduced us? Did I tell you that already?"

"Yes, sweetheart," Harry said. "You did."

"He's kind of a nerd, but actually all right."

After Jackie and Ann left, the two old men sat silent a long time. Finally Manny said diplomatically, "You want to get a snack, Harry?"

"She's happy, Manny."

"Yes. You want to get a snack, Harry?"

"She didn't even recognize him."

"No. You want to get a snack?"

"Here, have this. I got it for you this morning." Harry held out an orange, a deep-colored navel with flawless rind: seedless, huge, guaranteed juicy, nurtured for flavor, perfect.

"Enjoy," Harry said. "It cost me ninety-two cents."

glass

FOUR PEOPLE stood on the wide shallow steps in front of the library. One of them would be dead before dark.

As always, I couldn't tell which one. The moment came and went too fast, enveloping them in the familiar thickened air shot through with faint blue lines like living veins. Last summer, student-slumming through Europe with Janet, I stood frozen before the exquisite striped glass for sale all around the Piazza San Marco. Janet, puzzled and exasperated, had to pull me away: "What is it, Cath? For God's sake, if you want the vase, buy it—don't worship it!" Janet, who had landed at Kennedy customs with exuberantly fake cameos, four rosaries guaranteed blessed by the Pope, and seven dolls in different versions of native provincial dress, all made of shiny red satin.

She loped out of the library and down the steps, long skinny legs scissoring in counterpoint to her long skinny flying hair, calling to me from ten yards away. "Cath! You're on time, you're always on time, it's so incredibly boring!" She laughed, a laugh that would be straight from the belly if she had one, a laugh unchanged since we were both six years old. Then she came close enough, and her face changed. "What is it, what's wrong?"

She had rushed right past the four on the steps, noticing them only as obstacles, shapes to not bump into. I tried to not notice them either, but it was impossible. It always is. An overweight woman, a small child, an old man leaning on a cane, a young man holding a book. Still, I refused details. I have learned that much, at least.

I managed to say, "Nothing is wrong. You're late."

"And you're not." She laughed again and her head tilted back, toward the blue October sky. That made her blink and shake her head. I thought yet again how exaggerated Janet's gestures always were, how open. She leaned toward me and rolled her eyes. "Wait till you see him!"

I felt myself smiling, horribly, my face cracking open and gaping. I heard myself say, "Where are your glasses?"

"Broken again. Not to worry, roomie, I've got the fastest squint in the East. Wait—is that him over there, talking to whoever?"

The two men still stood on the steps. The woman and child had moved toward the street; another woman called, "Sue!" and hurried up to them. The two women embraced. The child, a girl with skimpy brown hair, stared at them from round eyes in a chinless face that would never be pretty. Like all toddlers, she had the look of knowing things she couldn't possibly know. I looked away, which made her transfer her ancient gaze to me.

"That *is* him," Janet said. "Hey, Jack! Yo!"

The young man raised his hand, then went back to talking to the old man. Janet whispered to me in her tough-guy imitation, "Check 'im out, Milecki." Then she noticed the little girl and began making faces at her. The child slithered to the safety of the back of her mother's legs, burying her face in the hollow between green polyester thighs.

The retreat did not deter Janet. Nothing deters Janet. She dropped to her knees, jeans scraping briefly against the leaf-covered sidewalk, and sang, "I seeeeeeeee you!" Twisting her head, she peered up at me. "Look at him talking to Dr. Jarlson. Physics Chair. Jack gets straight A's, every fucking test. Told you he was a brain, didn't I? And he's generous with it. Tim says if it weren't for Jack, he'd still think quasars were Japanese TV tubes. And all *you* have to do is just loosen up a little."

The child peeked around her mother's left knee, scowling. There was a tiny white scar, barely visible, on her chin. My little brother Roddy had exactly the same scar, from falling forward as he climbed into the school bus and hitting his chin on the top step. He couldn't catch himself; he had zipped his arms inside his jacket while pretending to be an earthworm.

"I seeeeeee you," Janet crooned. The child scowled harder, then stopped as sunlight flashed off Janet's ring. The mother glanced toward us, smiled. Blonde hair held by a green plastic barrette, no makeup, tired eyes, windbreaker with a shiny zipper. I watched helplessly, the mute panic starting to roll over me in waves.

"I seeeeee you. Can I ask what her name is?"

"Jennifer Ann. Jennie."

"See the pretty, Jennifer Ann?" Janet held out her hand. The engagement ring was glass, not diamond, a "stand-in" until Tim could afford the real thing. I suspected that Janet preferred the stand-in; she laughed the one time I accused her of this. As she moved the ring toward the little girl, her hand moved into shadow and the glass returned to dullness. Jennifer switched her gaze to Janet's face.

On the library steps, at the edge of my vision, the young man shook hands with Dr. Jarlson, turned, and started toward us. And then it happened, the thing I hate worse than the death itself, the thing I can sometimes avoid but not now, not this time, not when I wanted to. Everyone froze because the moment froze, deepened, turned lush with preternatural brightness. I felt it detach itself from the normal blur of ordinary sequential moments and become something else, a separate reality that would adhere to me in sharp and unfading detail the rest of my life. The ordinary metastasized to violation. Like cancer:

Dr. Jarlson, leaning on his cane, blue silk ascot and frayed cuffs, the lines in his face soft and eroded as sand gullies. The overweight mother's bitten nails, more ragged on the left hand than on the right; the tiny mole just above the collar of her windbreaker; a bluish bruise beside it: a hickey. The faint round corneal orbits of her friend's contact lenses. Jennifer scowling again at Janet, the stitching loose on her soiled pink Winnie-the-Pooh parka, sunlight lending gloss to the wispy hair. And Jack standing on the library steps, too tall and too thin in a brown cable-knit sweater with the lumpy seams of hand-knitting, his uplifted arm frozen forever in greeting to Janet.

Then she stood up and brushed the leaves from the knees of her jeans.

"Jack, this is Cath Milecki. Cath, Jack Naven."

"Hi," Jack said. "I've heard a lot about you."

"From *me*," Janet said. "All good, all true. She's wonderful, she's unique, ask anybody."

He smiled. "Rein it in, Janet. You're embarrassing your friend."

"*Me?* Embarrass anybody?"

"Well, look at her. Unless, Cath, you always go around with that stunned expression."

"She's stunned by you," Janet said. "What did I tell you?" She began a clumsy clog step on the sidewalk, humming "Love Is in the Air." "Well, since you two obviously want to go somewhere to discuss all my shining virtues. . . ."

Jack shook his head, smiling at me, an invitation to share his amusement at Janet's outrageousness. I could see his amusement. I could see his affection, his slight embarrassment, his physical reaction to me. I could see all of him.

He said, "Really, Janet . . . what do you say, Cath? Should we go have a cup of coffee and dig all the dirt on good old Janet?"

"No."

They both stared at me. I had heard my own tone. Jack looked as if I had slapped him; Janet gaped in astonishment. I curled the fingers of my left hand into my right and dug in until I could feel blood. An old trick. It let me speak.

"I'm sorry. I don't feel well. I'm sorry. I better go back to the dorm."

"Yes. Sure," Jack said awkwardly. The muscles around his mouth tightened. Janet grabbed an arm and pulled at me.

"Time out for a girlish huddle. Jack, you stay right there and don't move an inch. Think about black holes or something. Cath, in my office. On the double."

She tugged me toward the library steps. Jack gazed down the

street, his uncertain anger still uncertain, not yet hardened enough to let him stalk away. I thought he must feel like a perfect fool.

"What are you *doing?*" Janet hissed. "Here's this completely wonderful man asking to meet you, obviously bowled over by your gorgeous self when he does, and you cut him off at the knees. What's with you, Cath? Do you want to spend every last night studying alone in the dorm? Every last one?"

She glared down at me from her five-inch advantage, needing even for five inches to squint a little. My left palm was slippery with blood.

"He *likes* you, Cath. I can tell. Can't you?"

"Yes."

"Well, does he totally gross you out, or what? Could you maybe admit there's a slight chance you possibly might like him back, perhaps?"

I didn't answer.

Janet sighed. "Cath? I don't get it. Talk to me, Cath."

I felt dizzy. This was the first time it had happened like this. I never got to meet them. Janet held my arm too tight; there were needles in my wrist, in my fingers. I fought off that swooping black blur that meant fainting. Not here, not here.

"Janet—*he could be the one.*"

But there was no way she could understand that. "The one? The one for what? For love? For sex? For laughs? So have a cup of coffee and find out—what on earth do you have to lose?"

I made myself look away. Janet let go of my arm. I could feel her gaze move over my face, searching and concerned. Beyond her Jack stared pointedly at the line of the library roof against the sky. The two women gestured at each other and talked at the same time; the one who was not Jennifer's mother raised her hand to shield her eyes in theatrical despair, then laughed through spread fingers. At the end of the street, the limping figure of Dr. Jarlson turned the corner. The red car came from the library parking lot, already too fast, less than thirty feet away. I saw Jack turn, and I saw the moment his face changed as he dropped his book and barreled toward the street. Notebook paper fluttered from between the pages like white leaves.

Jennifer raised her small face. Brakes squealed. The mother's face went to pieces. Jack pushed past her but he was too late: her scream and Janet's came the same second as the thud of flesh on metal, both screams less shrill than the screech of brakes followed by the clash of metal on metal as the red car swerved broadside and plowed into a jeep parked across the street, Winnie-the-Pooh crushed in the grillwork between them.

We sat in the back booth of a bar none of us would have chosen, Janet and I together and Jack across from us. Janet's hands were still shaking. Her eyes, red and swollen from crying, kept darting around the table without meeting either of ours. I held her left hand tightly; on the tabletop Jack grasped the right. "It happened so fast!"

"I know," I said. She had said the same thing at least thirty times. Jack and I exchanged worried glances. Janet's glass ring, unseen, cut into my fingers.

"I keep seeing the mother, you know? Afterward. Kneeling in the street like that, with all the blood, and that baby . . ."

"Sshhh," I said, senselessly. "Sssshhhh, Janet."

Our drinks sat untouched, ice cubes melting. Jack bent his head a little and his hair fell forward over his face. The thick dark hair needed cutting. He hadn't cried like Janet, like me, but the skin around his mouth had a pinched, soft look; I thought confusedly of Dr. Jarlson's old face, his hurt leg.

"It just happened so *fast*." Suddenly Janet gathered up her coat, books, purse. "Look, I have to go. Tim gets out of class in ten minutes. I said I'd meet him."

"I'll go with you," Jack said.

"No, no—I'm fine."

I said, "We'll both go with you. Please, Janet."

She stopped scrambling for her things and looked directly at me from puffy eyes. Almost never, not in all our years together, had I seen Janet's face in repose, without her usual frantic animation, quiet clear to the skull.

"I'd rather you didn't come with me, Cath. You either, Jack. Tim will be waiting for me and I'd rather tell him by myself about . . . this, and just be with him, you know?"

"We know," Jack said. Janet smiled painfully and slid out of the booth. I watched her cross the bar and open the door. A rectangle of light fell inward, narrowed, disappeared.

Jack leaned toward me across the table. "You all right?"

"I'm all right."

"Are you sure? Sometimes it's the people who don't scream and cry over something like that, who hold it all in, who hurt the most."

Abruptly, incongruously, he blushed. "I don't mean to psychoanalyze you, I know I hardly know you. I'm sorry. I just thought that if you wanted to talk about what happened, or anything, I'd like to listen."

"Thanks," I said. I tried to smile at him, failed. To cover that, I reached for my coat and said, "Janet will be all right, too."

"I know. She has Tim. They have a good thing going."

"Yes. And she's brave. She's always been brave. I've known her all my life."

"Brave?" He looked for a moment as if he didn't understand, and then as if he did. "Yeah, you're right. I know what you mean. She is."

"I don't know what I would do if it had been her," I said, amazed that I could say it to him, amazed that I could say it at all.

He fumbled with his beer. "Can I walk you to your next class, Cath?"

I was afraid it might happen again but the moment stayed put, mercifully in sequence, no more distinct than any other. Still, I knew I would remember him in that particular moment: hopeful quizzical eyes, hair falling over his forehead, neck strong over the clumsy cable-knit of the brown sweater. There was no thickening around him, no blue-veined glass. He had not been the one, after all. Instead, he was like the others, the ones left behind: like Dr. Jarlson with his arthritic limp, like Jennifer's mother sobbing in the bloody street. Like me. He kept on looking at me and he smiled, uncertain and shadowed but still a smile, stronger than his blushing or his fumbling with the beer. They were brave people, Janet and Tim and Jack. Very brave.

"Well?" he said.

"You can't walk me anywhere," I said, and got up and went out and left him there.

people like us

PARKER BROUGHT the car around at seven; George was going to meet the dinner guests at the station. Sarah said incredulously, "They're coming up by *train?*"

"Buddy Calucci broke his wrist last week and can't drive," George said, "and his wife has some kind of phobia about it. And the alien of course can't drive either."

Of course. Of course *not*. Couldn't drive, couldn't wear pants, probably couldn't eat anything Sarah had had Cook prepare for dinner either. All the alien could do was put her poor old George's firm out of business with its strange advanced fuel products, whatever they were. Sarah stood before the fireplace and regarded her husband as he picked up his coat from a leather chair.

"If it's supposed to be such a discreet meeting that you can't have it in the city, why are they taking the *train?* Why didn't your Mr. Calucci order a car and driver?"

"I don't think it would occur to him."

"This is going to be horrible, George. It really is. I'd just as soon have Parker and Cook and Cook's criminal brother-in-law. The one in Attica."

George shrugged into his coat, crossed the room, and put his hands on Sarah's shoulders. "I know, darling; it's too bad. But necessary. And if they come by train, they can't stay late. The last train back is the ten forty-two. That's something, at least."

"At least," Sarah said. But she made herself smile at George; it wasn't his fault, after all, and whining like this was really terribly unattractive. These . . . people were coming, and that was that. Just the same, with George's florid face inches from her own, she suddenly remembered something Louise Henderson had said to her just that week at the gallery. *You know, darling, George is getting awfully fat. He should go back to tennis instead of golf. If he's not careful, he'll start to look like that man that runs the hardware store.* Sarah had laughed; Louise had a wicked eye. But Sarah had been stung, too: George *did* look a little like the man in the hardware store. The same shape to the brow, the same chin. Friends had joked about it before.

After George had left for the station, Denise brought in a tray of canapes and fresh ice. Sarah made herself a scotch and water, drank half of it, poked at the fire, finally settled on a chair. The living room looked well by firelight, she thought. She loved this house, even if it had seemed a little empty since Emily had gone off to Rosemary Hall four years ago. Brass and mahogany gleamed in the firelight; wainscoting and molding took on subtle curves; the colors of the old Orientals glowed. In the bookcases leather bindings and Chinese vases jumbled comfortably against each other, both slightly dusty. Emily's violin leaned against one corner. Had Emily, home for the weekend, practiced today? Probably not; too busy with the horses. Sarah smiled, finished her scotch, and considered moving a pile of old *Smithsonians* and *Forbes* off the wing chair beside the violin. She decided against it.

She heard the car, and they were here. Sarah rose to meet her guests. "Hello."

"My wife Sarah," George said. "Darling, Mr. Calucci, Mrs. Calucci, Mr. C'Lanth."

"Call me Buddy," Calucci boomed at the same moment that his wife said, "Pleased to meet you, I'm sure. I'm Mabel." Buddy Calucci seized Sarah's hand and pumped it. He wore a coat with hugely padded shoulders and a bright yellow tie, carefully knotted, printed with daisies. Mabel Calucci wore heart-shaped glasses and a red satin dress cut so low that Sarah blinked. She avoided altogether looking at the alien. Not just yet.

"Nice place you got here," Calucci boomed. "Looks real homey." His eyes, Sarah saw, missed nothing, scrutinizing the portraits as if appraising them.

"My, yes," Mabel Calucci said. Her mouth pursed slightly at the magazines tossed on the wing chair.

Sarah said, "Would you like a drink?" and started toward the sideboard. Calucci's words stopped her.

"No, no, Mabel and I never touch the stuff. Christian Temperance. But you folks go right ahead—feel free."

"You don't drink?"

"Lips that touch liquor shall never touch mine," Mabel said roguishly. "This must be your dog—let him right into the living room, do you?" Her eyes moved to the spot by the fireplace where Brandy usually lay; Labrador hair clung to the Oriental.

"We got a dog, too," Calucci said. "Doberman. Meanest guard dog you ever saw. Not that we need it now with the new security system on the country home. Del EverGuard. Seven thousand for the fencing alone."

"How interesting," Sarah murmured. George threw her a warning glance. She poured herself another scotch and water, then one for George.

The alien said, "I'd like one, too, please."

Sarah turned in surprise. She had assumed that an alien wouldn't drink alcohol. Not that she actually knew much about the aliens, really—she hadn't kept up. The television set, a small black and white, had broken a few months ago, and with Emily only home occasional weekends Sarah hadn't yet gotten around to getting it repaired. She didn't watch TV.

"Scotch and water is fine," the alien said. He had a deep, slightly hoarse voice. Sarah made herself look at him. Standing with his back to the fire, balancing with what looked like careless ease on both legs and the curving muscular tail, he wasn't quite as bad as Sarah had expected. The aliens she had seen on the now-dead TV had worn odd-looking shiny clothes on the top halves of their bodies, nothing below. But this one wore a soft white shirt, no tie, and a tweed jacket cut long enough to cover all but his hairy legs. His head hair, too, didn't look as strange as on the TV aliens; she supposed that a barber must have cut it. It fell thickly from a side part to just over the tops of his ears. Sarah handed him the drink.

"Didn't know you folks imbibed," Calucci said to the alien. He sat on the sofa, pulling up his pant legs at the knees: preserving the crease. "Didn't see *that* on TV."

"We just got a new set," Mabel Calucci said. "Sony. Hundred-inch screen, remotes, stereo, everything."

"Have to have you all to our big Super Bowl party in January," Calucci said. "C'Lanth, your folks like football?"

"No," C'Lanth said. Calucci waited, but the alien said no more, sipping his drink and smiling faintly. Sarah smothered a grin.

"Probably not your native pastime," Calucci said. "Stands to reason. What sports do you guys like? Earth sports, I mean. When in Rome, I always say."

"I like tennis."

"Tennis?" George said, looking surprised.

C'Lanth smiled. "Yes. I'm afraid I've become something of a fanatic. But I'm also afraid I have an unfair advantage—something about the joints of our thumbs. Do you play?"

"Not as much as I used to," George said ruefully.

"Mrs. Atkinson?"

"Yes," Sarah said, wondering where C'Lanth had learned such good English. But didn't she remember something in the papers about the aliens being natural mimics as well as shrewd businessmen? And about their avidly studying just everything? "I play, but not very seriously, I'm afraid. I prefer sailing."

"Buddy and I bowled in a league," Mabel Calucci said. Her plump rouged face clouded over. "In St. Pete I mean. Before we moved to New York. Now—I don't know." She suddenly looked wistful.

"Are there bowling alleys in this cute little country town of yours, George?" Calucci asked.

"I'm afraid I wouldn't know."

There was a slight pause. Then Calucci and the alien spoke simultaneously: "Well, now, let's get down to business!" and "I met a friend of yours, Mrs. Atkinson, at an art-gallery board meeting Tuesday. Louise Henderson."

George said to Calucci, "Oh, I rather think later might be better, Buddy."

Sarah said to C'Lanth, "You were at the gallery board meeting?"

"Not as a member, of course. Kyle Van Dorr was just showing me around. A tourist." He smiled; Sarah would have sworn it was a self-deprecating smile.

"When *do* we get down to business then?" Calucci said. His big body shifted restlessly. When he lowered his head like that, Sarah thought, it was the exact shape of a garden trowel. "We have to act fast on this one, George, if we're going to have any kind of alliance here. Before *your* pals" — he nodded at C'Lanth — "have their little rule-making meeting on mergers."

"We believe in competition," C'Lanth said mildly. He finished his drink and held out the glass, mouthing, "Please?" George made him another scotch and water. In front of the fireplace Brandy stretched, turned in a circle, and farted. Mabel Calucci looked delicately away, mouth pursed; C'Lanth smiled. Sarah found herself smiling back. What kind of nitwit acted so affected as to be offended by a dog? Denise came to the door and announced dinner.

Sarah ate little. She watched. C'Lanth also ate sparingly, but he tried everything. Mabel Calucci, in the presence of food, turned garrulous; each course seemed to swell her verbally, words coming out at the same rate that calories went in. She talked about her little grandson — "Cute as a button, and smart as a whip! He can already tell a Caddy from a Buick"; about the redecoration of her kitchen in apple-blossom pink; about a woman on a game show who had won $100,000, had a heart attack, and had to sell the prizes to pay her medical bills; about the street they used to live on in St. Pete when Buddy and her were first married, where people were so friendly they didn't even knock on each other's doors before visiting. Not like here, where you couldn't even see the houses from the street. Not that that was true in New York, of course, where they had their new penthouse, with the cutest terrace you ever saw twelve stories up and just filled with fresh flowers. Buddy Calucci let his wife talk, his eyes appraising the room's furniture, pictures, wallpaper, silver. George, good host that he always was, listened to Mabel Calucci, nodding and smiling.

The five of them had just returned to the living room when Emily came in with her boyfriend, the Walker boy, both of them in jeans and sweaters, laughing. Emily's dark hair had escaped its barrette and fallen around her face, thick and shining. She showed no reaction to finding an alien in her parents' living room beyond a friendly smile. Sarah felt her heart swell. Her daughter was beautiful, and smart, and mannerly. She was very lucky in Emily. Some of her friends' daughters had turned just impossible, but Emily was wonderful. George made the introductions.

"Enjoying Princeton, Taylor?"

"It's wicked, sir. Especially calculus." Taylor Walker smiled, an attractive easy flash of teeth. "No head for figures, I'm afraid. Professor Boyden is just out of control."

"Hughes Boyden?" C'Lanth asked.

"Yes, sir," Taylor said. "Do you know him?"

"Slightly. I did a lot of reading at Princeton when I first came here. Some of the professors were very helpful. In fact, I was up to Princeton this year for Bicker and Sign-ins."

Taylor and Emily grinned at each other: some private joke. Emily said, "Totally paralytic. I didn't get to bed until seven A.M."

Mabel Calucci looked at her. Her voice went slightly shrill. "I was always glad that my daughter Tammy had the chance to attend Bob Jones University. The moral standards there are very high."

Fury rose in Sarah. The sheer smug *stupidity* . . . Emily, who was dean's list and honor committee . . . this horrible stupid woman. . . .

But all she said was, "Can I get anyone a drink? Taylor? Emily?"

"No, thanks, we're off," Taylor said. "We'll be at the club, Mrs. Atkinson. Nice to have met you, Mr. C'Lanth."

"Pleased, I'm sure," Mabel Calucci said coldly. Taylor and Emily left.

"I liked the young people Hughes Boyden introduced me to at Princeton," C'Lanth said, almost musingly. "There was about them a sort of . . . playful ease."

Calucci said brusquely, "Not supposed to be easy, is it? Toney school like that. Probably has real high admission standards. Now, George, I really think we got to get down to business. I'm sure the ladies will excuse us."

Sarah didn't glance at Mabel Calucci. Nonetheless, she knew that the woman was staring at Brandy, now curled in the wing chair on top of the *Forbes* and *Smithsonians*, half of which had tumbled to the floor. She knew that Mabel Calucci was surreptitiously tug-ging at her red satin neckline, which had slipped even lower. She even knew that in a moment Mabel Calucci would say something conciliatory, bright and sweet and cheerful, from lips still pursed like lemons. "I'll come and listen," Sarah said.

George looked relieved. Calucci looked annoyed. C'Lanth smiled. "Glad to have you," the alien said.

When George came back from the short drive to the station, Sarah was already in bed. She sat up against the pillows and watched George undress. George said nothing until he had flung his coat on a chair, loosened his tie, kicked off his shoes. Finally it burst out.

"That C'Lanth is a cutthroat."

"Oh, I don't know, I thought he was rather amusing."

"*Amusing?*"

"I thought of seeing if he'd come down the weekend of the third, when we have the Talcotts and the Hendersons."

George turned slowly toward her.

"You know how John Talcott is always complaining that no one he meets can ever give him a really good tennis game. And Louise so enjoys talking to people who actually know something about art. Really, George, don't look at me like that—it's not such a bizarre idea."

"Sarah—he's an *alien*. And you heard how the business talk went, the part of it you stayed for, anyway—where the devil did you go? Mabel Calucci complained in the car that you never came back to the living room. C'Lanth is going to ruin me if we don't get this deal moving."

"Well, wouldn't a chance to get to know him better help that?" Sarah said reasonably. George went on staring at her; after a moment she looked away. He was a dear, but he got so worked up. Unnecessarily, really. After all, they had her money, which was much more than the firm brought in. And when George wrinkled his face like that, he *did* look like the hardware store man.

"It would be more useful to get to know Buddy Calucci better," George said heavily. "He's the one holding the real clout here. Although C'Lanth might—"

"Oh, really, darling, do come to bed. It's late, and I don't want to argue. You haven't signed any papers yet, after all. Anything could happen."

George didn't answer. He finished undressing, climbed into bed, turned out the light. Sarah waited. When a few minutes had passed, she said softly, "You might be a little nicer to me, George. I *did* just spend an evening for you with those two dreadful people."

"I know," George said. She felt him reach for her in the darkness, and she put her head on his shoulder.

"I'm sorry I didn't go back to the living room, darling. Truly I am. But her *smugness*. And that inane chatter. And those little frizzy dyed curls. And him—that eager hard-eyed grin."

"I know," George said again.

"I did try."

"Yes, you did."

"And you'll think about having C'Lanth down on the third?"

"Might be a good idea," George said sleepily.

Sarah snuggled in closer against his shoulder. She was glad George thought she had tried, glad he wasn't angry. Because of course the truth was that she *had* been rude to those terrible Caluccis, rude with a sort of reverse-English rudeness of not having been polite enough, not having picked up the cues, not having tried at all to enter into their territory. But, really, with some people you just couldn't, and it was no good pretending. Everybody knew that, really. With some people, do what you might, the gap was just too wide.

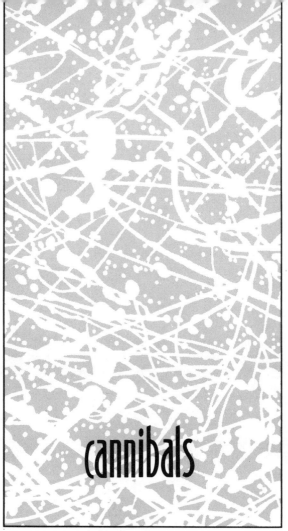

cannibals

T HE AIR WAS STARTING to close in on me again when Rachel and I met Ta-Nin on the path between the compound and the river. We had been having a desultory picnic at the water's edge, sitting on the dank spongy ground and talking through the filthy air, until I couldn't stand it anymore and Rachel led us back. Ta-Nin came crashing along the path in the opposite direction. Her flat bare feet broke foliage and stumbled over rocks the way they all did, raising noise even in this spongy squat forest where noise didn't seem a possibility.

"Something's wrong," Rachel said. "Look at her, Jake."

I looked, but without knowing what I was supposed to be see-ing. Planetside just a few months after two years in space, I was in that stage of acculturation where everything irritated: not just the air, which was a thick living soup of airborne spores and non-fungs and plant filaments, but the pulpy ground, the flaccid trees, the aliens themselves, too fat and too short and too unknown and too stupid. Everything.

Except Rachel Harbatu.

"Something must have happened," she said. Dropping to her knees beside Ta-Nin, Rachel talked with her in those rapid hack-ing coughs they called a language. I tried to figure out how she knew this was Ta-Nin and not another of the compound-tamed Sha. The alien, half my height, gazed at Rachel from dark, nearly cir-cular eyes set in a face that seemed all gray jowl. A strip of hair the color of pale grease ran from the top of her head along her spine and down the backs of both short legs.

"She won't tell me what's wrong." Rachel frowned; my irrita-tion increased. With the aliens she was always somehow a little dif-ferent: more obvious, less the ironic and detached scientist I en-joyed taking to bed, more like the Kelvin colonists—that is not true. She was nothing like the colonists. But with the Sha she was dif-ferent, and I didn't like it.

"She won't tell me," Rachel repeated. She rose to her feet; non-fungs dirtied her knees. "She just says nothing is wrong."

"Maybe nothing is."

"No. Look at her. They're such bad liars."

"Then why do they lie all the time?"

She threw me a cool look. The whole picnic had been like that: jumpy with things unsaid. Neither of us had mentioned her father. Or maybe it was only me that was jumpy. Rachel's cool look had no hurt in it; she never demanded that I share her interest in the Sha. She never demanded anything. I had known she would answer my question with that remote calm. It was why I had asked it.

Ta-Nin put her blobby four-fingered hand on Rachel's hip and pushed in a gesture even I could interpret. She wanted us to move along the path, back toward the river. Rachel shook her head.

"I can't be sure, but I think she—"

Something screamed.

Rachel glanced at Ta-Nin and began to run, veering off the path at a forty-five-degree angle, plunging through the shoulder-high plants in the direction of the scream. It sounded again, a horrible animal shriek. Ta-Nin made an unintelligible noise and crashed after Rachel. I followed them both, easily passing Ta-Nin but catching Rachel — God, she was fast — only when she stopped at the lip of a sudden shallow depression ringed with rocks. She paused but a second, then leaped the rocks and seized what crawled on the spongy ground.

"Get that one there, Jake! Off her leg!"

But I couldn't. My knees gave way and my stomach rose. I had never seen it happen before.

The Sha female within the dell screamed again. Rachel seized the maggoty whiteness on her leg and pulled hard. I expected the grub to scream too, but then I saw the circle of suckers fastening it to the alien fat. Rachel yanked again, wrapping both her arms around the slimy limbless body. The suckers did not come loose. Another of the things crawled from between the Sha's legs. Its head swayed, blind, and then it crept up its mother's side and its mouth closed on her warm belly.

Rachel's face never lost its expression of intense concentration. Kneeling beside the Sha, whose eyes had closed, she pried open the alien's mouth, forced her head to lean over her belly, and rammed two fingers down her throat. The Sha vomited over her child.

So did I.

When the last of the heaves had passed, I stumbled forward, too late to be of any use. But of course it had always been too late. The Sha had stopped struggling and lay with her eyes closed, head thrown back against the rim of the shallow dell. Her three offspring sucked at leg, belly, and chest. Smeared with vomit and slime, Rachel stood erect at the formless end of one of the grubs, staring down at them with her abstracted concentration.

Behind me, Ta-Nin wailed.

"Those things could have turned on you," I said, hours later. It took me hours to say it. If they had attacked Rachel, I would have been no help.

"They won't use human hosts," Rachel said. She stood in a short blue-green robe in front of my mirror, brushing her hair. I had pulled the standard utility lighting out of my quarters and put in old-fashioned lamps, heavy metal tubes ending in swells of glowing yellow. God knows that Kelvin, its one colony city stubbornly Basic Humanitarian, was already full enough of anachronisms without my anachronistic lamps. The colonists had chosen anachronism; the scientists in the compound were stuck with it, or leave. No light on Kelvin flowed into bioenhanced vision, or bioenhanced anything. I watched the compound personnel who entered my quarters catch sight of my lamps, glance at me warily, and pretend not to have noticed.

Or maybe I just liked the circles of yellow light overlapping on Rachel's skin.

She said, "Didn't I tell you the grubs won't feed on humans? I must have, Jake, at some point."

"I don't think so." I stretched out on the bed and watched her raise her arms to stick little red sparkly things in her hair.

"You probably weren't listening. The pheromones don't attract the offspring to human flesh. Wrong odor. We tried."

"You *tried?*"

"Under controlled circumstances."

"How the hell do you control circumstances like that?"

She turned her head and smiled at me. Light ricocheted off the red sparkles. I saw from the smile that she did not hold my squeamish failure of the afternoon against me—did not in fact hold it at all. Over and done. She was tough and clean as machinery, and nothing I did or did not do affected her much. I grinned and reached out to tug at the edge of her robe.

"Come on, how do you control circumstances like that?"

"You don't really care."

"Sure I do. I'm fascinated."

She laughed. "I'll tell you anyway. With the same elaborateness—stop that, Jake, the material will tear—with the same elaborateness you use to control tests on your life-support machinery."

"I don't test it. No, sir, ma'am—I just fix it. You got an airlock broke? Which one, this—no, that's the storage bay? Sure looked like an airlock to me, a lowly engineer."

She laughed. But a second later her face grew abstracted again.

I said, "Is your team any closer? To an answer?"

"No."

"Not even the hard-working and estimable Lemke?"

Rachel grimaced. Her team second was an ass. "The enzyme just isn't there anymore. We estimate that in nearly half the female population, the vomit shows not even a trace."

I pictured the controlled circumstances her team must have used to determine *that,* and let go of her robe.

"There's no logical answer," Rachel went on, almost to herself.

Her hands still moved in her hair, fussing with it. Healthy brown hair, masses of it. Despite myself, I looked away. "It can't be a spontaneous dominant mutation. Too dysfunctional. The Sha are literally consuming themselves. Self-genocide."

"Cannibalism," I managed to say.

"Well—no. That usually results from a protein deficiency, or else some mystical nonsense. Besides, human patterns don't apply. These people are used to a nonsentient host for the grub stage of their children. Cannibalism is deliberate."

"So where was the nonsentient this afternoon? Its absence looked pretty deliberate to me."

"The Sha know there's no point anymore. That woman today knew her vomit wouldn't counteract the suckers—she'd birthed before. But that time, her sisters had pulled her away in time. Ta-Nin told me."

"Woman." "People." "Children." And Rachel cautioned *me*, the mild xenophobe, not to think in human patterns. I said sourly, "Then why didn't her sisters pull her away this time?"

"They're all dead."

"Ta-Nin—"

"—is not her sister. It's a kinship thing. The only ones who are allowed to help with birthing are sisters or, in extreme cases, a male by whom one's sister has become pregnant." She frowned. "We think. It's still a little murky—informants give contradictory information."

"In other words, they lie like hell."

Rachel ignored that. "What bothers me more than all that is why the woman didn't even *try* to vomit until I forced her. There have been a few cases of spontaneous enzyme reappearance, and she must know that. But she didn't even try."

I saw again the repulsive alien and her monstrous grubs, not trying. Rachel stopped fussing with her hair and came closer. "You all right, Jake?"

"Yes." I reached for her, sliding one hand under her robe. She gave me her cool smile.

"Yes? What are you trying to prove now?"

"That you're smart enough to see what I'm trying to prove now." Which was, of course, a lie. I had told her a lot in the few months, more than I should have, probably. But never about Cassie. Rachel could not know what I needed to prove.

She laughed. "We don't have time for proof."

"Sure we do."

"I have to be in the lab in twenty minutes."

"That's time."

"Maybe for you. Not for me." She kissed me lightly and reached for her clothes, which she had draped over my tool case. I hadn't noticed that before. I glanced away from the case — a stupid, reflexive gesture that immediately killed my mood. Rachel went on dressing, and I watched her, and the yellow light from another time lay over the room.

"Rachel—"

She half turned toward me, her smile growing puzzled when she saw my face. What was I going to tell her? I didn't know; her name had just surfaced with that unexpected intensity, that involuntary suddenness I hated. My fists clenched at my sides.

"What is it, Jake?"

"Nothing."

She dropped whatever she was holding, reached for my right hand, and uncoiled my fingers. Her hair fell forward in a smooth brown river. I wanted to tell her not to look up, not to raise to me a face with any trace of question, or my arm would hit her.

Before I could say anything, someone pounded on the door, and I turned to open it.

"You witnessed another birth!" Lemke said. He pushed past me and rushed over to Rachel. She looked up and I saw that her face was as controlled and calm as ever, except for the allowable irritation of talking to Andrew Lemke.

Almost as short as the Sha, angular and brittle as corroded re-entry alloys, Lemke peered at his world from myopic eyes feverishly bright with envy. His world was Kelvin. Rachel told me he had been born to first-generation colonists, core-hot Basic Humanitarians, so convinced of the evolutionary wrongness of altering the human body that they had permitted their brilliant and misfit son neither eye implants nor the biogenetic altering that would have prevented his weak heart. Lemke had never been off Kelvin. He never would be. The transition from colony to compound had taken everything he had, consumed every skinny bitter tendon. He was Rachel's team second only because of Kelvin's stubborn refusal to allow on-planet any permanent scientist with significant biological engineering. There weren't many. Despite his education, Lemke was compound and not colony by default, and he knew it.

Once, by the river, I had seen him kick a Sha offspring, not a grub but a young maturant only days out of her safehouse. The Sha had crumpled, and Lemke had walked on.

"What happened at the birth? Tell me *everything*, Rachel."

"Nothing we haven't seen before." She sketched briefly the afternoon's events in the dell.

Lemke hit his open palm with the opposite fist, a ridiculous and theatrical show of frustration. "Didn't you have any enzyme with you?"

"I don't carry it on picnics," Rachel said calmly. "Do you?"

Lemke lowered his chin and looked at her; for a moment, his eyes glittered. It was impossible to picture him on anything as casual as a picnic. I said, "What enzyme?"

Rachel said, "An artificial synthesis of the enzyme the Sha have lost."

"You can do that?"

Lemke snorted, turning imperious with the machinery tech. "Of course we can do that, Razowski. A chemical formula is a chemical formula."

I spoke directly to Rachel. "Then why not just give the enzyme to the Sha? To use it when they birth?"

"They won't. We can synthesize chemicals to alter nearly any biological given, but we can't make them use it. At least, not so far, not even the few who communicate with the compound. It must touch on a taboo of some sort — we're not sure. The information is contradictory."

"Liars," Lemke said. "A Sha is a Sha." I had thought the same thing — but not with such native contempt.

"A colonist is a colonist," I murmured, too low for Rachel to catch it.

Lemke turned toward me with a peculiar slow swivel of his gaze that stopped just short of meeting my eyes and then turned slowly back. It was an eerie gesture, buried as the ponderous slide of tectonic plates under deep and muddy water.

Rachel said, "Ta-Nin tried to keep us away from the birth. The privacy thing. But she let me talk to her about it afterward, and I explained about the synthetic enzyme. Again. But really, Andrew, that was all. Nothing to add to what we already knew."

Lemke went through his palm-smacking theatrics again. Rachel reached for her shoes, a fluid graceful gesture that parted her robe enough to flash white thigh. Lemke stopped grimacing, and for a moment his face went still. Rachel didn't notice; she was pulling on her shoe. I suddenly wondered if there was any woman on Kelvin, colony or compound, who would not reject Andrew Lemke.

He said, his voice just slightly too shrill, "We're all looking forward to your father's performance tomorrow night."

She glanced at him and reached for her other shoe.

"It isn't often Kelvin gets a performance from somebody like Justin Harbatu."

Rachel pulled on her shoe. Lemke couldn't leave it alone.

"I hope he performs something from *Rage*. That's my favorite. I've seen it twice."

Rachel stood. Her face was calm as usual, smooth dark metal. *Rage* was based on the kidnapping and murder of her mother, when she was four years old. Rachel herself had been left alive by the same men. I strode past Lemke and opened the door.

"Out. Good-bye. We're busy."

He scuttled out; maybe he even felt a little ashamed. I doubted it. When I turned back to Rachel, she was smiling and shaking her head.

"God. Lemke." She stripped off the robe and reached for her tunic.

Relief burned my eyes. No averted face, no suppressed tears, no sudden moody quiet to have to question or ignore. No hurt clutching, not even about something as painful as *Rage* must be for her. Or maybe it wasn't even painful anymore; maybe her calm ran all the way through, the efficient cool energy of a solitary system.

Like Lemke, I couldn't leave it alone.

"Let's not go tomorrow night. To your father's show."

She fastened the front of her tunic. "We have to."

"No, we don't."

"Yes, we do. Or at least, I do. You can skip it if you want, Jake."

"You wouldn't mind going alone?"

"No. Why should I?"

Despising myself, I said, "Even if he does something from *Rage?*"

Rachel looked at me, level. "You can do what you want, Jake."

I saw that she meant it. No averted face, no suppressed tears. I put my arms around her and nuzzled her neck. Against my cheek, I could feel her mouth smile.

"No. I have to get to the lab. Stop that . . . later."

"Now."

"No. Later, Jake. I'll be back in a few hours, and we'll laser the floor if you want. There's plenty of time."

A memory stirred in my head. *There's never any time.* I pushed it away and stood up, a little ashamed of myself. I had been setting Rachel up, yet another petty test — when would I stop doing that? But she had passed. No tears, no clutching. She was not Cassie.

"I love you," I said. But she was already out the door, and I knew she would not hear.

Cassie and I had spent nearly a year on Janos, as the advance team for the Corps: life-support engineer and reconnaissance biologist. Janos was empty. No artistic performances, no scientific compounds, no colonists, no aliens with three-stage life cycles. There was only volcanic fire and rock and plants and worms and microbes, all of it, in memory, in shades of blood. And my wife, restless enough to want to breathe a barely breathable atmosphere whose heat slicked her skin with constant sweat, gleaming and sweet.

On Janos, Cassie suddenly refused to cut her hair. It grew wild in thick black masses that curled in the heat and clung to the sides of her neck. She pushed it back with a quick impatient gesture, both hands. At first only whenever the hair fell forward. Then as habit. Then more and more, until she did it constantly — her slim darting hands scraping raw the sides of her face, over and over, out of control.

"Don't do that, Cassie. Stop it."

"I can't."

"Why?"

"I don't know. Hold me, Jake, hold me tighter . . . I'm afraid!"

"Of what, for Christ sake?"

"I don't know. I don't know!"

"Cassie . . ."

"You don't love me. Not when I'm like this."

"I love you."

"But not enough."

"No matter what I say to you, it's not enough!"

"That's not true. It's inside, the fear, it's always inside . . . don't get up! Don't go!"

"Damn it, I have work to do!"

"I know. I know. I'm sorry. There's never any time."

But that had been in the beginning, when we still thought it was just we two, machinery wizard and gene wizard, on Janos.

Cassie never succeeded in isolating the microbe, despite her formidable equipment and training. Much later, the Corps medical officer told me that wasn't surprising.

"These slow viruses aren't really viruses, aren't genes as we define them. Not even life as we define it—no nucleic acids, no permanent structure. We can't find a trace in her brain, even with a TOL scanner."

"Then how the hell are you so goddamn sure it's there?"

He wouldn't look at me. He stood in the middle of his clean sick bay, surrounded by glassware that had not been hurled and walls that had not been pounded and furniture that had not been soaked with endless tears, and the son of a bitch would not look at me.

I shouted, "The drugs you give her aren't working! They don't calm her fears, they don't damp her emotions, they don't do anything!"

"I know. We don't understand what the alien virus does to brain transmitters. It's not chemical. We just don't understand."

"Damn it—"

"She can't help it, Razowski. What she does. Not any of it. The heightened emotionalism, all directed at one source . . . it's a part of the pattern. The most you can do is try to go on reassuring her."

"Try something else!"

"We can't. Anything else would kill her."

And I had said nothing, and the doctor had looked at me hard, because he had heard it anyway.

For months after Cassie finally died, I had had the same dream. She and I stood at the edge of a cliff that was both a dream place of red carbon steel, and the Great Rift on Janos. Below us the cliff face sheered straight down, without shadows. Cassie's legs were severed at the knees. Her blood pooled on the steel ground.

"Help me, Jake!"

"I can't. I *can't*, anymore!"

"Give me your legs."

"Cassie . . ."

"Give me your legs!"

And I did. Suddenly they were on her knees, and I lay with wriggling stumps at the edge of the red cliff. Cassie stood above me, her face momentarily calm. Into that shocking calm I spoke quietly, more quietly than I had spoken to my wife in that entire last tormented year.

"You're killing me, Cassie."

"I know," she said, and spat blood, and looked out over the empty rift into a sky white and hard as bleached bone. "I know."

When she died, the alien virus died with her. The doctor handed me the suicide note. "She didn't want to take the chance of transmitting it to you. Even though there was no chance. She knew that, but. . . ." He didn't finish.

I took the note. With my other hand I took from him my terragauss-field sterilizer. Positioned at Cassie's head, it had created for a brief moment such an intense magnetic field that the atoms of her brain had let go, collapsing into slimy jelly punctured by fragments of clean bone. The instrument, its fist-sized case made of a duraplas immune to magnetism, felt cool and hard under my fingers. A strand of Cassie's black hair curved down from the handle, the shining tail of a comet already lost against the sun.

"I'm sorry," the doctor said.

"Yes," I said. The terragauss sterilizer had gone back in my tool case. I had gone into space, working freighters until after two years I came to Kelvin, whose tiny Basic Humanitarian colony thought it needed a life-support engineer.

The shuttle skimmed over the thirteen klicks between the scientific compound and the one human "city" on Kelvin. Rachel chatted composedly with the rest of the overdressed scientists, half of them watching her slyly for signs of drama; that was the half who had seen the holovid of *Rage*. I couldn't stand to look at them, so I held Rachel's hand and stared at the ground below.

There was nothing much to see except limp shoulder-high trees mottled with the all-pervasive nonfungs, sliced by the freight road connecting the compound to the city. Whatever engineer had laid the road had known what he was doing. It was a good job, serviceable even after three generations of use. I watched it all the time I tried to figure out yet again why Justin Harbatu had chosen to perform on Kelvin.

It made no sense. Harbatu was an actor. Actors of his stature did not make unenhanced holovids, nor the public appearances at which they were filmed. Actors of his stature made either enhanced holovids or direct-interface brainies—both of which were of course illegal among Basic Humanitarians. Even the equipment for the simplest enhanced holovid—the audience brain-wave scanners, the feedbacks for scent and light and subaudios—were illegal. What

Harbatu was allowed to do on Kelvin was, essentially, to stand on a stage and talk, with preset music and pheromones behind him. That was it. Anything else was to rape the Basic Humanitarian skull, on the inside of which was engraved THE HUMAN MIND SUPREME, UN-TAINTED.

So why had he come?

There was Rachel, of course. But he had seen Rachel a few months ago, on the first loop of this tour, right after I met her. She hadn't been interested in seeing him then; she wasn't now.

"Someone should tell him," she had said, "that the mark of the minor artist is always strain."

"You tell him."

"He wouldn't believe me. He calls it something else." Rachel licked her fingers; we had been eating something sticky, something forgotten. She looked up at me and smiled. "He calls it passion."

I smiled, remembering; Rachel leaned toward my ear and whispered, "What could possibly be funny on this stupid shuttle?"

I shook my head and pointed at the auditorium below.

It stood on a slight rise at the far end of the city. Someone had told me that it was the first nonessential building the original settlers had put up. I could believe it. The Basic Humanitarians had rejected a century of space-colony alloys and construction techniques in order to build a Terran Greek temple out of crumbly gray stone, complete with four columns and a frieze. Blue nonfungs mottled the columns and cancered over the stone, eating slowly clear down to the structural supports. Silhouetted against the filthy sky that diluted the light from three moons into watery urine, the auditorium looked like an outhouse. I had never heard anywhere of original settlers who were not humorless romantics, but this was the far end of a bell-shaped curve. All by itself, the auditorium went far toward explaining Andrew Lemke.

He was inside, prowling among the off-worlders who had come in on Harbatu's ship. Crew, colonists, and scientists milled in artificial camaraderie.

"Christ," Rachel said, "there's Kleinstadt. The governor. A black hole if there ever was one."

"He's coming this way. Shall I dent his Schwarzschild radius for you?"

"Behave yourself, Jake. He can throw us both off-planet."

I thought it was an odd thing for her to say; the scientific research on Kelvin was funded completely by the Corps, and the colonists could only interfere if the compound threatened their colonizing. Kleinstadt bore down on us, picking up Lemke on the way.

"Rachel, my dear," Kleinstadt boomed. "You must be so proud of being queen of a Justin Harbatu live performance."

"We've all waited so long to see this," Lemke purred.

Rachel's smile was iron. Kleinstadt prided himself on being more cosmopolitan than most Basic Humanitarians; it made him feel daring. Once he had even been off-planet. Years ago he had tried to marry a technician from the compound; she had declined. With his gray tunic he wore an orange necklace.

From across the room I saw someone I could actually have talked with: Jameson, the Security chief at the compound. He stood in rumpled, outdated dress robes, looking as if he wished he were somewhere else. But then he caught sight of Rachel, and I saw the hungry expression on his face a bare moment before it vanished. That was something I hadn't known.

"What is this new work Justin is going to perform?" Kleinstadt asked genially. I would have bet my hydrogen torch that Harbatu was unaware of having become "Justin." "Here I am set to introduce him and he won't tell me even the title until the last second. All he will say is that it was created since his ship stopped here on the first leg of his tour. But surely he would have told you!"

"Afraid not," Rachel said. "Shall we sit down?"

Just before we took our seats, I whispered to her, "We don't have to stay."

She didn't even answer me.

There was a long wait before the lights dimmed and Kleinstadt strode on stage. He looked pale. I saw him glance out over the audience, as if he were looking for someone—Rachel?—and for a disbelieving moment I thought he would announce that Harbatu would perform scenes from *Rage*. But he did not.

Kleinstadt cleared his throat. "We are privileged to present to you tonight the galactic premiere of a new . . . a new concert, created in the months since we were . . . privileged to have Justin Harbatu last visit Kelvin. I say 'privileged' advisedly, and with two meanings." He was sweating. "Privileged first because this work is the first Justin Harbatu has created to honor Basic Humanitarian principles: 'The human mind supreme, untainted.' Privileged second because this work is the first . . . the first human celebration of our cousins in life, the Sha."

All over the room, bodies drew rigid. Kleinstadt fumbled on.

"There exists on Kelvin that understanding, that brotherhood, great enough to let us appreciate our sentient brothers across the gulf that must exist between any two peoples alien to each other. That brotherhood is made the more precious, the more poignant, by the tragedy befalling our fellow sufferers in the universe—"

Like the politician he was, Kleinstadt had regained his sonorous tones. The colonists sat like stone. They had given their lives to what they thought it meant to be human; an honored outsider was now going to impose on them what it meant to be Sha. I saw two of the technicians from the compound exchange amused glances. Beside me, Rachel's thigh felt like stone.

"—fellow sufferers who face, as humanity once faced, the issue of their own self-destruction. Having triumphed over such a burden, having thrown it off, we can perhaps reach out to help our sentient brothers within the Humanitarian protection of our science. We can certainly reach out with our fellowship, and our tears. And so it is with incalculable gratitude that I welcome to Kelvin the one artist capable of that reaching out, as no other performer of our time could do. Justin Harbatu, performing his new concert: *Cannibals.*"

Harbatu walked out onto the stage.

Behind him, the opaquing dissolved and three Sha musicians began to play their weird repetitive music on instruments of wood and bone. I had heard the music before—when all three moons were down I had heard it all one endless night—but I had never heard it in the presence of Kelvin's colonists. Nor of Justin Harbatu. Light came up behind him—there may have been scent, too, I couldn't tell—and in the irregular spaces between the notes of Sha music Harbatu began to speak.

None of his holovid classics had captured the sheer personal presence of the man. It was more than the presence of the actor, more than the huge bulk and the famous eyes: glowing, startling green. Rumor said the eyes were alien implants; official counter-rumor said that was not possible. After thirty seconds, it didn't matter. After Kleinstadt, Harbatu looked real, alive, and through him came alive the Sha.

His words were not poetry, although that antiquated art gasped once again on Kelvin. His words were just that: words, the only possible words to give us the Sha and their lives, before: the soft yielding stalks of the forest, the village, the hearth. The air thick and cradling as blankets. The grubs in their safehouses, soft damp mounds of fur and plants in a ring around the hearth. A young maturant clinging to coarse fur. The children. The words to bridge how that felt to humans, felt to Sha.

Only I wasn't feeling the words, I was feeling the Sha, and I was watching Harbatu hold his body still with some terrible control that he could not make extend to his eyes, and that was the measure of its terribleness.

He spoke of when it changed.

Against the thin tattered music, Harbatu's phrases rose and fell. He described what I had seen that afternoon, and I knew I had not seen it at all. Cannibals. I had seen the ugliness, the obscenity, and had wanted to slam it into extinction. What I had not seen was the woman, the children. What it meant to her as centuries of evolution failed and her own grubs closed their suckers on her living flesh.

Picture after picture pinned behind my eyes.

The musicians played, not understanding the human words, and finally I could not take my eyes from them. Their dark circular eyes did not watch Harbatu, did not watch anything at all. Lost.

Then, abruptly, after so long in stillness, Harbatu's body shifted, a graceless jutting of pelvis, a wrench of shoulders. The lights changed, the music changed—I don't know how. It wasn't Sha music. I couldn't feel where it was coming from. The light opaqued the Sha musicians and did something else, something that hit like a blow. Harbatu's voice followed it harshly. The audience, amputated too quickly from the first movement, jerked. A woman in front of me whimpered.

Harbatu threw the words at us, in syncopated phrases contemptuous of the vulnerability he himself had created. The contempt was worse than any direct accusation: I was guilty without knowing of what, and I fell into the guilt as into a gravity well, the smash looming up at me from below. No one moved. There was no escape. Harbatu built it slowly. The child crawling from between the legs, and the vomit rising like despair, and the dark eyes watching as the mouths closed—

Harbatu was saying that the Sha cannibalism had come to Kelvin with the human settlers.

The woman in front of me gasped. A man half rose in his seat and then sank back. Harbatu fixed his gaze on us out of that dangerous light and no one else moved—except Rachel.

It took me a moment to realize she was gone. Only that could have pulled me from the auditorium. I stumbled after her. Outside, I saw that my arms still flailed weakly. What was I fighting off?

Harbatu's voice.

I breathed deep. It hurt, as if the moonlight were acid being drawn into my lungs. As my head cleared it began to pound. Thought struggled through the pounding: *Harbatu used illegal subliminals.*

Rachel had strode to the bottom of the hill and stood leaning against the stone base of a statue of a colonist, its silly commemorative posturing mottled with the same blue nonfungs as the building. Her left hand gripped the stone hard enough to turn the knuckles white. She turned to face me.

"He had no right."

"Rachel, it didn't—it didn't happen that way. Did it?"

She hesitated, and in the space of that hesitation she seemed to physically flicker.

"No," Rachel said. "It didn't happen that way."

"Tell me."

She didn't answer. I gripped her by the shoulders. *"Tell me."*

"The absence of the enzyme showed up before the original human team. That's to a .05 confidence level. The only doubt is because . . .," she shook her head to clear it, "because the equations have to allow for the Sha's having so little sense of time that it's hard to be sure about what they give us, and because there was the usual time lapse in learning the language. But that's not the point about the drivel he was wallowing in!"

I didn't see how that could not be the point. Rachel's eyes were enormous and curiously filmed—what kind of subliminals had Harbatu used? Pheromones, subaudios—the whole arsenal, somehow, of mind-benders just short of direct interface. I didn't see how else he could have sucked me into that much emotion. I writhed at the memory of sitting in that auditorium.

Rachel was watching me closely. She slipped free from my grasp and closed her fingers on my arm, and I could feel grit from the statue between her palm and my skin.

"It's *not* the point. It's not. Don't you see what he did? This accusation against humans is no worse than the rest of it. He exploits it—all of it. That bleeding compassion for the tragedy of the Sha—what does he know of the tragedy of the Sha? He spent two weeks here once, and never learned enough Sha to give a ritual greeting. He feeds on it, swells himself with this 'horror' that never touched him personally, and then spews it back to us sodden with easy compassion."

I saw the musicians' eyes.

Rachel said, "He has no *right* to that suffering, not even artistically. It is not his. He hasn't earned it."

She turned her face away from me. Moonlight slid over her hair. I wanted to walk away, escape this, think straight somewhere else. This was not Rachel.

"Rachel, artists have always—"

"No. This is different. None of us have a right to this, the death of a whole race. It's *obscene*, Jake. Do you think he really did that to all those people without feedback equipment? It's there, somehow, somewhere, miniaturized—I don't know. How long since any of us have seen state-of-the-art equipment in this backwater? He may even have used illegal pheromones. You saw that audience, paralyzed—he wants that for the holovid. Reaction shots." Her face twisted into ugly ridges. " 'Look, look, world—see what Justin Harbatu can do to an audience even when they're Basic Humanitarians!' God—the cameras spent more time filming them than him, and in holo it will look . . . he manipulated our responses until they were as artificial as his emotion. He *fed* off us, as much as off the Sha!"

I had forgotten the cameras. What had my face shown?

Rachel raced on, the ridges on her face contorting into snaking lines. "His engineers will put together a performance that will break your heart. Then it will go out over the entire sector, billed as the first performance from a Basic Humanitarian colony, and two dozen worlds will file genocide protests with the Corps. They'll shut us down. They'll have to, from political pressure, no matter how the figures compare with the biological risk humans bring to *any* world we touch. Do you know what that risk is, Jake? Do you?"

I couldn't speak. Her intensity hammered behind my forehead; her eyes bored into me.

"Six percent. In six percent of the worlds we touch, we destroy something biological. Something major. Here we have a chance to save something, and he will stop us. He'll stop us because his transcendent art is worth more than just truth. Truth doesn't hold up to impassioned holovids, especially when they're created by *my father*."

She said the two words softly, white hot. I stepped back.

"But not this time, Jake. Not like when . . . not this time. He's not going to destroy the Sha, or the work I've done here, either. Let him feed off somebody else's pain."

She had not let go of my arm. Her face leaned into mine and her breath scorched me. It smelled stale, as if she had been sleeping a long time. It was that, more than all the rest of it, that brought the panic rising along my spine and made me reach for the cruelest thing I could have said.

"I never saw the resemblance between you two before."

Rachel's eyes widened. She dropped my arm. For a moment her face broke up, went to pieces. Then it was her own again, controlled and smooth, and she strode away from me around the statue, toward the parked shuttle. I did not follow her. No look she wore now would wipe the image of that other face: relentless, fierce, passionate beyond all reason.

Not Harbatu's, although that was what Rachel thought I meant. She left the moonlit path and the darkness devoured her.

The next day, the water purification system malfunctioned; nearly simultaneously, everyone in the compound developed diarrhea. The malfunction was easy to find, harder to repair with the limited electronic and mechanical parts inventory. My immediate predecessor, like Andrew Lemke a colonist wanting to be something else, either had not known what he was doing, or had come to not care. The maintenance assistant I inherited from him was shitting his guts out. Overload on the sewage refiltering strained most of the generations-old life-support system in one way or another, and I worked twenty-hour days for a week, much of it at the antiquated water purification plant by the river. Bioengineered filter bacteria would have solved the problem in a day.

I did not see Rachel. But information filtered through, floating to me in semibroken particles, osmosis through the clean barrier of work.

Harbatu and his technical team were editing *Cannibals*, sequestered in the visitors' hotel. Kleinstadt had introduced a colony law banning concerts not previously viewed by a member of the Basic Humanitarian Council. Lemke had said outright that Harbatu had used illegal pheromones.

Had it been any other scientist, he might have been listened to.

Rachel had visited her father the day after his performance. A short visit, osmosis murmured. Behind closed doors, osmosis murmured. No shouting, osmosis murmured. Rachel left with a face as blank and cold as when she went in.

I bent closer over my valves and pipes and circuit boards.

When I looked up, Ta-Nin stood watching me. I glanced sharply over my shoulder—I had left the door open. Hadn't Rachel said something about lone Sha being unwilling to enter human buildings without their sisters? But here she was, bare huge feet splayed over the damp floor, blinking at me. I had seen no Sha since the concert.

"Hello," I said. Stupidly.

She answered with a burst of gibberish like rocks scraping together. I nodded, smiled, and pointed toward the door.

Ta-Nin scraped some more. I walked over and took her firmly by the elbow, steering her toward the door. To my surprise, she broke free—I had not thought her that strong—and planted herself firmly. Staring up from the level of my waist, she rubbed her flabby belly. I smelled the stale mildew of her skin, and looked down into the dark circular eyes.

"I don't have any food."

She tilted her head, looked at me stupidly, and went on rubbing her belly. I tried to pantomime "no food," shaking my head and pointing to my mouth and cupping empty hands and feeling a total idiot. She went on rubbing the drooping rolls of fat beneath her flat chest. Then I got it.

"You're pregnant."

She tilted her head some more, and something moved in those dark eyes.

I dropped her elbow. Uncertain, she put a hand on my arm. It felt gritty, and I thought confusedly of the nonfungs on Rachel's palm, the blue grit from the decaying statue.

That Ta-Nin was here without her sisters could mean only that she had no sisters left. She had seen Rachel and me run to save a sisterless Sha, and somewhere in her dim alien mind she had lowered a barrier, or dissolved it, or shifted it. It was all right to ask me to help her survive her birthing. She did not want to die.

I pushed her hand away and snarled, "Rachel—ask Rachel!"

She tilted her head far enough to ruin her balance, tottered, righted herself. The thing moved behind her eyes. Around us, the stench of untreated Kelvin water festered on thick air.

"Rachel helped, remember? I'm the one who shit upward. *Ask Rachel.*"

"She can't," Rachel said from the doorway. She wore her bio-chemist's smock over pale clothing. Against the dimness outside she was hard-edged white.

"She can't ask me because I'm female but haven't ever been pregnant. But she can ask you. A male."

Her voice was cool, rational, invulnerable. All that I had loved in her. I looked away and said, "Then why not ask a Sha male?"

"She probably has. She's probably asked males by whom her sisters became pregnant, which are the only ones she can—we think. But you know the ratio, Jake—only five percent of the Sha are male. They spend most of their lives screwing."

"What a life," I said, and heard my own callous strain. But Rachel, the old Rachel, only smiled.

"You're the first human male a Sha has asked to help her, at least as far as I know. She saw you at that other birth. Most Sha aren't able to combine abstract transfer of an experience with breaking a taboo. But Ta-Nin is an unusually intelligent alien."

The unusually intelligent alien was still rubbing her belly, tilting her head, staring with complete incomprehension.

Rachel said quietly, "Please help her, Jake. You won't have to touch Ta-Nin or the offspring. You can use the synthesized enzyme. You just pour it over an offspring's mouth and the maternal flesh will repel it."

"Will she permit that?"

"I don't know. She says yes, but I think she may just expect you to carry away the offspring. The enzyme is more reliable."

I didn't answer.

"You'll need to stay near Ta-Nin when her time comes, in a few weeks. Or rather, she'll stay near you. She can sleep—"

"Not in my quarters."

"I wasn't going to say that. In my lab. She's been there enough to enter it more or less willingly. And there's that couch in my office, for you. I'll be in and out. I'd like to see the actual birth, although I won't distress Ta-Nin by letting her see me. By remote, I think."

That couch in my office. I'll be in and out. With another woman, I would have seen this as at least partly devious invitation to gloss over the night of her father's performance. But Rachel met my gaze steadily, without layers. If she wanted to talk about that night, she would say so. Not everything she did was driven by devious emotional need. She was not Cassie.

I said, "What about a host?"

"There are always jelkin in the animal lab, alive and just-dead. You can bring one in when Ta-Nin starts labor. Jelkin were traditional hosts for the Sha, before. The offspring will seize it greedily."

But that picture was too close to the day of the picnic. I said sharply, "Tell her to stop that!"

Rachel made a gesture, and Ta-Nin finally stopped fondling her flaccid belly. If Rachel wondered at my sharpness, the wonder did not show on her face. She had never remarked on my squeamishness, never asked why a life-support engineer could not tolerate smashed bodies. She began to talk to Ta-Nin, presumably explaining the plans for her birthing. Ta-Nin suddenly dropped to the floor and began rubbing her forehead against my left knee. I leaped backward.

"Christ! Make her stop *that!*"

Rachel laughed. She shot more gibberish at Ta-Nin, who rose and looked from me to her. Rachel took the Sha's arm and firmly guided her to the door. It seemed to me for a second that as Rachel maneuvered the Sha, I could actually see purposefulness shimmer around her, a kind of steady undistorted field. Maybe Ta-Nin felt it, too. Maybe it would calm her. If she rubbed my knee again, I would probably kick her, and knowing that bothered me. I didn't like the Sha, but I liked even less resembling Andrew Lemke.

"Jake. Would you like to have dinner together tonight?" Rachel's voice from the doorway was level.

I hesitated, and then hesitation—or something—turned my voice sharp.

"No, thanks. Not tonight."

"Sure?"

"Yes."

"All right." Her tone did not change.

I bent over my pipes and valves, oddly reassured.

That night my Link buzzed, long after midnight. Someone had broken into Justin Harbatu's rooms at the visitors' hotel and stolen the holofilm of *Cannibals.*

Security called me not because the door lock had been tampered with, which would not have been my concern, but because it hadn't. Door and window E-monitors recorded nothing. Instead, the thief had simply come up through the floor with a tunable laser saw set to infrared to avoid triggering the E-monitors with X-ray backscatter. The ragged hole in the floor, a few meters from Harbatu's bed, was matched by pitted burns on the ceiling; the laser saw had been ineptly wielded. All the laser saws in the compound were supposed to be under my jurisdiction.

Justin Harbatu sat on the bed, holding his head in both hands. The windows were flung open, and a strong breeze blew through. Jameson stood in the middle of the room, looking as if something inside him had died.

"How could anyone get hold of a tunable laser, Razowski? Don't you keep them locked up? Or is this one off one of the ships at the port?"

"No, it's not off a ship. Yes, I keep the compound saws locked up. One is missing. I checked when you called."

"Missing from where?"

"My quarters. My personal tool case."

Our eyes met. Jameson was looking at me with a hatred I did not understand.

"The tool case has an E-lock?"

"Of course."

"Who had the code?"

"To the tool case, nobody. To my quarters, just Security and Rachel Harbatu."

Harbatu raised his head. His skin was gray. Even so, even not looking directly at him, I was hit again by his peculiar personal force, radiating from the strange green eyes. It filled the room like heat.

"My daughter? To *your* quarters?"

I looked at him then; his tone was an insult. Jameson said, "Could Dr. Harbatu have somehow gotten or deduced the code to your tool case?"

I thought then of Rachel's teasing voice, the two of us lying naked in my room: "When were you born, Jake? By how much am I robbing the nursery?" But I hadn't used my birth date for the tool-case code; only amateurs did that. I had used the date of my fifth birthday, when my mother had given me my first tool kit. Miniature welder, calculator, saw, struts, pliers, scribe: miniature love. I had told Rachel about that birthday. It had, like so much else, come welling up after two years of silence, two years of celibacy.

God, the things I had told her.

"Razowski," Jameson repeated with that same inexplicable anger, "could Dr. Harbatu have gotten access to your tool case?"

"Yes."

Harbatu's eyes bored into me. I said, "A laser saw is not completely silent, not on that synthetic. It would sizzle. Didn't you hear anything? Didn't the staff below hear anything? Christ, isn't there any security around here?"

Jameson snapped, "The visitors' hotel isn't exactly an E-max prison. Watch your tone, Razowski. The room below is a kitchen and nobody's in it at night. Mr. Harbatu was knocked out. A K-gas, we think, either in his room or shot through the floor after the first cut from the laser. He thinks he remembers hearing something. That stuff fuddles you."

That's why the windows were open, why Harbatu looked gray. A K-gas.

"Anyone in Animal Control would have K-gas," I said. "That's what it's for."

"A lot of people could have it," Jameson said; the stress on the second word sliced the air. I wanted to smash something, with an intensity that frightened me.

With heavy formality Jameson said, "Mr. Harbatu, I have to ask you if you want to file charges for the theft. Colony laws apply in the compound if anyone chooses to file a complaint that evokes them; otherwise, only Corps regulations apply. Do you wish to file charges?"

"Of course I do!"

"Are you sure? Was that the only copy of the holovid?"

It hadn't occurred to me that there might be another print. I jerked my gaze to Harbatu. He sat up straighter on the edge of the bed, his face clearer as the last of the K-gas wore off. He hesitated just a fraction, and in that hesitation I read not paternal affection but a lightning calculation.

"It doesn't matter if there is another print or not. If no, an irreplaceable work of art is lost. If yes, and I let that sway me, an irreplaceable principle of justice is lost. There's already been enough disregarding of justice on Kelvin. Justice is what *Cannibals* is all about. It's not an abstract to me, Mr. Jameson."

I said, "And neither is free publicity."

He didn't even glance at me. His gaze was locked on Jameson, whom I saw struggling to find some impact of his own to match Harbatu's, to keep himself from disappearing into that intense personal field.

"Then you file charges."

Harbatu stood, dwarfing us both. He burned—with impatience, with outrage, with pain, with exploitation—I could no longer tell.

"Yes. Arrest both *him* and my daughter."

Jameson looked like a man choking on rivets. "I won't arrest Razowski, Harbatu, and neither would the colony police. He doesn't know it, but he's covered. There was a security agent watching his quarters all night. He never left. And Dr. Harbatu is covered as well, at least as far as having committed the theft herself. Any evidence the colony wants to bring against her would only be circumstantial, based on motive but not opportunity. She was . . . was with me all night."

He didn't look at me; neither did Harbatu. Harbatu said something, but I didn't hear it. I was already out the door, leaving them both there behind me.

      The strange thing was that after the first shock, I didn't really blame her.

I locked the door to my quarters, sat on the bed, and spread the contents of the tool case around me in a circle of yellow lamplight. Monocrystal steel scribe. Pliers: needle, bent nose, stubby, griplock, diagonal. Quantum spectrometer. Omnimeter. Hydrogen torch. And the terragauss-field sterilizer, fist-sized, shaped like a stoppered jar. In the lamplight it shone softly. I unpacked everything.

The tool-case lock showed that it had been opened at 15:06:24, not long after Rachel had followed Ta-Nin from the water purification plant. She had asked me to dinner first. I had refused, and only after that she had moved on to Jameson, a second cat's-paw. She had not begged me, or cajoled, or cried. She had—by whatever lies—gotten Jameson to set a watch on my quarters, removing me from complicity in her fight to save her work on Kelvin. It was a clean, tough, and purposeful fight, and in a curious way, impersonal. I did not blame her.

Once, I had insisted on fucking Rachel in her lab, in the middle of the working day. She had smiled that ironic mocking smile, and I knew nothing I could do would hurt her. We had screwed like animals. It was the only time I ever told her I loved her, and she had laughed and kissed me lightly, without answering.

I packed the tool case and reprogrammed the lock with a different code. I chose the date of Cassie's death on Janos. Harbatu would not say if there was another print of the holovid; my guess is that there was not. They liked that extra edge of intensity, Harbatu and Cassie. One print of the masterpiece. One cat's-paw.

I wondered if the Sha, in the sane generations before their enzymatic genocide, had provided not one but two hosts for the hungry sucker-edged mouths as they emerged.

Ta-Nin squatted beside the path outside my Quonset, watching as I reset the lock. I had not seen her in days. She waddled up to me, smelling subtly different: a heavy sweet-sick smell, like rotting flowers. Wordlessly, she handed me two stones.

I took them—what else? They were gray, irregular, featureless except for having been rubbed free of every trace of blue nonfung. Ta-Nin's dark alien eyes peered into mine. I shrugged ignorance; Ta-Nin went on peering. Finally I put the stones in my pocket and walked on toward the greenhouses. Ta-Nin followed, squatting just outside the doorway, a blurry image through the translucent synglass.

Was she going to begin labor—here? Now? From what Rachel had told me, it should not be for another week yet. Could the Sha time birth more accurately than humans? With Rachel arrested, was I still supposed to midwife for this blobby, doomed alien?

I went to work checking machinery that didn't need checking. No one came near me; Rachel's trial, with swift colony justice, was set for tomorrow. Time had been requested on the CorpsLink. Had anyone told Ta-Nin? Would she have understood if they had?

Half an hour later, I opened the door. Ta-Nin was still there, rolls of gray fat over huge flat feet. Directly in front of the doorway were two more stones.

I slammed the door shut and led her to Rachel's lab.

When we entered the building, it fell silent. Technicians and scientists alike avoided my eyes. Ta-Nin at first hung back, then crowded close to me, smelling foul. I hunted up Lemke.

"Razowski—I've been looking all over for you!"

He couldn't have looked very hard; I was on-call with the Link. I grunted something. Lemke looked at me, then away, blinking rapidly.

"Has Ta-Nin been with you all morning?"

"Yeah."

Curiosity showed in his face for a moment, followed again by that rapid blinking. He looked over my left shoulder and moved around the edge of a lab table. The corner jutted sharp between us.

"This is all ridiculous, you know. Rachel's arrest. They're just making a show for Harbatu's sake, and he's got his crew *filming* it. All of it."

I said nothing. Suddenly Lemke looked at me directly, still blinking.

"The colonists are afraid, you know. They're afraid that if Harbatu's holovid gets out and the Corps forces us to leave, then it's possible the whole planet might be quarantined. To colonists as well as research."

I reached for the stones in my pocket.

"Of course she's innocent," Lemke rushed on, "but if they find her guilty of the theft and that's the only print—I have to be at the trial, of course. I'm the only one who could explain what her work here consists of. The only one. I'm the only one who could carry on with it if she can't, if she—"

"If she what?"

"If she, well . . . if she can't." And he smiled.

The smile was involuntary: a sudden stretching of thin lips over sharp teeth. I saw Lemke's horror that the smile had happened at all. He fumbled to grip the jutting corner of the table. I threw the four stones down in front of him and said, "What are these?"

Lemke looked, not seeing them.

"I asked you what they are. She brought them to me, Ta-Nin, two at a time. These two first, then these two. What are they?"

Finally he seemed to see the stones. "When?"

"This morning. She was waiting outside my quarters. Then she put the other two outside the door at the greenhouse."

Lemke picked up the stones and fingered them. Professional blandness settled over him like smog. "We've only seen this a few times. The Sha are secretive, you know, and if we get too close, they lie. But see how all the nonfung has been ground off? These are ritual stones, a formal request for help to a sister's mate from a woman about to give birth, when her own sisters can't help. We think."

He frowned, a grotesque wrinkling of bony chin.

"She probably didn't know what other category to put you in." Suddenly his eyes gleamed with malicious pleasure. "This might mean she considers Rachel to be some sort of sister. A Corps research head . . . but maybe not. They're not very inventive, you know. At any rate, the stones mean that the Sha's very close to birth. Tonight maybe, or tomorrow night."

He looked at Ta-Nin. She turned clumsily in a circle and began to edge out of the room.

"Rachel is still confined to the city, of course. She told me the arrangements she made for you. To function as a *Sha male*." He grinned.

I shifted my weight against the table. Lemke said hastily, "There's a couch in Rachel's office. I know she thinks Ta-Nin will be willing to birth here in the lab, but I don't. I think once labor starts she'll revert to taboo and go on out to the forest alone. So the building will be locked. When the birth starts, she'll start walking in circles, over and over, and she'll probably wail to get out of the building. Her noise will wake you, and you can take the vial of enzyme—it's here in this case, the only one on this shelf, so you can't mistake it—and follow her. Buzz me first. And take a remote tracker so we can find you."

"All right," I said, to say something.

"Pour a third of the enzyme over each offspring as it emerges—Sha never have more than three. If Ta-Nin vomits on her own, don't worry. The enzyme doesn't have to be very concentrated to turn the offspring away. And she may not even try. In fact, she might not understand what we're trying to do here at all, despite what Rachel says. They're not very bright, you know. Despite Harbatu's sentimental grandstanding. They're just barely sentient."

"Then why do you want Rachel's credit for saving them?"

Lemke looked at me as if I were a dead fish. I shoved the table forward and left.

Outside, Ta-Nin handed me two more stones.

That night it rained. Even though I knew the gravity was .97 Terran, the rain seemed to fall slowly: great cold drops struggling through living smog, to reluctantly splatter on the spongy earth and be swallowed. There were no puddles on Kelvin.

The sparse gray fur on Ta-Nin's head and back matted, smelling worse than before. She lumbered slowly beside me, and it seemed that her belly had distended even more since that afternoon. I had found her squatting outside the power Till, outside the water purification plant, outside my quarters after a solitary dinner ordered in. Did she need to eat? I figured that if she did, she would.

At nearly midnight we set off for the lab, through the filthy rain.

As I had hoped, everyone had gone. I led Ta-Nin to Rachel's office, not letting her see me lock the building door behind us. She curled up under the table I had shoved at Lemke, which seemed odd—if Sha birth was supposed to be out in the open, wouldn't she try for as much open as the large room permitted? I didn't worry about it. Lemke's anxious insistence that I buzz him when labor started was so much crap; I didn't believe for a minute that the lab wasn't fully monitored by more than the Link.

Rachel's office, however, probably wasn't. She would have

known, and wouldn't have stood for it. I offered Ta-Nin a blanket, which she ignored. I left it on the floor beside her, went into Rachel's office, and stretched out on the couch.

An hour later I woke up, disoriented. Beyond the office door the lab was pitch black, although I knew I had not turned off the lows. I groped for the switch, flooded the place with light, and scooted to Ta-Nin's table.

She blinked up at me. I said, stupidly, "Are you all right?"

She blinked again and turned away. The rotting-sweetness smell rose from her like smoke. I made my way back to the darkened office and lay down.

A few minutes later I heard her drag heavily from under the table and across the floor. All the lights went off.

I grinned at Lemke and his monitors.

Hours later I bolted awake, listening. Noise. Around me the darkness pressed like dreams. But there was no walking in circles, no wailing. I heard the noise again: the scrape of a table leg across the floor. Ta-Nin must be shifting clumsily in her sleep.

I wondered what Justin Harbatu could create from Sha dreams.

Kleinstadt's judicial chambers were more B.H. romanticism: synthetics molded to look like heavy dark wood, oversized Link terminal with styling popular a generation ago, all needlessly bright memory chips visible behind permaplas. Schlock, but technically good quality schlock. Kelvinites jammed the seats, but they too gave me an unexpected feeling of quality, of a peculiar sort. Unexpectedly quiet, expectedly grim, they sat with a perverse dignity. If the Corps shut down the scientific compound, it would make little difference to them. If the Corps evacuated Kelvin, they would lose everything. Faced with this threat, however secondhand, to their homes, they sat stiffly and did not look at Harbatu, who on many worlds would already be dead. "The human mind supreme, untainted."

Or maybe they just wanted to look good for the camera.

"Mr. Harbatu," Governor Kleinstadt said, his jowly face stripped of all geniality, "your turn. Face the DataLink terminal, please. Statement."

"I came to Kelvin with an artistic purpose," Harbatu began quietly, "and found a humanitarian one. I am an artist. An artist's job is to make humanity look at itself, to show us things we sometimes might not want to see. An artist . . ."

The governor let him go on being artistic for several minutes more. Harbatu had not chosen to dress as I thought he would. I thought he would wear the gaudy trappings of one of the sophisticated worlds Kelvin colonists would never see, underlining his position as an outsider from somewhere less parochial, more passionate about beauty and truth and wide-angle justice. A phoenix in the void. But instead he wore a plain gray tunic. He had pitched his famous voice a little higher than at his concert, however; the Link is usually set for the middle vocal ranges. He was a pro, all right. When had I become immune to him?

The moment I saw Rachel sitting beside Kleinstadt.

She didn't avoid my eyes. Steady, unflinching, she looked at me and nodded. The nod said there would be no self-tortured apologies for the laser saw, no passionate justifications for Jameson, no desperate appeals wrenching my guts into water. She trusted me to understand that she had been protecting her work, and if I did not, tough reentry. Tough, and clean.

I nodded back.

Finally Harbatu began to actually recount what had happened the night the holovid disappeared.

"And you heard nothing?" the governor said.

"Nothing identifiable."

"DataLink?"

The colony Link coded and cross-checked the testimony. "No questions," it said.

"Anyone else want to ask Mr. Harbatu anything?" the governor said. Evidently Kelvin had purchased the very loose Reform Legal Package.

"I do. But later," Jameson said. His face was as blank as Rachel's, but not as clean. He did not look at her.

"Well, I do *now*," the governor said. The air in the room, Kelvin-thick, jerked taut. "What made you think, Mr. Harbatu, that the Corps researchers had anything to do with starting the Sha illness?"

Harbatu's gaze traveled the room. I saw that he had expected this, just as he must have expected the colonists' hostility. Love of home planet versus reverence for life, all set among the B.H. simpletons who claimed exclusive right to such reverence. It would make a great vid.

"Is this relevant, Governor, to the theft of my property?"

"If it's not, the Link will ignore it. *I* want to know."

"If you're asking, Governor, whether I have hard statistical data, replicable and publishable—no, I do not. That is the function of the scientist, not the artist. The artist moves on the wave front ahead of the replicable. He *must* do that, if he is to have any value at all." Harbatu leaned forward, gripping the arms of his chair with both hands. In my mind's eye I saw Lemke, gripping the edge of a lab table. "To struggle to name what hasn't yet been named. To show us all the possibilities, for good and for ill—don't you see? Don't any of you *see?*"

He looked at us, pleading in the alien green eyes, and I suddenly saw the one thing I did not want to see: he was sincere. Not playing for the holovid. He believed what he was saying, and he believed it because it was, at least in some sense, true.

"Art shows us to ourselves, and until we look, we don't know what we are. Not fully. We don't see our own greatness, or our own guilt. The artist—from *Genesis* on—has taken on that burden of human guilt nobody else can yet bear to assume, in order to *make* it assumable. Socrates, Christ, Sakharov, Pollidena—the performing artist has held a mirror to our guilt. Art itself—"

But he had gone too far. The governor's face mottled. "The 'burden of guilt' in this case, Mr. Harbatu, is being charged not to you but to your daughter!"

Harbatu shifted his gaze to Rachel. I think it was the first time he had looked at her. His eyes filled, horribly, with tears. They did not fall, merely shimmered in a green film. The governor's face lost its high color, looked uncertain. Finally he looked away. No one moved. No one, it seemed, could—except Rachel.

She met that terrible nakedness for a long time before her gaze dropped. Only that. But I had seen, and recognized, and something in my chest that I had not known was still there, that I had thought long since smashed, stirred and clawed.

"That's all," the governor said, finally. "You're done, Mr. Harbatu. Security Chief Jameson, please. Face the DataLink, Mr. Jameson."

Rachel never raised her eyes again. Jameson testified, in a dry voice spare with words. I did. Lemke did, and Jameson's agent, and Harbatu's holovid engineer. The colony Link asked a few questions.

"All right," the governor said wearily. "DataLink, connection to SectorLink 710. Request *amicus curiae* brief from Code 654-3210A, British-American-SpaceBeta tradition, Reform Legal Package copyright Juno Corporation. Hear ye, hear ye. Court in recess."

We sat and waited. To call the CorpsLink decision an *amicus curiae* brief was a judicial euphemism; Rachel was not a colonist but a Corps citizen, and the Reform Legal Package was accredited. The governor laboriously hand-wrote his legal opinion. Three and a half light-years away, the SectorLink retrieved the testimony from megalight, coded it mathematically, cross-checked in the indicated tradition: thousands of precedents, millions of facts, dozens of events as recent as an hour ago from as distant as the edge of the spiral arm. The governor wrote with his left hand, the thumb criss-crossed with thick, whitened scar tissue.

The Link said, "CorpsLink *amicus curiae* brief received."

"Just a minute, just a minute." Kleinstadt scratched some more, read it over, handed his paper to the court clerk. The clerk held the two papers, one in each hand. When he swallowed, long tendons in his neck surfaced like ropy fish.

"Hear ye, hear ye. Basic Humanitarian judicial opinion is that the accused, Dr. Rachel Susan Harbatu, is not guilty of theft."

It had not been in doubt. No one moved.

"*Amicus curiae* CorpsLink judicial opinion is that the accused, Dr. Rachel Susan Harbatu, is not guilty of theft, due to lack of substantial evidence."

"A match," someone said just behind me. His voice curdled with disappointment. It was Lemke.

Harbatu rose. He walked over to Rachel and said, with infinite gentleness, "You did it."

She stood. He said in that same gentle voice, "I filed a Priority-A Alien Protection Violation with the Corps. Yesterday."

Everyone heard; faces clenched in anger. But still Rachel said nothing.

"Rachel. You had no right to take that chance with these beings' lives. No matter how statistically small a chance. The Corps should have been notified a decade ago. You had no *right* to feed your career on their extinction."

She spat in his face. Harbatu stood there a long moment after she had turned to walk away and I saw both their faces clearly, stacked one beside the other. Rachel kept on walking, and people sank back out of her way as if mowed down with a scythe.

Harbatu said clearly, his daughter's spittle still running down his face, "There is another print of the holovid."

She did not even look back over her shoulder.

I didn't remember walking outside the building. Lemke's hand closed on my shoulder, the fingers like sharp wire. "An Alien Protection Violation. He'll shut us down. All for . . ." His bony jaw quivered and I saw that he could not finish speaking; all I thought was how ridiculous he looked.

"I have to get back, Lemke. To Ta-Nin."

"Why bother? We'll never finish the work now. Not before the Corps acts on that . . . that. . . ."

His fingernails felt too much like Rachel's, the night of the performance. I shook him off. "And if it hadn't been for Rachel, Harbatu wouldn't be here at all. Isn't that what you're thinking?"

Lemke's eyes glittered, and then his face went blank, as completely empty as if somewhere in his mind circuits had switched off. I thought that if the Corps shut down the research compound, the scientists would leave—but not Lemke. Physically and emotionally unfit for anywhere but the colony he hated, he would remain on Kelvin until he died.

"Everyone on the research team is of course concerned about Dr. Harbatu," Lemke said with such tinny pomposity that I nearly brayed. Lemke's face stayed deadly blank.

I didn't take the shuttle from the city back to the compound. I should have, because of Ta-Nin, but I thought of the whispered speculation, heads averted from me: *Who had taken the holovid? For whom? Jameson* . . . and I walked the ten klicks, on the road laid down by the original engineer. Strange plants I hadn't seen before, that must not grow near the compound, edged the hard duraperm. One was reddish-brown, thick and wavy, almost like human hair. Twice a vehicle passed overhead, and once on the road itself. Each time, I stepped off the road and deep into the alien forest, crouching down among the flaccid shoulder-high plants until they met over my head, the thick blue-mottled leaves closing over me like water.

Ta-Nin waited outside my quarters. When she handed me two more stones, I could see their imprint pressed into the fat of her palm.

By the time I took her to the lab, it was again silent and dark. Had there been even one light, I think I would have turned us both back. Maybe not; shambling heavy beside me, Ta-Nin smelled even worse than last night, but this time I knew what the smell was. It was fear. I didn't know what she had thought during the hours we had all been gone to the city, nor who had been with her in the hours since. Rachel? Lemke? No one? She seemed different, somehow: something in the dark alien eyes. She might have thought we had all abandoned her. She might have thought anything.

I went into Rachel's office only to take the stoppered vial from its rack, and did not look at the couch.

Ta-Nin crawled under her table and lay down. I turned off all the lights and sat under the switch, the small of my back resting against the wall. The last thing I thought was *I won't sleep,* before I did. Machinery chugged in and out of my dreams, the kind of machinery that has not existed for three hundred years: pistons thumping with hot steam, fans pumping coolant, gears turning with teeth sharp enough to bite bone.

Then I was awake, in the darkness, knowing somehow that Ta-Nin was gone.

"Ta-Nin!"

She was nowhere in the lab, nor in Rachel's office. I thought of all the places she could be in the unlocked portions of the rest of the building, all the dark crannies large enough for a panicked alien about to give birth to children who would eat her. In Animal Control, I scanned the pens; none of the jelkin seemed to be gone, but I couldn't be sure. Racing through the corridors, turning on lights as I ran, I called out again and again. No answer. When the first grub turned on her, would she scream? Would that be too late?

"Taaaaaaa-Niiiiiin!"

She had *asked* for my help; why would she go away without it? Lemke had said she would revert to ritual, go to the open woods. He had also said that Sha were stupid, barely sentient, whereas Rachel thought otherwise. . . .

I moved down the corridor to the building's outside door.

The door, which I had left carefully locked, stood wide open. I punched up the record of the last opening. It was half an hour ago. From the inside.

Ta-Nin is an unusually intelligent alien.

Things shifted in my mind, great subterranean realignments like tectonic plates. A Sha who could learn to punch in an E-code . . . how much harder would it be to learn to use a laser saw? To use it clumsily, ineptly, the tuning already set and locked in, just enough to burn a hole in a synthetic flooring. For a synthetic sister, who was going to save your life.

Stumbling over my own feet, I ran back to the lab. The stoppered flask, which I had left beside me under the light switch, was gone.

Outside, it had rained again. The spongy ground held no footprints, but I thought I knew where Ta-Nin would go. The shallow dell where she had seen one taboo broken lay to the north. But if she went there, why without me, after all those mute appeals for my help? And if she went there without a host. . . .

I started to run, but stopped a little way from the building and turned to retrace my steps. This time I punched up the building lock record for the last six hours. Five minutes before the last unlocking the door had been opened from the outside, and then closed. A generic code opened the door from the inside; from the outside, the codes were individualized. This was the only one I would recognize; I had used it myself. It was Rachel's.

Undoubtedly a visual monitor covered this door, but only Security would have access to that record. Rachel would know that. Had she come to check on Ta-Nin, closed the door behind her, opened it, and left with Ta-Nin five minutes later? But Ta-Nin would not accept Rachel's help with her birthing. Only a sister's mate would be acceptable as midwife. *We think.*

I stood in the filthy air, thick as damp smoke, staring at the lock record. When someone moved up behind me, I didn't hear movement before voice, and I jerked as if I'd been shot.

"Razowski. What are you doing?" Lemke.

He stopped two meters from me and I thought, crazily in the midst of all the other craziness, *out of arm's reach.*

"Ta-Nin is gone. With Rachel, I think."

"Rachel? No, she can't be. At least not with Rachel. I just spoke with her on the Link. I called to see if there was anything I could do. About Harbatu's protest to the Corps. About the research."

"You just spoke to Rachel? In her quarters?"

"Just a few minutes ago."

Rachel's quarters were much farther from mine than were Lemke's. I stared at him stupidly. In the light spilling from the open lab door, sweat gleamed on his bony face like thick ointment.

I pushed past him and began to run, covering the short distance from the lab to the edge of the compound, then along the path to the river. I couldn't find the place where Rachel and I had left the path and crashed through the squat forest. I thought I had passed it when I heard Ta-Nin wail, and immediately afterward a piercing shriek of agony. Human.

Even with moonlight, I couldn't find the dell. Thrashing through the plants, gritty leaves whipping against my face until they filled my mouth, I couldn't find the dell. Then the human shrieking rose again and the ground gave way under my feet and I was sliding down the rock-strewn side of the depression where Ta-Nin lay. Sharp pain stabbed through my right elbow.

The third grub had just emerged from between her spread legs. It crawled blind in the thick night, open mouth swaying at the sky. I heard what I had been too nauseous to hear the first time: its thin wailing, nearly lost under Ta-Nin's cry of pain and that other, agonized shrieking.

The thing crept toward its mother's flesh. Ta-Nin, visibly gathering all her strength, raised Rachel's vial and splashed the last of the clear liquid over its mouth. The offspring wailed again, swayed, and turned away from her. It thrashed a moment, then changed direction and sank its mouth onto what had been Justin Harbatu's face.

He still moved. With my left hand I grabbed the grub's other end and pulled. The suckers did not loosen. I tore at the thing with both hands; it flailed horribly but did not let go. My own voice sounded in my ears as I pulled and pulled and the thing stretched until finally it tore. The other two still fed on Harbatu, one on belly and one on thigh. The one fastened on his belly crawled beside a pointed rock, sticky with blood and hair from Harbatu's skull.

By the time I fell backward with half of Ta-Nin's child slimy in my hands, only she and the other two offspring still moved.

People came crashing through the forest. Lemke, others. There was shouting, unintelligible yelling. Pain coursed through my arm. Above her two living children, Ta-Nin watched me from exhausted unfathomable eyes.

"He was looking for Rachel," Jameson said. His face was as gray as Harbatu's had once been from K-gas. We sat in Security the next morning, me sprawled across my chair, Jameson sitting in his as if bound to it. We did not look at each other.

"He had called me first, and I told him I didn't know where she was. Then he called Lemke. All the calls show in the Link. Lemke says he told Harbatu that he didn't know where Rachel was either. Lemke called Rachel after that, to ask about the research. By then she was home. She says she went to your quarters—witnesses saw her. She wanted to make sure you were at the lab with Ta-Nin, without actually going to the lab herself."

Jameson stared at a blank wall. His whole office was blank, the cubicle of a man giving nothing away. I said carefully, "Who opened the lab building door from the outside?"

"Harbatu. It's on visual. He used Rachel's code; she must have given it to him, on his previous visit to Kelvin."

"Does she say so?"

"She says she can't remember."

The lock codes were in simple sequence. By seniority. I didn't mention this; neither did Jameson. He moved doggedly on, his voice a straight hard road.

"Harbatu was still looking for Rachel. He closed the door, went to the lab, must have found Ta-Nin. You were asleep. She must have led him out and to the woods, since only she would know where that same dell was. Rachel must also have given her father the generic code to unlock the door from the inside. It's a simple one."

Sprawled in my chair, I gazed at the gray ceiling.

"Ta-Nin just picked the rock from the ring of them surrounding the birth place; you can see the shallow imprint in the ground where the pointed end had once been driven in. She says. . . ." Jameson stopped, looked away. I waited.

"She says Harbatu was going to hurt Rachel and make her go away. The researchers who speak Sha have been at her for hours, all the time she was pulling out her fur to make those damn safehouses. She tells one of them one thing, another one another thing. But that stays constant: Harbatu was going to hurt Rachel and make her go away. And then the Sha would go on dying forever."

I thought of an alien mind catching at the misshapen particles that drifted through the membrane of language. Seeing the jagged shards, the broken edges, but not knowing how they had once fitted together—if they ever had. Did Ta-Nin know that Harbatu was Rachel's father? What would it have meant if she had? How had she twisted whatever she thought she was being told over the last weeks by the researchers who talked to her?

Or perhaps no twisting had been necessary.

Jameson said, "The Corps wouldn't even have to be called in, except for—alien customs have Corps protection, especially for a low-sentient endangered species. If it weren't for the accident about which vial you took from Rachel's office, if you hadn't got the one that didn't just turn the grubs away from the mother but also actually attracted them to . . . to. . . ." He didn't finish.

"Accident," I say, for the sound of it.

"Yes. That's what Kleinstadt says. He would be the one to start anything legal, if he thought there was a reason."

I said nothing.

After a while, Jameson repeated, "Accident. Rachel says—" He stopped, heaved himself to his feet, and looked away from me. I would never hear what Rachel had said. When Jameson moved to the Link, it was with the overly careful fumblings of a man carrying something large, and heavy, and too costly to let out of his sight for even an instant, ever again.

That was my last conversation on Kelvin. Jameson had witnessed what I had to say to the Link, in case it should, sometime, be wanted. By someone.

I thought of what I did not say to the Link. I did not say: on 6 percent of the worlds we touch, we destroy something biological. I did not say: sometimes the biological destruction flows the other way. I did not say: Cassie once had thick black hair.

Afterward, Jameson himself drove me to the port. Neither of us mentioned Rachel again. Under Jameson's hands the shuttle throttle shimmied lightly side to side, and I was careful to not notice.

When the *Somerset II* leaves tomorrow, I leave with her. It's the ship Harbatu would have taken, but if Jameson thought of that, neither of us named it, among the other things unnamed. "Harbatu made this call, Rachel made that call, Lemke that other call." None of it important, none of it real. What was real was all conjecture, moving on the wave front ahead of the replicable.

Rachel's voice, saying: "We can synthesize chemicals to alter nearly any biological given."

Lemke's voice, not quite saying: "If it hadn't been for Rachel, Harbatu wouldn't be here at all."

Ta-Nin, coming to me just before I closed my quarters, to put into my good hand a stick woven with yellowed leaves. Her two offspring were not with her. I lay the stick on the floor and did not touch it again, nor did I ask anyone what it meant. Thank-you note, murder threat, curse for infanticide, request to stand godfather.

My last days on Kelvin, Rachel never tried to see me.

Waiting for the *Somerset II*, lying in my small stifling room at the spaceport, I see Rachel's face. The room is dark, but even if I turn on the too-harsh utilitarian light, I still see her face. Harbatu's should be there, too, covered with spittle and stacked side by side with hers the way they were in Kleinstadt's chambers, but I don't see it. Only hers. One is enough.

I'm leaving Kelvin not because I think Rachel instructed Ta-Nin to kill her father, but because I think she did not.

This may not be what Jameson thinks. If he is protecting her, he may think she used Ta-Nin that way. I am not sure what Jameson thinks. Unlike Harbatu, I will not lay claim to another's self-destruction.

Lemke talked to Harbatu that night; Lemke had had more time after the trial to talk to Ta-Nin; Lemke spoke the language. He had been suckled on it. The words of need turned rage were his native tongue. Since Rachel's resignation, he has become the head of biological research on Kelvin. Today he announced to Corps Data-Link, hungry for news of Justin Harbatu's spectacular death, that the scientific compound on Kelvin has just had a major breakthrough. He says the Sha biochemistry is the victim of a slow virus. He says they are close to isolating it. He says the Corps cannot interrupt this vital work now, even though research results on slow viruses are so hard to replicate by another scientific team. By the time you're sure you've infected the subject, its life-support circumstances have so often changed.

On the Sector worlds, Lemke will—at least for a time—be The Man Who Saved the Sha. Just as Justin Harbatu will be The Artist Who Died Witnessing Their Agony. The second holovid of Harbatu's last concert plays to the entire Sector next week, a breathlessly anticipated performance of a great visionary assuming a guilt no one else could, as yet, bear to assume.

Including Rachel. What I saw burning in her eyes when she spat at her father was not guilt, and not murder. Not even hatred. It was something else.

The last thing Cassie ever said to me, just before I aimed the terragauss sterilizer at her head, was *We won't ever escape each other, Jake. No matter what I put you through. Never. Sometimes I think I was never alive until you were here.*

The *Somerset II* plans space runs for over a year. Quick orbits, lots of loading and unloading, docking machinery and life-support systems under constant use. And there are other ships. I can stay in space as long as I choose.

There are no cannibals in the void.

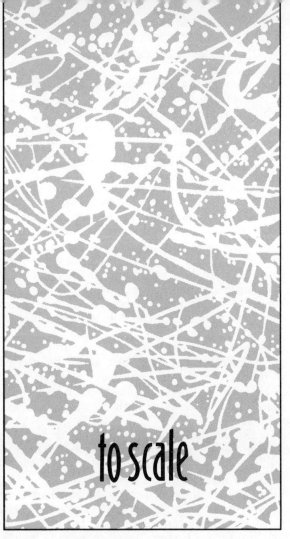

to scale

WHEN YOU GET home on Saturday night, your father is drunk again. He's a polite drunk; nothing in the living room is broken. There's only the spreading stain of his last whiskey on the worn carpet beside the overturned glass. You gaze down at the small wispy man lying there unconscious, the hems of his polyester suit pants twisted up over white sweat socks to reveal the skinny, hairy ankles underneath. One shoe off, one shoe on, diddle-diddle-dumpling my dad John. Everyone says you are the spitting image of him at your age—everybody, that is, who ever notices either of you. Usually you try to avoid mirrors. You are seventeen.

After you get him into bed—he's very light—you scrub hard at the whiskey spill on the roses-on-black carpet. It was your mother's. The smell disappears, replaced by pine-scented ammonia like hospitalized trees, but the petals of one rose stay discolored no matter what you do. Finally you give up and turn out the living-room lamp.

It's 11:00 P.M. Not very late; you didn't stay long in town. Just went to the hardware store, had a hamburger, drove around awhile in the battered pickup, watching couples whose names you know from school walking and laughing on the summer streets. Then home again, because where else was there to go.

There isn't anywhere else now, either. But you're restless. You can't sleep this early. You go through the kitchen out onto the porch, banging the screen door behind you.

A little wind murmurs in the trees. You put your hands on the splintery porch railing and lean out into the night. It smells of wild thyme, hemlock, mysteries. But through the open bedroom window comes the sound of your father's snoring, arhythmic and faltering. You go down the steps and start across the weedy lawn.

Here, the stars are magnificent: sharp and clean in a moonless sky. You tip your head back to study them as you walk. Halfway to the road, a huge black shape hurls out of the darkness straight at your throat.

You scream and throw up one arm. The shape hits and you both go down. You scream again, a high-pitched shriek that echoes off something, and try to roll away from the beast's jaws. Someone shouts, "King! King! Here, boy! Yo!"

The dog hesitates, then opens its mouth and snarls at you. From over your own upflung arm you see its eyes glow. Starlight reflects off its teeth. Frantically you keep rolling, but then the dog turns and trots across the road, where the voice is still yelling, "Yo! King, yo!"

Shakily you get to your feet. Mr. Dazuki strolls up, flicking cigarette ashes. "He get you?"

Your jeans are torn at the knee. Your arm is bloody, but that's from scraping the ground. "No," you say. And then, "Yes!"

"He break the skin?"

"No."

"Then you're all right," Dazuki says casually, and turns to leave. On the other side of the road he half turns. You can hear his grin in the darkness. "Don't be such a wimp, boy. Dogs're only afraid of you if you're afraid of them."

You are shaking too bad to risk an answer. You force yourself to walk slowly. Back inside your house, you lock the door and then stand for a long time against the refrigerator, your cheek pressed to its smooth coolness.

When your breathing has slowed, you go through the basement door down to the cellar.

Forty years ago the cellar had been subdivided into a maze of small rooms. Some have concrete or plywood walls; a few are walled in hard, bare dirt. You go past the discarded furniture, the broken washer/dryer set, the chamber with the sad piles of frayed rope and rusted fishing poles and paint cans whose contents have congealed into lumps of Slate Blue or Western Sky. Nobody but you ever goes down here.

At the far end of the house, in a cool windowless room that once was your mother's fruit cellar, you turn on bright two-hundred-watt bulbs wired into overhead sockets. The room springs into light. It is about twelve feet square, but less than half of the floor space is left. The rest is occupied by the dollhouse.

It started with the fruit shelves. After your mother died, you ate one jar of her preserves every day, until they were all gone. Strawberry jam, apple butter, peach jelly, stewed rhubarb. Sometimes you got queasy from so much sweetness. Your stomach felt like a hard taut drum, and that made you a little less empty. But then the fruit ran out. The shelves were bare.

You covered them with her collection of miniature glass animals: swans and rabbits and horses of cheap colored glass, bought at state fairs or school carnivals. They looked awful on the bare splintery shelves, so you brought in weeds and rocks and made a miniature forest. On the central shelf you put some dollhouse furniture you'd found in a box at the back of her closet. It looked old. You wanted to make it look better, so you found a scrap of carpet for a miniature rug. You found a doll's tea set at the Wal-Mart. You built a little table.

When the fruit shelves were full, you had no more reason to stay down here.

You built another row of shelves in front of the first. You've always been good with your hands, even at twelve. The shelves had a professional look. Making tiny furniture for each shelf wasn't hard. The scale was easy to work with, easier than real furniture would have been. You found you could make it look exactly how you saw it in your mind.

When you were fourteen, you read about a craft fair in the next town. You took your father's truck and drove there, even though fourteen is too young to drive legally in this state. Already your father didn't notice.

Miniature dishes for sale. Pillows, mailboxes, tea towels, cat bowls, weather vanes, scythes, doorknobs, toothpaste tubes, televisions, Tiffany glass, carpenter's chests. You couldn't believe it. You had seven dollars in your jeans. You bought a package of Fimo dough, a pamphlet on electrifying dollhouses, and a set of three tiny blue canning jars filled with miniature jelly.

By now the dollhouse is eleven or twelve layers deep. You build each one out in front of the next, with no way through except unseen doorways seven inches high. Official miniature scale is one inch to one foot. Each layer reaches to the ceiling and has twelve floors, with several rooms on each floor. Some rooms are furnished with cheap plastic dollhouse furniture you found in bulk at a factory closeout, dozens of pieces to the two-dollar pound. Some are furnished with simple straight-lined beds and tables of balsa, which you can turn out three to the afternoon. Some are elaborate period rooms over which you worked for months, with furnishings as authentic as you could devise or could buy mail-order. You work twenty hours a week at Corey Lumber for twice minimum wage, forty hours a week in the summer; Mr. Corey feels sorry for you. Your father never asks what you do with your money.

Somewhere in the impenetrable maze of tiny rooms is a Georgian drawing room with silver chandelier and grand piano from Think Small. Somewhere is a Shaker dining room with spare, clean lines in satiny cherry. Somewhere is a Tidewater Virginia bedroom, copied from a picture in *Nutshell News*, with blue velvet hangings, inlaid table, and blue delftware on the polished highboy. You will never see these rooms again; they've been covered over by newer layers. You don't have to see them again. You know they're there, hidden and unreachable. Untouched. Safe.

You pick up a piece of thirty-two-gauge two-conductor stranded wire and a twenty-five-watt pencil-tip soldering iron from your workbench. You are wiring a room for a pair of matching coach lights. They go well with a six-inch teak table you found cheap at a garage sale. Some kid had thoughtlessly carved "HD" across its top, but you can sand and restain that. The three matching side chairs are also restorable. You have learned to reupholster seats one and a quarter inches wide.

School lets out in mid-June. You work full time at the lumberyard. Your father gets up after you've left the house for his drive into the city, where he works as a data-entry clerk. You get home before he does, fix something to eat, leave his food in a covered dish in the oven, and go to the basement. By the time you come up, he is sitting in the living room, lights off in the summer dusk, drinking. His speech is very careful.

"Hello, Son."

"Hi, Dad."

"How was work?"

"Good," you say, on your way out.

"Going out?"

"Gotta meet some friends," you say, which is a laugh. But he nods eagerly, pleased you have such a social life. When you come home at ten or eleven, he's passed out.

This is the only way, you think, that either of you can bear it. Any of it. Most of the time, you don't think about it.

In July a girl comes into the lumberyard — not a woman looking for newel posts or bathroom tiles, but a girl your own age, with high teased bangs and long earrings and Lycra shorts. This is so rare in the lumberyard that you stare at her. She catches you.

"What're you staring at?"

"Nothing," you say. You feel yourself blush.

"Yeah? You saying I'm nothing?"

"No, I . . . no, you . . ." You wait to see if more words will emerge, but no more do. Now she stares at you, challenging and sulky. You remember that you don't like this kind of girl. She is the kind who combs her hair all class period, gives teachers the finger, sneers at you if you answer in history, the only class you like. You start to turn away, but she speaks to you again.

"You got a car? Want to drive me home after this dump closes?"

You hear yourself say, "Sure."

It turns out she is Mr. Corey's niece, sent to live with him for the summer. She works the register afternoons. You suspect she's been sent away from her own town because her family can't cope with her, and that Mr. Corey's taken her in out of the same sympathy that made him pay you more than he has to. You've never known how to think about that extra money, and you don't know how to think about Sally Corey, either. You still don't like her. But she tosses her head at the register and rolls her eyes at customers behind their backs and sticks out her ass when she dances in place between sales, and you feel a warm sweet hardness when you look at her. By the end of the week you have driven her to a roadside bar where neither of you got served, out to the lake, and to a drive-through ice cream place.

"Hey, let me see where you live," she says, for the third or fourth time. "What are you, too poor or something?"

"No," you say. At that moment, as in several others, you hate her. But she turns on the pickup's front seat and looks at you sideways over the lipstick she's smearing on her mouth, and maybe it's not hatred after all.

"Then what?" she demands. "What is it with you? You a fag?"

"No!"

"Then take me home with you. You said no one's there but your old man."

"He'll hear us."

"Not if he's *asleep*," she says with exaggerated patience. "We'll go downcellar or something. Don't you have a cellar?"

"No."

"Well, then, the backyard." She lays a hand on your thigh, very high, and something explodes inside your chest. You start the truck. Sally grins.

At home, your father's silhouette is visible through the living-room window. The television is on; sharp barks of canned laughter drift into the night like gunfire. You lead Sally in through the kitchen door, finger on your lips, and down the basement stairs. You lock the basement door behind you with a wooden bar you installed yourself.

In the first of the tiny cellar rooms, across from the broken Westinghouse washer, is an old sofa. You and Sally fall on it as if gravity had just been invented.

She tastes of wild thyme, strawberries, mystery. After several minutes of kissing and wild grabbing, she pushes you away and un-buttons her blouse. You think you might faint. Her breasts are big, creamy-looking, with wide dark nipples. You touch them just as she reaches for the zipper on your jeans. You forget to listen for footsteps above. You forget everything.

But later, afterward, something is wrong. She rolls lazily to her feet and looks down at you, splayed across the couch, gloriously empty.

"That's it?" she says. *"That?"*

You are apparently supposed to do something more. Shame grips you as you realize this. You can't think of anything more, can't imagine what else is supposed to happen. Her glare says this stupidity is your fault. You stare at her dumbly.

"What about *me?*" she demands. "Huh?"

What about her? She was there, wasn't she? Does that mean she didn't like it? That you—oh, God—did it wrong somehow? How? Can she tell you were a virgin? You go on lying across the sofa, a broken spring pressing into the small of your back, helpless as an overturned beetle.

"Christ," Sally says contemptuously. She drags her blouse across her chest and flounces off. You expect her to climb the steps, but instead she moves into the next room, idly flicking light switches and peering around.

In a second you are on your feet. But you're dizzy from getting up too fast, and your fallen jeans hobble your ankles. By the time you catch her, she has reached the fruit cellar and switched on the light.

"Jesus, Mary, and Joseph!" She stares at the looming density of the dollhouse. Only one shelf of the current outermost layer is still empty. *"You* do this?"

You can't answer. Sally fingers a miniature plastic chair, a stuffed cat, a tiny rolling pin from Thumbelina's. She walks to your workbench. You have been antiquing a premade Chippendale sofa: darkening the fabric with tea, wearing out the armrests with fine steel wool. Vaseline, you have discovered, makes wonderful grease stains on the sofa back.

Sally starts to laugh. She turns to you, holding the Chippendale, her face twisted under her smeared makeup. "Doll furniture! He plays with little dollies! So *that's* why your prick is so itty-bitty!"

You close your eyes. Her laughter goes on and on. You can't move. This is the end of your life. You will never be able to move again. It's all arrived here together, in this moment, under the two-hundred-watt bulbs, in the sound of this girl's ugly laughter. The kids at school who don't know you're alive (but they will now, when Sally meets them and spreads this around), your father's distaste for you because you're not good enough, the wussy way you're terrified of King's teeth, the endless days where the only words anyone ever says to you are "Twenty-pound bag of peat moss." Or "Hello, Son." And the two are the same words.

A howl escapes your lips. You don't know it's going to happen until it does, and at the sound of it your eyes fly open. Something has left you, gone out on the howl—you can feel it by its absence. Something palpable as the hiss of escaping gas under boiler pressure. You can feel it go.

Sally is gone.

At first you think she's gone back upstairs. But the wooden bar at the top of the steps is still in place. You grope your way back downstairs and stare at the dollhouse.

The plastic chair is tipped over, and the tiny rug askew, as if Sally had just dumped them contemptuously back into their miniature room. You look closer. There are tiny scuff marks on the floor beneath the far doorway, the one leading into the doll-house's inner regions.

The next morning Mr. Corey meets you at the lumberyard gate. "Billy, what time did you bring Sally home last night?"

You are amazed how easily you lie. "About nine-thirty. She wanted me to drop her off at the corner, so I did."

Mr. Corey doesn't seem surprised by this. "Do you know who she was meeting there?"

"No," you say.

The corners of his mouth droop. "Well, she'll be home when she's ready, I guess. It's not as if it's the first time." After a moment he adds hopelessly, "I knew you'd be too good for her."

You have nothing to say to this.

When you get home from work there is blood on the porch steps. Heart hammering, you start through the kitchen toward the cellar stairs, but your father calls to you from the living room.

"It's okay, Son. Just a flesh wound."

He is sitting in the rocker, his hand wrapped in a white pillow-case gone gray from washing. The whiskey bottle is a new one, its paper seal lying on the table beside his glass. The glass is unbroken. Your father's face looks pale and unhealthy. "I didn't see the dog in time."

"King? King attacked you?" A part of your mind realizes that these are the first nonstandard sentences the two of you have exchanged in weeks.

"Is that the dog's name?" your father says blearily.

"Did he break the skin?"

He nods. You feel rage just begin to simmer, somewhere below your diaphragm. It feels good. "Then we can sue the bastard! I'll call the police!"

"Oh, no," your father says. He fumbles for his glass. "Oh, no, Son . . . that's not necessary. No." He looks at you then, for the first time, a look of dumb beseeching undercut by stubbornness. He sips his whiskey.

"You won't sue," you say slowly. "Because then you'd have to go to court, have to stay sober—"

Your father looks frightened. Not the terror with which he must have met King's attack, but a muzzy, weary fear. That you will finish your sentence. That you will say something irrevocable. That you, his son, will actually talk to him.

You fall silent.

He says, "Going out, Son?"

You say, your voice thick, "Gotta see some friends."

On the porch, you start for the truck. Something growls from the hedge. King barks and breaks cover, rushing at you. You jump back inside and slam the door. After a minute, when you can, you pound your fists against the refrigerator, which rattles and groans.

Your father, who must surely hear you, is silent in the living room.

You go down the cellar stairs. You don't even turn on any lights. In front of the dollhouse, you close your eyes and howl.

The suffocating anger leaves you, steam from a kettle. Coolness comes, a satiny enameled coolness like perfect lacquer.

From somewhere deep inside the dollhouse comes a faint high-pitched bark.

You turn on the overhead bulbs and peer inside as far as you can. It appears that three layers in, a wing chair might be over-turned, but it's hard to be sure. Two layers in, a hunting print from Mini Splendored Thing is askew on a wall.

At the foot of the cellar stairs you notice something white. It's Sally's cotton panties, kicked into a corner. You don't remember the kicking. The panties aren't what you expect from hasty scans of *Playboy* at the Convenient Mart, not black lace or red satin or anything. They're white cotton, printed with small blue flowers. The label says "Lollipop." You dangle them from your fingers for a long time.

You go back to the dollhouse. You think about King hurtling

himself out of the darkness, the gleam of his teeth by starlight. Those teeth closing on your father's hand. The speck of blood already soaked through the gray pillowcase.

You close your eyes and concentrate as hard as you can. Afterward, you peer into the mass of the dollhouse, trying to gaze through tiny doorways, past Federal highboys and plastic refrigerators. You see nothing. There is no sound. Eventually, you give it up.

You feel like a wimp.

The next day Sally is back at the cash register. She wears no makeup, and her hair is wrapped tightly in a French braid. When you catch her eye, she shudders and looks wildly away.

"Where's my dog?" Dazuki demands. "I know you did something to my dog!"

"I never touched your dog," you say, truthfully.

"You got him in there, and I'm coming in to get him!"

"Get a search warrant," you hear yourself say.

Dazuki glares at you. To your complete amazement, he turns away. "You damn well bet I will!" But even to your ears this sounds like bravado. Dazuki believes you. He doesn't think you'd imprison his dog, whether from cowardice or honesty or ineptitude. There will be no warrant.

You glance at the living-room window, which was wide open. Your father must have heard how you told off Dazuki. Both you and the asshole were shouting. He must have heard. You go into the house.

Your father has passed out in his rocking chair.

Two days later, an upholstered Queen Anne chair on the fourth shelf of the first layer has been chewed. The bite marks look somehow desperate. But each one is only $\frac{3}{24}$ of an inch deep, to official scale. They are mere pinpricks, nothing anyone could actually fear.

The first day of school comes. By the end of third period, American Government, it is clear to you that Sally Corey has said something. When you walk into a room, certain girls snicker behind their hands. Certain boys make obscene gestures over their crotches. Very small obscene gestures.

You spend fourth period hiding out in the men's room. While you are there, hands bracing the stall closed while delinquent cigarette smoke comes and goes with the bang of the lavatory door, something happens to you. Fifth period you walk into Spanish III, coolly note the first boy to mock you, and listen for his name at roll call. Ben Robinson. You turn in your seat, look him straight in the eye long enough for him to start to wonder, then turn away. The rest of the period you conjugate Spanish verbs so the teacher can find out what useful information everybody already knows.

At home, in front of the dollhouse, you close your eyes. Ben Robinson. Ben Robinson. You howl.

There is a scuffling noise deep in the dollhouse.

For an hour you work at your bench. The Chippendale sofa is finished; you are building a miniature American Flyer sled of basswood. It will have a Barn Red finish and a rope of crochet cotton. You think of this sled, which you have never owned, as the heart of rural childhood.

After an hour, you close your eyes again and concentrate on Ben Robinson. When you're done, you inspect the dollhouse. The second-layer furniture that has been knocked over ever since the night with Sally Corey is now standing upright. On the bottom shelf of the first layer, which is coincidentally where you plan to put the American Flyer, you find very small, dry pellets. When you carefully lift them to your nose on the blade of an X-Acto knife, they smell like dog turds.

The second weekend in September there is a miniature show in the Dome Arena in the city. The pickup truck has something wrong with the motor. You take the bus, and spend time talking with craftsmen. To your own ears your voice sounds rusty; sometimes days go by without your speaking two sentences to the same person. At school you talk to no one. No one meets your eyes, although sometimes you hear people whispering behind you as you walk away from your locker or the water fountain. You never turn around.

But here you are happy. An artisan describes to you the lost-wax method of casting silver. A miniature-shop owner discusses the uses of Fimo. You study room boxes from the eighteenth century and dollhouses extravagantly fitted for the twenty-first. You buy some miniature crown molding, wallpaper squares in a William Morris design, a kit to build a bay window, and a bronze bust of Beethoven $\frac{7}{8}$ of an inch high.

At home, the fruit cellar is not completely dark. Tiny lights gleam deep inside the dollhouse, too deep for you to see more than their reflected glow through doorways and windows. You stand very still. Only the outer two layers of the pile have any electrified rooms. Only in the last year have you learned how to wire miniature lamps and fake fireplaces.

While you're standing there, the small lights go out.

You start skipping school one or two days a week. You aren't learning anything there anyway. What does it matter if the tangent of the sine doesn't equal the tangent of the cosine, or the verb *estar* doesn't apply to permanent states of being? You are tired of dealing in negatives. You can't imagine any permanent states of being.

"Going out, Son?" he asks. His hand trembles.

"No," you say. "Leave me alone!"

Sometimes there are lights on deep in the dollhouse, sometimes not. Occasionally furniture has been moved from one room to another. The first time this happens, you move the wicker chair back from the Federal dining room to the Victorian sun porch, where it belongs. The next day it is back in the Federal dining room, pulled up to the table, which is set with tiny ceramic dishes. On some of the dishes are crumbs. You leave the wicker chair alone.

At the end of September you find a tiny shriveled corpse on the third shelf of the bottom floor, in a compartment fitted like a garden. It's King. The dried corpse has little smell. You cover it with a sheet of moss and carve a tombstone from a half-bar of hand soap your mother once brought from a hotel in New York.

Once or twice, sitting late at your workbench, you catch the faint sound of music, tinny and thin, from an old-fashioned Victrola.

"Listen," Mr. Corey says, "this can't go on."

You wipe your hands on your apron, which says COREY LUMBER in stitched blue lettering. In your opinion, the stitching is a very poor job. You're thinking of reinforcing it at home. "What can't go on?"

He looks you straight in the eye, a big man with shoulders like hams, fat veined through the muscle. "You. You talk short and mean to customers. Yesterday you told old Mrs. Dallway her windows weren't worth repairing, and your voice said she wasn't worth it, neither. You never used to talk to people like that."

You say, "I keep the stock better than it's ever been before."

"Yeah, and that's another thing. It's too good. Too neat."

You just look at him. He rubs a hand through his hair in frustration.

"That's not what I mean. Not too neat. Just too . . . it doesn't have to be that exact. Paint cans lined up on the shelf with a ruler. The same number of screwdrivers in each bin. You fuss over it like an old hen. All the small crappy details. And then you're rude to customers."

You turn slowly, very slowly, away.

"Just forget the small stuff and concentrate on the service that people deserve, all right?" Mr. Corey's tone is pleading now. He always liked you. You don't care.

"Yeah," you say. "What they deserve. I will."

"Good kid," Mr. Corey says, in tones that convince neither of you.

Dazuki has a new dog, a pit bull. It's chained in his front yard just short of the road. You stand by your mailbox and watch it stretch its chain, leaping and snarling. You go downcellar and give the dog two hours in the dollhouse, while you work on a nanny-bench kit from Little House on the Table. Banging and yelping, very faint, come from deep in the dollhouse. Once there is grinding sound, like a dentist's drill. Glass breaks. For the last twenty minutes, you add Dazuki himself.

When you go back outside, about 7:30 P.M., the pit bull is lying across its chain. Its neck is bloody; one ear is torn. It catches sight of you and cowers. You go back inside.

The nanny bench turns out perfectly.

On Saturday afternoon Mr. Corey fires you. "Not for good, Billy," he says, and somehow he is the supplicant, pleading with you. "Just take a few weeks off to think about things. We're slow now anyway. In a few weeks you come back all rested, snap bang up to snuff again. Like you were."

"Sure," you say. The syllable tastes hot, like coals. You take off your apron — you reinforced the stitching last night — and hand it to him. You seem to be seeing him from the small end of a telescope. He is tiny, distant, with few details.

"Billy . . .," he says, but you don't wait.

The house is silent. In the mailbox is the new catalog from Wee Three. Holding it, you go in through the kitchen, down the stairs, and jab the light switch in the fruit cellar. Nothing happens.

You reach to the ceiling, remove one of the bulbs, and shake it. It doesn't rattle. The disk-belt sander on your workbench won't turn on. But inside the dollhouse are the reflections of lights. In the windowless dark of the fruit cellar they gleam like swamp gas.

Upstairs, the refrigerator doesn't hum. The kitchen lights won't turn on. In the living room your father lies in a pool of his own vomit on your mother's rug.

You yank open the drawer in the scarred rolltop where bills are kept. It's all there: three monthly warnings from the electric company, followed by two announcements of service cutoff. Threatening letters from collection agencies. Politer ones from the bank that holds the mortgage. Your father's pay stubs. The last one is dated four months ago.

Your father is shrinking. He looks like Corey did: a speck viewed from the wrong end of a telescope. The speck dances randomly, a miniature turd in Brownian movement on the end of an X-Acto blade. You realize you are shaking. You kick him, and he grows again in size, until he and his pool of vomit fill the living room and you have to get out.

You go downcellar.

More lights gleam inside the dollhouse, some of them a lurid red. The dentist-drill grinding is back. There are other noises, fitful and rasping but faint. Small. Very small.

You close your eyes and the howl builds, against your father, against Corey, against the world. It builds and builds.

Before the howl can escape, your mind is flooded with objects, all miniaturized, all familiar, whirling in the fireball path of some tiny meltdown. Your work apron is here — COREY LUMBER — and your mother's rug, with all its stains. Sally's Lollipop panties and the rolltop desk. The set of baseball cards you had when you were ten, and the set of Wedgwood china inexplicably left to you in your grandmother's will. Your mother's hairbrush, the old cookie jar with the faded green giraffes, even the pickup truck, littered with McDonald's wrappers. Everything rushes at you: small, petty, and in shreds. The rug has been chewed. The desk legs, broken off, lie among shredded books. Splinters that were once nursery toys catch at the inside of your eyelids. Shards of Wedgwood are razor sharp. Everything whirls together in a space of your soul that is shrinking still more, contracting like a postnova star, collapsing in on itself to the howl of a frightened dog.

Your yell comes out. "Noooooooooo . . ."

You open your eyes. The fruit cellar is completely dark.

You grope your way upstairs, outside, gulping huge drafts of air. It is later than it could possibly be. Orion hangs over the eastern horizon. It is past midnight.

You lean against the mailbox for support, and look up at the vast immensities of the stars.

In a few more minutes you will go back inside. You'll clean up your father and get him to bed. You'll start to sort through the bills and notices and make a list of phone numbers to call. In the morning you'll call Mr. Corey, set up an appointment to talk to him. You'll use ammonia on the rug.

And then you'll bring the dollhouse upstairs, layer by layer, piece by piece. Even though there's no place to put it all. Even though the miniatures that you made won't look nearly as realistic by sunlight, and some of the tiny pieces will surely end up lost among the large-scale furniture in the rest of the house.

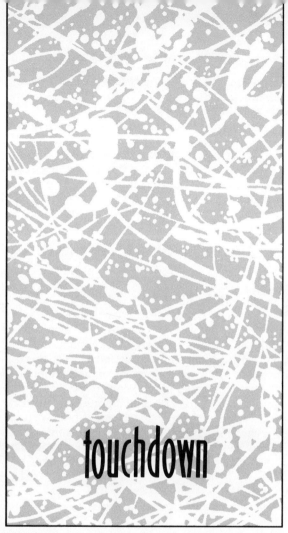

touchdown

MARIA TOLD ME that Team B had found Troy. It took me a moment to come up with the right answer (all we had found was Tokyo), and in that moment there was no way to tell how unprotected my expression had been. But I did come up with an answer. "That's impossible. Troy was *early*."

"Nonetheless, Team B found it. Excavated ruins."

"It wouldn't be big enough to carry any points!"

"It's on the exception list."

"I don't believe it."

Maria shrugged, watching (what had my face shown?). "So access the channel."

"But there wasn't anything *there*."

"There were enough exposed excavations or whatever to be on the list. Three hundred points. Leader just made the official acceptance." She smiled at me sweetly. "He said he was pleased."

Bitch. She knew I didn't access the open channel as often as she did; I work best with uninterrupted team-channel access. She also knew that Team B Leader had been my second husband. Her background psych research was always thorough. I toggled my 'plant to "record" and made a note to bid for her next season.

Tokyo was worth only forty-five points. *Anybody* can identify Tokyo, even starting from a fucking Pacific Island.

My Team Leader's voice buzzed in my 'plant. "Time's up, Cazie. Come on in."

"We have another four hours!"

"Touchdown city by Team A. Quarter's over."

Maria smirked; she was on Team A. Her 'plant had of course already told her about the touchdown. No appeal; someone on Team A had actually done it, gone out and touched an artifact from one of their cities. I turned away from her and pretended to study my console, my face under careful control. *She'll say it*, my 'plant said, programmed for this. The programming had been expensive, but worth it: no point in giving away rage if you can be warned those few seconds in advance that let you get your reactions under control. A few times the 'plant had even been wrong, audio context analysis being as uncertain as it is. A few times no one had even said it.

Maria said it.

"Don't be too upset. After all, Cazie—it's just a game."

Flying back is the part I hate the worst. Going out for the first quarter, of course, you can't see anything. The portholes are opaqued; even a loose chair strap could disqualify you in case it might let you glimpse something. During actual play, you're concentrating on the console readings, the team chatter as it comes over your 'plant, the hunches about where to search next, the feints to keep your flyer-mate off-balance. Especially the feints. You hardly notice the actual planet at all, even when you play in what passes for daylight.

But flying back to base, the quarter's over, the tension's broken, and there's nothing much going on over the 'plant to distract you from the place. And God, it was depressing. Even Maria felt it, she of the alloy sensitivity. We had been playing a day game in Tokyo; the computer flew us west, into the dying light. Ocean choked with slime or else just degree after degree of gray water, followed by great barren dusty plains howled over by winds of unbreathable air. Continents' worth of bare plains. Nothing hard, nothing bright or shiny, nothing cozy and compact. Just the bare huge emptiness. And overhead, the constant thick clouds that make it impossible to even guess where the sun is.

Once I told Ari—now Team Leader B—I wasn't sure the game was worth the aftermath, it was so depressing. He stared at me a long time and then asked, in that sweet voice that meant attack, whether the openness frightened me? And we were still married at the time. I said of course it didn't frighten me, what was there about such a dead world that was frightening? I kept my voice bored and disdainful. But he went on watching me anyway. And that was when we were even still *married*.

"Nothing," Maria said. She stood deliberately staring out the porthole as we whizzed over some dead plain. Showing off. Thinking she was outpsyching me. She even made a little song of it: "Nothing, no-thing, no-thing."

I didn't look at her. Maria smiled.

At the base we all gathered in the dome while the computer reffed the first quarter. The four members of Team A had found Sydney, Newcastle, Wollongong, Capetown, Oudtshoorn, Port Elizabeth, Shanghai, Beijing, and Hong Kong. The touchdown was for Sydney, but it was only a piece of bent metal, not a whole artifact, so it wasn't worth a lot of points. They had a lot of cities but the team had concentrated on coastal cities, which aren't worth as much overall because they're easier to find and to identify (although they did get extra points for Hong Kong, because it had sunk so deep).

Team B found Troy, Istanbul, Thessaloníki, New York, Yonkers, Greenwich, Stamford, Norwalk, Edmonton, Calgary, and Chikon: high initial points but a big loss after reffing because the North American cities were so close together and because they had misidentified Chikon—*twice*. I watched while the computer announced the adjusted score, but Maria went on smiling and her face gave away nothing. Neither did Ari's, damn him.

Team C found Rio de Janeiro, Santos, Campinas, Ourinhos—the actual Ourinhos, or what had been left of it after the earthquake—Bujumbura, Kigali, Dallas, Forth Worth, Waco, Austin, St. Petersburg, Tallinn, and Helsinki. An impressive score—and for nine of the cities they had been playing in the dark. The floating cameras zoomed in for close-ups of their smiles.

Team D found Tokyo, Jakarta, Bandung, Herāt, Farah, and (at the last minute, thanks to Nikos), Wichita. But we were saved from last place by Team E, who had found only *two* cities, Saskatoon and Kifta, and had misidentified Kifta. They couldn't hide their embarrassment, not even the Team Leader, not even when the cameras targeted him. The glances that went around the dome were almost compensation for our losing the quarter. Team Leader E stared straight ahead, mottled color rising on the back of his neck; unless he made a fast recovery in the next quarter, he'd be fucking his hand for *months*. And the fan reaction and betting back home on his orbital didn't even bear thinking about—let alone the sponsor's reaction. The team ended with only twenty-eight points adjusted.

Team C won the quarter, of course, 480 adjusted. Team Leader instructed me through my 'plant to try to find out their ID tactics in the coffee hour.

Larissa always does that to me. As if I were some kind of tactical genius, just because once I'd been quarterback for the team that racked up the record, 996 points in a single quarter. We'd found Pax. But you can't find Pax every quarter—after all this time, the accursed place is still floating around the Pacific—and underneath I'm always afraid some flyer-mate will psych out how bad I really am at team tactical programs.

What had Maria seen on my face?

I didn't find out. I didn't find out Team C's ID tactics either, because the coffee hour is only fifty-six minutes by strict rule before the blackout period, and Team B Leader had taken the risk of doping all of his people on Impenetrables set to kick in right after the ref announcements. God, he was self-confident. I looked at him sideways, when I was sure Maria or the cameras weren't watching. He hadn't changed much in the two years since our divorce. Short, muscled, smiling. Ari.

Then the coffee hour was over and the Leaders took the dome field down and Maria and I went back to the flyer and shot each other with the time-release knockout drugs. The camera hovered close as we laid the strips on each other's necks, and stayed close afterward. There's a hazy period while the stuff takes effect. Players are vulnerable: it's a warm sweet letting go, sometimes of words as well as consciousness. But I was pretty sure I didn't give anything away. Maria finally stopped talking to me and rolled over in her bunk, and I smiled to myself in the darkness.

Preparation for second quarter.

When I woke, Maria was blinking sleepily. The camera was already on. I felt rested, but of course that was no clue to how much time had elapsed—the drug made me feel rested. Had we been out two hours or twenty? However long it had been, the computer had moved all the flyers for the second round. I knew the latitude and longitude of where we had been, but now we could be literally anywhere in the world. Again.

Adrenaline surged, and my stomach tightened with pleasure. We strapped ourselves into the kickoff chairs. The portholes were shallow opaque caves. "Tallyho," Maria said. I ignored her. The computer kept us waiting for ten minutes. When the seat straps finally unlocked, Maria tried a direct run for her console (she's strong), but I was ready for her and made a flying tackle. She went down. I scrambled over her, reached my console, and activated it. The first half-hour control of the flyer was mine.

Maria got up slowly. She wasn't hurt, of course, but she made a show of rubbing her shoulder for the camera. She's a high-ranked player on a number of orbitals. Very dramatic.

The portholes deopaqued. Daylight. More barren plain, more dust blown by unbreathable air, some scraggly plant stuff in dull olive. Not much rock. No coast. No snow or frost, but of course with the greenhouse effect worsening every year that ruled out less than fifteen degrees of latitude. We could still be anywhere. You always hope the random patterns generated by the computer will set you down right at the edge of a qualifiable city, but that has only happened to me once. And it was Moscow, only ninety points unreffed.

I lifted the flyer for an aerial view, taking it up as high as the rules allowed. Maria and I both peered through every single porthole. Nothing but plain. Then I saw it, a quick flash of silver on the right horizon. Water. I headed right.

"Water over there!" I said excitedly, jazzing it up for the camera. It was watching Maria for the reaction shot, of course, but she just looked thoughtful: the serious young player concentrating for the fans back home.

A small river meandered across the dust. Along its banks, plants were a little greener, a little fuller. They disgusted me; pitiful things, trying to actually grow in this place. God knew what chemicals were in the river.

I followed it at top speed, needing to reach a city before my half-hour was up. With speed limited during play to sixty-five miles per hour, every minute counted. I didn't want to arrive at a city just as Maria's console cut in and mine shut down.

We flew for twenty minutes. Ruins appeared below us, some broken concrete and the mound pattern that means structures under the dust. But visual was enough to tell me that the place was too small to qualify as a city. Some stupid little town, not even enough left of it to get a fix on the architecture and make a guess what continent we were on.

Then the alarm bells went off.

"Lift! For God's sake, lift the fucking flyer!" Maria screamed. I thought she was overreacting for the camera until I saw her face. She was terrified.

Maria was—or rather, somewhere along the line had become— toxiphobic.

The computer had removed the aerial ceiling the second the radiation detectors had registered the toxic dump. I took the flyer up to forty thousand feet. It was the one time the rules allowed a major overview during a quarter, but Maria didn't even glance at a porthole. She stood breathing hard, eyes on the deck, pale as dust. By the time she had control of herself again, we had shot forward and I was dropping back to legal height.

Maria was toxiphobic.

And she hadn't even seen the ruins over the horizon at 342 degrees.

I used the five minutes I had left to take us as far in the other direction as I could. Five minutes would never be enough time to fly there and do an ID. My best bet was to hope she didn't fly that way during her half-hour.

She didn't. She veered off at twenty-eight degrees, and I kept careful track on my compass of everything she did after that. We came across three more polluter towns, but nothing big enough to qualify for points. When my console came back on, I headed straight back to my ruins, flying with that cocky grin that alerts fans that something is going to happen. Maria watched me sourly, at least when the camera was off her. "Know where we're going, do we?" I didn't answer. I didn't have to.

The city ruins were extensive, with roads leading in from all directions and a downtown section of fallen concrete and steel poking above the blowing dust. There were no clues, however, in the architecture, or at least none that I could identify. Ari had been the architectural whiz.

I started the chatter on the 'plant. "Cazie on. I've found one. Daylight, doesn't seem to be waxing or waning. No architectural clues to describe. Central downtown core, roads leading in from all directions, collapsed overpasses, plain with a 1.62-degree incline, small river flowing outside the city but not through it, no other still-existing visible waterways."

"Team Leader on. What's the diameter?"

"Crossing it now . . . I estimate three miles metropolitan . . . hard to be sure."

"Regular perimeter?"

"Circling now . . ." The detector shrilled.

I started to take the flyer up and to the right, but after a minute the alarm shut down.

"Cazie on. There's a toxic dump, but it's small—a few seconds moved me out of range."

"Did you see anything significant while you were lifting?"

"No. I'll circle in the other direction, try to get a shape for the perimeter."

By now the fans would be glued to their sets. They, of course, already knew what city we had. The name would be shimmering across their screens. The question now was, how would we players identify it? And who would get the points? I had 14.3 minutes left. Maria stood at her console, jaw clenched so tight her lips flared out slightly, like a flower.

"Cazie on. The shape is pretty regular. No, wait, it flattens out into a sort of corridor of ruins extending out at 260 degrees. There's a *river* here. Another one. A big one, but really muddy, clogged, and sluggish . . ." Not for the first time, I wished that soil analysis from inside the flyer was legal. Although then where would the challenge be?

"Jack on," he said through the 'plant. "Do the city ruins go right to the edge of the river or was there a park?"

"Cazie on. Seems to be extensive flat area between even the smallest ruins and the river."

"Team leader on. Vestigial vegetation?"

"None. The . . ." The alarm shrilled again.

This time the computer let me take the flyer all the way up. Maria started to tremble, clutching the edge of her console with both hands. Even over the alarms I could hear her: "Near cities. In their water, by their parks, goddamn fucking polluters, toxic dumps all over the place, they *deserved* to all die. . . ." But I didn't have time to gloat over her loss of control. Over twenty thousand feet the high-altitude equipment kicked in, all per game rules, and I got it all: aerial photos before we broke the cloud cover, sonar dimensions, sun position above the clouds, steel density patterns. Of course we couldn't access the computer banks, but we didn't have to. We had Jack, who had been a first-draft pick for his phenomenal memory. I passed him the figures right off the console, such a sweet clean information pass it almost brought tears to my eyes, and in less than a minute Jack said, "Syracuse, United States, North America!" Team Leader filed it, the computer confirmed, and the news went out over 'plants and cameras. The first score of the quarter. 185 points, plus points for initial continent identification, and no fouls for holding too long in toxic range. Mine.

I took the flyer down and grinned at Maria.

Once we knew where we were, the plays became a cinch. Chatter flew heavy over team channels: if you're in waning light and Cazie is in full light at 76°20′ W, 43°07′ N, where might I be in what seems to be dawn? I pictured fans flipping channels, listening, arguing, the serious bettors plotting flyer trails on map screens.

Maria found Rochester, United States. Her time ran out and I got Buffalo, United States, and Niagara Falls, Canada, which barely qualified for size and wasn't very many points, given that the falls are still there, torrents of water over eroded rock. Ari once told me that those falls are one of the few places on Earth with relatively clean water because water going that fast through rapids cleanses itself every hundred yards. He was probably teasing.

Time was called a few hours after we reached dusk. Maria looked tired and angry, the anger probably because she'd given away so much. She was behind in points, behind in psych-out, undoubtedly down in the betting back home.

I whistled some Mozart.

Maria stared at me coldly. "Did you know they buried him in an open grave for outcasts? With lime over him so the body wouldn't smell? Just threw him in like garbage?"

I shrugged. I couldn't see that it mattered. His music is glorious, but he was probably just as morally guilty as all the rest of them. Polluters do not deserve to live. That's the first thing children are taught: Do not foul the life systems. I had a sudden flash of memory: myself at four or five, marching around kindergarten, singing the orbital anthem and fingering the red stitching on my uniform: MY BODY, MY ORBITAL.

I said maliciously, "At least limestone isn't toxic." But she didn't even react. She really was depressed.

The screen in the corner suddenly flashed to life: Team Leader A. It startled both of us so much we turned in unison, like mechanical dolls. Only Team Leader A can use the screen to contact everyone during a game, and then only for game called, for an emergency, or for important news from home. He's the only one allowed direct orbital contact. My stomach tightened.

"Team Leader A. News flash. Don't panic, anyone, it's *not* an orbital. Repeat, no orbital is in danger. But something has happened: they've opened warfare on the moon."

Maria and I looked at each other. She was breathing hard. Not that she knew anybody on the moon, of course; it's been two generations since anybody but diplomats have made contact with those maniacs. Generations before that their ancestors chose their way off-planet, ours chose ours. To qualify for an orbital, you had to be a certain kind of person: nonviolent, nonpolluting, no criminal record of any kind, clearly self-supporting (you had to have money, of course, but money alone wouldn't do it), intelligent, and *fair*. You had to be able to respect rules.

Nobody else got in, not even relatives of qualifiers. Our founders knew they were choosing the future of the human race.

Everybody else with enough money but not enough decency tried to get to a moon colony.

"As far as orbital diplomats can tell, the war started when one underground moon colony mined another and detonated by remote. We don't yet know how many colonies are involved. But the orbitals agree that there is no danger to us. This war, if it is a war, is confined to themselves."

Team Leader A looked at us a minute longer. I couldn't read his expression. Then the screen went blank.

"Oh, God," Maria said. "All those people."

I looked at her curiously. "What do you care? There's no threat to any orbital."

"I *know* that. But even so, Cazie . . . that's not a game. It's real. Dying trapped underground while everything explodes around you. . . ."

I got out the third set of blackout strips. To tell you the absolute truth, I find attitudes like Maria's tiresome. She can't really care about moonies; how could she? They're no different from the maniacs who ruined Earth in the first place. She was just pretending because it made her look sensitive, cosmopolitan . . . to me it looked flabby. Moonies weren't like us. They didn't understand moral obligations. They didn't follow the rules. If they all blew each other up, it would just make space that much safer for the orbitals.

And her depression was ruining my triumph in the game.

That was when I realized that she must be doing it deliberately. And pretty neat it was. I had almost lost my edge for the game, thinking about moonies trapped underground . . . there's nothing so terrible about being underground anyway. It probably wasn't that much different from the coziness of an orbital. It was wide, open, unprotected spaces that were scary.

Unless you were scoping them from thirty thousand feet, making a high, clean information pass, the first one of the quarter and a total of two hundred points. . . .

I opened her blackout drug, grinning.

In the third quarter the computer set us down in darkness, on sand. Blowing sand as far as the high beams could see at maximum altitude. Miles and miles of blowing sand. Over my 'plant Nikos, our broad-base geography offense, ran me through the most likely deserts. Maria used a sweet triple-feint to get to her console first, and she called the first play.

We didn't find *anything* for hours. Team C reported Glasgow just as our sky began to pale in the east, and that gave us an approximate longitude. Jack found Colombo. Team A reported Managua and Baghdad. Then, slowly, mountains began to rise on our horizon. I calculated how far away they must be; they were *huge*.

"Nikos on," he said. "All right, I have to make this quick, Cazie, my play starts in forty-five seconds and we're coming into something. The mountains are part of the Rockies, and you're between them and the Mississippi River in the Great Central Desert of North America. Fly close enough to describe specific mountain profiles with degree separations to Jack, and he'll take it from there. Jack, can you take it now?"

"Jack on. Got it. Cazie, go."

I described for three minutes, and he suggested where I should look. I did, but not quick enough. Maria got La Junta, United States, North America. I got Pueblo, just barely. Then we hit a toxic dump and an announcement from Team Leader A simultaneously.

"Team Leader A. News flash. Orbital diplomats in three moon colonies have ceased communicating: Faldean, Troika, and Alpha. The assumption is that all three colonies are destroyed and our . . . our diplomats are dead."

His image stared straight ahead. After a minute he added, "I'll let you all know if they call the game."

Call the game.

"They won't do that, will they, do you think?" I said to Maria. She said, "I don't know."

I found Colorado Springs.

But how many fans were even watching?

They didn't call the game. We finished the day almost dead even. Right after we took the blackout drug, Maria crawled into my bunk. I was surprised—flabbergasted. But it turned out she didn't even want to fuck, just to be held. I held her, wondering what the hell was going on, if she thought I'd fall for some kind of sexual psych-out. The idea was almost insulting; I'd been a pro for nearly eight years. But she just lay there quietly, not talking, and when blackout was over she again seemed focused and tough, ready for the last quarter.

"Tallyho."

I never did learn what that meant. But I wasn't about to ask. I knew Maria had finished most of the two-year Yale software, and I've never even accessed a college program.

We deopaqued in rocky hills, in daylight. Twenty minutes later we found a saltwater coast. After that it was almost too easy: Algiers. Bejaïa. Skikda. Bizerte. Tunis. Not even any toxic dumps to speak of.

Too easy. And Maria and I were almost even in prereffed points.

"My play!"

"Take it, asshole. You won't reach Kairouan or Monastir by the time the quarter ends."

"The hell I won't."

Of course I didn't. It was too far. But I reached something else. The light had begun to fail. I gambled on sticking to the coast rather than flying inland toward Kairouan. Out of the gathering darkness loomed red cliffs. Piles of rubble clung to their sides, banked on terraces and ledges that had been folded by earthquakes and eroded by wind. From the sides of the cliffs twisted steel beams bristled like matted hair. "Cazie on. There's a city—maybe not a city —just below me. We're twenty-two minutes out of Tunis following the coast. Jack?"

"Jack on. Too small to qualify."

"Team Leader on. Sorry, Cazie. Come on in."

"It doesn't look too small!"

"It's too small."

"Maybe it's in the supplementary d-base." Nobody memorizes the supplementary database; it's all those cities and towns that don't qualify for points. Unless, of course, there's a tie, or a field goal at endgame. . . .

Seventeen minutes left.

"Team Leader on. We don't have any reason to think we're that close to a tie, Cazie. And if you earn a penalty by calling it wrong—"

Nobody can call in advance how the computer will ref points. Base points are of course known, but there are too many variables altering base points. If there's a flash of sunshine that the flyer registers as strong enough to count as a latitude clue, you lose points, even if you didn't notice that the fucking clouds parted. There are penalties assessed against other teams that you don't hear about until the quarter's over. There are points added for plays in darkness, subtracted for nuclear-radiation clues above a certain level, multiplied by a fractional constant for the number of cities already found during the quarter, factored for dozens of other things. But against all that, I *knew*. I did. We were close to a tie. You don't play this game for eight years without developing a sixth sense, a feeling. A hunch.

Sixteen minutes.

"Cazie on. I got a hunch. I just do. Let me try for a touchdown."

"Team Leader on. Cazie, last time you . . ."

"Larissa—*please*."

She didn't say anything. Neither did Jack or Nikos. Last time I tried for an endgame touchdown I froze. Just froze, out there alone in the howling unbreathable desert with no walls, no life-support, unprotected under that naked angry sky . . . We were disqualified. Disgraced. Odds on us lengthened to the moon, all four of us slept alone for a month. It took three flyers to get me in.

"Please. I have the hunch."

"Team Leader on. Go."

Fifteen minutes.

I slammed my fist onto the console code and struggled into my suit. The camera floated in for close-ups. Maria watched me through narrowed eyes. My 'plant said, *She's going to say it.*

"Cazie, it's only a game. It's not worth risking your life for a game."

I sealed the suit.

"You'll be exposed right at the edge of the ocean. God knows what toxins you'll be exposed to, even through the suit. You know that. We went right over that dump down the coast, and that ocean looks terrible. When your field's off, you'll be completely exposed."

I reached for my helmet. She was talking her fears, not mine.

"*And* you'll be right there in the *open.* God, all that open space around you, desolate, winds blowing—completely *exposed.* Unprotected. The winds could blow you off the—"

I sealed my helmet, shutting out her words.

The airlock took one minute to empty and open. Eleven minutes. The second the door opened, I was out.

The winds hit me so hard I cried out and fell against the flyer. The camera, buffeted by winds, was right behind me. I straightened and started away from the flyer. Almost immediately the fear was there, clawing at me from inside.

Open. Unprotected. Poisoned. Life systems fouled, death in the air and soil and water . . . Twenty-eight years of conditioning. And the fact that my conscious mind knew it was conditioning didn't help at all. Dead, foul, exposed, dead, dead, unprotected . . .

I made myself keep walking. Nine minutes.

The city—town, village—had been built down the cliff and, probably, along a coastal strip that was now all underwater. When they had built like that, often "richer" people lived higher up, in sturdier structures. Ahead of me the cliff turned in on itself a little, giving more shelter to whatever structures had been there. I made for the bend, running as fast as I could, the wind at my back, fighting the desire to scream. To fall. To freeze.

Around the curve of rock were twisted steel beams, welded together and extending back inside the rock. I wrenched at them, which was stupid; they were huge, and nothing was going to break off a piece that could be carried into a flyer. There were chunks of concrete all around, but concrete doesn't count. Below me, the poisoned ocean howled and thrashed.

I worked my way between the steel beams. Whatever walls had

been here had long since fallen down, the rubble blown away or washed away or just disintegrated. Dust blew all over everything; the steel and concrete were pitted by grit. It was the ugliest place I had ever seen. And it could shift under my feet any second. But between the steel beams a kind of cave, still roughly rectangular, led back into the cliff. The polluters had built into the earth before they destroyed it.

Three minutes.

I climbed over fallen rocks and rubble to get deeper into the cave house. For a moment I remembered the underground war on the moon and my breath stopped, but at the same moment I passed some kind of threshold and the sound from the horrible winds diminished abruptly. I kept on going.

Two minutes.

At the very back of the house I found it.

There was a loose fall of rock from the ceiling in the most protected corner; smashed wood stuck out from under it. Some piece of furniture. I tugged at the rocks; when they wouldn't move, I scrabbled with my hands behind them. Oh God, don't tear the suit, don't let the ground shift or more rocks fall from the ceiling, don't . . . my fingers closed on something smooth and hard.

And whole.

It was a keyboard, wedged between two rocks, slimy with some kind of mold but in one piece. I wiggled it free and started to run. For the first time in many minutes I became aware of the camera, floating along behind me. Not slowing, I held the keyboard in front of it, screaming words it couldn't hear and I couldn't remember. The winds hit me like a blow, but if I was clear enough of the cave for wind, I was clear enough for transmission.

"Cazie on! Larissa? Fuck it—*Larissa!*"

"Go!"

"I got it! A touchdown! A whole! A touchdown!"

"Touchdown by Team D!" Larissa screamed, on what I assumed to be all channels. "Touchdown!"

Thirty seconds.

The earth moved under me.

I screamed. I was going to die. The game was over but I was going to die, exposed unprotected poisoned dead on the fucking earth. . . .

The quake was small. I wasn't going to die. I swayed, sobbed, and began to fight my way back against the wind. Darkness was falling fast. But I could see the flyer, I was almost there, I had the whole, I was not going to freeze, and the treacherous earth was not going to take its revenge on me. On someone, almost certainly, eventually, but not on me.

Touchdown.

We won.

The reffed score among three teams—not just two, but *three*—was close enough to make the endgame play legal. We got 865 points adjusted, and beat the closest team, C, by 53 points. My keyboard gave us Sidi-bou-Zid, Tunisia, North Africa, from the supplementary database—a town no one had scored before.

The party at the base was wild, with fans at home flashing messages on the screen so fast you could barely read them. Drink flowed. I got pounded on the back so often I was sore. I had five whispered bids for the traditional postgame activity, *three* of them from Team Leaders. High on victory, I chose Ari. He had always been the best lover I had, and we even, in drunken pleasure, talked about getting together again back home. It was an astonishing party. Fans will talk about it for years.

Team Leader A says they'll put the keyboard in a museum in one of the orbitals, after the thing is cleaned up and detoxed. I don't care what they do with it. It served its purpose.

The moon war apparently was brief and deadly. No transmissions from any colony. They're assumed all dead. But while I was downing my third victory drink and Larissa and I were laughing it up for the cameras, I got a great idea. All the moon colonies were underground, so it won't take long for the surface marks to disappear: collapse the energy domes and in a few years meteors will make the surface look pretty much like the rest of the moon. But the colonies will still be there underground, or their ruins will, detectable to sonar or maybe new heatseekers. As long as the heat lasts, anyway. Looking for them will be a tremendous challenge, a new kind of challenge, with new plays and feints and tactics and brand new rules.

I can hardly wait.

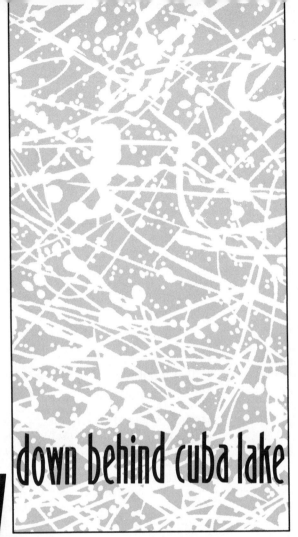

down behind cuba lake

WHEN JANE FINISHED reading the letter for the third time, she picked up the phone. Anger bubbled up through her like bad champagne, heady and perversely sweet. One hundred twenty miles away, Nick answered on the second ring.

"Hello?"

"This is Jane. I got your letter."

"Jane . . . "

"Yeah, Jane. You remember me. It was a lovely letter, Nick. Chatty and friendly and sweet."

Silence.

"It was really lovely to hear such great detail about the remodeling of your garage."

He said, very quietly, "Don't, Jane."

"Don't what?" she said automatically, before his quietness hit her. Then it did. This was Wednesday.

"Your wife is home."

"Yes."

Noncommittal, neutral. Was the woman in the same *room?* "You can't talk."

"No."

" 'Yes,' 'No'—what are you pretending, that I'm a fucking *construction client?*"

In his silence, Jane heard that he was doing just that. Tears bit her eyes. She moved to slam down the phone, stopping herself at the last possible moment before the receiver smashed into the erect double buttons.

"I'm coming down there, Nick. Tonight, after my evening class. I'll be there by eleven-thirty. Meet me at the bar, and you damn well better be there this time, I swear it. I have to talk to you. If you're not there, I'll come to your house and ring the bell and talk to you there."

She didn't wait for Nick's answer, but she heard part of it anyway while the receiver was on its way down: "Wait, tonight isn't—" The words already sounded tinny with distance, ghostly with loss.

She knew she was a better teacher when she was angry, was perhaps even at her best then. Even Freshman Composition sat up straight in its chairs, stopped doodling in its collective margins. During Romantic and Victorian Poetry, Jane sparkled with irony, grew passionate with the sort of literary scorn that impresses graduate students. Her notes strode across the board in a forceful hand she scarcely recognized as her own. The better students' eyes took on that thoughtful look that was at once public reward and a kind of private, sly seduction.

Not tonight, chickies. Sorry. Teacher has a headache.

Jane let them go at 8:45, fifteen minutes early, knowing she would need the time to peel them both off Wordsworth and off her, and escape to the car. By 9:02 she was pulling away from the campus, the lights of the high-rise dorms shining in her rearview mirror in erratic patterns like some indecipherable message from the sky itself. The October night was cold, desolately beautiful. She could feel her anger begin to slide away; she whipped it up again, afraid to feel what might take its place.

> *Dear Nick,*
>   *Don't write me, not even about the fascinating progress in remodeling your garage. I'll just have to live without finding out how much the insulation exceeds federal energy specifications. Don't write me, don't call me, don't try to drive up and walk into one of my classes—*

Fat chance.

She was crying again. *Fuck it.* She swiped at her eyes with a Kleenex, hunkered down over the wheel like a bad parody of a race car driver, and concentrated on the road. One hundred twenty miles south through the Allegheny foothills and over the border into Pennsylvania, the last section expressway but the rest New York State Route 19 south through decaying small towns and comatose cabbage farms. Two and a half hours, if it didn't rain. In two and a half hours she would slide into a booth in a roadside bar across from Nick and say . . . what?

Don't call me, don't write me.

Fat chance.

Not tonight, chickies. Teacher has a heartache.

She lost Route 19 at Pike, without at first realizing it. Clouds had rolled in from the west, and there were no streetlights except for the sole traffic light at the sole major crossroads of Pike itself. On campus, life went on twenty-four hours; this empty blackness, mile after mile of it broken only by an isolated farmhouse and her own headlights, was at first unsettling and then calming. Beyond the spectral sweep of her high beams lay sullen hills, sensed rather than seen even when the road rose and fell between them.

Jane rolled down the window. The air smelled of late autumn bitterness, wet leaves and wetter earth, violated out of season for the planting of winter wheat. Plows behind yellow tractors biting the ground. There would be thick raw furrows, naked without snow.

Twenty minutes past Pike, Jane knew she was lost. No more farmhouses, no more winter wheat, just dense woods crowding close to the road, which seemed to have shrunk. Jane scowled into blackness. *Let there be a road sign. And lo, there were road signs! It's a miracle, she's cured, she can . . . she can read again!*

There was no road sign.

A hundred feet, a quarter mile, a half mile more of nothing but sullen void. Even the trees had retreated back from the shoulder of the road. When she pulled over to consult a map, the quality of the silence startled her with its velvet indifference, its country blackness.

My dear Nicholas,
    Am writing this from the depths of nature, where I have gone to experience the fullness of the land and my own inner self, a Wordsworthian sentiment your pretty and illiterate little wife is incapable of feeling. Please forgive the turds smeared on the back of this birch bark. They are not a personal message but rather a social statement, as writing paper has come to seem a desecration of living timber which might provoke the ancient sleeping forces to retaliate—

The map was only limited help. The last landmark she remembered was Pike, where she must have missed the way Route 19 abruptly twisted southeast and instead had taken some branching local road. But the map, a gift from Mobil Oil, showed only main routes, and Jane had no idea in which direction she had branched, or if she had done so more than once. It was so damn dark. . . .

She could either retrace her route north back to Pike, or forge on ahead. She had come maybe ten miles off 19—retracing would lose her another fifteen or twenty minutes. Since she had not twisted east when 19 did, she was probably still heading south, and if that was so she ought to be able to keep going until she rejoined 19, or else came directly to the expressway at some point or other. The expressway ran east and west; if she drove south long enough, she would *have* to come to it.

On impulse, Jane twisted the door handle. Outside the car, the darkness seemed even more furry, soft in the way heaps of banked ashes are soft, with the underlying sense of something alive, mute but not extinguished. She could not remember the last time she had stood alone this deep in wooded countryside. Maybe she never had. There was no sound, not even insects. Was it too late in the year for insects, were they all dead? When in the fall did insects die? What if the car broke down out here?

Inside, she rolled up the window as tight as it would go. Three miles down the twisting road, just when she was beginning to eye panic warily, as if it were a potentially dangerous student, she saw the glow of curious green lights through the trees. Green, surrounding a red and glowing blob.

She had met Nick a year ago. As part of a Faculty Exchange Program that had started mostly because there was State Arts Council money to start it, the community college in Pennsylvania had requested a guest lecture on World War I poet Siegfried Sassoon, and Jane had lost the political tussle not to go deliver it. Why Siegfried Sassoon? She never found out.

Nick had sat in the second row, a big glum man with gray in his dark beard and the serious tan of someone who worked outdoors. Throughout the lecture he scribbled dutifully in a notebook, asking no questions and showing no real interest in Sassoon's sing-song and bitter pacifism. Nonetheless, Jane found herself aware of him throughout, and when he came up to her in the coffee hour afterward, she put on her best can-I-help-you-understand-some-point bullshit smile, slightly curious to hear what this aging undergraduate would ask. But she hadn't been prepared for what he did say.

"It's gone, you know. All that Georgian anguish over war, and then all that sixties pacifism. The men I know who didn't go to Nam wish they had."

Jane froze. Stupidly—later she would see it had been stupidly, had given him some early indefinable advantage she never regained—she said, "No, they don't."

He smiled. "Afraid so. Me, too. We missed something."

"*Missed?*"

He looked at her more closely, and his expression shifted.

"*Missed?*" She heard her own voice, scaling slightly upward, the acceptable contempt not quite enough to cover the unacceptable panic. "I lost a brother in Vietnam. The men you know must be fools, or bastards, or both!"

His glumness seemed to deepen, settle over him like a mist, out of which his eyes watched her with the first hint she had of his astonishing ability to turn an attack into an occasion for reassurance. "Oh yes, they are that. All of us. Both."

Jane had found herself grinning: coldly, reluctantly, her anger not completely gone. It was a strange sensation; the skin around her mouth tingled with it. She had raised her eyes to his, all glum compassion, and the dreary room had suddenly seemed too bright, full of glare and sunshine, hot with possibility.

The greenish light turned out to be Christmas tree lights, half of them broken into jagged ovals, circling a window with a red COCA–COLA sign. Even in the dark, Jane could see the wooden store was unpainted. Gutters sagged below the roof line. She parked her Chevette next to the biggest pickup truck she had ever seen, a monstrosity painted screaming yellow, and took the keys out of her ignition. To grasp the doorknob she had to reach through the soft worn ribbons of a screen door.

Inside, there were high half-empty shelves, one littered with the dusty yellow fallout from a bag of corn chips. Three people stood under a dim bulb, arguing fiercely. None of them looked at Jane.

"—paid last week, the full damn amount—"

"Like hell you did!"

"Like hell I didn't, Emma—"

"Excuse me," Jane said. The three looked up, annoyed. Uneasiness nibbled at Jane.

The woman—Emma—was huge, middle-aged muscle gone to fat stuffed into jeans and sweatshirt balanced over surprisingly small—even dainty—feet in Western boots. The boy, a gum-chewing ten or eleven, she would have passed a dozen times without noticing. But no one could not notice the man, if only because he matched the store too perfectly. In another setting Jane would have found him fascinating; in this one he seemed to her the creation of one of her second-rate students, a stale literary contrivance. Scrabbly-haired, wild-eyed, bearded, his knobby frame dressed in torn overalls and a dirty sheepskin-lined jacket.

"I'm lost," Jane said. "I'm trying to get back on Route 19, and I think I turned off it at Pike. What's the fastest way to pick it up south of here?"

The three stared blankly.

"Route 19," Jane repeated, more loudly. Were they all feeble? Rural inbreeding, exhausted chromosomes.

They went on staring. Then the woman stepped forward, a half-step in her delicate leather boots.

"Can't get there from here."

Exasperation flooded Jane, washing out her momentary uneasiness. "Of course you can get there from here—I just *was* there. I left Route 19 at Pike and now I could just drive back the way I came, but I thought there might be a faster way to rejoin 19 farther south. I'm heading for Pennsylvania."

"Can't get there from here," the woman said. Her voice had changed, gone curiously gentle.

The wild man said, "She can go by down behind Cuba Lake."

The boy stopped chewing gum. The woman whipped around her huge body to turn on the man. "Down behind Cuba Lake! I'd like to see her try to go down behind Cuba Lake, you big fool! She'd get lost on them back roads before she knew it!"

"Huh," the man said, and there the discussion stopped. Man and woman glared at each other, Jane apparently forgotten. Their fury was inexplicable to her, but obviously unconnected to getting back to Route 19. She scanned the Mobil map. There were numerous tiny splotches of blue, most of them unlabeled.

"Which one is Cuba Lake?"

Everyone ignored her.

"Look," Jane said, "I'll just retrace the route I came. Thanks anyway." She turned to the door.

"Wait," the man said. He stepped closer; she smelled fetid whiskey on his breath. "There's a faster way. You just follow me half a mile. Then the road splits in three, I'll pull over and get out and show you which way to go. It goes on a ways, put you back on a main road that hooks into 19 south of Oramel."

Jane looked at him. At the edge of his flannel collar, a roll of gray flesh worked up and down.

"No, thanks. It'll probably be simpler to just drive back to Pike."

He shrugged. "Suit yourself."

"Hold still a minute," the woman said sharply. She took the map, not asking first, from Jane's hand and studied it. "Lose you half an hour. Maybe more. Yeah—more."

More. And she had already lost time—she wouldn't get to Nick before 1:00 A.M. The bar would be deserted if it were open at all, the lights long since out behind Nick's Austrian pines.

"She can't even get down behind Cuba Lake," the woman said, still studying Jane's map. Her voice held a curious mixture of triumph and pique. Pique—that was reassuring, wasn't it? Pique wasn't an emotion that went with condoning a setup for crime. "Not on that split."

"Huh," the man repeated. He raised one scrawny leg and stood balanced on the other like some extinct waterfowl, yellowed teeth chewing on his bottom lip and eyes gone inward. He looked so bizarre that Jane was suddenly sick of both of them, suddenly longed for the slick normality of a Safeway. Clean plastic, college kids buying chips and beer, housewives with whining kids. An hour and a half.

"Look," she said with sudden decision, "when the road splits in three, which one do I take? Left, right, or middle?" She watched not the man but the woman, searching for some sign of complicity, some shifting of eyes or muscles that would map the woman as knowing him capable of . . . whatever. She didn't find it.

"Left," the man said. "But you could miss it, the middle curves a trick left too. I'll stop, get out, show you."

"Just honk," Jane said. "Honk at the split and I'll find it." She was still watching the woman, who showed only annoyance at having her opinion ignored. At the edge of her vision the man, still on one foot, nodded.

"Okay. I honk, you bear far left. Come on, boy."

Outside, the boy climbed into the cab of the huge yellow pickup. Jane felt further reassured. It didn't seem likely a man bent on rape or robbery would bring along a child, did it? She locked her car doors and started the engine.

The road seemed even darker, more desolate than before. Jane's high beams glared off the rear of the pickup. Despite herself, she peered at the window: no gun rack.

Dear Nick,

Literary models, like Newtonian physics, cause equal and opposite reactions. Put it in your course notes. I start to love you because you say something so outrageous that you can't possibly mean it. I follow a hillbilly derelict because he looks so much like a crazed killer that he can't possibly be one. The world is not that anthropomorphic, except in bad novels, which I've been reading a lot of lately in a stupid effort to not think about you —

The pickup honked, slowed, and veered right. Jane caught her breath, unexpectedly panicked that it had after all been some sort of trap, that the man would shoot out her tires or follow her down what would turn out to be a deserted dead end. "Dead end" . . . who the hell coined these metaphors?

The yellow truck honked a second time and picked up speed, disappearing around a bend. Jane pushed her foot to the floor. Pebbles clattered against the underside of the Chevette. She slowed down, angry at herself: even if there were some sort of cutoff and the yellow truck suddenly bore down on her, it wouldn't help to be piled up against the dark woods.

Crouched over the wheel, she strained to see the twists and turns of the dirt road. Her high beams were unaccountably focused too high; they showed clearly the undersides of leaves clawing at each other from opposite sides of the road.

A few miles after the fork, the road ended.

First it climbed an abrupt rise, which descended even more abruptly. Jane's headlights, now pointed down, shimmered over a flat blackness. She slammed on the brakes and skidded, stopping inches from the water's edge.

Panic gripped her. Mud—the bank could be soft mud, cars sank in mud and then the pressure kept the doors from being opened from the inside—

Flinging open the door, Jane hurled herself out of the car and clambered back up the rise. Her heart slammed in her chest as she stood looking down on the smooth top of the Chevette, still shining its lights out over the lake.

Minutes passed. The top did not move. When Jane finally crept back down the slope, she tested the ground with each step. It held firm. Cautiously she reached into the car for her purse and pulled out a penlight. Hard ground, covered with tough weeds, extended clear to the water's edge. Beyond, the lake sighed softly. A breeze sprang up; the surface rippled like black muscle.

Cuba Lake?

In her haste at the triple fork, she must not have veered far enough left, and so had ended up on the middle road. The man had said . . . the man. . . .

Jane scrambled back into the car, slammed the door, and switched off both headlights and flashlight. But after a moment anger began to burn away fear. She yanked the key to the right and started to back up the rise. Her beams again pointed down onto the lake, and for a moment it seemed something moved over the surface, far from shore. Jane turned her head back over her shoulder and tried to stay out of the underbrush.

At the top of the rise she did a three-point turn in seven points, then barreled back under the leaves that were like dark hands.

> Nick—
>
> I do not believe in ancient terrors stirring to life in the menacing countryside, shaping the lives of men as in some modern horror novel, any more than I believe in ancient benevolence stirring to life in the pastoral countryside as in the sentimental Romantic poets you unaccountably love so much—

Poets. What was she doing in possibly mortal danger, thinking about *poets? Nick, Nick, you corrupted me, my dissertation was on Zola — stay on the road, Jane you idiot, it turns here —*

Beyond the turn, the yellow pickup blocked the road.

It was positioned with hood touching the dense trees on one side of the road, rear bumper on the other. There was no way around. Jane peered at the truck, one hand frozen halfway in the act of hitting the lights. The yellow cab seemed empty.

Then where was he, where were they . . . the boy, too —

Nick —

Carefully, fingers trembling on the wheel, she backed the car through the overhanging trees. A hundred yards before the turn, there had been a gap in the woods, something that might have been the remnant of another dirt track. If it angled upward, it might bypass the occupants of the pickup, wherever they were.

She found the track, choked with weeds at its beginning but becoming surprisingly clear as she pushed along it. At one point Jane had the eerie sensation that she was driving on fresh asphalt, not dirt. The road seemed neither to curve back toward the lake nor to angle upward — until it precipitately descended and Jane was again staring at the dark water of the lake.

She hit the brakes, stopped just short of the bank, and laid her forehead against the cold plastic of the steering wheel.

In her headlights, something dark moved over the water.

She tried to pull herself together, to think rationally. Of course all the dirt tracks would lead back to the lake; the lake was probably where everyone — or such "everyone" as there was around here — wanted to go. Kids fishing. Hunters out after deer. Lovers looking for a lane.

She resisted the impulse to open the car door and let the penlight search for used condoms.

This time there was room to turn the Chevette around by the water's edge, a wide shelf of weedy ground that nonetheless left her shaking each time the wheels approached the bank. The shaking made her inch up the rise, and so she was going slow enough to notice the nearly hidden fork at the top. On the right, the clear road she had come down; on the left, a weed-choked path.

She turned left. The path, wherever else it took her, headed away from the yellow truck. And after a hundred yards, it was even easier to drive on than the previous road. Caught between curiosity and dread, Jane stopped the car, opened the door just wide enough

to take the width of the penlight, and shined it straight down.
Asphalt.

As she again drove forward, a sudden giddiness seized her. She
even laughed out loud, a sound so high and abrupt that it made
her shake her head ruefully. The car shimmied lightly.

Dear Nicky,
      *You my love are a fool to prefer your domestic little wife to
a woman who can—single-handedly! yes!—defeat a mad hillbilly
rapist AND a child-midget murderer AND—not to mention!—
the dark forces rising from the gaseous swamps to ooze around
the souls of the sinful, a group for which you and I definitely
qualify. A pioneer of femininity, hacking her way through this
slightly banal underbrush while your—*

Ahead, the pickup blocked the road.

Jane cried out. This time she nearly smashed into the passenger
side of the cab before she was able to make her foot hit the brake.
The tires squealed, laying rubber. Scabs of scrofulous yellow paint
loomed at her.

There was no sound. After unbearable moments of dark silence,
Jane leaned into the horn. Thin blatting leaked out into the thick
air, was absorbed by it as by soggy wool. No one came.

The truck could not be there. There hadn't been time, the road
beyond angled even farther to the left, even farther away from
where the pickup had been parked before. It could not be there.
It could not.

Shaking, Jane studied the truck. The front bumper was jammed
against an outcropping of New England granite. But between the
rear bumper and the trunk of a pulpy-looking tree Jane couldn't
identify, was a gap that might be just large enough to ease the
Chevette through. Or might not.

And if there *was* someone hunkered down in the yellow cab—
someone small, a child—who reached up to turn on the ignition,
to pull the clutch into reverse, to lean with both hands on the ac-
celerator as the Chevy was easing through the gap, the pickup could
crush the passenger door. Would that make it easier or harder for
someone to get inside? If the pickup kept on crushing, would it
twist the steering wheel into her chest?

She could back up again, look for yet another side road. But
this time she had been watching; there were no more side roads.
Behind her was only the lake.

For a long moment Jane squeezed shut her eyes, opening them only when the images inside the lids became worse than the one outside. Carefully she edged the Chevy toward the rear of the pickup.

The right door handle caught the bottom edge of the bumper, scraping a bright gash in the dirty chrome. On the driver's side, bark smeared across the window. Once off the asphalt, the Chevette sank a few inches into loam and rotten leaves, and there was a moment where Jane thought it would not continue to move forward. But it did.

Clear of the truck, Jane accelerated wildly. Four hundred yards down the road the trees suddenly withdrew and she was flying past flat fields, empty as deserts. The rearview mirror revealed the pickup still motionless, still solitary.

A drink—what she would give for a Jack Daniel's, how late did Pennsylvania bars serve. . . .

Her watch said 10:03.

Shocked, Jane slowed the car. That wasn't possible. She had left Pike perhaps an hour ago, at roughly 10:00. There was no way it could be that early—

Directly ahead, her high beams skimmed out over water.

She stopped at the water's edge, the road behind her both flat and straight, stretching like a plumb line to where she had left Cuba Lake receding in the other direction.

Another lake . . .

But she knew it was not. Even as she watched numbly through the windshield still spattered with leaves and pulpy bark, something spectral moved over the distant surface.

Wearily, with muscles that no longer seemed her own, Jane opened the door and walked toward the water. She sat at its very edge, knees clasped to her chest, tough weeds rustling under her weight and pressing their shapes through the wool of her slacks. It no longer seemed to matter whether she protected herself by staying in the car; whether she tried another road; whether she tried at all. There was no other road. There was only the yellow pickup and the derelict with gray in his dark beard and the black thing over the water, and all roads led to Cuba Lake.

"You can't get there from here."

Dispassionately, with the curious clarity that comes from having worn out all emotion, Jane studied the darkness moving over the water. A kind of mist, without form, neither rising from the

lake nor descending from the sky. "*And darkness was upon the face of the deep, and the Spirit of God moved upon the face of the waters.*" *Breshith, en arkhei, Beginning,* Jane thought and, despite herself, smiled jeeringly. A professor to the last. The quotation created the reality.

> *Dear Nick,*
> > *Ask for me tomorrow and you shall find me a grave man —*

Nick . . .

Her purse was in her hand, although she didn't remember carrying it from the car. On impulse, eyes still hopeless on the dark lake, she fumbled among the makeup and wallet and glasses case for his letter. When she held it again, lukewarm colorless tasteless hemlock on sixteen-pound bond, anguish pierced her so sharply that she bent her head over her raised knees and rested it there. She thought it would be helpful to cry, thought it in just those detached pop-theory bullshit words: "It would be helpful, Jane, to cry." But she knew she wouldn't. The thought of the echoes of sobs returning to her from across that lake — that alone would have been enough to stop her.

A long time later she released the straining clasp around her knees and lay, exhausted, on her back. The sky above was featureless. Jane stared at it, equally empty. She stared until the gray blank might have been either miles or inches above her eyes. Until the boundary between the flat void of the sky and her skull disappeared. Until her clothing was soaked with dew and her fingers so chilled they would not open around Nick's letter.

It took that long.

Her watch said 10:03.

Eventually, Jane rose, staggering on numb legs. She got into the car and started back along the flat, perfectly straight road. Glancing in the rearview mirror she saw, as she knew she would, the surface of the water empty behind her. After a few miles, the road roughened, swerved, and joined New York State Route 19. A little farther along, road signs reappeared; farther still, she came to a caution light, blinking like a single yellow eye.

> *Dear Nick,*
> > *Not Wordsworth, not Byron, not even Stephen King. They all had it backward. We shape it.*

Just before Pike, halted at a barren intersection, Jane rolled down the car window. The crumpled paper arced over the dirt shoulder and into an unseen ditch. There was the faint splash of water. Driving only slightly faster than the speed limit, she was able to glimpse the last light in Lehman Science Hall before whoever was still up there working winked it off.

Dear Nick,
  But not each other.

Her watch said 11:30.

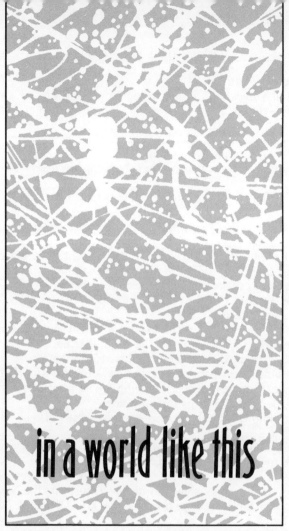

in a world like this

MY WIFE MAKES OUT her shopping lists not in single words but in dependent clauses and prepositional phrases. She will write "fruit but not apples, which we have," or "kuchen, for Sunday A.M." This habit sparks in me a deep primal dislike—for its manneredness, its pretentious completeness. Emily knows this.

"You realize you're being ridiculous," she says.

"I know it," I answer, having already been put at a disadvantage by the pettiness of my objections, and now at a further one by admitting them. "I can't help it."

"Of course you can."

"I'll tell you what," I say, trying to salvage dignity through jocularity—always a risky move. "So long as you don't end the clauses with a period."

Emily smiles at me, the slant-eyed smile that she often wears in bed. "Fair enough. No periods."

The next time I come across her shopping list, it says "tampons, for my;"

She has left it on the kitchen table, where I am sure to see it.

"Look at this, John," Kip Lowry says after we settle ourselves on the 7:42. He has opened his newspaper, and it is flapping over into my half of the seat. Kip works for some scientific/political think tank downtown and reads the morning newspaper with an intensity that would make me wonder exactly what he expects to see there, except that I suspect it of being a pose to look more knowledgeable than he is.

"*Two* earthquakes last night. Mexico City and Miskolc. And both registered exactly the same on the Richter scale."

"I didn't think the Reds released that information." I poke at the edge of the newspaper, nudging it back toward Kip. He frowns and glances at me evasively. Watching Soviet information may or may not be something his institute does.

"Who knows? Look at this—another burglary in Hickory Village."

Hickory Village is the subdivision in which we both live. I crane my neck toward the paper I have just pushed away.

"The cops don't have any leads," Kip reports. "When do they ever? Hey, look at this—some guy in Albany just won the New York State Lottery for the second time! Do you know what the odds are against that?"

"High," I say, apparently too sourly. Kip gives me that evasive glance once more. He does this at parties as well—starts a subject that touches on his specialty, something called information theory, and then suddenly shies away as if his listeners were moving toward something politically sensitive. I dislike the habit intensely. He also wears wide-brimmed, overly dramatic hats.

"A Russian last name for that lottery winner," Kip says slowly. I close my eyes and pretend to sleep. Whatever Kip thinks he is looking for, or wants me to think he is looking for, he can look alone.

The lobby of Jefferson Tower rings with jackhammers. I

step over chunks of floor and rolls of sodden carpet to scream at the receptionist, "What happened?"

She screams back, "Water leaking from someplace. They can't find where. Damnedest thing—ruined the carpet!"

I can't consider the carpet, which has always looked like cold oatmeal with pebbles in it, to be much loss. The noise, on the other hand, is unbearable. Even in my office on the eighth floor the jackhammers are audible, like a steady whine from huge but distant insects.

Helen, my secretary, comes in with a sheaf of papers. She looks distracted.

"This is the agenda for Ken Robinson's meeting at ten, because he wants to be sure everyone sticks to both the topic and the time frame. This is the script for the new training film, because the production studio is booked for next Tuesday and they need copy approval. Your report for the senior staff isn't done yet because the Xerox copier is down again."

"Christ."

"I think the copier is down because either the corotron needs rewiring or the baffle spring is pulled off the shaft."

I stare at her. Helen has trouble getting the top off a jar of coffee. "How do you know that?"

"I looked inside. I also leafed through the manual because I thought maybe I could fix it."

"But you can't. Nobody can fix those things, not even the tech rep, or they would stay fixed longer than ten minutes after he leaves."

"The machines don't stay fixed because we run too much volume on them. That's because—"

"Helen," I say, with some irritation, "you aren't by any chance related to my wife, are you?"

She looks confused. "I don't think so."

"Good."

On the 6:17, Kip Lowry smacks his knee with his folded newspaper—the evening edition this time. He has pulled his hat brim down lower than usual, and this strikes me as an ominous sign. Visible is his lower jaw, bristling with a day's worth of dark stubble, which gives him a dangerous look. The hints Kip drops about his project in information theory seem to mostly involve such tame and academic things as mathematical formulas and high-speed computers, but it has nonetheless always seemed to me that there is something inflamed about the look of Kip's jaw. Something needing only the right environment to erupt into possibly contagious boils. The 6:17 seems an unlikely environment, but I don't like that smacking newspaper.

"Colder tonight," I say. I am trying to make up for my morning rudeness.

Kip doesn't answer.

"Thought I'd cover the roses, even though it's early in the year for that. No pattern to the weather lately. You should cover yours, too." Kip's roses are the most neglected in Hickory Village: spindly stems and sparse blossoms. This gives me an obscure sense of cheerfulness.

Kip says, "Sandra is leaving me." Smack, smack.

After a pause I say, "I'm sorry." I know this is inadequate, but what else would be better? We don't look at each other.

"After seventeen years," he says. A tear appears from beneath the lowered hat brim, and I am disgusted with myself for feeling a profound distaste. Kip is, I suppose, the closest thing I have to a friend. But on the 6:17?

"You'd think," he says, "that after seventeen years she'd be willing to ride this thing out."

"What thing?" I say, because I see I'm supposed to and despite a strong reluctance to ask.

"Lara Kashinsky."

"Lara *Kashinsky?*"

He stiffens. "Lara just happens to be one of the best random-information specialists in the world."

"I remember your saying that she's brilliant," I say hastily. I also remember her picture in the newspapers, at the time of her defection. She must be well over fifty.

"I never thought Sandy would find out," Kip says gloomily. "And now she won't even listen. I didn't plan the thing with Lara. It just happened."

"Ummm."

"These things happen," Kip says. He stops smacking the newspaper and stares out the train window, at trees flashing past too fast to be counted.

"Janice called," Emily says over a late-night brandy. She tucks her hair behind her ears; this is a characteristic gesture of agitation. "There was another burglary, two doors down from her. The police questioned her and Jim and the kids. No clues. They looked in all the soft mud in the yard for tracks, because—"

"I can guess why they looked for tracks without your telling me," I cut in. There is a silence while Emily stares into her brandy. We are sitting up in bed, and the bedside lamp casts a pearly glow on Emily's shoulders, bisected by the lacy straps of her nightgown. At thirty-eight she is beautiful still, and my irritation vanishes and is replaced by affection. Emily is very precious to me, although it is hard for me to say so. I have always found it hard. Emily knows this; she is one of the few women who will forgive it. I reach for her.

She frowns. "Why now?"

"Just because."

"Because why?"

Irritation returns, swamping affection. "Do I need a reason? I want to make love to you. If you don't want to, say so."

"Sandy Lowry is leaving Kip."

So that is what the agitation is about, not the burglary. I see that the Hickory Village phones have been buzzing all day. I see, too, the trickiness of the conversation ahead. When one husband strays, all husbands are somehow implicated, in some weird web I have never understood but learned to recognize.

"Ummm," I say, noncommittally.

"It's because he's having an affair with that Russian scientist."

Emily is watching me closely; another "ummm" will probably not do. I decide instead on honesty.

"I know. Kip told me today on the train."

She stops fiddling with her hair, and her shoulders relax; apparently she knew I knew. "It's that ridiculous house. It's strapped him with debt, and he was looking for some sort of cheap release. Sandy didn't even want such a huge place. Kip only wanted it because he grew up so poor, because his father died when he was three and his mother's eyesight was too poor for her to work, and *her* father was an immigrant who never understood about childhood corrective surgery before it was too late."

"I don't think you have to go back three generations and produce such an elaborate explanation. Anyway, you probably couldn't pin down any definitive reasons. These things happen."

Emily shifts against the headboard and reaches out to set her glass on the nightstand. One shoulder strap slides down. Her eyes narrow. "What do you mean—'these things happen'?"

"They just do. Kip and Lara work together on that information project, whatever it is."

"So?"

"So it just . . . happens." Even to me these words have started to sound curiously lame, and I resent it.

Emily punches up her pillow and lies back. "That's irresponsible. It lets everybody off the hook—it lets *Kip* off the hook. Things don't just happen. They're connected, they happen for good and sufficient reasons!"

"Emily—"

"There are always *reasons*."

I suddenly think of my secretary, Helen. "Women always want things so definite. Black and white. The world simply isn't that way. Things fall into shades of gray, into unpredictable subtleties. Why can't you just *accept* that!"

I hear, to my own surprise, that I am shouting. Emily turns her head on the pillow to look at me. Perhaps it is a trick of the lighting, some passing effect, but her eyes look like those of a woman I don't know. They are both thoughtful and outraged; violation sparkles in them like stained glass.

There is a long silence, which slowly turns unbearable. To break the silence without having to break it, I reach again for Emily. She doesn't resist, but she lies passive in my arms while I stroke her. Then she half turns and clutches me almost desperately, and we make very definite and unsubtle love.

The carpet in the corridor outside my office is sopping. Inside the office, water meanders down the walls, drips from the ceiling onto my desk, pools on chairs and file cabinets. As I stand in the doorway staring at this, Helen hurries around the corner, looking harried.

"Oh, Mr. Catton—it's the sprinkler system, they think. That's what was wrong in the lobby yesterday, too. They think that while they were jackhammering the floor someone hit something vital and jammed the whole thing."

"How long—?"

"They won't say!" Helen cries. I have never seen her so overwrought; she is usually the calmest and most efficient secretary on the floor, making consistent sense out of my chaotic meeting and memo flow. "They think it happened because of a workman who is very inexperienced, he had only been on the job two weeks and three days. His supervisor was out sick because he caught the flu from his little boy, who got it at day-care because the supervisor's wife died in a car crash two years ago and he's raising the little boy alone."

I stare at her. "Helen—how do you know all that?"

She makes a vague gesture, flinging her palms upward as if begging for mercy. "The control thing for the sprinkler system was manufactured in Japan, because it cost sixteen dollars and forty-two cents less per unit to do it there. The engineer said it appeared to be functioning perfectly, because he took it out and tested it, but he won't say how long it will be before you can use your office!"

"Well," I say helplessly—could Helen be having some sort of secretarial burnout?—"we can work around the mess, I suppose. Where did you put my phone and the Hentschel files?"

"In George Schwartz's office. The water isn't too bad in there, and George is out because he took a vacation day to go up to his daughter's college, because she's failing two subjects, due to excessive partying with Kappa Delta Omicron. But I don't know *why* there's less water in his office than in yours!"

"Well," I say, more helplessly than before, "I don't suppose it matters. So long as we can get on with the day. So it goes."

And at my last words Helen calms down instantly, moving rapidly past calm to a set and rigid face, from which she stares at me in silence like stone.

"Look at that!" Kip says, his face pressed to the train window. I obediently look; Kip has had a hysterical edge to him for a week, ever since Sandra moved out with their girls.

"John—did you see it?"

"Did I see what?"

"On that other track. A train went by and it . . . shimmered. Like a ghost image on TV."

"There are three sets of track there."

"No—it wasn't on the third set! You didn't see it?"

"I wasn't looking."

Kip grimaces abstractedly beneath his hat brim. When the brim dips forward, I brace myself. Kip has been twirling his self-aggrandizing veils of information theory all week: message channels. Noise level. Algorithms. Context-sensitive redundancy. If he does it yet again, I will change my seat. This time, I will. But he says something else.

"Lara called Sandy and told her that I said I wanted to marry her. Marry Lara."

I am somehow not surprised by this. "Do you want to marry her?"

"Of course not. I still care everything for Sandy."

"Did you say anything to Lara that might lead her to think—?"

"Oh, hell, how should I know? You know how it is. You're in bed, you say things—and then women try to hold you to them in a goddamned court of law. Sandy had a fit. She called me after Lara called *her*, and then Lara called on the line in the den, and it seemed I was on the phone with one or the other of them all night. Christ, the hysteria all around."

I can picture it and am meanly glad that Kip lives at the other, richer end of Hickory Village.

At the station, he trudges toward the Depot, a bar-cum-restaurant built in an antiquated baggage office for commuters grabbing a quick orange juice in the morning, or a quick drink instead of going home. He has been heading for the Depot every night; I don't know what time he leaves it. I turn my steps in the other direction, toward my street. I am halfway down it when two police cars dash up to the Lindstrom house.

They swerve to the edge of the lawn, black-and-white doors fly open, and two cops run to the back of the house and two more to the front. The Lindstroms, I remember vaguely, are on vacation. I prepare to tell this to the cop approaching me when Kitty Sue Cunningham comes running out of her house across the street and begins babbling in the Georgia accent that somehow becomes thicker each year in New Jersey.

"Ah saw him go in, just sneak around the side of the house, and Ah called the police right away. Ah just *know* he's the one who's been doin' all these *horrible* robberies. . . ."

She goes on and on, an anxious syrupy flow, her eyes never leaving the Lindstrom house, hands twisting the material of a pink dress too young for her lacquered blonde beehive. The cop listens stoically.

". . . lookin' so long at the window because Ah was cleanin' the glass, because of those horrible fly spots every time the weather goes and warms up again and the eggs hatch, and that's all just because a single housefly can lay one hundred fifty eggs at a time, all hatching in just twelve hours—"

"What?" I say. There is lead in my lungs.

"—because the rate they get eaten up by birds and toads and all those bitty creatures is so high—"

"*Kitty Sue*—"

"Nothing," a cop says to me, in a tone I recognize as intentional reassurance. "The lady must have been mistaken. There aren't any tracks anywhere, and in that soft mud, there would have to be."

"But Ah *saw*—"

"No tracks, ma'am," the cop says in the same reassuring tone, but Kitty Sue is not listening. She is not even there. A faint bluish shimmer, and Kitty Sue Cunningham—pink dress, Georgia drawl, dyed blonde hair, reasons for the mating habits of flies—has vanished.

Another faint shimmer a second later, and she is back. "—might have been the Wozniak boy, he's breakin' his poor mother's heart with his shenanigans, but that's all because—"

The cop's eyes slide toward mine. I see the shock on his face; but the next moment it, too, is gone, locked behind a stony blank-cop look—*Make something of it, buddy*—that gives him a jawline like an erection.

"—stealin' money from his daddy's wallet, and doin' it more than once, Ah was told, because—"

"Just *because*," I say—loudly, angrily, pointlessly, and with fear. Neither of them answers, and I walk away, trembling a little. I don't look back but go straight home, where I find Emily in tears: while she was out at the shopping mall, our house had been burglarized.

"They said it was random," I say to Emily as we prepare for bed. Both of us are exhausted from talking to the police, soothing the kids, notifying the insurance people, listing the stolen possessions. Who knows exactly what the stolen possessions are? Months from now we will discover things missing that we had forgotten we owned.

"Random, Emily. Not personal. They probably didn't know us, or anything about us. You shouldn't take it personally. It happens."

Emily looks up, shimmers, and is gone.

In a moment she is back, yanking her slip over her head and flinging it into an open drawer. I stand completely still, unable to speak. Perhaps I hallucinated about Kitty Sue Cunningham; perhaps I am hallucinating now. . . . Terrible thoughts chase themselves through my head: cerebral arteriosclerosis. Alzheimer's disease. Brain tumors.

Emily, in bra and panties, begins a frenzied straightening of the jars and tubes on her dresser. "The burglars took my mother's silver candlesticks, because they are worth four hundred fifty-eight dollars with silver at current market prices. He didn't know my mother because she died in 1978 and never visited us in Hickory Village because we hadn't moved here yet. He *does* need the money because he's the only child of a single-parent female-headed household with an average taxable income of only six thousand four hundred thirty-two dollars, and he dropped out of high school ten months ago because—"

"Stop it!" I shout, and seize her by the shoulders. She twists savagely away from me, and we face each other at arm's length, Emily panting hard and I shaking with a primordial fury I no longer care to control. I recognize that there is some elemental abyss here, some deep lack in her that I have always despised. Almost I could strike her.

Emily glares at me with hatred.

The moment spins out, frozen, unbearable. Then Emily breaks, putting her hands over her face and starting to sob.

"I want things to make sense. I just want things to *make sense.* . . ."

And the naïveté of this, the sheer lost longing, fills me with a rush of pity. I take her in my arms. Pity, exasperation—and, unaccountably, desire. Her breasts through the lacy bra are soft against my chest, her breath silky against my face. The whole moment has taken one of those unpredictable turns into sweetness, into grace. There is a profound mystery in the circle of yellow lamplight on the floor, in the random movements of the air, in the improbable longings of the fragile and sweet-limbed body in my arms. Emily. I press her closer.

"No," Emily says. Carefully she detaches herself, turns her back, and yanks a flannel nightdress over herself, bra and all. She crawls into bed and lies on the far edge, facing away from me. I do not understand. She does not explain.

The next day it all happens.

Kip is not on the train. I enter Jefferson Tower, get on the elevator, press the button for the eighth floor. When the door opens, I am on the sixteenth.

Jefferson Tower has fourteen floors.

I have never seen this place before. The elevator faces a bank of copiers and telecommunications equipment, as in my building, but the signs above them are sheer gibberish: HY*CAFK OIG TYH MB K. Only the "16" on the lighted elevator panel makes sense. Music fills the air, a woman singing softly in gibberish. Out of sight, around a corner, someone laughs, and a sudden nauseating smell, strong enough to make my stomach lurch, wafts from that direction. The light is a soft purple. I stand frozen, until the elevator doors close and the elevator descends. It opens on the eighth floor. Helen, her back to me, is fiddling with the Xerox copier.

I let the doors close again, ride to street level, and leave the building. Some part of my mind notes that I am not trembling, not even when I insert coins into the newspaper vendor and buy a morning edition I cannot quite make myself read on the deserted train. At the Hickory Hill station, however, among the familiar wooden platform and red-painted metal railing and late-blooming fall wildflowers in straggling clumps, I open the paper.

STRANGE RADIO BROADCASTS MYSTIFY CITY
MASS DELUSIONS SUSPECTED IN JPLCO
GT& BHO + P SAYS "NEVER AGAIN"

A woman, expensively dressed in linen and mink, walks by me. She is talking to herself with intense preoccupied concentration. "—can't go along with it because of previous commitments, and *that* came about because—"

I squeeze my eyes shut. She sounds like Helen, like Kitty Sue, like Lara Kashinsky. Like Emily. When I open my eyes, Kip Lowry is standing on the station platform in front of me, looking as if he has not slept for days. Wordlessly he puts a hand on my shoulder, a gesture I normally dislike from anyone but Emily, and drags me into the Depot.

I have lost all power to resist.

Inside, we sit at the long bar, which at this hour—10:32 A.M.— is empty of all but a dour bartender polishing glasses. Kip orders a double scotch, downs it with a single snap of his wrist, then orders another. Perversely, the cheap theatricality of this deepens my dazed numbness. We sit for several minutes in complete silence.

Eventually Kip looks around him and says hollowly, "Low information content."

"What?"

"This bar. Dark paneling, stools and booths, mirror over the bar—all predictable. The greater the predictability, the less the new information. This bar is a boring information system."

I say carefully, "I hadn't thought of it as an information system."

"It is. Everything is." He drinks off the second double scotch, motions for a third, and then gives a bark of laughter. "Everything. All of it out there."

"Kip," I say, but only because I cannot stop myself, "just what is going on out . . . out there?"

"What Lara predicted."

"What *Lara* predicted?"

"She warned them," he says, and I am appalled to hear under the strain in his voice another, unmistakable note: dramatic satisfaction. "Them. Us. At the institute. Of course nobody believed her, except me. Then nobody believed either of us: a female defected Russki and a second-rate researcher."

"Believe what?" I say, and wonder if I am humoring him or believing him myself. Suddenly, without reason, I know that Kip has been fired from his institute. Today, yesterday, or the day before. There has been a scene, one of Kip's messy dramas, and he is making me part of the third act. I want no part of that, after all the rest of it, and I am rising to leave when Kip says, "See this glass?"

I don't answer.

"This glass is an information system. The molecules in the ice cube are in one state, the molecules in the scotch in a very different state. Entropy in this glass is low. Sit down, John."

"I don't want to hear about entropy in that glass!"

"Yes, you do," he says, with utter conviction. "That glass is what happened to you out there."

I lower myself onto the barstool.

"This glass has low entropy, or, to put it another way, the information system has a high degree of order. You know which is the ice and which is the scotch, and where the molecules of each are located, at least roughly." He stirs the scotch with a red plastic swizzle stick. "See—there's only a few places the ice can go. Or—in terms of information theory—there are only a few possible messages. High order, low entropy, limited possible states."

Why do I sit and listen? "Kip—"

"But even now, even as we speak, it changes!" Kip shouts. The bartender gives us a startled glance. Kip drops his voice, shoves his face close to mine, and says in a stage whisper, "Watch—don't miss it—keep your eyes peeled every second! Entropy increases!"

"You damned—"

"Yes, indeed. As are we all. Entropy in this glass is increasing. The ice is melting. Soon you won't be able to tell which is scotch and which is ice. All the molecules will be mixed. You won't be able to predict where any single one is. There will be low order,

high entropy, an infinite number of possible states. That's what
Lara says the Russians are doing."
Despite myself, I look at Kip's glass and think of vodka. "What's
what the Russians are doing?"
"Information theory. The whole world is an information system:
a glass of booze, DNA, Sandy's angry little mind."
"I don't see it."
"Increase the amount of disorder, you increase the number of
the possible arrangements of the parts. Thirty minutes from now,
those scotch molecules could be anywhere in the system. Lara says
it was a sort of skunkswork project, blue-skying it, way apart from
their official scientific establishment. They might not have even
tried it if the last grain harvest hadn't been such a bust. But it's
working, isn't it?" Kip makes a vague gesture toward the door.
"They're revving up the flow of chaotic information, artificially increasing it exponentially, and so increasing both the entropy and
the number of possible states for the whole planetary system."
"How would you increase the flow of chaotic infor—" I say, and
think suddenly of all the high-speed computers in the world—the
communications satellites, datalinks, phone lines, banking networks,
electromagnetic broadcasts. Kip is watching me.
"Exactly," he says softly—too softly. I see once again that some
theatrical part of him is *enjoying* this.
"That's all insane, Kip. Just theory. What goes on in the real
world . . . there are physical laws. *Rules.*"
Kip smiles slyly. "Ah, but Lara says they are not mutating just
the information. They're mutating the rules by which 'molecules'
of information act on each other."
"But that can't be possible. To change the *rules?*"
"Rules are just more information, differently coded. That code,
too, can become entropic. That's what cancer is: a DNA code that
has managed to gain in entropy, and so in the number of possible
states it can produce."
"But—"
"Stop saying 'but.' There's a complexity barrier—Von Neumann
proved the equations for that."
"But—"
Kip picks up my glass—untouched—and pours it into his. Liquid overflows and begins to meander in rivulets along the polished
surface of the bar.
"Too much individual information. The old system can't con-

tain it. Complexity is a decisive property. Above some critical level, too much information — even high-possibility random information — becomes explosive. You get an exponential leap in the number of possible states. Lara says the Other Side probably wants a different state. This one is slow economic suicide for them."

The longer Kip talks, the more of what he says makes a weird distorted sense, just out of grasp, like an object at the bottom of a shallow but murky pond. One second you think you know it's a tire iron, a perfectly familiar object — except that no tire iron was ever bent in that peculiar way. But then, was Kip's abstruse theory any more bent than what had happened in the Jefferson Tower elevator?

Some objection, some half-remembered piece of learning, surfaces in my mind. "Wait," I say, and hear the triumph in my own voice, as earlier it had sounded in Kip's: the perverse triumph of proving a connection wrong. "Wait, no — things don't always tend toward entropy. There's biological life and evolution: living beings tend to become *more* orderly, not more random!"

"The complexity barrier," Kip says. His mercurial theatrics have faded by now, and he sits in quiet gloom. "Vertebrates passed it. But you're right — when they did, another force entered the information system — a drive to create order, connections, meaning. And that's why I'm scared shitless."

I am confused all over again. "Why?"

"I don't know." He starts drawing meaningless pictures in the spilled scotch: a flower, a house, a long-tailed squiggle that might have been a sperm. "Who knows? That drive for meaning isn't random, isn't entropic, isn't high possibility. It seeks the probable. If I write a letter that starts 'Dear Sadny' — spelled S-a-d-n-y — the brain will read it S-a-n-d-y. At least, some brains would. Not everyone's. Some types of mind just like order. Some search compulsively for connections. Some don't."

I think of Kip's messy life, his hysterical nights. He has sketched a woman in the scotch; she has long hair. Lara, I remember, has long hair, which she wears in a neat twist.

"Fuck it," he says suddenly, violently.

I say, "I don't believe any of this."

"You don't want to believe it. Too much of a comic book. Look at you — you're red in the face. *You!*"

I say stiffly, "Do you think you can get home all right?"

Kip throws back his head and laughs, a sound of such reckless amusement that I am shocked.

"Christ, John, you're priceless! Prissy to the end. Don't you see it, even now? *This is the end of this information system.* Any hour now—"

The bartender has been walking toward us, rag in hand and eyes disapprovingly on the mess Kip has made all over the bar. As we watch, the rag bursts into flames. The bartender yells and hurls it into the sink; the stainless steel begins to stain, then abruptly stops.

"Different information systems operating there," Kip says conversationally, and laughs again. I hit him on the arm, hard.

"Stop it!"

He grins at me. "Why, John, you man of few words, I never knew you cared." His grin widens. "About anything." Then he says, in a different voice, "In living things, the very complex system divides. Like with sexual reproduction."

And for some reason this statement—no less abstract than the rest of his crazed theory—makes sense. The pond drains away, and I see the tire iron nearly clear, only it's not a tire iron but a dangerous club, covered now only by a passing wave, a watery shimmering—

A *shimmering*—

"Oh, my God."

"What now?" Kip says, still smiling.

A *different state of information. Some types of mind search compulsively for order. Black and white, with no gray.*

"You damn fool!" I shout. "All of you damn fools!" Kip rises from the barstool, combative or concerned, I don't care which. I am running out of the Depot, hitting the doorjamb with my shoulder as I hurl through.

The doorjamb responds by turning from brown to yellow.

All the four blocks home it is like that. Things happen as in dreams. Trees turn purple, shade through indigo to blue, return to green as information about the wavelength of light alters its coding. The sky is red. A parked car serenely floats two feet straight up, then drops. The air fills with staticky noise, weird chaotic droning that turns briefly into the theme from Handel's Suite no. 5. It is hot and then freezing. I reach the street end of my driveway, which has begun to melt. One moment I am running, and the next I feel my legs and arms and heart pump as hard as ever, but I do not move. I am suspended. Time itself does not move, hangs suspended.

The complexity barrier. This is the decisive passage, the crossing point.

I am too late.

I am xjj sbeg.

v yp *c#1/4mm;p—

Then the moment passes, and I am standing, dazed, in the middle of the new information state.

The trees stand straight. The sky is blue. Parked cars are parked; the McMillans' BMW has a ticket stuck under the wiper. A quiet breeze blows. At my feet, the green grass thrusts upward through cracks in the asphalt in its eternal bid to extend roots, reproduce itself, control my driveway. At the end of the driveway stand two houses.

One is the familiar center-door Colonial I left this morning in hurried disorder: socks on the bathroom floor; an unanswered letter from my sister on the coffee table; no silver candlesticks because they have been burglarized; newspapers filled with airline disasters and stock market gains, multiple lottery winners and simultaneous earthquakes, random muggings and paragraphs of garbled gibberish. The letter from my sister was one I wasn't going to answer. I never particularly liked my sister.

The other house is a bluish shimmer, Colonial lines still in the process of fading in and out. Right now it is hard to see clearly, like a house under deep water. But I know perfectly well what will be inside: all the shopping lists will be written with explanatory clauses.

Desperately I glance down the length of street. Number 54 stands alone; old Mr. Ashrider is a widower. Number 56 is a double shimmer; Elizabeth Hauser stays home with her and Ed's small children. Number 58, double; Jane and Carl Romano recently reconciled. Number 60, not; the Griswolds are off vacationing in Jamaica. Number 62, double; Chuck Dugan has remarried.

Anger seeps through me, but there is no time for anger. Already the blue shimmer of my second house is fading. I can't remember— did Kip say that information states, like galaxies, all move farther away from each other?

Shopping lists in dependent clauses. Burglars and infidelities with life histories. Answered letters. Sex talk that means exactly what it says, no more and no less. A low-possibility state with few shades of gray. Everything personal, connected.

And Emily.

I stand rooted to the asphalt, uncertain. But there is no longer room for uncertainty. Still, even as my feet carry me forward, I do not know which of the two houses I will enter.

philippa's hands

It is not contrary to reason to prefer the destruction of the whole world to the scratching of my finger. — DAVID HUME

THEY CAME AGAIN at dawn, like last time, distilling out of the washed-out gloom under the bedroom window. Or perhaps they came through the window, floating through the chilly glass and worn flowered curtains — how could you tell? They were crying again. They were always crying. Philippa thought, through her sleepy dread, *I could see if the curtains are damp. Then I could tell.*

The bandage still covered her right middle finger from last time.

They stood grouped at the foot of her bed, three rosy transparent hideous shapes that might have been old women. Or might not. Pinkish areas would swell into sketchy pseudopods suggesting a bent arm, a shawl draped over a head, a hunched back. Then the swellings would shift before she could be sure. Only the tears were constant, great rosy globes of sorrow welling and falling in arcs so beautiful that Philippa had to look away. In the morning, when it was all over, the carpet would still be soaked clear through.

No no no no no no no no no went the part of her that never understood, the most part, and her left hand clutched at the edge of the quilt. The central blue vein sprung out sharply. On the back of her hand two liver spots, for some reason clear in the gloom, echoed brown stains on the quilt that not even her diluted bleach on a clean rag had been able to touch.

One of them stepped forward. This time it was the one on the left. Philippa never knew. Their hierarchy, if they had one, was a mystery to her. If they were angels they should have a hierarchy, shouldn't they? It was one of the reasons she had given up on the idea that they were angels.

Philippa let go of the quilt and clasped her hands together to pray, but of course she couldn't do it. She never could while they were in the room. It wasn't only that fear kept her from concentrating properly. It was that she forgot what prayers were for, whom they were addressed to, what the whole thing was supposed to accomplish. There was no room in this for prayer, a thing that left the edges of hope intact and a little fuzzy. You never really knew if prayers were answered or not. Here you always knew, in concrete terms: this for that. It was a bargain, a contract, a hard Yankee deal.

She reached over to switch on the bedside lamp. Once, the first time, she had actually thought that would make them vanish. Things that go bump in the night, begone with the light. She hadn't known. She hadn't known anything. She had burned with terror, smoked black at the edges with it, ignited with the fear that either she was going crazy or she wasn't. She hadn't known anything. And 416 people had died.

At the click of the lamp switch the three glowing nebulous old women drew closer together. They always did that. They also cried harder, the rosy tears silently welling, coursing a short way down the glow, trembling a minute like perfect-cut rubies come alive to breathe in sorrow, breathe out pain. Then they fell.

Philippa waited.

The one who had stepped forward—although now that the light was on and they had moved into a bright amorphous huddle it was even more difficult to see where one left off and the next began—reverently laid the clipping on the foot of the bed. Against the faded chintz of the quilt, inherited from Philippa's mother, the newsprint looked almost white. The rosy huddle stepped back. Tears flowed.

"Who are you?" Philippa said to the old women, but not because she expected an answer. Just for something to say. In the still room her voice sounded rusty. Well, it was rusty. You don't speak when there's nobody to speak to.

The second and third times, Philippa had torn apart the library in Carter Falls, looking for those clippings. She had read every newspaper the library carried, and then the ones you had to use the microfiche machine for, sticking her head into the strange contraption and trying at least to match the typeface to the pieces of paper in her hand. She had even thought of driving into the college library in Plattsburgh, but it had been hard enough to get into Jim's car for the first time in the eight months since the funeral and drive just to Carter Falls. The thought of the trucks on Route 3 undid her. She had no driver's license, no need to go to Carter Falls, and no answer. The clipping was nowhere. It was never anywhere. This new one wouldn't be, either, until the grocery boy delivered next week's *Time*.

About four inches square, the clipping on the bed was paper-cut sharp on two joining edges, furred on the other two, as if it had been torn from the bottom-right corner of a page. But then there should be a date or page number or part of the paper's name, shouldn't there? Philippa could see without moving that there wasn't. The clipping was uncreased, unyellowed, crisp. But that made sense, since it hadn't appeared yet.

Made sense. O my God.

She could curse but not pray.

Another thing she knew she couldn't do, not until it was all over, was look at the crucifix on the wall. Just flat couldn't swivel her head that way. The whole wall—faded green-striped wallpaper, her grandmother's bureau with the chipped green paint and newel-post mirror and hand-tatted dresser scarf, Douay Bible on the scarf beside the cut-glass bowl holding hairpins and rubber bands—was off limits, until this was over. The first time, she had even thought this made a terrible sense. If the three weird women came from the Antichrist, the Evil One, then of course she would be barred from looking at the crucifix while they were there . . . she had been so stupid. And so afraid.

The clipping bore only one small headline. With type that small, and coming from the bottom of a page, it must not be too important. That was a good sign. "An outward and visible sign of an inward and spiritual grace."

Now how had *that* bit of catechism gotten through? Startled, Philippa tried again to clasp her hands for prayer. Her left ring finger, where once Jim's band had gone and where she would have worn the silver band making her a Bride of Christ, looked to her bonier and whiter than the rest. But that was just trashy fancy. It was important to keep clear what was fancy, what was not.

Philippa slid out of bed. That too was necessary; the clipping couldn't be reached otherwise, no matter how far forward she leaned. Her long flannel nightdress, the nap worn off at the elbows, wound itself around her hips. She jerked it down with a quick glance at the sobbing women, who only went on sobbing in their eerie silence.

Impatience stabbed Philippa. They weren't the ones going to do it. Some people just liked carrying on. Some like that from the parish had tried to visit her after Jim, clutching her hand and sniffing enough to turn your stomach, when they had never come near Jim during his illness. One visit was all she let them try.

She picked up the news clipping. The paper felt heavier than the ones the grocery boy delivered once a week. The type was smaller, too: serious type, and brief:

MARRAKECH—An earthquake here earlier today killed at least 34 people, including 22 children. Although officials at the Seismographic Institute in Rabat say the quake measured no more than 5.8 on the Richter scale, structures it toppled included a government-sponsored orphanage that stood near its epicenter. The orphanage housed 60 children and 17 adults. Rescue crews working around the clock have
Please turn to page 4A

Philippa closed her eyes. She couldn't picture the orphanage, the quake, any of it. She didn't know where Marrakech was, although she vaguely remembered a song about it when she had been in high school, the kind of song Johnny Mathis had never sung. Was it in Asia? Africa? Had the orphanage been whitewashed, with a dome? But it was only their pretty heathen churches that had domes, wasn't it?

Twenty-two dead children.

Philippa opened her eyes and looked at the ghostly wailing women. Suddenly they reminded her of the black-clad old ladies attending 6:00 A.M. Mass at St. Stanislaw's, every single morning of her childhood. Every single morning. Shuffling up the steps in heavy black-laced shoes, dipping holy water with two gnarled fingers from the font by the carved wooden door, lighting endless candles for the dead. What had there been in those pious figures to fill a child with such horror?

"All right, then," Philippa said, "I'm ready. Tell me."

The figure on the right raised her sketchy arm. A line of rosy light stretched from its end to Philippa's left hand, ending at the first joint of her index finger. A faint tingle, and the glowing line vanished. The knife appeared on the quilt: the same ordinary, murderously sharp hunting knife as always, the same one Philippa could have bought at Wayne Clarke's in Carter Falls. The old women wailed without comfort, their rosy tears cascading to the floor, pooling on the carpet, pristine in falling and sodden when done. Philippa looked at the whole spectacle with sudden distaste.

"Oh, stop that racket!"

Which was funny, because there was no noise.

Twenty-two dead children: babies with their skulls crushed before the soft spots had closed, toddlers carrying . . . whatever toys toddlers carried in Marrakech.

She picked up the knife and hacked off her left index finger at the first joint.

Much later, the doorbell rang. Tuesday—the weekly grocery delivery. Philippa sat weak and sick in the old rocker with the bottom rung missing, her head thrown back against a tied-on cushion. The grocery boy wouldn't come in; he would leave the groceries on the porch and take away the check made out to Hall's Superette, as he always did.

She had forgotten to put a check out on the porch.

The bell rang again. Philippa tried to think, but the pain still wouldn't let her. She sat pressing several folds of a bed sheet to the amputated joint; as the outer folds reddened she had moved on to a different section. Much of the sheet was red, and the air swelled with the rich metallic scent of blood. But Philippa knew she would not lose enough blood to die, would not get gangrene in the amputated tissues, would not even faint from shock. So many things that never happened. She sat pressing the blood-sodden sheet

to her maimed left hand with the thumb and one whole finger of the right, and listened to the doorbell ring.

A school-bus crash in Calgary, a cholera epidemic along the Indus River, a dam burst in Colorado, a political massacre in El Salvador.

Could the grocery boy see through the dingy curtains covering the front window?

And the two she hadn't believed, the first times: the bridge collapse in Florida, the crop failure in a Chinese province she couldn't pronounce.

The curtains had a hole just above the windowsill nearest the door; the fabric had been clawed through by a cat that had run away the day after Jim's funeral. Jim's cat. If the grocery boy stooped, he could peer through the hole. Philippa tried to inch her rocker in the other direction, but the effort just made her dizzy. It would be a few hours yet before she could eat anything, clean up the bedroom, change the quilt. She was running out of quilts.

The doorbell stopped ringing, and the knob rattled. Philippa made a small noise; from the rocker she could see that the chain was off. But the door was locked, she was sure of that, she'd locked it last night.

The door heaved twice, the first heave curving the wood gracefully inward like the bow of a violin, the second springing it back on its hinges and bouncing it so hard against the faded wallpaper that the doorknob punched a round hole in the plasterboard beneath. A hand caught the door on the rebound. It wasn't the grocery boy from Hall's Superette but Sam Hall himself, walking into the room with the deliberate shambling step Philippa knew since high school. He wore his mechanic's coveralls, boots leaving sloppy snow on the carpet and grease at the knees in splotches like the outlines of distant countries.

Philippa glared at him, furious and embarrassed. He gazed mildly around the room, and she had the idea that he missed nothing, saw it all through to the buckling bones: her mother's clock ticking heavily in the corner, the piles of newspaper furred with dust, the ashtray from Niagara Falls filled with paper clips and pennies and thread, the rounded corners of the overstuffed sofa tufted with dangling buttons, the unwashed curtains and scrupulously washed ceramic Madonna, with its beautiful draperies and foolish simper. Saw it all, as if it were the engine of a truck he was taking apart behind the Superette, removing one part after another in his slow way, running a careful thumb over each to feel its essential soundness under the necessary grease. Then he looked again at Philippa, at the bloody sheet and four healed stumps, and behind his eyes moved something that she didn't like.

"Philippa, you oughtn't be doing that to yourself here."

She meant to say furiously, *And you oughtn't be breaking and entering into people's houses, Sam Hall!* but those weren't the words that came. Instead she heard herself say, "There wasn't anything else I could do," and after that the mortifying tears—in front of Sam Hall!—rolling hot and stinging on her dry skin, spraying outward when she swiped at her dripping nose, turning pink where they fell on the bloody sheet in her hands.

They talked about it only once. Sam Hall took her to Mass on Sunday, Mass at a reasonable 10:00 a.m., and he didn't assume the five dollars he put in the collection plate was for both of them. Philippa liked that. When women she hadn't seen since the funeral rushed up afterward to exclaim over her hands and gawk at Sam, he took Philippa firmly by the elbow and guided her back toward his truck. After church came a movie in Carter Falls, a thing neither of them found funny, about people chasing and killing one another over something that fit inside a computer. The movie was redeemed by a drive along the lake on an afternoon bursting with lilacs. Then came a dinner at the Apple Tree in Carter Falls, and another one with Sam's grown daughter home from college in Plattsburgh. The daughter never mentioned Philippa's hands. Another movie, only this one was funny, another dinner out, a political picnic for John Crane, who had gone to school with Philippa and Sam and Jim and now was running for county sheriff. And all those weeks they talked about it only once, in Sam's truck, parked in Philippa's driveway just before she went inside and he started the long drive back to town.

Philippa said abruptly, out of one of their long comfortable silences, "Do you believe in aliens?" The word sounded foolish there in the cab of the pickup, so she added, "Like in the movies?"

"Nope," Sam said.

"Ghosts?"

"No."

"Angels?"

"In Bible times."

"Not now?"

"No."

Philippa nodded. "I wanted to be a nun, after Jim died. Can you imagine? I got books to study, and I wrote to the convent at Plattsburgh."

"What did they say?"

"They said they were a teaching order, and I wasn't a teacher."

Sam slapped at a mosquito above his collar. A moth lit on the windshield: ghostly pale wings translucent in the light from the porch. He said, "People do weird things sometimes. From loneliness."

He glanced at her hands. Philippa laid them defiantly on the dashboard, side by side. "It wasn't from loneliness." That was true.

He considered this. She breathed in the smell of his shirt—cigarettes and thirty-weight oil and fabric softener. Finally he said, "You needed rescuing."

Rescuing! Hysterical laughter rose in her, heady as whiskey. Rescuing! Her! When it was she who had saved . . . single-handedly . . . *single-handedly*. . . . Philippa put her palm over her mouth and leaned forward against the dashboard. As soon as she shifted, the moth flew toward the porch light.

"Philippa," Sam said, "Philippa—" She knew then it was all he would ever say, all he would ever ask, and that she didn't have to answer. It was all right if she never answered. She shifted the other way, to lean against his shoulder.

"Sometimes there just isn't any choice," she said.

"Uh-huh," he agreed, and laid his hand on her breast, and she heard the sudden laughter in his slow voice.

They came at dawn, three days before Philippa's wedding. The window was open, and the room smelled of a heavy rich August night too warm for dew. Three glowing nebulous figures at the foot of the bed, welling with rosy tears. Philippa woke and her spine went rigid.

The one on the left laid the newspaper clipping on the bed. The bedspread was new, a frivolous green quilted in shiny squares and edged with six inches of eyelet ruffle. Sam was painting the bedroom green. Through the outlines of the wailing women Philippa could see the outlines of the paint cans, both ghostly against the bare plaster Sam had already stripped and washed.

This time the clipping was large, more than half a page, the headline in thick black letters. Right and left edges were clean, top and bottom torn. The top, Philippa thought: where the name of the newspaper would be. She never would find out what it was called. Against the bright shiny green of the bedspread the paper looked unnaturally white, like someone about to faint.

No no no no no no.

Philippa's feet slid out of bed. The carpet had been rolled up for the painting. The bare wide-planked hardwood floor was cool enough to make her toes curl under. The newspaper felt light and dry in her hand, even lighter than paper should feel. Without turning on the lamp, Philippa carried the clipping across the room to the window, where there was just barely enough light to read it.

TWA JET CRASHES IN BOSTON HARBOR
FATALITIES FEARED HIGH

BOSTON—A TWA 707 jetliner failed to take off at Logan Field late last night and plummeted into Boston Harbor, killing at least 257 people. The plane, Flight 18 from Boston to Washington, achieved takeoff speed but failed to leave the ground at the end of the runway, which ended at the harbor. The plane sped forward and sank in the 63-degree water.

The jetliner remained two-thirds submerged in the water, enabling at least 9 passengers and airline personnel to escape through the two doors they managed to open.

"There was this roar and then a huge splash," said Elizabeth Brattle, who witnessed the crash from the deck of her sailboat moored in the harbor. "Waves rolled in, nearly swamping the boat. You could hear people screaming. It was horrible."

By 20 minutes after the disaster, diving teams were on the scene to assist in the recovery. Divers are expected to remain on the scene throughout the night.

The cause of the plane's failure to lift into the air is unknown. TWA spokesperson Richard Connington expressed shock and concern but cautioned against speculation that
Please turn to back of section

There was a second article, an eyewitness account from one of the passengers who escaped, and a picture of the drowning plane. Philippa didn't read the second article. The three rosy hideous women bent nearly double with wailing and grief, and their beautiful tears pooled on the wooden floor. Philippa watched them, feeling their pain, feeling all the pain and terror of the great plane reaching the end of the runway and still rolling along the ground, of the dizzying lurch into the water, the sudden impact. Did the

water come in right away? Did the lights go out? People screaming, choking in the darkness, and later that other choking and
darkness, of the survivors.

Sam had taken down the crucifix when he took down the ancient dingy needlepoint worked by one of Philippa's great-aunts and
the framed painting of a woodland brook that Philippa had bought
at The Art Shoppe in Carter Falls. She wondered if she would have
been able to see the crucifix this time. The pink thread of light
shot out from one of the crying women, Philippa couldn't see which
one, and touched the first joint of her right thumb.

At the base of the thumb, just below the knuckle, was a burn
blister where she had foolishly touched the pan taking an apple
pie for Sam out of the oven. Sam, eating the pie at her kitchen
table. Holding the square of heated metal of the wallpaper strip-
per against this room, while she followed him with the scrub bucket.
Holding the tips of her fingers while they watched TV and never
saying anything against them, anything at all about stupidity or
pride or need.

At least 257 people. "You could hear people screaming."

The knife appeared on the bed. The glowing women cried and
wailed. All the sorrow of the world seemed to flow through them,
the world beyond this room, that Philippa had once thought to re-
nounce and go be a middle-aged nun because there was nothing
left here anyway.

Philippa whispered, "No," and the knife vanished.

She stood shivering in a sudden breeze from the window as the
silently keening women also vanished, leaving only the pool of rosy
tears on the scarred floor that she and Sam planned to wax shining
and hard and golden.

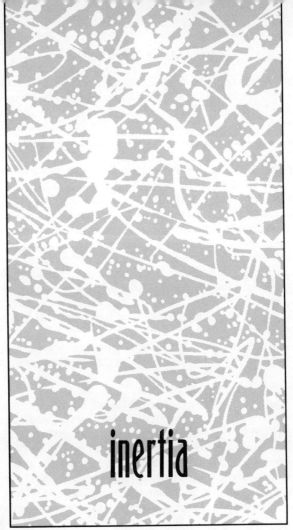

inertia

AT DUSK the back of the bedroom falls off. One minute it's a wall, exposed studs and cracked blue drywall, and the next it's snapped-off two-by-fours and an irregular fence as high as my waist, the edges both jagged and furry, as if they were covered with powder. Through the hole a sickly tree pokes upward in the narrow space between the back of our barracks and the back of a barracks in E Block. I try to get out of bed for a closer look, but today my arthritis is too bad, which is why I'm in bed in the first place. Rachel rushes into the bedroom.

"What *happened*, Gram? Are you all right?"

I nod and point. Rachel bends into the hole, her hair haloed by California twilight. The bedroom is hers, too; her mattress lies stored under my scarred four-poster.

"Termites! Damn. I didn't know we had them. You sure you're all right?"

"I'm fine. I was all the way across the room, honey. I'm fine."

"Well—we'll have to get Mom to get somebody to fix it."

I say nothing. Rachel straightens, throws me a quick glance, looks away. Still I say nothing about Mamie, but in a sudden flicker from my oil lamp I look directly at Rachel, just because she is so good to look at. Not pretty, not even here Inside, although so far the disease has affected only the left side of her face. The ridge of thickened ropy skin, coarse as old hemp, isn't visible at all when she stands in right profile. But her nose is large, her eyebrows heavy and low, her chin a bony knob. An honest nose, expressive brows, direct gray eyes, chin that juts forward when she tilts her head in intelligent listening—to a grandmother's eye, Rachel is good to look at. They wouldn't think so, Outside. But they would be wrong.

Rachel says, "Maybe I could trade a lottery card for more drywall and nails, and patch it myself."

"The termites will still be there."

"Well, yes, but we have to do *something*." I don't contradict her. She is sixteen years old. "Feel that air coming in—you'll freeze at night this time of year. It'll be terrible for your arthritis. Come in the kitchen now, Gram—I've built up the fire."

She helps me into the kitchen, where the metal wood-burning stove throws a rosy warmth that feels good on my joints. The stove was donated to the colony a year ago by who-knows-what charity or special interest group for, I suppose, whatever tax breaks still hold for that sort of thing. If any do. Rachel tells me that we still get newspapers, and once or twice I've wrapped vegetables from our patch in some fairly new-looking ones. She even says that the young Stevenson boy works a donated computer newsnet in the Block J community hall, but I no longer follow Outside tax regulations. Nor do I ask why Mamie was the one to get the wood-burning stove when it wasn't a lottery month.

The light from the stove is stronger than the oil flame in the bedroom; I see that beneath her concern for our dead bedroom wall, Rachel's face is flushed with excitement. Her young skin glows right from intelligent chin to the ropy ridge of disease, which of course never changes color. I smile at her. Sixteen is so easy to excite. A new hair ribbon from the donations repository, a glance from a boy, a secret with her cousin Jennie.

"Gram," she says, kneeling beside my chair, her hands restless on the battered wooden arm, "Gram—there's a visitor. From Outside. Jennie *saw* him."

I go on smiling. Rachel—nor Jennie, either—can't remember when disease colonies had lots of visitors. First bulky figures in contamination suits, then a few years later, sleeker figures in the sanisuits that took their place. People were still being interned from Outside, and for years the checkpoints at the Rim had traffic flowing both ways. But of course Rachel doesn't remember all that; she wasn't born. Mamie was only twelve when we were interned here. To Rachel, a visitor might well be a great event. I put out one hand and stroke her hair.

"Jennie said he wants to talk to the oldest people in the colony, the ones who were brought here with the disease. Hal Stevenson told her."

"Did he, sweetheart?" Her hair is soft and silky. Mamie's hair had been the same at Rachel's age.

"He might want to talk to you!"

"Well, here I am."

"But aren't you excited? What do you suppose he wants?"

I'm saved from answering her because Mamie comes in, her boyfriend Peter Malone following with a string bag of groceries from the repository.

At the first sound of the doorknob turning, Rachel gets up from beside my chair and pokes at the fire. Her face goes completely blank, although I know that part is only temporary. Mamie cries, "Here we are!" in her high doll-baby voice, cold air from the hall swirling around her like bright water. "Mama darling—how are you feeling? And Rachel! You'll never guess—Pete had extra depository cards and he got us some chicken! I'm going to make a stew!"

"The back wall fell off the bedroom," Rachel says flatly. She doesn't look at Peter with his string-crossed chicken, but I do. He grins his patient, wolfish grin. I guess that he won the depository cards at poker. His fingernails are dirty. The part of the newspaper I can see says ESIDENT CONFISCATES C.

Mamie says, "What do you mean, fell off?"

Rachel shrugs. "Just fell off. Termites."

Mamie looks helplessly at Peter, whose grin widens. I can see how it will be: they will have a scene later, not completely for our benefit, although it will take place in the kitchen for us to watch. Mamie will beg prettily for Peter to fix the wall. He will demur, grinning. She will offer various smirking hints about barter, each hint becoming more explicit. He will agree to fix the wall. Rachel and I, having no other warm room to go to, will watch the fire or the floor or our shoes until Mamie and Peter retire ostentatiously to her room. It's the ostentation that embarrasses us. Mamie has always needed witnesses to her desirability.

But Peter is watching Rachel, not Mamie. "The chicken isn't from Outside, Rachel. It's from that chicken yard in Block B. I heard you say how clean they are."

"Yeah," Rachel says shortly, gracelessly.

Mamie rolls her eyes. "Say 'thank you,' darling. Peter went to a lot of trouble to get this chicken."

"Thanks."

"Can't you say it like you *mean* it?" Mamie's voice goes shrill.

"*Thanks,*" Rachel says. She heads toward our three-walled bedroom. Peter, still watching her closely, shifts the chicken from one hand to the other. The pressure of the string bag cuts lines across the chicken's yellowish skin.

"Rachel Anne Wilson—"

"Let her go," Peter says softly.

"No," Mamie says. Between the five crisscrossing lines of disease, her face sets in unlovely lines. "She can at least learn some manners. And I want her to hear our announcement! Rachel, you just come right back out here this minute!"

Rachel returns from the bedroom; I've never known her to disobey her mother. She pauses by the open bedroom door, waiting. Two empty candle sconces, both blackened by old smoke, frame her head. It has been since at least last winter that we've had candles for them. Mamie, her forehead creased in irritation, smiles brightly.

"This is a special dinner, all of you. Peter and I have an announcement. We're going to get married."

"That's right," Peter says. "Congratulate us."

Rachel, already motionless, somehow goes even stiller. Peter watches her carefully. Mamie casts down her eyes, blushing, and I feel a stab of impatient pity for my daughter, propping up mid-thirties girlishness on such a slender reed as Peter Malone. I stare at him hard. If he ever touches Rachel . . . but I don't really think he would. Things like that don't happen anymore. Not Inside.

"Congratulations," Rachel mumbles. She crosses the room and

embraces her mother, who hugs her back with theatrical fervor. In another minute, Mamie will start to cry. Over her shoulder I glimpse Rachel's face, momentarily sorrowing and loving, and I drop my eyes.

"Well! This calls for a toast!" Mamie cries gaily. She winks, makes a clumsy pirouette, and pulls a bottle from the back shelf of the cupboard Rachel got at the last donations lottery. The cupboard looks strange in our kitchen: gleaming white lacquer, vaguely Oriental-looking, amid the wobbly chairs and scarred table with the broken drawer no one has ever gotten around to mending. Mamie flourishes the bottle, which I didn't know was there. It's champagne.

What had they been thinking, the Outsiders who donated champagne to a disease colony? *Poor devils, even if they never have anything to celebrate.* . . . Or *Here's something they won't know what to do with.* . . . Or *Better them than me—as long as the sickies stay Inside.* . . . It doesn't really matter.

"I just love champagne!" Mamie cries feverishly; I think she has drunk it once. "And oh look—here's someone else to help us celebrate! Come in, Jennie—come in and have some champagne!"

Jennie comes in, smiling. I see the same eager excitement that animated Rachel before her mother's announcement. It glows on Jennie's face, which is beautiful. She has no disease on her hands or her face. She must have it somewhere, she was born Inside, but one doesn't ask that. Probably Rachel knows. The two girls are inseparable. Jennie, the daughter of Mamie's dead husband's brother, is Rachel's cousin, and technically Mamie is her guardian. But no one pays attention to such things anymore, and Jennie lives with some people in a barracks in the next Block, although Rachel and I asked her to live here. She shook her head, the beautiful hair so blonde it's almost white bouncing on her shoulders, and blushed in embarrassment, painfully not looking at Mamie.

"I'm getting married, Jennie," Mamie says, again casting down her eyes bashfully. I wonder what she did, and with whom, to get the champagne.

"Congratulations!" Jennie says warmly. "You too, Peter."

"Call me Pete," he says, as he has said before. I catch his hungry look at Jennie. She doesn't, but some sixth sense—even here, even Inside—makes her step slightly backward. I know she will go on calling him "Peter."

Mamie says to Jennie, "Have some more champagne. Stay for dinner."

With her eyes Jennie measures the amount of champagne in

the bottle, the size of the chicken bleeding slightly on the table. She measures unobtrusively, and then of course she lies. "I'm sorry, I can't—we ate our meal at noon today. I just wanted to ask if I could bring someone over to see you later, Gram. A visitor." Her voice drops to a hush, and the glow is back. "From *Outside*."

I look at her sparkling blue eyes, at Rachel's face, and I don't have the heart to refuse. Even though I can guess, as the two girls cannot, how the visit will be. I am not Jennie's grandmother, but she has called me that since she was three. "All right."

"Oh, thank you!" Jennie cries, and she and Rachel look at each other with delight. "I'm so glad you said yes, or else we might never get to talk to a visitor up close at all!"

"You're welcome," I say. They are so young. Mamie looks petulant; her announcement has been upstaged. Peter watches Jennie as she impulsively hugs Rachel. Suddenly I know that he, too, is wondering where Jennie's body is diseased, and how much. He catches my eye and looks at the floor, his dark eyes lidded, half ashamed. But only half. A log crackles in the wooden stove, and for a brief moment the fire flares.

The next afternoon Jennie brings the visitor. He surprises me immediately: he isn't wearing a sani-suit, and he isn't a sociologist.

In the years following the internments, the disease colonies had a lot of visitors. Doctors still hopeful of a cure for the thick gray ridges of skin that spread slowly over a human body—or didn't, nobody knew why. Disfiguring. Ugly. Maybe eventually fatal. And *communicable*. That was the biggie: communicable. So doctors in sani-suits came looking for causes or cures. Journalists in sani-suits came looking for stories with four-color photo spreads. Legislative fact-finding committees in sani-suits came looking for facts, at least until Congress took away the power of colonies to vote, pressured by taxpayers who, increasingly pressured themselves, resented our dollar-dependent status. And the sociologists came in droves, minicams in hand, ready to record the collapse of the ill-organized and ill colonies into street-gang, dog-eat-dog anarchy.

Later, when this did not happen, different sociologists came in later-model sani-suits to record the reasons why the colonies were not collapsing on schedule. All these groups went away dissatisfied. There was no cure, no cause, no story, no collapse. No reasons.

The sociologists hung on longer than anybody else. Journalists have to be timely and interesting, but sociologists merely have to publish. Besides, everything in their cultural tradition told them that Inside *must* sooner or later degenerate into war zones: deprive people of electricity (power became expensive), of municipal police (who refused to go Inside), of freedom to leave, of political clout, of jobs, of freeways and movie theaters and federal judges and state-administered elementary-school accreditation—and you get unrestrained violence to just survive. Everything in the culture said so. Bombed-out inner cities. *Lord of the Flies.* The Chicago projects. Western movies. Prison memoirs. The Bronx. East L.A. Thomas Hobbes. The sociologists *knew.*

Only it didn't happen.

The sociologists waited. And Inside we learned to grow vegetables and raise chickens, which, we learned, will eat anything. Those of us with computer knowledge worked real jobs over modems for a few years—maybe it was as long as a decade—before the equipment became too obsolete and unreplaced. Those who had been teachers organized classes among the children, although the curriculum, I think, must have gotten simpler every year. Rachel and Jennie don't seem to have much knowledge of history or science. Doctors practiced with medicines donated by corporations for the tax write-offs, and after a decade or so they began to train apprentices. For a while—it might have been a long while—we listened to radios and watched TV. Maybe some people still do, if we have any working ones donated from Outside. I don't pay attention.

Eventually the sociologists remembered older models of deprivation and discrimination and isolation from the larger culture: Jewish shtetls. French Huguenots. Amish farmers. Self-sufficient models, stagnant but uncollapsed. And while they were remembering, we held goods lotteries, and took on apprentices, and rationed depository food according to who needed it, and replaced our broken-down furniture with other broken-down furniture, and got married and bore children. We paid no taxes, fought no wars, wielded no votes, provided no drama. After a while—a long while—the visitors stopped coming. Even the sociologists.

But here stands this young man, without a sani-suit, smiling from brown eyes under thick dark hair and taking my hand. He doesn't wince when he touches the ropes of disease. Nor does he appear to be cataloging the kitchen furniture for later recording: three chairs, one donated imitation Queen Anne and one Inside genuine Joe Kleinschmidt; the table; the wood stove; the sparkling new Oriental lacquered cupboard; plastic sink with hand pump; woodbox with donated wood stamped GIFT OF BOISE-CASCADE; two eager and intelligent and loving young girls he had better not try to patronize as diseased freaks. It has been a long time, but I remember.

"Hello, Mrs. Pratt. I'm Tom McHabe. Thank you for agreeing to talk to me."

I nod. "What are we going to talk about, Mr. McHabe? Are you a journalist?"

"No. I'm a doctor."

I don't expect that. Nor do I expect the sudden strain that flashes across his face before it's lost in another smile. Although it is natural enough that strain should be there: having come Inside, of course, he can never leave. I wonder where he picked up the disease. No other new cases have been admitted to our colony for as long as I can remember. Had they been taken, for some Outside political reason, to one of the other colonies instead?

McHabe says, "I don't have the disease, Mrs. Pratt."

"Then why on earth—"

"I'm writing a paper on the progress of the disease in long-established colony residents. I had to do that from Inside, of course," he says, and immediately I know he is lying. Rachel and Jennie, of course, do not. They sit one on each side of him like eager birds, listening.

"And how will you get this paper out once it's written?" I say.

"Shortwave radio. Colleagues are expecting it," but he doesn't quite meet my eyes.

"And this paper is worth permanent internment?"

"How rapidly did your case of the disease progress?" he says, not answering my question. He looks at my face and hands and forearms, an objective and professional scrutiny that makes me decide at least one part of his story is true. He is a doctor.

"Any pain in the infected areas?"

"None."

"Any functional disability or decreased activity as a result of the disease?" Rachel and Jennie look slightly puzzled; he's testing me to see if I understand the terminology.

"None."

"Any change in appearance over the last few years in the first skin areas to be affected? Changes in color or tissue density or size of the thickened ridges?"

"None."

"Any other kinds of changes I haven't thought to mention?"

"None."

He nods and rocks back on his heels. He's cool, for someone who is going to develop nondysfunctional ropes of disease himself. I wait to see if he's going to tell me why he's really here. The silence lengthens. Finally McHabe says, "You were a CPA," at the same time that Rachel says, "Anyone want a glass of 'ade?"

McHabe accepts gladly. The two girls, relieved to be in motion, busy themselves pumping cold water, crushing canned peaches, mixing the 'ade in a brown plastic pitcher with a deep wart on one side where it once touched the hot stove.

"Yes," I say to McHabe, "I was a CPA. What about it?"

"They're outlawed now."

"CPAs? Why? Staunch pillars of the establishment," I say, and realize how long it's been since I used words like that. They taste metallic, like old tin.

"Not anymore. IRS does all tax computations and sends every household a customized bill. The calculations on how they reach your particular customized figure are classified. To prevent foreign enemies from guessing at revenue available for defense."

"Ah."

"My uncle was a CPA."

"What is he now?"

"Not a CPA," McHabe says. He doesn't smile. Jennie hands glasses of 'ade to me and then to McHabe, and then he does smile. Jennie drops her lashes, and a little color steals into her cheeks. Something moves behind McHabe's eyes. But it's not like Peter; not at all like Peter.

I glance at Rachel. She doesn't seem to have noticed anything. She isn't jealous, or worried, or hurt. I relax a little.

McHabe says to me, "You also published some magazine articles popularizing history."

"How do you happen to know that?"

Again he doesn't answer me. "It's an unusual combination of abilities, accounting and history writing."

"I suppose so," I say, without interest. It was so long ago.

Rachel says to McHabe, "Can I ask you something?"

"Sure."

"Outside, do you have medicines that will cure wood of termites?"

Her face is deadly serious. McHabe doesn't grin, and I admit—

reluctantly—that he is likable. He answers her courteously. "We don't cure the wood, we do away with the termites. The best way is to build with wood saturated with creosote, a chemical they don't like, so that they don't get into the wood in the first place. But there must be chemicals that will kill them after they're already there. I'll ask around and try to bring you something on my next trip Inside."

His next trip Inside. He drops this bombshell as if easy passage in and out were a given. Rachel's and Jennie's eyes grow wide; they both look at me. McHabe does, too, and I see that his look is a cool scrutiny, an appraisal of my reaction. He expects me to ask for details, or maybe even—it's been a long time since I thought in these terms, and it's an effort—to become angry at him for lying. But I don't know whether or not he's lying, and at any rate, what does it matter? A few people from Outside coming into the colony—how could it affect us? There won't be large immigration, and no emigration at all.

I say quietly, "Why are you really here, Dr. McHabe?"

"I told you, Mrs. Pratt. To measure the progress of the disease." I say nothing. He adds, "Maybe you'd like to hear more about how it is now Outside."

"Not especially."

"Why not?"

I shrug. "They leave us alone."

He weighs me with his eyes. Jennie says timidly, "I'd like to hear more about Outside." Before Rachel can add, "Me, too," the door flings violently open and Mamie backs into the room, screaming into the hall behind her.

"And don't ever come back! If you think I'd ever let you touch me again after screwing that . . . that . . . I hope she's got a diseased twat and you get it on your—" She sees McHabe and breaks off, her whole body jerking in rage. A soft answer from the hall, the words unintelligible from my chair by the fire, makes her gasp and turn even redder. She slams the door, bursts into tears, and runs into her bedroom, slamming that door as well.

Rachel stands up. "Let me, honey," I say, but before I can rise— my arthritis is much better—Rachel disappears into her mother's room. The kitchen rings with embarrassed silence.

Tom McHabe rises to leave. "Sit down, Doctor," I say, hoping, I think, that if he remains Mamie will restrain her hysterics— maybe—and Rachel will emerge sooner from her mother's room.

McHabe looks undecided. Then Jennie says, "Yes, please stay. And would you tell us"—I see her awkwardness, her desire to not sound stupid—"about how people do Outside?"

He does. Looking at Jennie but meaning me, he talks about the latest version of martial law, about the failure of the National Guard to control protesters against the South American war until they actually reached the edge of the White House electrowired zone; about the growing power of the Fundamentalist underground that the other undergrounds—he uses the plural—call "the God gang." He tells us about the industries losing out steadily to Korean and Chinese competitors, the leaping unemployment rate, the ethnic backlash, the cities in flames. Miami, New York, Los Angeles—these had been rioting for years. Now it's Portland, St. Louis, Eugene, Phoenix. Grand Rapids burning. It's hard to picture.

I say, "As far as I can tell, donations to our repositories haven't fallen off."

He looks at me again with that shrewd scrutiny, weighing something I can't see, then touches the edge of the stove with one boot. The boot, I notice, is almost as old and scarred as one of ours. "Korean-made stove. They make nearly all the donations now. Public relations. Even a lot of martial-law congressmen had relatives interned, although they won't admit it now. The Asians cut deals warding off complete protectionism, although of course your donations are only a small part of that. But just about everything you get Inside is Chink or Splat." He uses the words casually, this courteous young man giving me the news from such a liberal slant, and that tells me more about the Outside than all his bulletins and summaries.

Jennie says haltingly, "I saw . . . I think it was an Asian man. Yesterday."

"Where?" I say sharply. Very few Asian-Americans contract the disease; something else no one understands. There are none in our colony.

"At the Rim. One of the guards. Two other men were kicking him and yelling names at him—we couldn't hear too clearly over the intercom boxes."

"We? You and Rachel? What were you two doing at the *Rim?*" I say, and hear my own tone. The Rim, a wide empty strip of land, is electromined and barbwired to keep us communicables Inside. The Rim is surrounded by miles of defoliated and disinfected land, poisoned by preventive chemicals, but even so it's patrolled by unwilling soldiers who communicate with the Inside by intercoms set up every half mile on both sides of the barbed wire. When the colony used to have a fight or a rape or—once, in the early years—a murder, it happened on the Rim. When the hateful and the hating came to hurt us, because before the electrowiring and barbed wire we were easy targets and no police would follow them Inside, the soldiers, and sometimes our men as well, stopped them at the Rim. Our dead are buried near the Rim. And Rachel and Jennie, dear gods, at the *Rim* . . .

"We went to ask the guards over the intercom boxes if they knew how to stop termites," Jennie says logically. "After all, their work is to stop things, germs and things. We thought they might be able to tell us how to stop termites. We thought they might have special training in it."

The bedroom door opens and Rachel comes out, her young face drawn. McHabe smiles at her, and then his gaze returns to Jennie. "I don't think soldiers are trained in stopping termites, but I'll definitely bring you something to do that the next time I come Inside."

There it is again. But all Rachel says is, "Oh, good. I asked around for more drywall today, but even if I get some, the same thing will happen again if we don't get something to stop them."

McHabe says, "Did you know that termites elect a queen? Closely monitored balloting system. Fact."

Rachel smiles, although I don't think she really understands.

"And ants can bring down a rubber tree plant." He begins to sing, an old song from my childhood. "High Hopes." Frank Sinatra on the stereo—before CDs, even, before a lot of things—iced tea and Coke in tall glasses on a Sunday afternoon, aunts and uncles sitting around the kitchen, football on television in the living room beside a table with a lead-crystal vase of the last purple chrysanthemums from the garden. The smell of late Sunday afternoon, tangy but a little thin, the last of the weekend before the big yellow school bus labored by on Monday morning.

Jennie and Rachel, of course, see none of this. They hear light-hearted words in a good baritone and a simple rhythm they can follow, hope and courage in silly doggerel. They are delighted. They join in the chorus after McHabe has sung it a few times, then sing him three songs popular at Block dances, then make him more 'ade, then begin to ask questions about the Outside. Simple questions: What do people eat? Where do they get it? What do they wear?

The three of them are still at it when I go to bed, my arthritis finally starting to ache, glancing at Mamie's closed door with a sadness I hadn't expected and can't name.

"That son of a bitch better never come near me again," Mamie says the next morning. The day is sunny and I sit by our one window, knitting a blanket to loosen my fingers, wondering if the donated wool came from Chinese or Korean sheep. Rachel has gone with Jennie on a labor call to deepen a well in Block E; people had been talking about doing that for weeks, and apparently someone finally got around to organizing it. Mamie slumps at the table, her eyes red from crying. "I caught him screwing Mary Delbarton." Her voice splinters like a two-year-old's. "Mama—he was screwing Mary Delbarton."

"Let him go, Mamie."

"I'd be alone again." She says it with a certain dignity, which doesn't last. "That son of a bitch goes off with that slut one day after we're engaged, and I'm fucking alone again!"

I don't say anything; there isn't anything to say. Mamie's husband died eleven years ago, when Rachel was only five, of an experimental cure being tested by government doctors. The colonies were guinea pigs. Seventeen people in four colonies died, and the government discontinued funding and made it a crime for anyone to go in and out of a disease colony. Too great a risk of contamination, they said. For the protection of the citizens of the country.

"He'll never touch me again!" Mamie says, tears on her lashes. One slips down an inch until it hits the first of the disease ropes, then travels sideways toward her mouth. I reach over and wipe it away. "Goddamn fucking son of a bitch!"

By evening, she and Peter are holding hands. They sit side by side, and his fingers creep up her thigh under what they think is the cover of the table. Mamie slips her hand under his buttocks. Rachel and Jennie look away, Jennie flushing slightly. I have a brief flash of memory, of the kind I haven't had for years: myself at eighteen or so, my first year at Yale, in a huge brass bed with a modern geometric-print bedspread and a redheaded man I met three hours ago. But here, Inside . . . here sex, like everything else, moves so much more slowly, so much more carefully, so much more privately. For such a long time people were afraid that this disease, like that other earlier one, might be transmitted sexually. And then there was the shame of one's ugly body, crisscrossed with ropes of disease

. . . I'm not sure that Rachel has ever seen a man naked.

I say, for the sake of saying something, "So there's a Block dance Wednesday."

"Block B," Jennie says. Her blue eyes sparkle. "With the band that played last summer for Block E."

"Guitars?"

"Oh, no! They've got a trumpet *and* a violin," Rachel says, clearly impressed. "You should hear how they sound together, Gram — it's a lot different than guitars. Come to the dance!"

"I don't think so, honey. Is Dr. McHabe going?" From both their faces I know this guess is right.

Jennie says hesitantly, "He wants to talk to you first, before the dance, for a few minutes. If that's all right."

"Why?"

"I'm not . . . not exactly sure I know all of it." She doesn't meet my eyes: unwilling to tell me, unwilling to lie. Most of the children Inside, I realize for the first time, are not liars. Or else they're bad ones. They're good at privacy, but it must be an honest privacy.

"Will you see him?" Rachel says eagerly.

"I'll see him."

Mamie looks away from Peter long enough to add sharply, "If it's anything about you or Jennie, he should see *me*, miss, not your grandmother. I'm your mother and Jennie's guardian, and don't you forget it."

"No, Mama," Rachel says.

"I don't like your tone, miss!"

"Sorry," Rachel says, in the same tone. Jennie drops her eyes, embarrassed. But before Mamie can get really started on indignant maternal neglect, Peter whispers something in her ear and she claps her hand over her mouth, giggling.

Later, when just the two of us are left in the kitchen, I say quietly to Rachel, "Try not to upset your mother, honey. She can't help it."

"Yes, Gram," Rachel says obediently. But I hear the disbelief in her tone, a disbelief muted by her love for me and even for her mother, but nonetheless there. Rachel doesn't believe that Mamie can't help it. Rachel, born Inside, can't possibly help her own ignorance of what it is that Mamie thinks she has lost.

On his second visit to me six days later, just before the Block dance, Tom McHabe seems different. I'd forgotten that there are people who radiate such energy and purpose that they seem to set the very air tingling. He stands with his legs braced slightly apart, flanked by Rachel and Jennie, both dressed in their other skirts for the dance. Jennie has woven a red ribbon through her blonde curls; it glows like a flower. McHabe touches her lightly on the shoulder, and I realize from her answering look what must be happening between them. My throat tightens.

"I want to be honest with you, Mrs. Pratt. I've talked to Jack Stevenson and Mary Kramer, as well as some others in Blocks C and E, and I've gotten a feel for how you live here. A little bit, anyway. I'm going to tell Mr. Stevenson and Mrs. Kramer what I tell you, but I wanted you to be first."

"Why?" I say, more harshly than I intend. Or think I intend.

He isn't fazed. "Because you're one of the oldest survivors of the disease. Because you had a strong education Outside. Because your daughter's husband died of axoperidine."

At the same moment that I realize what McHabe is going to say next, I realize, too, that Rachel and Jennie have already heard it. They listen to him with the slightly openmouthed intensity of children hearing a marvelous but familiar tale. But do they understand? Rachel wasn't present when her father finally died, gasping for air his lungs couldn't use.

McHabe, watching me, says, "There's been a lot of research on the disease since those deaths, Mrs. Pratt."

"No. There hasn't. Too risky, your government said."

I see that he caught the pronoun. "Actual administration of any cures is illegal, yes. To minimize contact with communicables."

"So how has this 'research' been carried on?"

"By doctors willing to go Inside and not come out again. Data is transmitted out by laser. In code."

"What clean doctor would be willing to go Inside and not come out again?"

McHabe smiles; again I'm struck by that quality of spontaneous energy. "Oh, you'd be surprised. We had three doctors inside the Pennsylvania colony. One past retirement age. Another, an old-style Catholic, who dedicated his research to God. A third nobody could figure out, a dour persistent guy who was a brilliant researcher."

Was. "And you."

"No," McHabe says quietly. "I go in and out."

"What happened to the others?"

"They're dead." He makes a brief aborted movement with his

right hand, and I realize that he is, or was, a smoker. How long since I had reached like that for a nonexistent cigarette? Nearly two decades. Cigarettes are not among the things people donate; they're too valuable. Yet I recognize the movement still. "Two of the three doctors caught the disease. They worked on themselves as well as volunteers. Then one day the government intercepted the relayed data and went in and destroyed everything."

"Why?" Jennie asks.

"Research on the disease is illegal. Everyone Outside is afraid of a leak: a virus somehow getting out on a mosquito, a bird, even as a spore."

"Nothing has gotten out in all these years," Rachel says.

"No. But the government is afraid that if researchers start splicing and intercutting genes, it could make viruses more viable. You don't understand the Outside, Rachel. *Everything* is illegal. This is the most repressive period in American history. Everyone's afraid."

"You're not," Jennie says, so softly I barely hear her. McHabe gives her a smile that twists my heart.

"Some of us haven't given up. Research goes on. But it's all underground, all theoretical. And we've learned a lot. We've learned that the virus doesn't just affect the skin. There are—"

"Be quiet," I say, because I see that he's about to say something important. "Be quiet a minute. Let me think."

McHabe waits. Jennie and Rachel look at me, that glow of suppressed excitement on them both. Eventually I find it. "You want something, Dr. McHabe. All this research wants something from us besides pure scientific joy. With things Outside as bad as you say, there must be plenty of diseases Outside you could research without killing yourself, plenty of need among your own people"— he nods, his eyes gleaming—"but you're here. Inside. Why? We don't have any more new or interesting symptoms, we barely survive, the Outside stopped caring what happened to us a long time ago. We have *nothing*. So why are you here?"

"You're wrong, Mrs. Pratt. You do have something interesting going on here. You *have* survived. Your society has regressed, but not collapsed. You're functioning under conditions where you shouldn't have."

The same old crap. I raise my eyebrows at him. He stares into the fire and says quietly, "To say Washington is rioting says nothing. You have to see a twelve-year-old hurl a homemade bomb, a man sliced open from neck to crotch because he still had a job to go to and his neighbor doesn't, a three-year-old left to starve because someone abandoned her like an unwanted kitten. . . . You don't know. It doesn't happen Inside."

"We're better than they are," Rachel says. I look at my grandchild. She says it simply, without self-aggrandizement, but with a kind of wonder. In the firelight the thickened gray ropes of skin across her cheek glow dull maroon.

McHabe says, "Perhaps you are. I started to say earlier that we've learned that the virus doesn't affect just the skin. It alters neurotransmitter receptor sites in the brain as well. It's a relatively slow transformation, which is why the flurry of research in the early years of the disease missed it. But it's real, as real as the faster site-capacity transformations brought about by, say, cocaine. Are you following me, Mrs. Pratt?"

I nod. Jennie and Rachel don't look lost, although they don't know any of this vocabulary, and I realize that McHabe must have explained all this to them, earlier, in some other terms.

"As the disease progresses to the brain, the receptors that receive excitatory transmitters slowly become harder to engage, and the receptors that receive inhibiting transmitters become easier to engage."

"You mean that we become stupider."

"Oh, no! Intelligence is not affected at all. The results are emotional and behavioral, not intellectual. You become—all of you— calmer. Disinclined to action or innovation. Mildly but definitely depressed."

The fire burns down. I pick up the poker, bent slightly where someone once tried to use it as a crowbar, and poke at the log, which is a perfectly shaped molded-pulp synthetic stamped DONATED BY WEYERHAEUSER-SEYYED. "I don't feel depressed, young man."

"It's a depression of the nervous system, but a new kind—without the hopelessness usually associated with clinical depression."

"I don't believe you."

"Really? With all due courtesy, when was the last time you—or any of the older Block leaders—pushed for any significant change in how you do things Inside?"

"Sometimes things cannot be constructively changed. Only accepted. That's not chemistry, it's reality."

"Not Outside," McHabe says grimly. "Outside they don't change constructively or accept. They get violent. Inside, you've had almost no violence since the early years, even when your resources tightened again and again. When was the last time you tasted butter, Mrs. Pratt, or smoked a cigarette, or had a new pair of jeans? Do you know what happens Outside when consumer goods become unavailable and there are no police in a given area? But Inside you just distribute whatever you have as fairly as you can, or make do without. No looting, no rioting, no cancerous envy. No one Outside knew *why*. Now we do."

"We have envy."

"But it doesn't erupt into anger."

Each time one of us speaks, Jennie and Rachel turn their heads to watch, like rapt spectators at tennis. Which neither of them has ever seen. Jennie's skin glows like pearl.

"Our young people aren't violent either, and the disease hasn't advanced very far in some of them."

"They learn how to behave from their elders—just like kids everywhere else."

"I don't feel depressed."

"Do you feel energetic?"

"I have arthritis."

"That's not what I mean."

"What do you mean, Doctor?"

Again that restless furtive reach for a nonexistent cigarette. But his voice is quiet. "How long did it take you to get around to applying that insecticide I got Rachel for the termites? She told me you forbade her to do it, and I think you were right; it's dangerous stuff. How many days went by before you or your daughter spread it around?"

The chemical is still in its can.

"How much anger are you feeling now, Mrs. Pratt?" he goes on. "Because I think we understand each other, you and I, and that you guess now why I'm here. But you aren't shouting or ordering me out of here or even telling me what you think of me. You're listening, and you're doing it calmly, and you're accepting what I tell you even though you know what I want you to—"

The door opens and he breaks off. Mamie flounces in, followed by Peter. She scowls and stamps her foot. "Where were you, Rachel? We've been standing outside waiting for you all for ten minutes now! The dance has already started!"

"A few more minutes, Mama. We're talking."

"Talking? About what? What's going on?"

"Nothing," McHabe says. "I was just asking your mother some

questions about life Inside. I'm sorry we took so long."

"You never ask *me* questions about life Inside. And besides, I want to dance!"

McHabe says, "If you and Peter want to go ahead, I'll bring Rachel and Jennie."

Mamie chews her bottom lip. I suddenly know that she wants to walk up the street to the dance between Peter and McHabe, an arm linked with each, the girls trailing behind. McHabe meets her eyes steadily.

"Well, if that's what you *want*," she says pettishly. "Come on, Pete!" She closes the door hard.

I look at McHabe, unwilling to voice the question in front of Rachel, trusting him to know the argument I want to make. He does. "In clinical depression, there's always been a small percentage for whom the illness is manifested not as passivity, but as irritability. It may be the same. We don't know."

"Gram," Rachel says, as if she can't contain herself any longer, "he has a *cure*."

"For the skin manifestation only," McHabe says quickly, and I see that he wouldn't have chosen to blurt it out that way. "*Not* for the effects on the brain."

I say, despite myself, "How can you cure one without the other?"

He runs his hand through his hair. Thick brown hair. I watch Jennie watch his hand. "Skin tissue and brain tissue aren't alike, Mrs. Pratt. The virus reaches both the skin and the brain at the same time, but the changes to brain tissue, which is much more complex, take much longer to detect. And they can't be reversed — nerve tissue is nonregenerative. If you cut your fingertip, it will eventually break down and replace the damaged cells to heal itself. Shit, if you're young enough, you can grow an entire new fingertip. Something like that is what we think our cure will stimulate the skin to do.

"But if you damage your cortex, those cells are gone forever. And unless another part of the brain can learn to compensate, whatever behavior those cells governed is also changed forever."

"Changed into depression, you mean."

"Into calmness. Into restraint of action . . . The country desperately needs restraint, Mrs. Pratt."

"And so you want to take some of us Outside, cure the skin ropes, and let the 'depression' spread: the 'restraint,' the 'slowness to act'. . . ."

"We have enough action out there. And no one can control it —

it's all the wrong kind. What we need now is to slow everything down a little—before there's nothing left to slow down."

"You'd infect a whole population—"

"Slowly. Gently. For their own good—"

"Is that up to *you* to decide?"

"Considering the alternative, yes. Because it *works*. The colonies work, despite all your deprivations. And they work because of the disease!"

"Each new case would have skin ropes—"

"Which we'll then cure."

"Does your *cure* work, Doctor? Rachel's father died of a cure like yours!"

"Not like ours," he says, and I hear in his voice the utter conviction of the young. Of the energetic. Of the Outside. "This is new, and medically completely different. This is the right strain."

"And you want me to try this new right strain as your guinea pig."

There is a moment of electric silence. Eyes shift: gray, blue, brown. Even before Rachel rises from her stool or McHabe says, "We think the ones with the best chances to avoid scarring are young people without heavy skin manifestations," I know. Rachel puts her arms around me. And Jennie—Jennie with the red ribbon woven in her hair, sitting on her broken chair as on a throne, Jennie who never heard of neurotransmitters or slow viruses or risk calculations—says simply, "It has to be me," and looks at McHabe with eyes shining with love.

I say no. I send McHabe away and say no. I reason with both girls and say no. They look unhappily at each other, and I wonder how long it will be before they realize they can act without permission, without obedience. But they never have.

We argue for nearly an hour, and then I insist they go on to the dance, and that I go with them. The night is cold. Jennie puts on her sweater, a heavy hand-knitted garment that covers her shapelessly from neck to knees. Rachel drags on her donated coat, black synthetic frayed at cuffs and hem. As we go out the door, she stops me with a hand on my arm.

"Gram—why did you say no?"

"*Why?* Honey, I've been telling you for an hour. The risk, the danger . . ."

"Is it that? Or"—I can feel her in the darkness of the hall, gathering herself together—"or is it—don't be mad, Gram, please don't be mad at me—is it because the cure is a new thing, a change? A . . . different thing you don't want because it's *exciting?* Like Tom said?"

"No, it isn't that," I say, and feel her tense beside me, and for the first time in her life I don't know what the tensing means.

We go down the street toward Block B. There's a moon and stars, tiny high pinpoints of cold light. Block B is further lit by kerosene lamps and by torches stuck in the ground in front of the peeling barracks walls that form the cheerless square. Or does it only seem cheerless because of what McHabe said? Could we have done better than this blank utilitarianism, this subdued bleakness— this peace?

Before tonight, I wouldn't have asked.

I stand in the darkness at the head of the street, just beyond the square, with Rachel and Jennie. The band plays across from me, a violin, guitar, and trumpet with one valve that keeps sticking. People bundled in all the clothes they own ring the square, clustering in the circles of light around the torches, talking in quiet voices. Six or seven couples dance slowly in the middle of the barren earth, holding each other loosely and shuffling to a plaintive version of "Starships and Roses." The song was a hit the year I got the disease, and then had a revival a decade later, the year the first manned expedition left for Mars. The expedition was supposed to set up a colony.

Are they still there?

We have written no new songs.

Peter and Mamie circle among the other couples. "Starships and Roses" ends and the band begins "Yesterday." A turn brings Mamie's face briefly into full torchlight: it's clenched and tight, streaked with tears.

"You should sit down, Gram," Rachel says. This is the first time she's spoken to me since we left the barracks. Her voice is heavy, but not angry, and there is no anger in Jennie's arm as she sets down the three-legged stool she carried for me. Neither of them is ever really angry.

Under my weight the stool sinks unevenly into the ground. A boy, twelve or thirteen years old, comes up to Jennie and wordlessly holds out his hand. They join the dancing couples. Jack Stevenson, much more arthritic than I, hobbles toward me with his grandson Hal by his side.

"Hello, Sarah. Been a long time."

"Hello, Jack." Thick disease ridges cross both his cheeks and snake down his nose. Once, long ago, we were at Yale together.

"Hal, go dance with Rachel," Jack says. "Give me that stool first." Hal, obedient, exchanges the stool for Rachel, and Jack lowers himself to sit beside me. "Big doings, Sarah."

"So I hear."

"McHabe told you? All of it? He said he'd been to see you just before me."

"He told me."

"What do you think?"

"I don't know."

"He wants Hal to try the cure."

Hal. I hadn't thought. The boy's face is smooth and clear, the only visible skin ridges on his right hand.

I say, "Jennie, too."

Jack nods, apparently unsurprised. "Hal said no."

"*Hal* did?"

"You mean Jennie didn't?" He stares at me. "She'd even consider something as dangerous as an untried cure—not to mention this alleged passing Outside?"

I don't answer. Peter and Mamie dance from behind the other couples, disappear again. The song they dance to is slow, sad, and old.

"Jack—could we have done better here? With the colony?"

Jack watches the dancers. Finally he says, "We don't kill each other. We don't burn things down. We don't steal, or at least not much and not cripplingly. We don't hoard. It seems to me we've done better than anyone ever hoped. Including us." His eyes search the dancers for Hal. "He's the best thing in my life, that boy."

Another rare flash of memory: Jack debating in some long-forgotten political science class at Yale, a young man on fire. He stands braced lightly on the balls of his feet, leaning forward like a fighter or a dancer, the electric lights brilliant on his glossy black hair. Young women watch him with their hands quiet on their open textbooks. He has the pro side of the debating question: *Resolved: Fomenting first-strike third-world wars is an effective method of deterring nuclear conflict among superpowers.*

Abruptly the band stops playing. In the center of the square Peter and Mamie shout at each other.

"—saw the way you touched her! You bastard, you faithless prick!"

"For God's sake, Mamie, not here!"

"Why not here? You didn't mind dancing with her here, touching her back here, and her ass and . . . and. . . ." She starts to cry. People look away, embarrassed. A woman I don't know steps forward and puts a hesitant hand on Mamie's shoulder. Mamie shakes it off, her hands to her face, and rushes away from the square. Peter stands there dumbly a moment before saying to no one in particular, "I'm sorry. Please dance." He walks toward the band, who begin, raggedly, to play "Didn't We Almost Have It All." The song is at least twenty-five years old. Jack Stevenson says, "Can I help, Sarah? With your girl?"

"How?"

"I don't know," he says, and of course he doesn't. He offers not out of usefulness but out of empathy, knowing how the ugly little scene in the torchlight depresses me.

Do we all so easily understand depression?

Rachel dances by with someone I don't know, a still-faced older man. She throws a worried glance over his shoulder: now Jennie is dancing with Peter. I can't see Peter's face. But I see Jennie's. She looks directly at no one, but then she doesn't have to. The message she's sending is clear: I forbade her to come to the dance with McHabe, but I didn't forbid her to dance with Peter and so she is, even though she doesn't want to, even though it's clear from her face that this tiny act of defiance terrifies her. Peter tightens his arm and she jerks backward against it, smiling hard.

Kara Desmond and Rob Cottrell come up to me, blocking my view of the dancers. They've been here as long as I. Kara has an infant great-grandchild; one of the rare babies born already disfigured by the disease. Kara's dress, which she wears over jeans for warmth, is torn at the hem; her voice is soft. "Sarah. It's great to see you out." Rob says nothing. He's put on weight in the few years since I saw him last. In the flickering torchlight his jowly face shines with the serenity of a diseased Buddha.

It's two more dances before I realize that Jennie has disappeared.

I look around for Rachel. She's pouring sumac tea for the band. Peter dances by with a woman not wearing jeans under her dress; the woman is shivering and smiling. So it isn't Peter that Jennie left with. . . .

"Rob, will you walk me home? In case I stumble?" The cold is getting to my arthritis.

Rob nods, incurious. Kara says, "I'll come, too," and we leave Jack Stevenson on his stool, waiting for his turn at hot tea. Kara chatters happily as we walk along as fast as I can go, which isn't as fast as I want to go. The moon has set. The ground is uneven and the street dark except for the stars and fitful lights in barracks windows. Candles. Oil lamps. Once, a single powerful glow from what I guess to be a donated stored-solar light, the only one I've seen in a long time.

Korean, Tom said.

"You're shivering," Kara says. "Here, take my coat." I shake my head.

I make them leave me outside our barracks and they do, un-questioning. Quietly I open the door to our dark kitchen. The stove has gone out. The door to the back bedroom stands half open, voices coming from the darkness. I shiver again, and Kara's coat wouldn't have helped.

But I am wrong. The voices aren't Jennie and Tom.

"—not what I wanted to talk about just *now*," Mamie says.

"But it's what I want to talk about."

"Is it?"

"Yes."

I stand listening to the rise and fall of their voices, to the petulance in Mamie's, the eagerness in McHabe's.

"Jennie is your ward, isn't she?"

"Oh, Jennie. Yes. For another year."

"Then she'll listen to you, even if your mother . . . the decision is yours. And hers."

"I guess so. But I want to think about it. I need more informa-tion."

"I'll tell you anything you ask."

"Will you? Are you married, Dr. Thomas McHabe?"

Silence. Then his voice, different. "Don't do that."

"Are you sure? Are you really sure?"

"I'm sure."

"Really, really sure? That you want me to stop?"

I cross the kitchen, hitting my knee against an unseen chair. In the open doorway a sky full of stars moves into view through the termite hole in the wall.

"Ow!"

"I said to stop it, Mrs. Wilson. Now please think about what I said about Jennie. I'll come back tomorrow morning and you can—"

"*You* can go straight to hell!" Mamie shouts. And then, in a different voice, strangely calm, "Is it because I'm diseased? And you're not? And Jennie is not?"

"No. I swear it, no. But I didn't come here for this."

"No," Mamie says in that same chill voice, and I realize that I have never heard it from her before, never. "You came to help us. To bring a cure. To bring the Outside. But not for everybody. Only for the few who aren't too far gone, who aren't too ugly — who you can *use*."

"It isn't like that—"

"A few who you can rescue. Leaving all the rest of us here to rot, like we did before."

"In time, research on the—"

"Time! What do you think time matters Inside? Time matters shit here! Time only matters when someone like you comes in from the Outside, showing off your healthy skin and making it even worse than it was before with your new whole clothing and your working wristwatch and your shiny hair and your . . . your. . . ." She is sobbing. I step into the room.

"All right, Mamie. All right."

Neither of them reacts to seeing me. McHabe just stands there until I wave him toward the door and he goes, not saying a word. I put my arms around Mamie, and she leans against my breast and cries. My daughter. Even through my coat I feel the thick ropy skin of her cheek pressing against me, and all I can think of is that I never noticed at all that McHabe wears a wristwatch.

Late that night, after Mamie has fallen into damp exhausted sleep and I have lain awake tossing for hours, Rachel creeps into our room to say that Jennie and Hal Stevenson have both been injected with an experimental disease cure by Tom McHabe. She's cold and trembling, defiant in her fear, afraid of all their terrible defiance. I hold her until she, too, sleeps, and I remember Jack Stevenson as a young man, classroom lights glossy on his thick hair, spiritedly arguing in favor of the sacrifice of one civilization for another.

Mamie leaves the barracks early the next morning. Her eyelids are still swollen and shiny from last night's crying. I guess that she's going to hunt up Peter, and I say nothing. We sit at the table, Rachel and I, eating our oatmeal, not looking at each other. It's an effort to even lift the spoon. Mamie is gone a long time.

Later, I picture it. Later, when Jennie and Hal and McHabe

have come and gone, I can't stop picturing it: Mamie walking with her swollen eyelids down the muddy streets between the barracks, across the unpaved squares with their corner vegetable gardens of rickety bean poles and the yellow-green tops of carrots. Past the depositories with their donated Chinese and Japanese and Korean wool and wood stoves and sheets of alloys and unguarded medicines. Past the chicken runs and goat pens. Past Central Administration, that dusty cinder-block building where people stopped keeping records maybe a decade ago because why would you need to prove you'd been born or had changed barracks? Past the last of the communal wells, reaching deep into a common and plentiful water table. Mamie walking, until she reaches the Rim, and is stopped, and says what she came to say.

They come a few hours later, dressed in full sani-suits and armed with automatic weapons that don't look American-made. I can see their faces through the clear shatterproof plastic of their helmets. Three of them stare frankly at my face, at Rachel's, at Hal Stevenson's hands. The other two won't look directly at any of us, as if viruses could be transmitted over locked gazes.

They grab Tom McHabe from his chair at the kitchen table, pulling him up so hard he stumbles, and throw him against the wall. They are gentler with Rachel and Hal. One of them stares curiously at Jennie, frozen on the opposite side of the table. They don't let McHabe make any of the passionate explanations he had been trying to make to me. When he tries, the leader hits him across the face.

Rachel—*Rachel*—throws herself at the man. She wraps her strong young arms and legs around him from behind, screaming, "Stop it! Stop it!" The man shrugs her off like a fly. A second soldier pushes her into a chair. When he looks at her face he shudders. Rachel goes on yelling, sound without words.

Jennie doesn't even scream. She dives across the table and clings to McHabe's shoulder, and whatever is on her face is hidden by the fall of her yellow hair.

"Shut you fucking 'doctors' down once and for all!" the leader yells, over Rachel's noise. The words come through his helmet as clearly as if he weren't wearing one. "Think you can just go on coming Inside and Outside and diseasing us all?"

"I—" McHabe says.

"Fuck it!" the leader says, and shoots him.

McHabe slumps against the wall. Jennie grabs him, desperately trying to haul him upright again. The soldier fires again. The bullet hits Jennie's wrist, shattering the bone. A third shot, and McHabe slides to the floor.

The soldiers leave. There is little blood, only two small holes where the bullets went in and stayed in. We didn't know, Inside, that they have guns like that now. We didn't know bullets could do that. We didn't know.

"You did it," Rachel says.

"I did it for you," Mamie says. "I did!" They stand across the kitchen from each other, Mamie pinned against the door she just closed behind her when she finally came home, Rachel standing in front of the wall where Tom died. Jennie lies sedated in the bedroom. Hal Stevenson, his young face anguished because he had been useless against five armed soldiers, had run for the doctor who lived in Barracks J, who had been found setting the leg of a goat.

"You did it. You." Her voice is dull, heavy. *Scream,* I want to say. *Rachel, scream.*

"I did it so you would be safe!"

"You did it so I would be trapped Inside. Like you."

"You never thought it was a trap!" Mamie cries. "*You* were the one who was happy here!"

"And you never will be. Never. Not here, not anyplace else."

I close my eyes, to not see the terrible maturity on my Rachel's face. But the next moment she's a child again, pushing past me to the bedroom with a furious sob, slamming the door behind her.

I face Mamie. "Why?"

But she doesn't answer. And I see that it doesn't matter; I wouldn't have believed her anyway. Her mind is not her own. It is depressed, ill. I have to believe that now. She's my daughter, and her mind has been affected by the ugly ropes of skin that disfigure her. She is the victim of disease, and nothing she says can change anything at all.

It's almost morning. Rachel stands in the narrow aisle between the bed and the wall, folding clothes. The bedspread still bears the imprint of Jennie's sleeping shape; Jennie herself was carried by Hal Stevenson to her own barracks, where she won't have to see Mamie when she wakes up. On the crude shelf beside Rachel the oil lamp burns, throwing shadows on the newly whole wall that smells of termite exterminator.

She has few enough clothes to pack. A pair of blue tights, old and clumsily darned; a sweater with pulled threads; two more pairs of socks; her other skirt, the one she wore to the Block dance. Everything else she already has on.

"Rachel," I say. She doesn't answer, but I see what silence costs her. Even such a small defiance, even now. Yet she is going. Using McHabe's contacts to go Outside, leaving to find the underground medical research outfit. If they have developed the next stage of the cure, the one for people already disfigured, she will take it. Perhaps even if they have not. And as she goes, she will contaminate as much as she can with her disease, depressive and nonaggressive. Communicable.

She thinks she has to go. Because of Jennie, because of Mamie, because of McHabe. She is sixteen years old, and she believes—even growing up Inside, she believes this—that she must do something. Even if it is the wrong thing. To do the wrong thing, she has decided, is better than to do nothing.

She has no real idea of Outside. She has never watched television, never stood in a bread line, never seen a crack den or a slasher movie. She cannot define napalm, or political torture, or neutron bomb, or gang rape. To her, Mamie, with her confused and self-justifying fear, represents the height of cruelty and betrayal; Peter, with his shambling embarrassed lewdness, the epitome of danger; the theft of a chicken, the last word in criminality. She has never heard of Auschwitz, Cawnpore, the Inquisition, gladiatorial games, Nat Turner, Pol Pot, Stalingrad, Ted Bundy, Hiroshima, My Lai, Wounded Knee, Babi Yar, Bloody Sunday, Dresden, or Dachau. Raised with a kind of mental inertia, she knows nothing of the savage inertia of destruction, that once set in motion a civilization is as hard to stop as a disease.

I don't think she can find the underground researchers, no matter how much McHabe told her. I don't think her passage Outside will spread enough infection to make any difference at all. I don't think it's possible that she can get very far before she is picked up and either returned Inside or killed. She cannot change the world. It's too old, too entrenched, too vicious, too *there*. She will fail. There is no force stronger than destructive inertia.

Except maybe one.

I get my things ready to go with her.

phone repairs

WHEN THE PHONE rang, Dave Potter seized it with a desperate relief he tried not to let Caroline see. From the way her face froze and she turned her back away from him and toward the sink full of dirty dishes, Potter knew he had failed. She had seen the relief. It would only make worse the fight that was already bearing down on them, inevitable and dreary, like one of those unstoppable cold fronts picked out on weather maps in little blue spikes.

The phone call was from his son Brendan, sixteen, whom Potter had not seen in three days. Their hours at home barely overlapped since school had let out for the summer.

"Dad. I wrecked the car." And—belatedly, laconically—"Sorry."

"What do you mean, you wrecked the car?" Potter said, his voice scaling upward in some subtle combination of fear and outrage. Caroline stopped clattering dishes. Her green eyes widened. "Are you all right?"

"Sure," Brendan answered.

"He's all right," Potter said to Caroline at the same moment that Brendan said, "Why the hell were you on the phone so long? I've been trying to get through for forty-five minutes."

"No one was on the phone. Look, what happened? Is anyone hurt? Did you hit another car?"

"Nah. Telephone pole."

"Was anyone in the car with you?"

"Nah. Look, Dad, it's no big deal, all right?"

"No big *deal*? What shape is the Buick in?"

"Well . . .," Brendan said, and Potter heard the drawn-out reluctance and clamped down hard on his temper.

"Where are you, Brendan?"

"Cathy's Towing. Corner of Elm and Hackett."

"I'll be right there. Stay put."

"Can't. Kelso's already here to pick me up. We got the track meet in fifteen minutes. Why were you on the phone so goddamn long?"

"No one was on the phone!" Potter yelled. "Stay put until I get there!"

"Hey, I said I was sorry!" Brendan snarled, the snarl now justified by Potter's yelling, by Potter's unreasonable order, by Potter's failure to be an understanding parent.

"Just stay there," Potter repeated. Caroline, tight-lipped, began running water into the sink. On the other end, the phone clicked dead.

When Potter arrived at Cathy's Towing, Brendan wasn't there. Potter's Buick was symmetrically caved in on the passenger side in a deep **U**. Raw metal gleamed like fangs. Cathy, a beautiful midthirties blonde in the dirtiest overalls Potter had ever seen, regarded the car with something close to artistic satisfaction. "Been the other side, your kid've been a goner. If he hadn't of been belted in, even." Potter turned his back on her.

At home, Caroline was on her hands and knees, scrubbing the kitchen floor and crying. Potter put a hand on her shoulder; she shrugged it off so violently that Potter nearly slipped on the soapy Congoleum. "Don't touch me!"

"All right," Potter said wearily and went into the living room to make himself a drink. Caroline scrubbed more savagely; he could hear the stiff bristles of her brush rasp across what was supposed to be an E-Z-Care floor. The blue spikes moved closer.

Money. Sex. Kids. In-laws. Those were supposed to be the big four, but Potter knew that this was something else entirely, something both less visible and more pervasive, like lethal radiation. His and Caroline's marital rage seemed to come from everything and nothing, a meltdown at the core, beyond the puny firefighting of mere words. It had been going on for months now. Potter saw that it would go on for months more, while both of them watched helplessly, until at some point it no longer did. His hands shook as he poured himself a J & B.

The phone rang.

"Hello?" Potter said.

"Bill!" a woman's voice cried, low-pitched and husky with warmth. "Just a minute — *now*, kids!" Children began to sing "Happy Birthday."

"This isn't Bill," Potter tried to say, but was drowned out by the song. All the children — it sounded like three of them — stayed in tune, their voices high and sweet. When they had finished, the woman's voice returned; Potter could hear the laughter in it.

"And from me, too — happy birthday, darling. You don't know *how* I wish we were home with you!"

"This isn't Bill. You must have the wrong number," Potter said. He felt a perfect fool.

A pause at the other end. "Isn't this 645-2892?"

"No, I'm sorry. This is one digit off that number."

"No, *I'm* sorry," the woman said, a little stiffly. Stiffness didn't destroy the husky timbre of her voice. "I must have dialed wrong."

"I'm sorry," Potter said again, inanely, and hung up. In the other room, Caroline scrubbed and cried. Potter drank off the J & B and poured himself another, staring at the phone.

Potter's daughter Melissa sat cross-legged on the living-room floor, scissors in her hand, bent over paper dolls. Her dark hair, a little too long at the bangs, fell in a shiny, tangled curtain over the shoulders of her yellow pajamas. Saturday morning cartoons blared from the television, mindless and irritating as blowing sand. The faded rug bore the wreckage of a Friday night at home: spilled potato chips, sticky glasses, Potter's unopened briefcase, the discarded sections of last evening's newspaper mixing with the discarded sections of this morning's as Potter tossed them down from the sofa.

Caroline, barefooted, padded in from the bedroom. Potter glanced at the smooth line of her thigh beneath her short summer robe, and looked away. Caroline began shrieking.

"Damn it, Dave, why the hell are you letting her cut those up!"

Potter raised himself on one elbow. What he had assumed were paper dolls were in fact photographs, all the family pictures kept in a red-topped dress box that Potter had failed to recognize because the red top was removed and upside down. Melissa had methodically sliced into at least three dozen of the photos, cutting off all the people's heads. The little girl's eyes, raised suddenly to Potter's face, horrified him.

"Can't you watch her while I at least get some sleep on a Saturday morning? Can't you at least do that?" Caroline shouted, her voice gone shrill with hysteria. She grabbed for the scissors in Melissa's hand. Potter saw beheaded pictures of Caroline waving in front of the Washington Monument, of Melissa and Brendan at the beach, of a dog they had owned briefly three years ago. He saw his wedding pictures.

"That's not too goddamn much to ask!" Caroline shrieked. Melissa moved her gaze from Potter, stlll stunned by it, to her mother's contorted face. Eluding Caroline's grab for the scissors, she twisted her small body to plunge them into Potter's briefcase. The leather released air and a pungent smell like riding tack.

Caroline gasped and seized Melissa. Her eyes met Potter's over the child, their green wiped perfectly blank by shock. Melissa wrapped her legs around her mother and began to sob into her neck. Caroline carried her into the bedroom and closed the door. Potter heard it lock.

On his knees he sorted numbly through the photos, looking for some clue to what Melissa had done, some of the reassurance that might come from finding a pattern to the pictures she had chosen to destroy. There was none. Pictures of relatives, friends, people Potter no longer recognized—all had been equally defaced. In the wedding photo, Caroline, Potter, the best man, and maid of honor had each been decapitated. Caroline's white gown floated around what was left of her, tight at the waist and a billowing cloud below, a silk so light and delicately scented that it had once seemed like mist against his hands.

Potter squeezed his eyes shut as tightly as they would go.

The voice on the phone was deep, with a reckless lilt of gaiety. "Connie? Listen, darling, we finished up early here and I'll be coming home on the eight forty-five flight TWA tomorrow night, and wait till you hear the news I've got for you, you lucky sexy broad!"

"I'm sorry," Potter said, a little resentfully. He knew his voice was pitched a little high for a man and the husky-voiced woman's was low, but there was still a difference. "I'm sorry. You have the wrong number."

Silence, and then the man said in a changed tone. "Is this Dave? At 645-2872?"

Surprised, Potter nodded, caught himself, and said, "Yes. How did you know?"

"We've been getting your phone calls for a few weeks now. The lines must be crossed. Have you been getting our calls?"

"When you all stay home long enough to get any," Potter said, out of a sudden spitefulness that took him by further surprise. The man's—Bill's—voice hardened.

"I'll call the phone company. Don't sweat it. Sorry for the inconvenience."

"Yeah," Potter said. "Me, too."

"She needs therapy," Caroline said to Potter during a commercial for laundry detergent. They had been watching TV in isolated silence for two hours, only one dim bulb left on in the shabby living room. Both children were asleep. Potter had gone to check on them during the previous commercial: Brendan scowling even in sleep, his ungainly adolescent face a clenched fist; Melissa's features so smooth and soft that Potter's heart had clutched in his chest.

"She should go at least four times a week, Dr. Horacek says," Caroline continued. In the semidarkness Potter could not see her face, was glad of it. "That's at first. Maybe more, maybe less after he gets a feel for her disturbance. That's what he said: 'a feel for her disturbance and what might be causing it.'"

"Four times a week. Jesus, Caroline, the company insurance only pays half of any nonphysical therapy. I checked today."

"Yes," Caroline said. She didn't sound surprised. The TV commercial ended and the program, whatever it was, resumed.

"Look at it this way," Caroline suddenly added in a hard voice he didn't recognize but knew immediately had carried them over some border, into a new descent in terrain, "now I couldn't divorce you. We can't afford it."

She jackknifed off the sofa and went into the bathroom. Potter sat there, reaching for the drink he had already finished. The phone rang.

"Congratulations, Mr. and Mrs. William Boylan!" said a professionally cheery voice. "Your entry has just won an all-expense-paid trip to Hawaii."

Potter said nothing.

"Hello? Is this the Boylan residence? Hello?" The voice sounded a little less professional.

"Yes," Potter said, "but which Boylan did you want? There are a lot of us, and the listings in the phone book are wrong."

"Let me see," the voice said uncertainly. "Mr. and Mrs. William Boylan at . . . I have it right here someplace, here . . . at 5542 Lapham Park Road."

"No, I'm sorry," Potter said, "this is James Boylan on East Main."

"Oh, I *am* sorry," the voice said, all professionalism restored. It added roguishly, "Especially for you!"

"Happens," Potter said. He hung up and went back to stare at Melissa's sleeping face.

There was no 5542 Lapham Park Road. Potter, driving out after work in Caroline's Chevette, which he knew she needed that evening, followed the street from its origins at a city park out to its last suburban house, 5506. The builders had not yet put up the rest of the development, although there were signs they might: a half-finished road, red X's on certain trees. The finished houses were big, surrounded by healthy mature trees left standing during the building process, and sparse new lawns. There were in-ground swimming pools, bay windows, twin chimneys, landscaped lots large enough for that urban luxury, privacy. The smells of summer evening hung in the air: cut grass, warm asphalt, overblown roses, the sweet sweat of healthy toddlers. Lawn sprinklers whirled.

On the way home, Potter stopped at a restaurant with a public phone and directory. There was no listing for William Boylan.

"I needed the car," Caroline said stiffly to Potter when he

returned. Her green eyes sparkled with resentment. "You knew I needed it tonight."

Potter didn't answer. Anything he said would only make it worse. Sadness welled up from his belly to his throat, choking him.

"I *told* you," Caroline said. Melissa, standing beside her mother, looked at him flatly. When he reached out to smooth her beautiful hair, she flinched.

Brendan slouched into the living room. It was the first evening he had been home in over a week; more and more he stayed at his friend Kelso's house, with Kelso's family. Potter had at first protested this, but Caroline had said wearily, "Oh, let him stay there. Why would he want to stay *here?*" and Potter had not fought her. He knew he was losing some quality essential for fighting, some fundamental vigor.

"Phone, Dad."

"For me?"

Brendan's face twitched in disgust. "No. For Superman." He slouched out.

Potter walked on trembling legs to the extension in the bedroom. A girl's voice said, "Daddy? It's Jeanine." He recognized the voice; it had last sung "Happy Birthday" to him, sweet and tuneful. How had Brendan come to pass on the call? Whom had she asked for?

"Daddy?"

Potter closed his eyes and heard himself say, "Yes."

"Guess what? I won!"

"You did."

"Yes! You sound funny, Daddy. Are you okay?" The young voice radiated concern.

"I have a cold, honey."

"Oh, I'm sorry. Anyway, I won! I played a wrong note in the first movement, you wouldn't believe how dumb, but I didn't let it rattle me and I played the second movement like we rehearsed, and I won! And one judge said I was the youngest to win in the violin division *ever!*"

"That's wonderful."

"Yes," the voice burbled, "and you should have seen Gary and Susie, they were jumping up and down in the first row and clapping like crazy, even Susie. Mom, too. Here she is."

"Bill?" said the voice Potter remembered, its huskiness and warmth as full of light as the child's. Potter could see it, that light:

shimmering auroras, silver and pearl, behind his eyelids. He hung up.

For a long time he stood there, finally whispering, "No," but so softly no one else could hear.

"No what?" Melissa said. She had unaccountably appeared at his elbow. He looked at her, at the horrible flatness in her eyes that had drifted there out of some imbalanced chemical weather in her brain, out of Potter's and Caroline's misery, out of some unknown country that, Potter realized, he did not really believe Dr. Horacek would ever map.

"No nothing, baby," he said, and reached to gather her into his arms. Melissa kicked him and squirmed away, running from the bedroom. At the doorway she turned, her little face full of the anguished and pointless fury that modern medicine said was part of her illness, and spat.

"Don't touch me! I wish you weren't my daddy!"

She whirled and was gone. Potter grabbed the phone and yanked the cord from the wall. With all the strength he had left, he hurled it across the room at the mirror over the dresser. Glass shattered and flew wildly in silver splinters of flashing light.

AT&T Subsidiary Repair Operator Number 21 claimed that the company had already acted on Complaint #483-87A, cross-wired phones in the same digital decad, but would look into the situation yet again. Potter said that the address on file for the other digits did not exist, and possibly the digits did not either, and there would be nothing to look into. Repair Operator Number 21 did not reply.

Potter took to calling 645-2892 from his office, from the kitchen extension when there was no one else at home or the bedroom extension when there was, once from a pay phone outside Melissa's therapist's office. He never called twice at the same time of day; he never spoke. Jeanine or Connie or Bill or Gary would answer, and Potter would listen a moment and hang up. Susie never answered; Potter guessed she was too young, perhaps even a baby. Gary's voice had the huskiness of his mother's. Only Bill Boylan ever reacted with suspicion to the silence at the other end of the phone, and Potter imagined his suspicion to smell of protection, not fear. Connie and Jeanine answered liltingly — "He*llo?*" — Gary with offhand confidence. Often there was laughter in their voices, as if the phone had interrupted some blithe conversation or ongoing family joke.

On a Saturday night in late October, calling at 10:30 P.M. when Caroline had stormed out after a fight and Brendan had not been home for two weeks and Melissa had gone on one of her increasingly frightening rampages and then, exhausted, had fallen asleep, Potter heard two receivers lift simultaneously. Bill's voice said, "*Hello*," the first syllable heartier than the second, and Jeanine said, "Hi there!" and then burst into laughter that echoed from what sounded like a dozen feminine young throats. A slumber party.

"Get off the phone, honey," Bill said. "I got it."

"Yes, Daddy."

"Hello," Bill repeated to the silent Potter. And then, "Now you listen to me. I don't know who you are or what you think you're doing calling my family every few days like this, but you better cut it out now, buddy, or you'll wish you had. The phone company can put a tracer on this line. I've already spoken to them about it. Do this again and you'll be in deep shit. From both them *and* me, if I find out who and where you are. Got that?"

"Yes," Potter said, not caring if Boylan recognized his voice, if he connected the crossed-wires malfunction with this newer, less mechanical one. But apparently Boylan did not make the connection. In his world, Potter thought, malfunctions were separate, manageable. They did not mutate and crossbreed and turn cancerous, feeding on their own deformed tissues until the center itself could no longer hold.

"Scum," Boylan said, and hung up.

Potter put his own receiver down gently, as if it were alive.

He gathered together all the photographs Melissa had decapitated, and put them into a nine-by-twelve manila envelope. With them he folded one of Melissa's therapy reports, a heartbreaking document in prophylactic prose: "Subject systematically destroys toys in playroom environment. One-to-one observation reveals no symbolic preference in plaything destruction." Potter put into the envelope a notice from the bank stamped INSUFFICIENT FUNDS. He added a torn piece of foil from the packet of birth control pills he had found in Caroline's drawer and had left there, after a long sightless moment in which he felt the knife he had not minded at his actual vasectomy. He even put in a paint flake from the Buick.

He addressed the envelope in clear block letters:

MR AND MRS WILLIAM BOYLAN
5542 LAPHAM PARK ROAD
WINTHROP, NEW YORK

At the post office, he looked up the zip code for such of Lapham Park Road as existed. He was careful to include his return address. Five days later, the manila envelope was delivered to Potter's mailbox, stamped NO SUCH ADDRESS—RETURN TO SENDER.

So it would have to be the phone.

He stayed home from work on a Tuesday, when Caroline was at her part-time job and Brendan and Melissa at school. Just before he picked up the receiver, Potter had a moment of clarity, unwelcome as sudden nakedness. Why had he mailed the envelope? What had he hoped? To somehow poison the other, luminous world he could not have, or to send a cry of help for his own? He hated both alternatives, writhed in humiliation just thinking of them. Boylan's voice saying, "Scum . . ."

But as he had hoped, it was Connie who answered. That husky voice, vibrant with warmth. "Hello?"

"My name is Dave Potter. Listen, please don't hang up on me, Connie. You don't know me, but our phone lines were crossed a few months ago and I spoke to you and your family. Since then things here have just fallen apart, you can't know, I don't know how or why but I'm about at the end of my rope and I need to talk to you for a while. Just talk. I'm harmless to you, I swear it, and your house doesn't exist anyway so I couldn't come there to—" Potter stopped, appalled. What was he saying?

Connie was silent. Potter felt her bewilderment, coming over the phone line in waves. He clutched the receiver tighter.

"Please don't hang up. Please. I know how this must sound to you, but there isn't anything here like your family, your marriage, *nothing*, do you hear me, we can't do it anymore—" He realized he was shouting, made himself lower his voice.

"Connie—"

"Please leave me alone," she said, and even through her fear and his grief some part of Potter's mind still registered that "please," a grace note grown so alien that it stunned him and he groaned.

"*Connie—*"

"I'm sorry," she whispered, "I can't help you," and hung up.

Potter remained standing in his bedroom, listening to silence. After a while, it was replaced by a dial tone, and then by a high whining drone like wind in dead trees.

In January, after the holidays, Caroline asked Potter for a divorce. He didn't contest it; in New York State, there would have been little point. He and Caroline argued bitterly over financial and custody arrangements, but by Valentine's Day she was gone.

Potter moved into a two-bedroom apartment, to which he brought his children every other weekend and Wednesday nights.

Shortly before his share of the furniture arrived but after his phone had been installed, Potter surrendered to impulse and dialed 645-2892. Standing there in the bare wooden box with its sterile walls and cheap Scotch-guarded carpet, Potter felt his heart begin a slow hammering against his ribs, which kept up even after a voice answered.

"The number you have reached has been disconnected. The new number for that party is unlisted. Thank you for using AT&T."

In June, Melissa was taken off Ritalin by her doctor. Without the medication, her rages increased for a brief time, but then began to subside. It was decided at a tense conference of Potter, Caroline, Dr. Horacek, and the clinic staff that Melissa should repeat kindergarten at a public school. This announcement did not seem to upset her. "Okay," she said, not looking up from dressing her Cabbage Patch doll.

On a Friday afternoon the following October, Potter was driving in an unfamiliar part of the city. He had had a business appointment that had taken far longer than it should have. His watch said nearly 6:30, and he still had to pick up the circus tickets before the Ticketron closed and get to the bank before it closed. He needed a hefty wad of cash for tomorrow. Early, before the bank opened, he was driving Brendan upstate to visit two community colleges that were supposed to have strong programs in mechanical arts. The colleges were 250 miles apart; they had appointments at the first one at 10:00 A.M. and the second at 4:00 P.M., and would spend Saturday night at a motel somewhere. Sunday afternoon was the circus for Melissa, and Potter hadn't gotten around to doing any laundry in two weeks. It would be tight, very tight. He drove with one hand drumming on the dashboard, leaning forward over the wheel to arrive at the Ticketron three inches earlier.

He passed the intersection of Lapham Park Road.

Potter wrenched the wheel to the right. Before he had time to think about it, he was driving east on Lapham, away from the city park, past the row houses separated by narrow concrete driveways, past the 1950s ranches and split-levels, to the old trees and new development where the road ended.

The builders had done a lot in fifteen months. The last house was now 5573. Beyond it, bulldozers and backhoes stood yellow and silent against the bloody Indian summer sunset, looming over stacks of lumber and bags of cement and spools of cable. Kids climbed on the bulldozer, shrieking at each other in delight. As Potter watched from his parked car, one of them, a small boy, climbed off the heavy equipment and wandered down the street to stare at the moving van in front of 5542.

The new owner was carrying in furniture himself, along with the uniformed movers. He balanced a hall table, silky amber-colored wood with a matching chair upholstered in rose, against his muscular chest. The chair, upside down on the table, slid a little. A woman ran lightly down the steps, smiling, and steadied the chair. She had sleek chestnut hair, bright blue eyes, and long slim legs in crisp jeans. Behind her a child appeared in the doorway, waddling on bare legs beneath a plastic diaper; an older girl dashed up behind the toddler and grabbed her before she could try to navigate the steps. The older girl grinned and shook her head, her long hair cutting the air. From around the corner of the house, Gary tentatively approached the neighbor boy and smiled shyly.

Potter started his engine, made a three-point turn, started back up Lapham Park Road. The hall table had had an underslung open shelf instead of a drawer. He wondered if the table would stand in an upstairs hall or a downstairs one, and if the phone placed on it would be a desk model, a Trimline, or some fancy custom job to match whatever the Boylans' idea of home decoration might be.

Potter pushed his foot down on the gas pedal. The bank closed in half an hour, the Ticketron an hour after that, and if he didn't get to the bank before it closed, he wouldn't be able to be on time for his trip with Brendan tomorrow. He stopped thinking about the phone. It had nothing to do with him; it never had.

the battle of long island

OVER BY THE mess tent one of my younger nurses is standing close to a Special Forces lieutenant. I watch her face tip up to his, her eyes wide and shining, moonlight on her cheekbones. He reaches out one hand—his fingernails are not quite clean—and touches her brown hair where it falls over her shoulder, and the light on her skin trembles. I know that later tonight they will disappear into her tent, or his. Later this week they will walk around the compound with their arms around each other's waists, sit across from each other at mess, and feed each other choice bits of chow,

oblivious to the amused glances of their friends. Later this month—
or next month, or the one after that, if this bizarre duty goes on
long enough—she will be pale and distraught, crumpling letters in
one hand. She will cry in the supply tent. She will tell the other
nurses that he fed her lies. She will not hear orders, or will carry
them out red-eyed and wrong, endangering other lives and despising her own.

She will be useless to me, and I will have to transfer her out
and start over with another.

Or maybe it won't happen that way. An alternate future: *He*
will snap at his buddies, volunteer for extra duty near the Hole,
become careless with some red- or homespun-coated soldier stumbling forward with musket or bayonet. He'll kill somebody or—less
likely—get killed himself. Or maybe he'll just snap at the wrong
person: his captain, say. He'll be transferred out. If he kills an Arrival, General Robinson will personally crucify him. General Robinson's wife and daughters are members of the DAR.

The two people by the mess tent, of course, don't see it this
way. They like the same movies, were snubbed by the same people in high school, voted the same way in the last presidential election. Both volunteered for duty by the Hole. It follows that they're
in love. It follows that they understand each other, can see to the
bottoms of each other's soul. The other military couples they
know—the ones who have divorced, or who haven't: the affairs on
leave, the angry words on the parade ground at dawn—have nothing
to do with *them*. They are different. They are unique.

When people can see the truth so plain around them, why do
they persist in believing some other reality?

"Major Peters! You're needed in Recovery! Quick!"

I leave my tent and tear across the compound at a dead run.
We have only three people in Recovery; one of the weird laws of
the Hole seems to be that they seldom come through it if they're
going to recover. Musket balls in the belly or heart, shell explosions
that have torn off half a head. Eighty-three percent of the Arrivals
are dead a few minutes after they fall through the Hole. Another
11 percent live longer but never regain consciousness. That leaves
us with 6 percent who eventually talk, although not to us. After
we repair the flesh and boost the immune system, the Army sends
heavily armored trucks to move them out of our heavily armored
compound to somewhere else. The Pentagon? We aren't told.

Somewhere there are three soldiers from Kachlein's Riflemen, a field-grade officer under Lord Percy, and a shell-shocked corporal in homespun, all talking to the best minds the country thinks it can find.

This time I want to talk first.

The soldier who has finally woken up is a grizzled veteran who came through dressed in breeches, boots, and light coat. It's summer on the other side of the Hole: the Battle of Long Island was fought on August 27, 1776. Unlike most Arrivals, this one staggered through the Hole without his rifle or bayonet, although he had a hunting knife, which was taken away from him. He'd received a head wound, most likely a glancing shell fragment, enough to cause concussion but, according to the brain scan, not permanent damage. When I burst into Recovery he's sitting up, dazed, looking at the guards at the door holding their M-18s.

"The general and Dr. Bechtel are on their way," I say to the guards, which is approximately true. I sent a soldier walking across the compound to tell them. My phone seems to be malfunctioning. The soldier is walking very slowly.

"General Putnam?" the soldier asks. His voice is less dazed than his face: a rough, deep voice with the peculiar twist on almost-British English that still sends a chill through me, all these months after the Hole opened.

"Were you with the Connecticut Third Regiment? Let me check your pulse, please, I'm a nurse."

"A nurse!" That seems to finish the daze; he looks at my uniform, then my face. When the Hole first opened, there was wild talk of putting the medical staff in Colonial dress—"To minimize the psychological shock." As if anything could minimize dying hooked to machines you couldn't imagine in a place that didn't exist while being stuck with needles by people unborn for another two centuries. Cooler heads prevailed. I wear fatigues, my short hair limp against my head from a shower, my glasses thick over my eyes.

"Yes, a nurse. This is a hospital. Let me have your wrist, please."

He pulls his hand away. I grab his wrist and hold it firmly. Two Arrivals have attacked triage personnel and one attacked a Recovery guard; this soldier looks strong enough for both. But I served in the minor action in Kuwait and the major ones in Colombia. He lets me hold his wrist. His pulse is rapid but strong.

"What is this place?"

"I told you. A hospital."

He leans forward and clutches my arm with his free hand while I'm reaching for the medscan equipment. "The battle—*who won the battle?*"

They're often like this. They find themselves in an alien, impossible, unimaginable place, surrounded by guards with uniforms and weapons they don't recognize, and yet their first concern is not their personal fate but the battle they left behind. They ask again and again. They have to know what happened.

We aren't supposed to tell Arrivals anything not directly medical. No hint that this is more than a few days into their future. That's official policy. Not until the Military Intelligence experts are finished with whatever they do, wherever they do it. Not until the Pentagon has assured itself that the soldier, the Hole itself, is not some terrorist plot (whose, for Christ's sweet fucking sake?). We're "not qualified for this situation" (who do they imagine is?). Those are my orders.

But he hasn't asked for very much future: the Battle of Long Island was over in less than twenty-four hours. And I, of all people, am not capable of denying anyone the truth of his past.

"The colonists lost. Washington retreated."

"Ahhhhhhhhhhh . . ." He lets it out like escaping gas. In Bogotá, in the '95 offensive, lethal gas wiped out three thousand men in an hour. I don't look directly at his face.

"You were hit in the head," I say. "Not badly."

He puts his hand to his head and fingers the bandage, but his eyes never leave mine. He has a strong, fierce face, with sunken black eyes, a hooked nose, broken teeth, and a beard coming in red, not gray. He could be anywhere from forty to sixty. It's not a modern face; today the Army would fix the teeth and shave the beard.

"And the general? Put survived the battle?"

"He did."

"Ahhhhhhhh . . . And the war? *How goes the war?*"

I have said far too much already. The soldier sits straight on his bed, his fingers still clamped around my wrist, his fierce eyes blazing. Behind us I hear the door open and the guards snap into salute. In those Colonial eyes is a need to know that has nothing in it of weakness. It isn't a plea, or a beseeching. It's a demand for a right, as we today might demand a search warrant, or a lawyer, or a trial by jury—all things whose existence once depended on what this soldier wants to know. He stares at me and I feel in him an elemental power, as if the need to know is as basic as the need for water, or air.

"How goes the war, Mistress?"

Footsteps hurry toward us.

I can't look away from the soldier's eyes. He doesn't know, can't know, what he's asking, or of whom. My mouth forms the words softly, so that only he hears.

"You won. England surrendered in October of 1781."

Something moves behind those black eyes, something so strong I draw back a little. Then they're on us, General Robinson first and behind him chief of medical staff, Colonel Dr. William Bechtel. My father, who has denied me truth for thirty-five years.

I have never stood by the mess tent with a young soldier. If you are posted at twenty, right out of nursing school, and you stay in it for nineteen years, and you never wear a skirt or makeup, there is only one question your fellow soldiers come to ask. I know the answer: I am not homosexual. Neither, as far as I can tell, am I heterosexual. I have never wanted to feel anyone's touch on my hair in the moonlight.

Dr. Bechtel was assigned to duty at the Hole the day it appeared. If I'd known this, I never would have requested a transfer. I was en route to the U.S. European Command in Stuttgart; I would have continued on my way there. I use my dead mother's surname, and I don't think General Robinson knows that Bechtel is my father. Or maybe he does. The Army knows everything; often it just doesn't make connections among the things it knows. But that doesn't matter. I run the best nursing unit under fire in the entire Army. I'd match my nurses with any others, anywhere. I myself have performed operations alongside the doctors, in Bogotá, when there were five doctors for three hundred mangled and screaming soldiers. I never see my father outside the OR.

The new Arrival's name is Sergeant Edward Strickland, of the Connecticut Third Regiment. No modems are permitted in the Hole compound, which used to be Prospect Park in Brooklyn, but officers are issued dumb terminals. The Army has allowed us access to its unclassified history databanks. By this time we all know a lot about the Battle of Long Island, which a year ago most of us had never heard of.

Strickland rates two mentions in the d-banks. In a 1776 letter to his wife, General Israel Putnam praised Strickland's "bravery and fearlessness" in defending the Brooklyn Heights entrenchments. A year later, Strickland turns up on the "Killed in Action" list for the fighting around Peekskill. A son, Putnam Strickland, became a member of the Pennsylvania legislature in 1794.

My father never had a son. The criminal charges against him resulted in a hung jury, and the prosecutor chose not to refile but to refer the case to the Family Court of Orange County. After he was barred by the judge from ever seeing me again, he lived alone.

In the afternoon a Special Forces team shows up to make a fourth assault on the Hole. During the first two, medical staff had all been bundled into concrete bunkers; maybe the Pentagon was afraid of an explosion from antimatter or negative tachyons or whatever the current theory is. By the third attempt, when it seemed clear nothing was going to happen anyway, we were allowed to stay within a few yards of the Hole, which is as far as most Arrivals get.

And farther than the assault team gets. The four soldiers in their clumsy suits lumber toward the faint shimmer that is all you can see of the Hole. I pause halfway between OR and Supply, a box of registered painkillers in my hand, and watch. Sun glints off metal helmets. If the team actually gets through, will they be bullet-proof on the other side? Will the battle for Brooklyn Heights and the Jamaica Road stop, in sheer astonishment, at the monsters bursting in air? If the battle does stop, will the assault team turn around and lumber back, having satisfied the Pentagon that this really is some sort of time hole and not some sort of enemy illusion? (Which enemy?) Or will the team stay to give General Israel Putnam and his aide-de-camp Aaron Burr a strategy for defeating twenty thousand British veterans with five thousand half-trained recruits?

Head nurses are not considered to have a need to know these decisions.

The assault team lumbers forward. When they reach the shimmer — I have to squint to see it in the sunlight — they stop. Each of the four suited figures bends forward, straining, but nothing gives. Boxlike items — I assume they're classified weapons — are brought out and aimed at the shimmer. Nothing. After ten minutes three soldiers lumber back to the command bunker.

The fourth stays. I wouldn't have seen what he did except that I turn around as three British soldiers fall through the Hole from the other side. An infantryman first, blood streaming from his

mouth and nose, screaming, screaming. By the time I reach him, he's dead. The other two come through twenty feet east, and as I straighten up from bending over the infantryman, his blood smearing my uniform, I see the Hole guards leap forward. A musket discharges, a sound more like an explosion than like the *rat-a-tat-tat* of our pieces. I hit the dirt. The guards jump the other two redcoats.

Beside me, just beyond the dead Brit, I see the assault-team lieutenant finish his task. He's undogged the front of his suit, and now he reaches inside and pulls out something that catches the sunlight. I recognize it: Edward Strickland's hunting knife. He lobs it gently toward the Hole. It cuts through the shimmer as easily as into butter and disappears.

"Major! Major!" One of my young nurses runs toward me. For the second time I crawl up from the English soldier's body.

Another musket discharges. A fourth British soldier, an officer, has stumbled through the Hole and fired. The ball hits the young nurse in the chest, and she staggers backward and falls in a spray of blood just as the *rat-a-tat-tat* of assault rifles barks in the hot air.

We're in OR all afternoon. I think that's the only reason they don't get to me until evening. My nurse, Lieutenant Mary Inghram, dies. The British major who killed her dies. One of the other British soldiers dies. The infantryman was already dead. The last Brit, a Captain John Percy Healy of His Majesty's Twenty-third Foot under the command of Lord William Howe, is conscious. He has arterial bleeding, contusions, and a complex femoral fracture. We put him under. To treat him and to autopsy the other three English soldiers, we have to remove heavy winter uniforms, including watch coats and gloves. The cockade on Healy's tricorne is still wet with snow.

I am just finishing at the dumb terminal when the aide comes for me. I haven't even showered after OR, just removed my scrubs. The terminal screen says: **JOHN PERCY HEALY, THIRD SON OF VISCOUNT SHERINGHAM, 1747–1809. (1) ARRIVAL IN VIRGINIA WITH TWENTY-THIRD FOOT, 1781, JUST PRIOR TO CORNWALLIS SURRENDER AT YORKTOWN. SEE BURKE'S PEERAGE.**

"Major Peters? The general wants to see you in his quarters, ma'am."

Seventeen eighty-one. Five years after the Battle of Long Island.

"Ma'am? He said right away, ma'am."

What battle had Captain Healy been fighting on his side of the Hole?

"*Ma'am . . .*"

"Yes, soldier." The screen goes blank. After a moment red letters appear: **ACCESS DENIED ALL PERSONNEL UNTIL FURTHER NOTICE.**

General Robinson's quarters are as bleak as the rest of the compound: a foamcast "tent" that is actually a rigid gray-green dome, furnished with standard-issue cot, desk, locker, and terminal. He's made no effort at interior decoration, but on the desk stand pictures of his wife and three daughters. They're all pretty, smiling, dressed up for somebody's wedding.

Bechtel is there.

As I stand at attention in front of the two men, I have a sudden memory of a doll I owned when I was a child. By the time the doll came to me from some other, forgotten child, its hair was worn to a fragile halo through which you could see the cracked plastic scalp. One eye had fallen back into its head. It wore a stained red dress with a raveling hem where one sleeve should have been. My mother told me much later that whenever I saw the doll around our house I picked it up and carried it everywhere for a few days, but when I lost it, I didn't hunt for it. When it appeared again at my father's trial, it must have seemed natural to me to once more take hold of its battered, indifferent familiarity. I think now that I didn't understand to what use it was being put; I don't remember what I thought then. I was four years old.

Nor do I remember anything about the actual trial, only what I was told much later. But I know why I remember the doll. I even know why I think of it now, in the general's bunker. After the trial my mother took the doll away and substituted another with the same shape, the same dress, the same yellow hair. Only this doll was new and unused, its red satin dress shiny and double-sleeved. I remember staring at it, puzzled, knowing something had changed but not how, or why. It was the same doll—my mother told me it was the same doll—and yet it was not. I looked at my mother's face, and for the first time in what must have been the whole long mess of the trial, I felt the floor ripple and shake under my feet. My mother's smiling face looked suddenly far away, and blurred, as if she might be somebody else's mother. I remember I started screaming.

The general says, "Major Peters, Sergeant Strickland says you were the first person to talk to him after he gained consciousness. He says you told him the American colonists won the Revolution, and that England surrendered in 1781. Is that correct?"

"Yes, sir." My shoulders are braced hard. I look directly at the general, and no one else. The general's face is very grave.

"Were you aware of explicit orders that no medical personnel shall supply information concerning these men's future, under any circumstances?"

"Yes, sir. I was."

"Then why did you disobey the order, Major?"

"I have no good reason, sir."

"Then let's hear an un-good one, Major."

He's giving me every chance to explain. I wonder if General Israel Putnam was like this with his men, all of whom followed him with a fanatic devotion, even when his military decisions were wrong. Even when a movement started to have him court-martialed for poor military judgment after the disaster of Long Island. Robinson watches me with grave observant eyes. I might even have tried to answer him, if Bechtel hadn't been there. Bechtel is responsible for the conduct of his entire medical staff, of course, and for a sudden horrified moment I wonder if that's really why I disobeyed orders. To get back at my father.

But I can't say all that out loud, not even if Bechtel were still posted halfway around the world.

"No reason at all, sir," I say, and wait for my reprimand, or transfer, or court-martial. I'm not sure how seriously the Army takes this gag order with Arrivals. I've never heard of anybody else disobeying it.

The general shuffles some papers on his desk. "There is a complication, Major." He looks up at me and now I see something else in his eyes besides fairness. He is furious. "Sergeant Strickland refuses to talk to anyone but you. He says he trusts you and no one else, and unless you're present, he won't cooperate with Military Intelligence."

I don't know what to say.

"This is obviously an undesirable situation, Major. And one for which you may eventually be held responsible. In the meantime, however, you're needed to assist in the debriefing of Sergeant Strickland, and so you will report immediately to Colonel Orr and arrange a schedule for that. If that represents a conflict with your other duties, I will arrange to relieve you of those."

Relief fills me like sunlight. No court-martial. If I cooperate, the whole thing will be overlooked — that's what the offer to keep my nursing duties means. Robinson doesn't want an issue made of this one slip, any more than I do. Slavering beyond the perimeter of the high-security compound, along with the Brooklyn zoo, are hundreds of journalists from around the world. The less we have to say to them, and they about us, the better. No duty goes on forever.

"Yes, sir. There will be no conflict of duties. Thank you, sir."

"You logged onto the library system last night."

"Yes, sir." Of course log-ons would be monitored. The Army knows what I discovered about the Brit captain. The Army knows that I know they know. I like that. I joined the service for just these reasons: actions are measurable, and privacy is suspect.

"What did you learn about Captain Healy?"

I answer immediately. "That he must come from a different past on the other side of the Hole. A past in which events in the Revolution were somehow different from ours."

Robinson nods. The carefully controlled anger fades from his eyes. I have passed some test. "You will say nothing of that speculation to Sergeant Strickland, Major. Anything you tell him will concern only history as it exists for us."

He's asking me to not do something I would never have done anyway. I am the last person to offer Strickland a doubtful past. "Certainly, sir."

"You will answer only such questions as Colonel Orr thinks appropriate."

"Yes, sir."

"There will be no more anomalies in any communication in which you are involved."

"No, sir."

"Fine," Robinson says. He rises. "I'm going for a walk."

Without dismissing me. The general knows, then. He has cross-filed the personnel records. Or Bechtel told him. Bechtel requested this "walk" to leave us alone for a moment. The skin over my belly crawls — Robinson *knows*. I stare straight ahead, still at attention.

A long silent moment passes.

Bechtel makes a noise, unclassifiable. His voice is soft as smoke. "Susan — I didn't do it."

I stare straight ahead.

"No matter what the judge decided. I never touched you. Your mother wanted the divorce so bad she was willing to say anything. She *did* say anything. She —"

"Will that be all, sir?"

This time there is no soft noise. "Susan—she *lied*. Doesn't that matter to you?"

"She said you lied," I say, and immediately am furious with myself for saying anything at all. I clench my jaw.

My fury must somehow communicate itself to my father. In the stiffness of my already stiff body, in the air itself. He says tiredly, "Dismissed," and I hear in the single word things I don't want to examine. I walk stiff-legged from the tent.

After the trial, I never touched the doll in the red dress again.

My first interview with Sergeant Edward Strickland, Connecticut Third Regiment, First Continental Army, takes place the next morning. He's been moved from Recovery to a secure bunker at the far end of the compound, although he still has an elevated temperature and the remains of dysentery. Even in a standard-issue hospital gown he doesn't look like a man from our time. It's more than just the broken teeth. It's something unbroken in his face. He looks as if ass-covering is as foreign to him as polyester.

"Sergeant Strickland," commands the Military Intelligence expert, Colonel Orr. Unseen recording equipment whirrs quietly. "Tell us all your movements for the last few days, starting with General Putnam's fortification of the Brooklyn Heights works."

Strickland has apparently decided he is not enlisted in this Army. He ignores the colonel and says directly to me, "Where am I, Mistress Nurse?"

Orr nods, almost imperceptibly. We've rehearsed this much. I say, "You're in an Army hospital on Long Island."

"What date be today?"

"July 15, 2001."

I can't tell if he believes me or not. The fierce black eyes bore steadily, without blinking. I say, "What work did you do before you joined the army, Sergeant?"

"I was a smith."

"Where?"

"Pomfret, Connecticut. Mistress . . . if this be the future, how come I to be here?"

"We don't know. Three months ago soldiers from the Battle of Long Island began to stumble into a city park out of thin air. Most of them died. You didn't."

He considers this. His gaze travels around the foamcast bunker, to my glasses, to the M-18 held by the guard. Abruptly, he laughs.

I see the moment he refuses the idea of the future without actually rejecting it, like a man who accepts a leaflet on a street corner but puts it in his pocket, unread, sure it has nothing to do with his real life.

He says, "What losses did we suffer at Long Island?"

"A thousand dead, seven hundred taken prisoner," I answer, and he flinches.

"And the enemy?"

"Howe reported sixty-one dead, twenty-nine missing."

"How did the enemy best us?"

"Surprised you with a flanking march down the Jamaica Road, with a force you couldn't possibly match."

"How did Put retreat?"

"By water, across the river to New York."

It goes on like that, reliving military history 225 years dead. Six months ago, I knew none of it. Orr doesn't interrupt me. Probably he thinks that Strickland is learning to trust us. I know that Strickland is learning to trust his own past, checking the details until he knows they're sound, constructing around himself the solid world that must hold this mutable one.

From the direction of the Hole comes the muffled sound of musket fire.

This time it's a Hessian, one of the mercenary force serving the British under von Heister in front of the Flatbush pass. He's the first Hessian to come through the Hole. Screaming in German, he fights valiantly as the OR personnel put him under. By the time I see him, swaddled in a hospital gown, in Recovery, his face is subdued in the unnatural sleep of anesthesia, and I see that although as big as Strickland, the Hessian mercenary is no more than sixteen. By our standards, a child.

Strickland walks in, accompanied by the MI colonel and a very attentive MP. Are they trying to build his trust by giving him the illusion of free movement within the compound? He's the first Arrival who's ambulatory and still here. I think about how easily the Special Forces lieutenant slid Strickland's hunting knife back through the Hole, which not even our tanks had been able to penetrate, and I bet myself that Old Put's sergeant's free movement has no more latitude than Put himself did on the Jamaica Road.

Strickland gazes at the Hessian. "A boy. To do their fighting for 'em." The rough voice is heavy with sarcasm.

"From von Heister's troops," I say, to say something.

"Put always traded 'em back."

"It must have been hard for them, to go so far from their homes," the nurse on duty says tentatively. She has a high fluttery voice. Strickland looks at her with irony, a much more surprising expression on that rough face than sarcasm, and she flushes. He laughs.

The German boy opens his eyes. His blurry gaze falls on Strickland, who again wears his own breeches and shirt and coat, with the strip of red cloth of a field sergeant sewn onto the right shoulder. The Hessian is probably in a lot of pain, but even so his face brightens.

"*Mein Feldwebel! Wir haben die Schlact gewonnen, nicht wahr?*"

The Military Intelligence colonel's eyes widen. Strickland's face turns to stone. Orr makes a quick gesture, and the next minute both Strickland and I are being firmly escorted out of Recovery. Strickland shakes off the MP's arm and turns angrily to me.

"What did he mean, '*Mein Feldwebel*'? And '*Wir haben die Schlact gewonnen*'?"

I shake my head. "I don't speak German."

Strickland looks at me a moment longer, trying to see if I'm telling the truth. Evidently he sees from my face that I am. We stare at each other in the sunlight, while I wonder what the hell is happening. Orr emerges from Recovery long enough to snap an order at the MP, who escorts Strickland back to his quarters.

In my own quarters I fish out the German-American dictionary I bought when I thought I was being sent to Stuttgart instead of Brooklyn. It takes a long time to track down spellings in a language I don't speak, especially since I'm guessing at the dialect, and at words I've only heard twice. Outside, two passing soldiers improvise a songfest: "There's a Hole in the battle, dear Gen'ral, dear Gen'ral; there's a Hole in the battle, dear Gen'ral, a Ho-oo-ole." Finally I piece together a translation of the German sentence.

"*My sergeant! We won the battie, yes?*"

I try to think about everything that would have had to be different in the world for Frederick II of Hesse-Kassel to furnish mercenaries to the Colonial patriots instead of to the British. I can't do it; I don't know enough history. A moment later, I realize how dumb that is: there's a much simpler explanation. Von Heister's Hessian could simply have deserted, changing sides in midwar. Loyalties were often confused during the Revolution. Desertion was probably common, even among mercenaries.

Desertion is always common.

My mother was born in 1935, but she didn't graduate from college until 1969. All her life, which ended in a car crash, she kept the conviction of her adopted generation that things are only good before they settle into formula and routine. She marched against the draft, against Dow Chemical, against capitalism, against whaling. She was never *for* anything. Shoulder to shoulder with a generation that refused to trust anyone over thirty, this thirty-three-year-old noisily demonstrated her hatred for rules.

All my childhood I never knew if I was supposed to be home for dinner by 6:00, or 6:30, or at all. I never knew if the men she dated would return again, or be showered with contemptuous scorn, or move in. I never knew if the electricity would suddenly be cut off while I was doing my algebra homework, or when we would move again in the middle of the night, leaving the gas bill shredded and the rent unpaid. I never knew anything. My mother told me we were "really" rich, we were dirt-poor, we were wanted by the law, we were protected by the law. At seventeen I ran away from home and joined the Army, which put me through nursing school.

My mother is buried in Dansville, New York, which I once saw from a Greyhound bus. It's a small town with orderly nineteenth-century storefronts and bars full of middle-aged men in John Deere caps. These men, who pay their mortgages faithfully, stand beside their barstools and argue in favor of capital punishment, confiscation of drug dealers' cars, the elimination of welfare, and the NRA. On summer weekends they throw rocks at the Women's Peace Collective enclave off Route 63. The Dansville cemetery is kept neatly mowed and clipped. I chose the burial plot myself.

Captain John Percy Healy of His Majesty's Twenty-third Foot is kept under close guard. Strickland couldn't get anywhere near him, even if he knew that Healy and his winter-clad Battle of Long Island existed. Nor can he get near the Hole, although he tries. The summer sun is slanting in long lines over the compound when he breaks away from the MI colonel and the bodyguard MP and me, and sets off at a dead run toward the Hole. His head is down, his powerful legs pumping. As each leg lifts, I see a hole in the sole of his left boot flash and disappear, flash and disappear.

"Halt!" shouts Colonel Orr. The guards at the Hole raise their weapons. The MP, whose fault this escape is, starts to run after Strickland, realizes he can't possibly catch him, and draws his gun. "Halt, or we'll fire!"

They do. Strickland goes down, hit in the leg. He drags himself toward the Hole on his elbows, his body thrashing from side to side on the hard ground, a thin line of blood trickling behind. I can't see his face. The MP reaches him before I do and Strickland fights him fiercely, in silence.

Three more soldiers are on him.

I've seen more direct combat nursing than any other nurse I've met personally, but in OR I can't look at Strickland's eyes. If he had reached the Hole he could have gone through, and I'm the only person in the room who knows this. Not even Strickland knows it. He only acted as if he did.

Dr. Bechtel sends for me the next morning. He's the chief of medical staff. I go.

"Susan, I think. . . ."

" 'Major,' sir. I would prefer to be called 'Major.' Sir."

He doesn't change expression. "Major, I think it would be a good idea if you requested a transfer to another unit."

I draw a deep breath. "Are you rotating me out, sir?"

"No!" For a second some emotion breaks through—anger? fear? guilt?—and then is gone. "I'm suggesting you voluntarily apply for a transfer. You're not doing your career any good here, with Strickland, not the way things have turned out. There are too many anomalies. The Army doesn't like anomalies, Major."

"The entire Hole is an anomaly. Sir."

He permits himself a thin smile. "True enough. And the Army doesn't like it."

"I don't want to transfer."

He looks at me directly. "Why not?"

"I prefer not to, sir," I say. Is a nonanswer answer an anomaly? I can feel every tendon in my body straining toward the door. And yet there is a horrible fascination, too, in staring at him like this. Somewhere in my mind a four-year-old girl touches a one-eyed doll in a raveled red dress. *Here. He touched me here. And here* . . . But did he?

The four-year-old doesn't answer.

"Strickland is asking to see you," he says wearily. "No— *demanding* to see you. Somewhere he saw Healy's uniform. Being carried across the parade ground from the cleaning machine, maybe—I don't know. He won't say."

I picture Healy's heavy watch coat, his red uniform with the regimental epaulets on both shoulders, his crimson sash.

"Strickland's smart," I say slowly, and immediately regret it. I'm participating in the conversation as if it were normal. I don't want to give him that.

"Yes," my father says, a shade too eagerly. "He's figured out that there are multiple realities beyond the Hole. Multiple Battles of Long Island. Maybe even entirely different American Revolutions . . . I don't know." He passes a hand through his hair and I'm jolted by an unexpected memory, shimmery and dim: my daddy at the dinner table, talking and passing a hand through his hair, myself in a high chair with round beads on the tray, beads that spin and slide. . . . "The Pentagon moves him out tomorrow."

"Strickland?"

"Yes, of course, that's who we've been talking about." He peers at me. I give him nothing, wooden-faced. Abruptly he says, "Susan—ask for a transfer."

"No, sir," I say. "Not unless that's an order."

We stand at opposite ends of the bunker, and the air shimmers between us.

"Dismissed," he says quietly. I salute and leave, but as I reach the door he tries once more. "I recommend that you don't see Strickland again. No matter what he demands. For the sake of your own career."

"Recommendation noted, sir," I say, without inflection.

Outside, the night is hot and still. I have trouble breathing the stifling air. I try to think what could have prompted my father's sudden concern with my career, but no matter how I look at it, I can't see any advantage to him in keeping me away from Strickland. Only to myself. The air trembles with heat lightning. Beyond the compound, at the Brooklyn zoo, an elephant bellows, as if in pain.

The next day the Hole closes.

I'm not there at the time—0715 hours—but one of the guards retells the story in the mess tent. "There was this faint pop, like a kid's toy gun. Yoder hit the dirt and pissed his pants—"

"I did not! Fuck you!" Yoder yells, and there are some good-natured insults and pointless shoving before anybody can overhear what actually did happen.

"This little pop, and the shimmer kinda disappeared, and that was it. Special Forces showed up and they couldn't get in—"

"When could they ever?" someone says slyly, a female voice, and there is laughter and nudges.

"And that was it. The Hole went bye-bye," the guard says, reclaiming group attention.

"So when do we go home?"

"When the Army fucking says you do."

They move Strickland out the next day. I don't see him. No one reports if he asks for me. Probably not. At some point Strickland decided that his trust in me was misplaced, born of one of those chance moments of emotion that turn out to be less durable than expected. I wasn't able to help him toward the Hole. All I was able to do was tell him military information that may or may not be true for a place and time that he can't ever reach again.

Curiously enough, it is the Brit, Captain John Healy, to whom we make a difference.

He is with us a week before they move him, recovering from his injuries. The broken leg sets clean. Military Intelligence, in the form of Colonel Orr, goes in and out of his heavily guarded bunker several times a day. Orr is never there while I'm changing Healy's dressings or monitoring his vitals, but Healy is especially thoughtful after Orr has left. He watches me with a bemused expression, as if he wonders what *I'm* thinking.

He's nothing like Strickland. Slight, fair, not tall, with regular features and fresh-colored skin. Healy's speech is precise and formal, courteous, yet with a mocking gaiety in it. Even here, which seems to me a kind of miracle. He's fastidious about his dress, and an orderly actually learns to black boots.

Between debriefings, Healy reads. He requested the books himself, all published before 1776; but maybe that's all he's permitted. *Gulliver's Travels. Robinson Crusoe.* Poems by somebody called Alexander Pope. I've never been much of a reader, but I saw the old movie about Crusoe, and I look up the others. They're all books about men severely displaced. Once Healy, trying to make conversation, tells that he comes from London, where his family has a house in Tavistock Place, also a "seat" in Somerset.

I refuse to be drawn into conversation with him.

On the day they're going to move him, Bechtel does a complete medical. I assist. Naked, with electrodes attached to his head and vials of blood drawn from his arm, Healy suddenly becomes unstoppably talkative.

"In London the physicians make use of leeches to accomplish your identical aims."

Bechtel smiles briefly.

"In *my* London, that is. Not in yours. There is a London here, I presume, Doctor?"

"Yes," Bechtel says. "There is."

"Then there exist two. But there's rather more, isn't there? One for the Hessian. One for that Colonial who attempted escape back through the . . . the time corridor. Probably others, is that not so?"

"Probably," Bechtel says. He studies the EKG printout.

"And in some of these Londons we put down the Rebellion, and in others you Colonials succeed in declaring yourself a sovereign nation, and perhaps in still others the savages destroy you all and the Rebellion never even occurs. Have I understood the situation correctly?"

"Yes," Bechtel says. He looks at the Brit now, and I am caught by the look as well: by its unexpected compassion.

The vial of blood in my hand seems to pound against my temples.

My mother told me, when I was eight, that my father had caused the war then raging in Vietnam.

I say nothing.

"Then," Healy continues in his beautiful, precise, foreign voice, "there must exist several versions of this present as well. Some of them must, by simple deduction, be more appealing than this one." He glances around the drab bunker. Beyond the barred window, an American flag flies over the parade ground. Couldn't we have spared him the constant sight of his enemy's flag?

Then I remember that he probably doesn't even recognize it. The Stars and Stripes wasn't adopted by the Continental Congress until 1777.

"This compound is not the whole of our present," Bechtel says, too gently. "The rest is much different."

Healy waves a hand, smiling. "Oh, quite. I'm convinced you have marvels abounding, including your edition of London. Which, since I cannot return to my own, I hope to one day visit." The smile wavers slightly, but in a moment he has it back. "Of course, it will not be even the descendant of my own. I must be prepared for that. In *this* history, you Colonials fought the Battle of Long Island in the summer."

"Yes," Bechtel says.

"My own history is apparently quite unrecoverable. Your historical tactician tells me that no connection appears to exist between this place and whichever of those histories is mine. And so I cannot, of course, know what might have happened in the course of my own war, any more than you can know." He watches Bechtel closely. All this is said in that same mocking lighthearted voice. I can hear that voice in London drawing rooms, amid ladies in panniers and high-dressed curls, who know better than to believe a word such an amusing rake ever says.

Bechtel lays down the printout and steps toward Healy's cot. Instinctively the Brit reaches for the coat of his uniform and pulls it around his shoulders. Bechtel waits until Healy is draped in his remnants of the British empire. Then Bechtel speaks in a voice both steady and offhand, as if it were calculated to match the careless facade of Healy's own bravery.

"You must choose the reality you prefer. Look at it this way, Captain. You don't know for sure who won the war in your time, or who survived it, or what England or the United States became after your November 16, 1776. Your past is closed to you. So you're free to choose whatever one you wish. You can live as if your choice *is* your past. And in so doing, make it real."

I move carefully at my station, feeding Healy's blood samples into the Hays-Mason analyzer.

Healy says, with that same brittle gaiety, "You are urging me to an act of faith, sir."

"Yes, if you like," Bechtel says. He looks at me. "But I would call it an act of choice."

"Choice that I am not a prisoner *de guerre*, from a losing army, of a war I may or may not have survived?"

"Yes."

"I will consider what you say, sir," Healy says, and turns away. The epaulets on his shoulders tremble, but it may have been the light. From the parade ground beyond the window comes the sound of a jeep with a faulty muffler.

"I've finished here," Bechtel tells the guard, who relays the information over his comlink.

They remove Healy in a wheelchair, although it's obvious he doesn't like this. As he's wheeled past, he catches at my arm. His blue eyes smile, but his fingers dig into my flesh. I don't allow myself to wince. "Mistress Nurse — are there ladies where I'm going? Shall I have the society of your sex?"

I look at him. Not even a hint of how Lieutenant Mary Inghram died has leaked to the outside press. Her parents were told she died in an explosives accident; I signed the report myself. When the Pentagon takes the Arrivals from our compound, they vanish as completely as if they'd never existed, and not even an electronic-data trail, the hunting spoor of the twenty-first century, remains. Ladies? The society of my sex? How would I know?

"Yes," I say to Healy. "You will."

The tent is empty except for Bechtel and me. I clean and stow the equipment; he scrubs at the sink. His back is to me. Very low, so that I barely hear him over the running water, he says, "Susan. . . ."

"All right," I say. "I choose. You did it."

I walk out of the bunker. Some soldiers stand outside, at parade rest, listening to their sergeant read the orders for move-out. Guards still ring the place where the Hole used to be. In the sky, above the Low Radar Barrier, a sea gull wheels and cries. The elephant is silent. I have never seen my father since.

You might think I should have chosen differently. You might think, given the absence of proof, that like any jury empowered by the Constitution of the United States, I should choose the more innocent reality. Should believe that my father never molested me, and my mother, who is now beyond both proof and innocence, lied. The trial evidence is inconclusive, the character evidence cloudy. If I choose that reality, I gain not only a father but also peace of mind. I free myself from the torments of a past that might not even have happened.

But I would still be *this* Susan Peters. I would still watch my nurses tremble with love in the moonlight, and I would still see clearly the deceptions and hurt ahead, the almost inevitable anger. I would still recoil if a man brushes against me accidentally away from the hospital, and still pride myself on never wincing at anything within a hospital. I would still know that I chose Army nursing precisely because here dangerous men are at their weakest, and most vulnerable, and in greatest need of what I can safely give them.

I would still know what Strickland learned: the Hole always closes.

One version of the past has shaped all my choices. If I decide it never happened, what remains? Will I exist? I, Susan Peters, who runs the best combat nursing unit in the entire Army? I, Susan Peters, who have earned both the Commendation Medal and the Distinguished Service Cross? I, Susan Peters, who can operate on a patient myself if the doctors are occupied with other screaming and suffering men? And *have?*

I, Susan Peters.

Who was sexually abused by her father, ran away from home, joined the Army, became a nurse, served honorably in the Special Medical Unit assigned to the Battle of Long Island, and have never lied to a patient except once.

And maybe it wasn't a lie.

Maybe there *will* be ladies where they are taking Captain John Percy Healy of His Majesty King George III's Twenty-third Foot. Maybe Healy will stand with some young woman, somewhere, in the moonlight and touch her face with gentle fingers. It's possible. I certainly don't know differently. And if there are, then it wasn't even a lie.

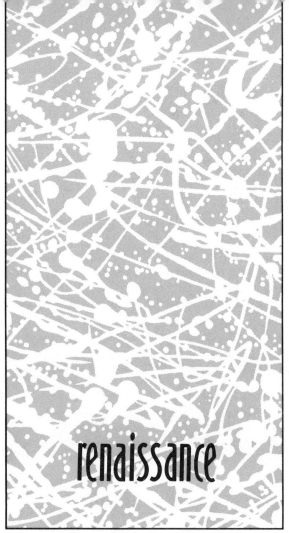

renaissance

HER LADYSHIP was late to breakfast again, and when she did appear it was in a cobwebby lace robe stained with Bloody Marys, blonde mane hanging in artful mats, eyes big and shadowed with Gray-Violet No. 6. So we were doing Camille this morning. Brad, already through his melon and severe in pinstripes, glanced up and frowned. The tiniest possible frown, almost imperceptible: you don't upset a wife eight months pregnant with God-knows-what, *no matter what*. But the frown said he was not prepared to play Armand. Not dressed for the part, my dear. Did her ladyship care? She did not.

"Mother Celia, such a dream I had!" she breathed. I detest being called "Mother Celia." Cherlyn knows this.

"What did you dream, darling?" Brad asked fondly. His tie was wrong for his suit: too flashy, too slick. Unlike his father, Brad had no style. Was there a gene for tackiness? And if so, had they edited it out of the monstrous bulge under Cherlyn's Bloody Marys?

Cherlyn breathed, "I was walking up these stone steps, right? White marble steps, like at a state capitol or something? Only it was in a foreign country, like in a Club Med ad, and I'm the only one there. The sun is beating down. It's very hot and the sky is very blue and the steps are very white and the place is very quiet and I'm very all by myself."

Not a dialogue writer, our Cherlyn. In the old days, Waldman would have had her off the set for that singsong voice and sticky-cheery expression, as if just below the smooth flawless skin lay smooth flawless marzipan. But Brad only leaned forward, elbows on the table and face wrinkled in concern—my son does this very well—to prompt, "Were you afraid, darling?"

"Not yet. That's the weird thing. On either side of the steps were these two humongous stone things, really strange, and even when the first one spoke to me I wasn't scared. They were half lion and half some kind of bird."

"Griffins," I said, despite myself. "Fierce predators who guard treasure and eat humans." Both looked at me blankly. I added— also despite myself—"Paramount once did the movie. You must have seen it, Cherlyn, you pride yourself on your knowledge of your profession's history. B-movie. Nineteen, uh, thirty-seven. *The Griffin That Ate Atlanta.*"

"Oh, yes," Cherlyn said vaguely. "Wasn't that Selznick?"

"Waldman," I said. Brad shot me a warning look.

"I remember now," Cherlyn said. "I remember thinking there was a part in there I would have been *great* for."

"I'm sure," I said. In her present condition, she could play Atlanta.

"*Anyways,*" Cherlyn said, "in my dream this griffim spoke to me. Actually, they both did. The one on the left—no, wait, it was the one on the right—the one on the right said, 'Soon.' Right out loud, real as life. Then the one on the left said, 'We shall return.' "

"Old griffins don't die, they just fade away," I said.

"Huh?"

Brad frowned at me. I said, "Nothing."

"Well, *anyways*, that did sort of give me the spooks, right? This weird stone griffim looks me right in the eye and says, 'We shall return.' No, wait—it was 'We can return.' No, no, wait—it was '*Now* we can return.' That was it."

In the midst of the dialogue editing, the phone rang. The quality of mercy, and it wasn't even raining. I reached backward from my chair to answer it, but Brad leapt up, knocked over his coffee, and made an end run around the table to get there first. Excilda appeared with a sponge, clucking. Brad listened and handed the receiver to me without meeting my eyes.

"Expecting a call, are we?" I said. Excilda disappeared, still clucking. Brad's eyes met Cherlyn's, then slid sideways to the table in nonchalance as phony as his tie. I felt a brief cold prickling at the back of my neck.

"Celia?" the phone said. "You there, darling?"

It was Geraldine Michaelson, née Gerald Michaelson, my lawyer and oldest friend. She had on her attorney voice, which was preferable to his all-us-girls-together voice, and I prepared to listen to whatever she had to say. But she was merely confirming our monthly lunch date.

"There's one or two things we might discuss, Celia."

"All right," I said, watching Brad. His blue eyes did not meet mine. Handsome, handsome man—his father had been gorgeous, the dear dead bastard.

"Some . . . irregularities," Gerry said.

"All right," I said. There are always irregularities. The biggest irregularity in the world kicked under my daughter-in-law's negligee.

"Fine," Gerry said. "See you then."

I passed the phone to Cherlyn, who instead of hanging it up as anyone else would, sat holding it like a party drink. "And *then* in my dream, the stone griffim sort of shook itself on the steps—"

"You told someone," I said to Brad. He turned on his dazzling grin. I was not dazzled; I knew him when. "Cut the bullshit. You broke your word and leaked it. And that phone call was supposed to be the story breaking. Who did you give it to?"

"—even though it was *stone*," Cherlyn said loudly. "And then—"

"Who, Brad?"

"Really, Mother, you worry too much. You always have." More grin: his repertoire is limited. If he were an actor instead of a broker, he'd be as execrable as Cherlyn. He took the phone from her limp

hands and hung it up. "You shouldn't have to worry now, at your time of life. You raised your family and now you should just relax and enjoy life and let us worry about this baby."

"*Who*, Brad?"

"—the griffim stood right up—are you listening, Mother Celia?—stood *right up*—"

"You could have waited. You promised the doctors and researchers. You signed a contract. There would have been plenty of money later without selling a tawdry scoop."

"Now just wait a minute—"

"—on the stone steps big as life and said again 'Soon,' and I liked to died because—"

"You never did have any style. Never."

"Don't you—"

Cherlyn half rose in her chair and shouted, "—like to died because those stone lion-things just shook out this huge set of stone-cold wings!"

We turned our heads slowly to look at her. Cherlyn's pretty vapid eyes opened wide enough to float L.A.

The phone rang.

Reporters. TV cameras. Cherlyn in a blue maternity smock, blue bows in her hair, no more Camille. Auditioning for the Madonna. Brad in his flashy tie, good suit, coffee-stained cuff, reveling with a sober face. Sleaze and charm. My son.

Miss Lincoln's pregnancy has been completely normal. No, we are not apprehensive about the baby's health. All fetal monitoring shows normal development.

Got two dice?

My wife and I regard it as a singular honor to be chosen to bear the first child with this particular genetic adaptation, the first in a breathtaking breakthrough that will let mankind finally realize all its century-long aspirations.

Got two hundred dice?

Ten years ago, it was barely possible to genetically select for hair color. Ten years from now, the human race will be poised at the start of a renaissance that will dwarf anything that has gone before. And our little Angela Dawn will be among the first.

I had not heard the name before. From the window, I could imagine Brad and Cherlyn scanning the crowd of reporters before them on the lawn, looking beyond for the next wave: agents, book publishers, studio people. How much did a story like this go for these days? Yahweh and Technicolor Mary.

My wife and I talked this over at great length, and agreed it was momentous enough to interrupt her film career for a brief time in order to participate in this, uh, momentous research. We both felt it's what my father, the late Dr. Richard Felder, would have wanted.

He wasn't missing a trick. But Richard, whatever else he was, was not stupid. Physicists seldom are. Richard would not have stood there in the wrong tie speaking overconfident platitudes. Richard could have told Brad something about the unseen risks, the unseen connections, in universes more complex than Universal Pictures.

This opportunity represents the greatest treasure any parents could give their child. But Miss Lincoln and I do regret that the story has broken prematurely. I have asked Dr. Murray at the Institute to investigate how this could have happened. However, since it has happened, it seems better to answer your questions honestly than to permit possibly irresponsible speculation.

I didn't stay to hear any more. While the reporters were still enthralled, I ducked out the back door, struggled over the orchard wall, and called a cab from the Andersons' housekeeper's room. Juana eyed my torn skirt with bemusement, shrugged, and went back to polishing silver. She once, in a burst of confidence after seeing Cherlyn's sole film, told Bruce Anderson that Cherlyn looked like "Alicia in Wonderland, only Alicia, in that book, she keep on her clothes," a remark that endeared Juana to me for life. The Mad Tea Party. The Queen of Hearts. Off with her head. In Cherlyn's case, redundancy.

I suddenly remembered that it was a griffin who conducted Alice to the trial of the Jack of Hearts.

It must have been that thought that gave me Cherlyn's dream. Eyes closed in the cab on the way to Gerry's office, I walked up the shallow marble steps to the temple. The griffins, *en regardant,* watched me from wild carved eyes, but did not speak. I crept toward the one on the left. The great predatory stone head swung toward me, so that I was forced to step back to avoid the hooked beak. Manes of spiral curls, writhing as if alive, stretched toward me. The lion's tail swished from side to side. Stone talons gripped tighter on unhewn rock. But the beast remained silent.

I said, "Are you returning?" Dreams permit one inanity.

The griffin remained silent. But then the eyes suddenly

changed. They turned black, a black deeper than any night, more ancient than the marble underneath my feet. The griffin rose and shook its wings: pointed, deeply veined stone flesh over muscled bone.

But to me it said nothing.

"Celia!" Gerry cried, coming toward me with both hands extended and both eyes averted. That was bad; Gerry considered eye contact very important. In the days when he was an agent and I was Waldman's chief scripter, he would make eye contact on the L.A. Freeway at seventy.

"What is it," I said.

"You're looking wonderful."

"What is it?"

Gerry rubbed her jaw. Under the makeup, she needed a shave. "Your portfolio."

I found that somewhere inside, I'd known. "How bad?"

"Pretty bad. Come inside."

She closed the office door. I sat by the window. Brad had had my portfolio for a little over a year. *To get the business started, Mother.* Desperate dignity in his unemployed voice. A gesture of maternal faith.

"He's been stock churning," Gerry said. "Turned over the entire damn portfolio twenty times in the last ten months. And chose badly. There's almost nothing left."

"How do you know? I gave him complete power of attorney. He wouldn't tell you."

"No."

"How do you *know?*"

"Don't ask. I know."

"You never trusted him." She didn't answer me. I said, "The real estate?"

"I don't know yet. Being looked into now. I only found out about the other this morning."

"When will you know?"

"Possibly tonight. I'll call you if . . . the portfolio was a *lot* of money, Celia. What'd he need it for?"

"Had your TV on this morning?"

She hadn't. We both stared out the window. Black dots whirled in the blue distance. They might have been sea gulls. Finally Gerry said, "This much churning is actionable."

"He's my son."

She didn't look at me. I remember Gerry when he was married to Elizabeth. After Geraldine's operation, Elizabeth took the boys back to Denmark and changed all their names. I was the one who scraped Gerry up off the bathroom floor, called the ambulance, stuck my fingers down his throat to make her vomit however many pills were still in her stomach.

We sat watching the flying black dots, which at this distance might have been anything at all.

I took a cab to the Conquistador, stopping on the way at the Book Nook on Sunset. The cabbie was delighted to go all the way up the coast to the Conquistador. He had even heard of it. "You know, industry people used to stay there. Sam Waldman and his people, they used to go there all the time. Take over the whole place for planning a movie or editing or maybe just partying. Place was a lot grander then. You know that?"

I told him I did.

Nobody recognized me. Nobody commented that my only luggage was three hundred dollars worth of oversized books. Nobody appeared to carry the books to my room, which had one cracked windowpane and a bedspread with cigarette burns. My books were the newest thing in the room, and the *Historia Monstrorum* was a 1948 reprint.

I learned that the griffin was the most mysterious of tomb symbols. That it dated back to the second millennium. That the Minoan griffin was the one with the mane of black spiral curls. That the griffin was the most predatory of all mythical monsters, guarding treasures and feeding on live human hearts. That Milton had mentioned a "hippogriff," presumably a hybrid of a hybrid. The Sumerians, Assyrians, Babylonians, Chaldeans, Egyptians, Mycenaeans, Indo-Iranians, Syrians, Scythians, and Greeks all had griffins. And so did Greater Los Angeles.

I sat by the window past midnight, smoking and watching the sky, waiting for Gerry to call. Clouds scudded over the moon: fantastic shapes, writhing and soaring. Smoke rose from the end of my cigarette in spiral curls. Somewhere, beyond the window in the unseen darkness, something snapped.

Once, when Brad had been very small, I had fallen sick with something-or-other; who can remember? But there had been fever, chills, nausea. The housekeeper had run off with the gardener and sixteen steaks. My soon-to-be-ex had been off doing what already-exes do; Richard always did like a jump on deadlines. The phone line had gone down in a windstorm. For forty-eight hours, it had been me, Brad, and several million germs. And at one point I had lost it, wailing louder than both wind and baby, lead performer in the Greek chorus.

Brad had stopped dead and crept close to my bed. He peered at me, screwing up his small face. Then he had called jubilantly, "Towl! Towl!" and run to fetch a grimy dishrag with which to smear Liquid Gold across my face. This had become one of my most precious memories. *What will I be when I grow up, Mommy?*

There was wind tonight, blowing from the sea. I could smell it. Sometime past midnight, the phone rang.

"Celia? Gerry. Listen, love—I'm coming up there."

"That bad? Come on, Gerry, tell me. We're both too old for drama."

I could hear her thinking. As an agent, he used to conduct deals while pulling leaves off the *Ficus benjamina* by his office phone. In a good year, his exfoliation topped United Logging's.

"He sold the waterfront properties, Celia. Both of them. Not a bad price, but invested wildly. And he's too far extended. You can recover some if you clip his wings right now, today, but the whole house of cards will still be shaky. You'll come out with less than a fourth of what you had, with the stock churning counted in. You're not a bag lady on Sunset yet, but it's not good. And it's actionable."

"I hear something else you're not telling me."

"The media is going wild. Cherlyn's in labor."

"*Now?*"

"Now."

"It's only eight months!"

"Yeah, but with this . . . baby, they're saying the womb just couldn't hold on any longer. That's what they're saying—what the hell do I know? I'm leaving now to get you."

"I'll take a cab."

"You can't afford it," Gerry said brutally, and hung up. I understood. She would do whatever she could to persuade me to sue Brad. Maybe I would let her. I packed up my books and called a cab. Then I left the books on the ratty unused bed. The Conquistador seemed a good place for them.

The cab could only get a block away from the hospital. I pushed my way on foot through the crowds, argued my way through the police cordon, slunk my way past the TV cameras, blustered my way through the lobby. "I'm Miss Lincoln's mother-in-law." "I'm Miss Lincoln's mother." "Miss Lincoln . . . the baby . . . the grand-mother . . ."

More TV, more reporters. Shouts, chaos, trampled Styrofoam cups. A huge nurse in a blinding pink uniform grabbed my arm and hauled me into an elevator, closing the doors so fast I lost my purse.

"Pretty fierce, huh?" she said, and laughed. Jowls of fat danced on her shoulders. She winked at me. I wished Brad had married *her*.

He was in the recovery room with Cherlyn, but the main show was already over and a helpful intern hauled him out and then tact-fully disappeared. I wished Brad had married *him*. Half-lit, the cor-ridor had the hushed creepiness of all hospitals late at night.

"Mother! You're a grandma!"

He wore a surgical gown and mask, looking like a natural. I opened my mouth to say — what? I still don't know — but he rushed on. "She's perfect! Wait till you see her! Little Angela Dawn. Perfect. And Cherlyn's fine, she's resting up for the press conference. Of course, we want you there, too! This is a great day!"

"Brad—"

"*Perfect*. You never saw such a baby," which had of course to be true enough. "We're going to bring her out wrapped up at first, let them see her face and hair — she's got all this hair, dark like yours, Mother — and just gradually be persuaded to unwrap her. Maybe not even today. Maybe not even tomorrow. We've forbidden cameras in the hospital, of course."

"I—"

"Wait till you see her!" And then he stopped.

And I knew. Knew before he turned to me in the middle of the hall, before he took my arm, before he smiled at me with that blind-ing sincerity that could sell vacuum tubes to Sony. I knew what he was going to say, and what I was going to say, although up till that moment it had been as much in doubt as Cherlyn's cerebrum.

He laid his hand on my shoulder. "You'll want to set up a trust fund for your first grandchild."

"I'm suing you for mismanagement of funds."

We stared at each other. I felt suddenly exhausted, and sickened, and old. *Towl, towl.*

"Wait!" a voice croaked. "Wait, wait, don't start the press without me, you bastard!"

Cherlyn wheeled herself around the corner in a pink motorized wheelchair, followed by a shocked and gibbering nurse. Cherlyn wore a pink gown with bunnies on it, but her hair still lay against her head in damp coils and sweat glistened on her forehead. One of the nurses grabbed at her hand to snatch it away from the "Forward" button; Cherlyn half turned in her chair, clawed with three-inch nails at the nurse, and gasped with pain herself. I winced. An hour ago she had been in labor.

"You were going without me! You were going *without* me!"

I saw Brad's state-of-the-art calculation. "Of course we weren't, darling! Cherlyn, honey, you shouldn't be up!"

"You wanted to start without *me*, you bastard!"

The nurse gasped, pressing a tissue to the wicked scratches on her arm. Brad knelt tenderly beside the wheelchair, murmuring endearments. Cherlyn gave him the look of Gorgon for Perseus. She tried to slap him, but winced again when she raised her hand.

Brad shuffled backward to avoid the slap and backed into the knees of a scandalized nurse carrying the baby. "Miss Lincoln! Miss Lincoln! You shouldn't be up!"

"Well, that's what *I* told her," said the first nurse, still holding her arm and glaring at Cherlyn.

The baby nurse tried to squeeze past. Brad reached out and tried to take the baby, a pink-wrapped bundle, from her arms.

"Mr. Felder! You don't have on your surgical mask! This baby is going straight to the high-security nursery!"

"Nuts," Brad said. "This little darling has a press conference to go to."

He reached for the baby with both hands. The nurse held it tighter. Cherlyn reached up from the wheelchair, grimacing with pain and fury. "Give me that baby! I *had* that baby!"

I leaped forward to—what? Add two more hands to the ones pulling the baby? Brad, being the strongest, won. He wrenched the blanketed bundle from the nurse and pushed her hard enough so she staggered back against the corridor wall. Somewhere in the distance I heard a low rumble, like an advancing horde of barbarians.

"Brad!" Cherlyn shrieked. "Give me that baby!" She began to pound at his knees.

Brad hesitated. One nurse huddled, wild-eyed, against the wall. The other, made of sterner stuff, suddenly sprinted down the corridor in the unblocked direction, probably going for help. That seemed to decide him. He turned on his blinding grin and lowered the baby—tenderly, tenderly—into its mother's arms.

"There, Cherlyn, darling—don't fret, you've been through hell, poor darling. Here she is. You have her now, everything's all right, here she is."

Cherlyn clutched the baby, shooting him a look of pure hatred. "You were *going without me!*"

"No, no, never, darling, you misunderstood. God, look at you, look at both of you!" Overcome by the sight of so much maternity, Brad passed his hand in front of his eyes.

Cherlyn glared at him. "That nurse will have doctors here to take her to the nursery in a minute. If we're going to hit the press, let's go!"

"In one second. Just after *Mother* sees the baby. Your first grandchild, Mother—God, I remember how important Grammy was to me growing up! I would have known a real and profound loss if that special grandparent-grandchild bond had ever been interfered with!"

There were tears in his eyes. Until he was six, Grammy had thought his name was Rod.

Brad took my arm and led me over to the wheelchair. At the other end of the corridor, doors were flung open. I saw a long look pass between Cherlyn and Brad, and then I forgot them both because Cherlyn was peeling the pink blanket back from the quiet bundle.

The baby opened her eyes.

I looked at little Angela Dawn and stepped back. The room faded, righted itself. There were people in it: doctors ordering, Cherlyn shouting, Brad. Brad, my son. He was looking at me levelly, for the moment giving me his whole attention, that treasure all children are supposed to want from their parents. Backward, backward. It's always been clear who holds the treasure, who is the thief that risks being torn apart to approach it. Who is the predator that feeds on whose human hearts.

Brad said softly, "Isn't she beautiful?"

"Yes," I said. She was.

He went on, "You wouldn't wreck her future, would you, Mother? You wouldn't let her little life start with her grandmother suing her father?"

I said nothing, but he knew. With a satisfied smile he kissed me and went back to fighting off the doctors who would interfere with his press conference for such a trivial purpose as the baby's health. I slipped away in the other direction, past the elevators, down corridors, till I found an empty waiting room and sat down.

He didn't know. Being Brad, he might not know for a long time. Being Brad, he might never know. But I knew. The second I saw the baby, I *knew*.

The unseen risks, the unseen connections. I started to laugh. Poor Brad—and he might never even really know. And neither would anyone else unless Cherlyn related her dream, which I doubted she could even remember. Probably not even Angela Dawn, beautiful little Angela Dawn, would ever know. Only I. Unless one day, in a fit of grandmotherly affection, I held her firmly from rising up off my lap and told her. I would tell her about the moment I first knew: the moment she opened her beautiful eyes.

They were black, not the blue of most newborns but black: night-black, ancient-black. Silky black curls spiraled over her soft head. Babies are not supposed to see well, but it seemed to me that she saw me, saw us all with those dark fierce predator's eyes fixed on her parents' faces.

Someone rushed into the little room, jabbered at me, and turned on the TV. I didn't stay. I didn't need to see the press conference for this little genetically engineered living marvel. I had seen Angela Dawn's eyes.

I didn't need to see the wings.

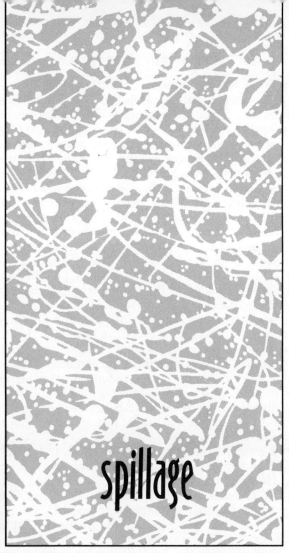

spillage

WHEN THE COACH broke for the third time, the second
coachman was flung sideways over the shrieking axle and down an
embankment. He rolled in the moonless darkness, over and over,
brambles tearing at the velvet of his livery and whipping across his
face. He uttered no sound. There was water at the bottom, a desultory and dirty little stream; the coachman lay in it quietly, blinking
in pain at the stars, blood trickling from one temple.

A rat fell on top of him, squeaked once, and scurried off into
the brush.

From far above, the coachman heard a sudden feminine cry. It was not repeated, but after a while there came to his dazed ears a muffled sound, not quite footsteps, as if someone were dragging along the road above. *The lady in the coach, or the First Coachman himself —* The sound receded and died, and no other took its place.

He lay in the ditch without moving, at first frightened that some bone might have broken in the darkness without, later more frightened by the greater darkness within. No matter how hard he looked, there was nothing there. Not a name, not a place, not a history.

Only the lady in the coach, and the First Coachman: the lady more beautiful than stars, the First Coachman portly and sharp-eyed as he peered back over his shoulder at his apprentice hanging on behind, to make sure he was doing it right. He had been doing it right. He had stood tall and unsmiling on the perch; the jeweled night had flown past the shining sphere of the coach; the horses' hooves had struck sparks from the stone road. They had passed other coaches, each a glow in the darkness growing to an exhilarating rush of beast and metal, and then the thlock-thlock dying away behind, leaving the scent of perfume and oiled leather, with never a word spoken. And finally the destination: leaping from the perch to let down the carriage steps onto cobblestones so polished they reflected perfect rectangles of yellow light from the windows above. Lowered eyes and the lady's hand as she alighted, the rustle of silk glimpsed only at the hem, the small gloved hand briefly in his.

I am a coachman, he thought with relief, and searched for something else in the darkness, something more. There was nothing. He was a coachman, and that was all.

Too frightened to move, he lay in the wet ditch until he began to shiver. Water had soaked from velvet to skin. He sat up slowly, holding his head, and crawled out of the stream and back up the embankment. At first he wasn't sure he had reached the top. Sudden darkness, eclipsing the stars, rolled over him like fog.

He crouched by the road, not knowing where it led to, or from. Neither end reached his memory. Cold, bleeding, frightened, the coachman hunkered down into the long grass. His hand touched something nasty: pulpy and wet. He jerked his fingers away and wiped them on his ruined livery.

When dawn came, he saw that it was a shattered pumpkin, and next to it lay a slipper of glass.

The village lay at one end of the stone road. He reached

it after hours of walking in the direction opposite to the long skid of coach wheels, his belly rumbling and the midsummer sun too bright and hot in his eyes. When he tried to shade them with one hand, the hand stopped five inches from his face.

A bulky woman drawing water from a well looked up and burst into laughter.

"Oh, I'm sorry, I'm sorry, it's just . . . your nose. . . ." She went off again, backing a little away from him, her gray eyes wide with mirthful fear.

The coachman touched the end of his preposterous nose and opened his mouth to say—what?—and found that he was mute. There were words in his head, but none left through his lips.

The woman stopped laughing as jerkily as she had begun. Too carefully, she set the bucket on the lip of the well and walked closer. She was not young. There were lines around her eyes, and heaviness in the solid set of each foot on the earth. In her voice he heard again the fear. It was the sound of the breaking axle, the brambles on the embankment.

"They're careless up there, sometimes, with the . . . with that. It doesn't always go cleanly. Bits and pieces get . . . spilled over."

He stared at her, having no idea what she meant, saying nothing.

I am a coachman.

As if he had spoken aloud, she said with sudden brutality, "Not anymore you aren't. Not here."

Picking up her bucket, she started toward the village. The coachman stared after her dumbly, hands dangling loose at his sides, belly rumbling. She had gone nearly beyond hearing before calling roughly over her shoulder, "You can go to the baker's. Last house on the left. He needs a man for rough work, and he doesn't. . . . You can ask, anyway. Before you fall over."

She walked away. The weight of the water bucket made her broad hips roll. Hair straggled from its topknot in wispy hanks. Her back bent as if from more than the bucket, as if in pain.

The baker hired him at two pence a week, with as many stale rolls as he could eat and a pallet in the kitchen. After staring a full minute at the coachman's nose, and at his inept gesture that was supposed to indicate dumbness, the baker hardly ever glanced at him again. Monthly the bakery sank a little deeper into the compost of debt; monthly the baker himself became more nearly as silent as his wretched hireling.

The coachman worked all day within an arm's reach of the sagging kitchen hearth, where no one saw him and he saw no one. There he mixed, scrubbed, kneaded, swept, hauled, mended, and baked. He didn't mind the hard labor; he scarcely noticed it. There was an embankment in his mind.

Again and again he sped through the jeweled night, behind the gleaming coach and the silken lady. Again and again came the thlock-thlock of the horses, the lady's hand in his as she stepped onto the cobblestones, the rectangles of yellow light—until the embankment loomed and he fell.

At night the hearth grew cold, and the coachman lay in darkness and breathed in the powdery tickle of floating ash. Sometimes he wondered why he had left the slipper of glass; why he had not taken it with him away from the embankment. There was no answer.

At the end of a month, the woman from the well bustled through the baker's kitchen door, stooping under the splintered lintel. She wore a clean apron and carried a pile of brown cloth.

"I brought you a shirt. Velvet doesn't wear at all, does it? This was my late husband's; you're of a size, I think. Try it."

The coachman did, torn between gratitude and irritation. The brown wool felt clean and warm against his arms. When he saw the woman staring at his thin chest, he turned his back to do up the laces.

"Good enough," she said briskly. "Tomorrow I can bring the breeches. You look queer enough with wool above and velvet below." She laughed, an unmusical booming straight from the belly, then abruptly fell silent.

The coachman had no choice but to be silent.

Finally the woman said, "I'm called Meloria."

The flowery name made her ridiculous. The coachman nodded and smiled, pantomiming thanks for the shirt. He could not have told his name even had he known it. Meloria regained her briskness as abruptly as she had lost it, and bustled out the door. Even without a bucket full of water, she waddled.

The coachman thought of the small gloved hand, a slim ankle beneath lifted silk.

He kneaded the bread.

Meloria came the next day with the brown wool breeches, on the day after that with stout boots. A hat to keep off rain. A sour-grape pie, a plaid blanket, a pillow stuffed with pine needles, a yellow cheese.

"You look like you need this," she would boom, and the coach-man, who did need that, would smile weakly and nod two or three times. He was falling off another embankment, or was being pushed. He saw the edge clearly, but not how to avoid it. The shining boots of his livery had fallen apart. The nights had grown colder. When he looked at the sour-grape pie, after weeks of stale rolls, his mouth filled with a savage juice.

After she had gone, he swept the hearth sullenly, not caring that cinders flew up into the air and floated down again, ashy gray snow, on the cooling rolls.

One night he dreamed. After he had lowered the steps to the cobblestones, he turned around to look toward the yellow light. It came from a fortress, windows blazing with candles, gates thrown wide. As he gazed, he felt a touch on his shoulder. It was the lady's hand; she stood behind him, and he could see just the tips of her gloved fingers, delicate as white moths. He turned, her perfume taking him first, to smile on her face.

Moonlight woke him. It fell through the baker's broken window, full on the coachman's face. Blinking into that cold and colorless light, he saw a rat creep along the hearth. Its fur was matted in mangy patches around an open sore. The coachman leapt up and began flailing at it with the poker, murderous despairing blows he did not understand, nor try to. The rat screamed and escaped between damp stones, but not before the poker struck the last third of its tail and smeared it, hairless and pulpy pink, across the floor. The poker clanged and dented.

The coachman sank to his knees and noiselessly wept.

In midwinter the kingdom held a festival. Even in this mean village, under the hunger moon, there were feasts and fires and the pervasive scent of wine mulled with spices.

"Sundown. At Meloria's," the baker growled at noon on the second day of the festival. The coachman, who was breaking the ice on a pail of water and who had all but forgotten what the baker's voice sounded like, looked up in surprise.

"She says," the baker said, and smirked.

The coachman shook his head.

I am a coachman.

The baker smirked again.

Nonetheless, he went. The night was clear and star-sharp, the ashes in the hearth had gone cold, the whole village smelled of cooking, and in Meloria's cottage window shone a yellow light.

"I'm glad you've come," Meloria said, and handed him a cup of steaming wine, red and hot in his bare hands. "Drink to mid-winter's passing!"

He did. They ate, a greedy sating with meat pies, new bread, fruits stewed in wine and honey, gravy and fowl and soup and ripe cheeses and wine, always wine, more wine.

"Drink to midwinter," Meloria said.

While they ate, there was no talk. Juice ran down their chins, rich grease slicked their fingers, succulent skin crackled in their teeth. When they had finished and the table lay stained and bone-strewn as a battlefield, Meloria talked, as the coachman could not.

She spoke slowly, in her plain unmusical voice, of growing up a tenth daughter of twelve girls, of marrying her husband, of their childlessness, of his death. He had been struck by lightning from a blue sky. The coachman half listened, his belly tight as a drum, his mind a slow empty whirling of wine-colored sparkles. Only when she spoke of her childlessness did he rouse a little, at something new in her voice, something splintered that made him frown and look across the table with fuddled eyes.

"Drink to midwinter," Meloria said, and the splintered tone, which had reminded him of something, was gone.

Later—how much later, he didn't know—he woke. It was unac-customed warmth that woke him, as shocking after his hearth and cinders as would have been ice water. Meloria's vast breasts lay against his cheek. Blue lines dribbled across their fatty slackness. He shifted a little, and the breath came to him from her open mouth, heavy and stale with used wine.

His stomach lurched.

He made it out of the bed but not out of the cottage. Vomit spewed onto the hearth, making a paste of cinders. When the rack-ing heaves became too bad, the coachman dropped to his hands and knees, naked on the stone, long nose inches from the floor. Eventually the last of the wine came up, a thin pink trail across the stone.

I am a coachman—

When he could stand, he fetched water, cleaned the hearth, and dressed with trembling fingers. A gray winter dawn had drained all color from the village, and all sound. It was only hours later, well along the road, that he thought it odd that Meloria had not been wakened by his retching, and hours after that before he remembered that she had, and that he had seen in her eyes, staring sightlessly at the roof, that splintered thing: the breaking axle, the brambles on the embankment.

Her dead husband's boots were better than his living ones had been; they kept his feet dry the whole long day.

The fortress stood hard-lined against the gray dusk, spilling no rectangles of light onto the cold cobblestones. But the coachman had no time to ponder this; at almost the moment he trudged in view of the nearest tower, he was seized by two armed soldiers. They dragged him into the fortress. He was taken first before a young captain with close-cropped hair and jawline like an erection, who brought him before. . . .

"A stranger, my prince. Creeping by the edge of the castle road, in cover of the trees. And he will say nothing."

"And of her tracks you found—"

The captain looked at the floor.

"*You found*—"

"Nothing yet, my prince. But this man—"

The prince made a chopping gesture, and the captain was silent. Everyone stood absolutely still except the coachman, who fearfully raised his eyes for a first look at the prince, and the prince himself, who frowned. The coachman dropped his eyes and shuddered.

"Two days."

"Yes, my prince."

"*This* time."

"Yes, my prince."

"I want her found *now*. And if anything has happened to the child. . . ."

"Yes, my prince."

The prince put out one hand in a useless unfinished gesture. The hand was strong and brown, with tiny golden hairs at the wrist and a single square-cut ring carved with a wax seal.

"How does she go? And why?" On the last word his voice splintered, and no one answered.

"Can you talk, man?" the prince said to the coachman, who shook his head.

"Not even sounds?"

The coachman remembered the sounds of his retching, but did nothing.

"Have you come here at anyone else's bidding?"

The captain shifted his weight, not quite impatiently. The prince ignored him. The coachman shook his head.

"Did you see anyone on the road? Anyone or . . . anything? Anything unusual?"

The captain said, "My prince, we don't even know if he lied when he answered the first question. Perhaps he can talk and perhaps he cannot. I can find that out easily enough, if you will but leave him to me. . . ."

The prince raised the coachman's chin with one fist and looked steadily into his eyes, shadowed blue into muddy brown. The coachman stepped back a pace. The inside of his head shouted—*I am a coachman!*—but no words came.

"No," the prince said finally. "Can't you tell by looking that he is harmless? Because if you cannot, Captain, if you must substitute force for sight, you are not as much use to me as if—"

He did not finish. A great commotion moved through the corridor beyond, and a page ran into the room. "She is found! She is found!"

The prince bolted for the door. Before he could reach it, a second captain entered, older than the first, carrying the limp body of a woman. The first captain bit his lip and scowled. The prince took the lady into his own arms and laid her on a low couch. The coachman saw in a daze that she was heavily pregnant, and dressed in rags. Without volition, he glanced at her ankle, bare now, and dirty under the torn skirt.

When she opened her eyes, they were the same clear blue as the prince's. He said gently, and even the coachman saw how the gentleness could not quite cover the anguish, "Another fit."

"Yes," she said, and then in a rush: "I'm sorry, love! I don't remember!"

"Not anything? Not how you left the castle, or why, or . . . or this?" He touched the rags she wore.

"No," the lady said, and in the sound of her voice the coachman lay again in the wet ditch, blackness without, even more within.

The prince held her tighter. "Are you hurt anywhere?"

"No, I . . . no. Just very tired. I was asleep this time, I think, when it came over me."

"And no one saw? Your women, the men-at-arms—"

"No. Please—it wasn't their fault, don't. . . . I don't know how I went past them all, but I know it was not their fault. It was—"

Her voice faltered. The prince murmured against her hair, his face hidden. The younger captain, who had begun to sweat when the prince said, "the men-at-arms," seized the coachman's arm with one hand and the page's with the other and pushed them from the room. The older captain followed, closing the door.

"Where this time?" the younger demanded.

"In the forest. Like before. But she could not have been there more than a few minutes; she would have frozen, in those rags at midwinter."

The other swore. "And *she* will be queen."

The older man pursed his mouth disapprovingly, an odd look for a soldier, and said nothing. The coachman saw again the tightening of the prince's arm around the lady, the trembling of the square-cut ring.

The first captain said, too hastily, "Not that I would speak any word against such a beautiful and virtuous princess!"

The other man merely smiled.

"Well, you two get out!" the first captain shouted. He shoved the page between the child's shoulder blades, and kicked the coachman with his boot. The blow caught the coachman behind the left knee, which buckled. "You heard me—get out or you'll wish you had!"

The page scurried away. The coachman staggered to his feet and took one step before the knee collapsed for a second time. The captain kicked him again.

"Enough," said the older man. "You know he don't like that. Nor she either."

The other looked sullen. The coachman put both palms flat against the wall, bit his tongue, and heaved himself upright. Through a gray haze, he followed the page down the corridor, onto the cobblestones. The early dark of midwinter had fallen; yellow rectangles of light lay on the cobblestones under the cold moon.

Limping along the road, he nearly froze; not moving he surely would have. He had no tinder to make a fire, no coals, no flint. There was moonlight, this time, enough to see, but by the time he came to the place where the shoulder of the road dropped into a steep embankment, he was beyond seeing. He moaned, when the chattering of his teeth and the shivering of his bones let him, and he kept his feet more or less on the road even when he fell into it. But he saw neither the road nor the embankment, bristling with frozen weeds like little spears. He saw darkness, and a rushing jeweled night, and the shining sphere of the coach . . . and something more.

Presently his moaning grew. It became muttering, and the muttering grew to the frozen shapes of deformed words.

"Spilled over. Bits and pieces of magic . . . spilled over. Bits and pieces and pieces . . ."

He fell down, and this time could not rise, although he tried. Once he put out his hand and groped on the icy roadway, his fingers splayed and bent as if he expected to touch something softer, nastier.

"I am a coachman!" he shouted to the thing that was not there. Body and mind gave out; laying his cheek against the frost, he closed his eyes.

The coach, and the exhilarating rush of horses in the jeweled night, and the thlock-thlock dying away behind. But the thlock-thlock grew louder, and a shape catapulted out of the darkness.

"Oh, no, no—"

Meloria dismounted, all but falling off the borrowed ass, and lifted the coachman. He was nearly too heavy for even her strength and mass, but somehow—heaving, pushing, cursing, sweating—she wrestled him across the back of the mangy ass. She rubbed his hands and cheeks; she raged at his stupidity; she pried open his mouth and scalded his throat with hot soup. She wept and cursed and waddled along the road, leading the ass, carrying the coachman away from the embankment steep in the frozen moonlight.

"It was you," the coachman said when he finally woke again in the cottage, under piles of stifling blankets. Then he realized: slowly his fingers went to his lips where the words had appeared, and he looked at Meloria in hatred and fear.

She took a step away from him and studied a crack in the hearth. "I can speak."

She said nothing, watching him from the corner of her eye. "Your doing."

"No."

"Then bits and pieces. Spillage. Like the other. 'When they're careless.' That's what you said."

"Yes," Meloria answered, looking suddenly older, suddenly weary. In the one word the coachman heard again the breaking of the axle, the tearing of the brambles on the embankment.

He turned his head away from her and saw that he lay on the

hearth, as close to the fire as possible. It burned too hot. He yanked the blankets down from his chin; under them, he discovered, he was naked.

Suddenly he shouted, as he had on the road, "I am a coachman!"

"Not before me, you were not."

He jerked his head around so quickly that the bones in his neck snapped. Meloria said it again, in a rougher voice:

"Not before me, you were not. No more than *she* was . . . what she is."

He said, in a perfect rage, "She changes back! Without warning, without help, and then he can't even find her!"

"He always does."

"He—"

"Would she have been better off without me, without any of it, as she was before? Without him or the child? Without even those dangerous bits and pieces. Just because the magic goes away sometimes—would she have been better off without it entirely?"

He was tired. His knee was in pain, and his neck hurt where it had snapped, and a great listlessness came over him, as if the cold had claimed him on the road after all, as if Meloria had not come. He closed his eyes. After a while he could hear Meloria moving around the cottage preparing food, drawing water, clanking a pot down on a table with clumsy, heavy movements.

She drew the blankets back up to his chin.

The coachman opened his eyes and looked up at her. Meloria set her lips hard together. Her chin quivered.

"None of us is that free of spillage. None. Not even . . . such as I."

The coachman nodded. He raised one hand and touched her cheek. It took all the strength he had, without and within, more strength even than not remembering what had hurled after him down the embankment. Then he closed his eyes, exhausted, and slept.

the mountain to mohammed

A person gives money to the physician.
Maybe he will be healed.
Maybe he will not be healed.
　　　　　　　　　　—The Talmud

WHEN THE SECURITY buzzer sounded, Dr. Jesse Randall was playing *go* against his computer. Haruo Kaneko, his roommate at Downstate Medical, had taught him the game. So far nineteen shiny black-and-white stones lay on the grid under the scanner field. Jesse frowned; the computer had a clear shot at surrounding an empty space in two moves, and he couldn't see how to stop it. The buzzer made him jump.

Anne? But she was on duty at the hospital until one. Or maybe he remembered her rotation wrong. . . .

Eagerly he crossed the small living room to the security screen. It wasn't Anne. Three stories below a man stood on the street, staring into the monitor. He was slight and fair, dressed in jeans and frayed jacket with a knit cap pulled low on his head. The bottoms of his ears were red with cold.

"Yes?" Jesse said.

"Dr. Randall?" The voice was low and rough.

"Yes."

"Could you come down here a minute to talk to me?"

"About what?"

"Something that needs talkin' about. It's personal. Mike sent me."

A thrill ran through Jesse. This was it, then. He kept his voice neutral. "I'll be right down."

He turned off the monitor system, removed the memory disk, and carried it into the bedroom, where he passed it several times over a magnet. In a gym bag he packed his medical equipment: antiseptics, antibiotics, sutures, clamps, syringes, electromed scanner, as much equipment as would fit. Once, shoving it all in, he laughed. He dressed in a warm pea coat bought secondhand at the Army-Navy store and put the gun, also bought secondhand, in the coat pocket. Although of course the other man would be carrying. But Jesse liked the feel of it, a slightly heavy drag on his right side. He replaced the disk in the security system and locked the door. The computer was still pretending to consider its move for *go*, although of course it had near-instantaneous decision capacity.

"Where to?"

The slight man didn't answer. He strode purposefully away from the building, and Jesse realized he shouldn't have said anything. He followed the man down the street, carrying the gym bag in his left hand.

Fog had drifted in from the harbor. Boston smelled wet and gray, of rotting piers and dead fish and garbage. Even here, in the Morningside Security Enclave, where that part of the apartment-maintenance fees left over from security went to keep the streets clean. Yellow lights gleamed through the gloom, stacked twelve stories high but crammed close together; even insurables couldn't afford to heat much space.

Where they were going there wouldn't be any heat at all. Jesse followed the slight man down the subway steps. The guy paid for both of them, a piece of quixotic dignity that made Jesse smile. Under the lights he got a better look: the man was older than he'd thought, with webbed lines around the eyes and long thin lips over very bad teeth. Probably hadn't ever had dental coverage in his life. What had been in his genescan? God, what a system.

"What do I call you?" he said as they waited on the platform. He kept his voice low, just in case.

"Kenny."

"All right, Kenny," Jesse said, and smiled. Kenny didn't smile back. Jesse told himself it was ridiculous to feel hurt; this wasn't a social visit. He stared at the tracks until the subway came.

At this hour the only other riders were three hard-looking men, two black and one white, and an even harder-looking Hispanic girl in a low-cut red dress. After a minute Jesse realized she was under the control of one of the black men sitting at the other end of the car. Jesse was careful not to glance at her again. He couldn't help being curious, though. She looked healthy. All four of them looked healthy, as did Kenny, except for his teeth. Maybe none of them were uninsurable; maybe they just couldn't find a job. Or didn't want one. It wasn't his place to judge.

That was the whole point of doing this, wasn't it?

The other two times had gone as easy as Mike said they would. A deltoid suture on a young girl wounded in a knife fight, and burn treatment for a baby scalded by a pot of boiling water knocked off a stove. Both times the families had been so grateful, so respectful. They knew the risk Jesse was taking. After he'd treated the baby and left antibiotics and analgesics on the pathetic excuse for a kitchen counter, a board laid across the nonfunctional radiator, the young Hispanic mother had grabbed his hand and covered it with kisses. Embarrassed, he'd turned to smile at her husband, wanting to say something, wanting to make clear he wasn't just another sporadic do-gooder who happened to have a medical degree.

"I think the system stinks. The insurance companies should never have been allowed to deny health coverage on the basis of genescans for potential disease, and employers should never have been allowed to keep costs down by health-based hiring. If this were a civilized country, we'd have national health care by now!"

The Hispanic had stared back at him, blank-faced.

"Some of us are trying to do better," Jesse said.

It was the same thing Mike—Dr. Michael Cassidy—had said to Jesse and Anne at the end of a long drunken evening celebrating the halfway point in all their residencies. Although, in retrospect, it seemed to Jesse that Mike hadn't drunk very much. Nor had he actually said very much outright. It was all implication, probing masked as casual philosophy. But Anne had understood, and refused instantly. "God, Mike, you could be dismissed from the hospital! The regulations forbid residents from exposing the hospital to the threat of an uninsured malpractice suit. There's no money."

Mike had smiled and twirled his glass between fingers as long as a pianist's. "Doctors are free to treat whomever they wish, at their own risk, even uninsurables. *Carter v. Sunderland.*"

"Not while a hospital is paying their malpractice insurance as residents, if the hospital exercises its right to so forbid. *Janisson v. Lechchevko.*"

Mike laughed easily. "Then forget it, both of you. It's just conversation."

Anne said, "But do you personally risk—"

"It's not right," Jesse cut in—couldn't she see that Mike wouldn't want to incriminate himself on a thing like this?—"that so much of the population can't get insurance. Every year they add more genescan pretendency barriers, and the poor slobs haven't even got the diseases yet!"

His voice had risen. Anne glanced nervously around the bar. Her profile was lovely, a serene curving line that reminded Jesse of those Korean screens in the expensive shops on Commonwealth Avenue. And she had lovely legs, lovely breasts, lovely everything. Maybe, he'd thought, now that they were neighbors in the Morningside Enclave. . . .

"Another round," Mike had answered.

Unlike the father of the burned baby, who never had answered Jesse at all. To cover his slight embarrassment—the mother had been so effusive—Jesse gazed around the cramped apartment. On the wall were photographs in cheap plastic frames of people with masses of black hair, all lying in bed. Jesse had read about this: it was a sort of mute, powerless protest. The subjects had all been photographed on their deathbeds. One of them was a beautiful girl, her eyes closed and her hand flung lightly over her head, as if asleep. The Hispanic followed Jesse's gaze and lowered his eyes.

"Nice," Jesse said. "Good photos. I didn't know you people were so good with a camera."

Still nothing.

Later, it occurred to Jesse that maybe the guy hadn't understood English.

The subway stopped with a long screech of equipment too old, too poorly maintained. There was no money. Boston, like the rest of the country, was broke. For a second Jesse thought the brakes weren't going to catch at all and his heart skipped, but Kenny showed no emotion and so Jesse tried not to, either. The car finally stopped. Kenny rose and Jesse followed him.

They were somewhere in Dorchester. Three men walked quickly toward them, and Jesse's right hand crept toward his pocket. "This him?" one said to Kenny.

"Yeah," Kenny said. "Dr. Randall," and Jesse relaxed.

It made sense, really. Two men walking through this neighborhood probably wasn't a good idea. Five was better. Mike's organization must know what it was doing.

The men walked quickly. The neighborhood was better than Jesse had imagined: small row houses, every third or fourth one with a bit of frozen lawn in the front. A few even had flower boxes. But the windows were all barred, and over all hung the gray fog, the dank cold, the pervasive smell of garbage.

The house they entered had no flower box. The steel front door, triple-locked, opened directly into a living room furnished with a sagging sofa, a TV, and an ancient daybed whose foamcast headboard flaked like dandruff. On the daybed lay a child, her eyes bright with fever.

Sofa, TV, headboard vanished. Jesse felt his professional self take over, a sensation as clean and fresh as plunging into cool water. He knelt by the bed and smiled. The girl, who looked about nine or ten, didn't smile back. She had a long, sallow, sullen face, but the long brown hair on the pillow was beautiful: clean, lustrous, and well-tended.

"It's her belly," said one of the men who had met them at the subway. Jesse glanced up at the note in his voice, and realized that he must be the child's father. The man's hand trembled as he pulled the sheet from the girl's lower body. Her abdomen was swollen and tender.

"How long has she been this way?"

"Since yesterday," Kenny said, when the father didn't answer.

"Nausea? Vomiting?"

"Yeah. She can't keep nothing down."

Jesse's hands palpated gently. The girl screamed.

Appendicitis. He just hoped to hell peritonitis hadn't set in. He didn't want to deal with peritonitis.

"Bring in all the lamps you have, with the brightest watt bulbs. Boil water—" He looked up. The room was very cold. "Does the stove work?"

The father nodded. He looked pale. Jesse smiled and said, "I don't think it's anything we can't cure, with a little luck here." The man didn't answer.

Jesse opened his bag, his mind racing. Laser knife, sterile clamps, scaramine—he could do it even without nursing assistance provided there was no peritonitis. But only if . . . The girl moaned and turned her face away. There were tears in her eyes. Jesse looked at the man with the same long, sallow face and brown hair. "You her father?"

The man nodded.

"I need to see her genescan."

The man clenched both fists at his side. Oh, God, if he didn't *have* the official printout. . . . Sometimes, Jesse had read, uninsurables burned them. One woman, furious at the paper that would forever keep her out of the middle class, had mailed hers, smeared with feces, and packaged with a plasticene explosive, to the President. There had been headlines, columns, petitions . . . and nothing had changed. A country fighting for its very economic survival didn't hesitate to expend frontline troops. If there was no genescan for this child, Jesse couldn't use scaramine, that miracle immune-system booster, to which about 15 percent of the population had a fatal reaction. Without scaramine, under these operating conditions, the chances of postoperation infection were considerably higher. If she couldn't take scaramine. . . .

The father handed Jesse the laminated printout, with the deeply embossed seal in the upper corner. Jesse scanned it quickly. The necessary RB antioncogene on the eleventh chromosome was present. The girl was not potentially allergic to scaramine. Her name was Rosamund.

"Okay, Rose," Jesse said gently. "I'm going to help you. In just a little while you're going to feel so much better. . . ." He slipped the needle with anesthetic into her arm. She jumped and screamed, but within a minute she was out.

Jesse stripped away the bedclothes, despite the cold, and told the men how to boil them. He spread Betadine over her distended abdomen and poised the laser knife to cut.

The hallmark of his parents' life had been caution. *Don't fall, now! Drive carefully! Don't talk to strangers!* Born during the Depression — the other one — they invested only in Treasury bonds and their own one-sixth acre of suburban real estate. When the marching in Selma and Washington had turned to killing in Detroit and Kent State, they shook their heads sagely: *See? We said so. No good comes of getting involved in things that don't concern you.* Jesse's father had held the same job for thirty years; his mother considered it immoral to buy anything not on sale. They waited until she was over forty to have Jesse, their only child.

At sixteen, Jesse had despised them; at twenty-four, pitied them; at twenty-eight, his present age, loved them with a despairing gratitude not completely free of contempt. They had missed so much, dared so little. They lived now in Florida, retired and happy and smug. "The pension" — they called it that, as if it were a famous diamond or a well-loved estate — was inflated by Collapse prices into providing a one-bedroom bungalow with beige carpets and a pool. In the pool's placid, artificially blue waters, the Randalls beheld chlorined visions of triumph. "Even after we retired," Jesse's mother told him proudly, "we didn't have to go backward."

"That's what comes from thrift, Son," his father always added. "And hard work. No reason these deadbeats today couldn't do the same thing."

Jesse looked around their tiny yard at the plastic ducks lined up like headstones, the fanatically trimmed hedge, the blue-and-white striped awning, and his arms made curious beating motions, as if they were lashed to his side. "Nice, Mom. Nice."

"You know it," she said, and winked roguishly. Jesse had looked away before she could see his embarrassment. Boston had loomed large in his mind, compelling and vivid and hectic as an exotic disease.

There was no peritonitis. Jesse sliced free the spoiled bit of tissue that had been Rosamund's appendix. As he closed with quick, sure movements, he heard a click. A camera. He couldn't look away, but out of a sudden rush of euphoria he said to whoever was taking the picture, "Not one for the gallery this time. This one's going to *live.*"

When the incision was closed, Jesse administered a massive dose of scaramine. Carefully he instructed Kenny and the girl's father about the medication, the little girl's diet, the procedures to maintain asepsis that, since they were bound to be inadequate, made the scaramine so necessary. "I'm on duty the next thirty-six hours at the hospital. I'll return Wednesday night, you'll either have to come get me or give me the address, I'll take a taxi and—"

The father drew in a quick, shaky breath like a sob. Jesse turned to him. "She's got a strong fighting chance, this procedure isn't—"

A woman exploded from a back room, shrieking.

"No, no, noooooo . . ." She tried to throw herself on the patient. Jesse lunged for her, but Kenny was quicker. He grabbed her around the waist, pinning her arms to her sides. She fought him, wailing and screaming, as he dragged her back through the door. "Murderer, baby killer, nooooooo—"

"My wife," the father finally said. "She doesn't . . . doesn't understand."

Probably doctors were devils to her, Jesse thought. Gods who denied people the healing they could have offered. Poor bastards. He felt a surge of quiet pride that he could teach them different.

The father went on looking at Rosamund, now sleeping peacefully. Jesse couldn't see the other man's eyes.

Back home at the apartment, he popped open a beer. He felt fine. Was it too late to call Anne? It was—the computer clock said 2:00 A.M. She'd already be sacked out. In seven more hours his own thirty-six-hour rotation started, but he couldn't sleep.

He sat down at the computer. The machine hadn't moved to surround his empty square after all. It must have something else in mind. Smiling, sipping at his beer, Jesse sat down to match wits with the Korean computer in the ancient Japanese game in the waning Boston night.

Two days later, he went back to check on Rosamund. The row house was deserted, boards nailed diagonally across the window. Jesse's heart began to pound. He was afraid to ask information of the neighbors; men in dark clothes kept going in and out of the house next door, their eyes cold. Jesse went back to the hospital and waited. He couldn't think what else to do.

Four rotations later the deputy sheriff waited for him outside the building, unable to pass the security monitors until Jesse came home.

COMMONWEALTH OF MASSACHUSETTS
SUFFOLK COUNTY   SUPERIOR COURT

To __Jesse Robert Randall__ of __Morningside Security__ __Enclave, Building 16, Apartment 3C, Boston__, within our county of Suffolk. Whereas __Steven & Rose Gocek__ of Boston within our County of Suffolk has begun an action of Tort against you returnable in the Superior Court holden at Boston within our County of Suffolk on __October 18, 2004__, in which action damages are claimed in the sum of __$2,000,000__ as follows:

TORT AND/OR CONTRACT FOR MALPRACTICE

as will more fully appear from the declaration to be filed in said Court when and if said action is entered therein:

WE COMMAND YOU, if you intend to make any defense of said action, that on said date or within such further time as the law allows you cause your written appearance to be entered and your written answer or other lawful pleadings to be filed in the office of the Clerk of the Court to which said writ is returnable, and that you defend against said action according to law.

Hereof fail not at your peril, as otherwise said judgment may be entered against you in said action without further notice.

Witness, __Lawrence F. Monastersky, Esquire__, at __Boston__, the __fourth__ day of __November__ in the year of our Lord two thousand __four__.

Alice P. McCarren
Clerk

Jesse looked up from the paper. The deputy sheriff, a soft-bodied man with small light eyes, looked steadily back.

"But what . . . what happened?"

The deputy looked out over Jesse's left shoulder, a gesture meaning he wasn't officially saying what he was saying. "The kid died. The one they say you treated."

"Died? Of what? But I went back. . . ." He stopped, filled with sudden sickening uncertainty about how much he was admitting.

The deputy went on staring over his shoulder. "You want my advice, Doc? Get yourself a lawyer."

Doctor, lawyer, Indian chief, Jesse thought suddenly, inanely. The inanity somehow brought it all home. He was being sued. For malpractice. By an uninsurable. Now. Here. Him, Jesse Randall. Who had been trying only to help.

"Cold for this time of year," the deputy remarked. "They're dying of cold and malnutrition down there, in Roxbury and Dorchester and Southie. Even the goddamn weather can't give us a break."

Jesse couldn't answer. A wind off the harbor fluttered the paper in his hand.

"These are the facts," the lawyer said. He looked tired, a small man in a dusty office lined with secondhand law books. "The hospital purchased malpractice coverage for its staff, including residents. In doing so, it entered into a contract with certain obligations and exclusions for each side. If a specific incident falls under these exclusions, the contract is not in force with regard to that incident. One such exclusion is that residents will not be covered if they treat uninsured persons unless such treatment occurs within the hospital setting or the resident has reasonable grounds to assume that such a person is insured. Those are not the circumstances you described to me."

"No," Jesse said. He had the sensation that the law books were falling off the top shelves, slowly but inexorably, like small green-and-brown glaciers. Outside, he had the same sensation about the tops of buildings.

"Therefore, you are not covered by any malpractice insurance. Another set of facts: over the last five years jury decisions in malpractice cases have averaged 85 percent in favor of plaintiffs. Insurance companies and legislatures are made up of insurables, Dr. Randall. However, juries are still drawn by lot from the general citizenry. Most of the educated general citizenry finds ways to get out of jury duty. They always did. Juries are likely to be 65 percent or more uninsurables. It's the last place the have-nots still wield much real power, and they use it."

"You're saying I'm dead," Jesse said numbly. "They'll find me guilty."

The little lawyer looked pained. "Not 'dead,' Doctor. Convicted—most probably. But conviction isn't death. Not even professional death. The hospital may or may not dismiss you—they have that right—but you can still finish your training elsewhere. And malpractice suits, however they go, are not of themselves grounds for denial of a medical license. You can still be a doctor."

"Treating who?" Jesse cried. He threw up his hands. The books fell slightly faster. "If I'm convicted I'll have to declare bankruptcy—there's no way I could pay a jury settlement like that! And even if I found another residency at some third-rate hospital in Podunk, no decent practitioner would ever accept me as a partner. I'd have to practice alone, without money to set up more than a hole-in-the-corner office among God-knows-who . . . and even that's assuming I can find a hospital that will let me finish. All because I wanted to help people who are getting shit on!"

The lawyer took off his glasses and rubbed the lenses thoughtfully with a tissue. "Maybe," he said, "they're shitting back."

"What?"

"You haven't asked about the specific charges, Doctor."

"Malpractice! The brat died!"

The lawyer said, "Of massive scaramine allergic reaction."

The anger leached out of Jesse. He went very quiet.

"She was allergic to scaramine," the lawyer said. "You failed to ascertain that. A basic medical question."

"I—" The words wouldn't come out. He saw again the laminated genescan chart, the detailed analysis of chromosome eleven. A camera clicking, recording that he was there. The hysterical woman, the mother, exploding from the back room: *noooooooooo* . . . The father standing frozen, his eyes downcast.

It wasn't possible.

Nobody would kill their own child. Not to discredit one of the fortunate ones, the haves, the insurables, the employables . . . No one would do that.

The lawyer was watching him carefully, glasses in hand.

Jesse said, "Dr. Michael Cassidy—" and stopped.

"Dr. Cassidy what?" the lawyer said.

But all Jesse could see, suddenly, was the row of plastic ducks in his parents' Florida yard, lined up as precisely as headstones, garish hideous yellow as they marched undeviatingly wherever it was they were going.

"No," Mike Cassidy said. "I didn't send him."

They stood in the hospital parking lot. Snow blew from the east.

Cassidy wrapped both arms around himself and rocked back and forth. "He didn't come from us."

"He said he did!"

"I know. But he didn't. His group must have heard we were helping illegally, gotten your name from somebody—"

"But why?" Jesse shouted. "Why frame me? Why kill a child just to frame *me*? I'm nothing!"

Cassidy's face spasmed. Jesse saw that his horror at Jesse's position was real, his sympathy genuine, and both useless. There was nothing Cassidy could do.

"I don't know," Cassidy whispered. And then, "Are you going to name me at your malpractice trial?"

Jesse turned away without answering, into the wind.

Chief of Surgery Jonathan Eberhart called him into his office just before Jesse started his rotation. Before, not after. That was enough to tell him everything. He was getting very good at discovering the whole from a single clue.

"Sit down, Doctor," Eberhart said. His voice, normally austere, held unwilling compassion. Jesse heard it, and forced himself not to shudder.

"I'll stand."

"This is very difficult," Eberhart said, "but I think you already see our position. It's not one any of us would have chosen, but it's what we have. This hospital operates at a staggering deficit. Most patients cannot begin to cover the costs of modern technological health care. State and federal governments are both strapped with enormous debt. Without insurance companies and the private philanthropical support of a few rich families, we would not be able to open our doors to anyone at all. If we lose our insurance rating we—"

"I'm out on my ass," Jesse said. "Right?"

Eberhart looked out the window. It was snowing. Once Jesse, driving through Oceanview Security Enclave to pick up a date, had seen Eberhart building a snowman with two small children, probably his grandchildren. Even rolling lopsided globes of cold, Eberhart had had dignity.

"Yes, Doctor. I'm sorry. As I understand it, the facts of your case are not in legal dispute. Your residency here is terminated."

"Thank you," Jesse said, an odd formality suddenly replacing his crudeness. "For everything."

Eberhart neither answered nor turned around. His shoulders,

framed in the gray window, slumped forward. He might, Jesse thought, have had a sudden advanced case of osteoporosis. For which, of course, he would be fully insured.

He packed the computer last, fitting each piece carefully into its original packing. Maybe that would raise the price that Second Thoughts was willing to give him: *Look, almost new, still in the original box.* At the last minute he decided to keep the playing pieces for *go*, shoving them into the suitcase with his clothes and medical equipment. Only this suitcase would go with him.

When the packing was done, he walked up two flights and rang Anne's bell. Her rotation ended a half hour ago. Maybe she wouldn't be asleep yet.

She answered the door in a loose blue robe, toothbrush in hand. "Jesse, hi, I'm afraid I'm really beat—"

He no longer believed in indirection. "Would you have dinner with me tomorrow night?"

"Oh, I'm sorry, I can't," Anne said. She shifted her weight so one bare foot stood on top of the other, a gesture so childish it had to be embarrassment. Her toenails were shiny and smooth.

"After your next rotation?" Jesse said. He didn't smile.

"I don't know when I—"

"The one after that?"

Anne was silent. She looked down at her toothbrush. A thin pristine line of toothpaste snaked over the bristles.

"Okay," Jesse said, without expression. "I just wanted to be sure."

"Jesse—" Anne called after him, but he didn't turn around. He could already tell from her voice that she didn't really have anything more to say. If he had turned it would have been only for the sake of a last look at her toes, polished and shiny as *go* stones, and there really didn't seem to be any point in looking.

He moved into a cheap hotel on Boylston Street, into a room the size of a supply closet with triple locks on the door and bars on the window, where his money would go far. Every morning he took the subway to the Copley Square library, rented a computer cubicle, and wrote letters to hospitals across the country. He also answered classified ads in the *New England Journal of Medicine*, those that offered practice out-of-country where a license was not crucial, or low-paying medical research positions not too many people might want, or supervised assistantships. In the afternoons he walked the grubby streets of Dorchester, looking for Kenny. The lawyer representing Mr. and Mrs. Steven Gocek, parents of the dead Rosamund, would give him no addresses. Neither would his own lawyer, he of the collapsing books and desperate clientele, in whom Jesse had already lost all faith.

He never saw Kenny on the cold streets.

The last week of March, an unseasonable warm wind blew from the south, and kept up. Crocuses and daffodils pushed up between the sagging buildings. Children appeared, chasing each other across the garbage-laden streets, crying raucously. Rejections came from hospitals, employers. Jesse had still not told his parents what had happened. Twice in April he picked up a public phone, and twice he saw again the plastic ducks marching across the artificial lawn, and something inside him slammed shut so hard not even the phone number could escape.

One sunny day in May he walked in the Public Garden. The city still maintained it fairly well; foreign tourist traffic made it profitable. Jesse counted the number of well-dressed foreigners versus the number of ragged street Bostonians. The ratio equaled the survival rate for uninsured diabetics.

"Hey, mister, help me! Please!"

A terrified boy, ten or eleven, grabbed Jesse's hand and pointed. At the bottom of a grassy knoll an elderly man lay crumpled on the ground, his face twisted.

"My grandpa! He just grabbed his chest and fell down! Do something! Please!"

Jesse could smell the boy's fear, a stink like rich loam. He walked over to the old man. Breathing stopped, no pulse, color still pink . . . No.

This man was an uninsured. Like Kenny, like Steven Gocek. Like Rosamund.

"Grandpa!" the child wailed. "Grandpa!"

Jesse knelt. He started mouth-to-mouth. The old man smelled of sweat, of fish, of old flesh. No blood moved through the body. "Breathe, dammit, breathe," Jesse heard someone say, and then realized it was him. "*Breathe,* you old fart, you uninsured deadbeat, you stinking ingrate, breathe—"

The old man breathed.

He sent the boy for more adults. The child took off at a dead run, returning twenty minutes later with uncles, father, cousins, aunts, most of whom spoke some language Jesse couldn't identify. In that twenty minutes none of the well-dressed tourists in the Garden approached Jesse, standing guard beside the old man, who breathed carefully and moaned softly, stretched full-length on the grass. The tourists glanced at him and then away, their faces tightening.

The tribe of family carried the old man away on a homemade stretcher. Jesse put his hand on the arm of one of the young men. "Insurance? Hospital?"

The man spat onto the grass.

Jesse walked beside the stretcher, monitoring the old man until he was in his own bed. He told the child what to do for him, since no one else seemed to understand. Later that day he went back, carrying his medical bag, and gave them the last of his hospital supply of nitroglycerin. The oldest woman, who had been too busy issuing orders about the stretcher to pay Jesse any attention before, stopped dead and jabbered in her own tongue.

"You a doctor?" the child translated. The tip of his ear, Jesse noticed, was missing. Congenital? Accident? Ritual mutilation? The ear had healed clean.

"Yeah," Jesse said. "A doctor."

The old woman chattered some more and disappeared behind a door. Jesse gazed at the walls. There were no deathbed photos. As he was leaving, the woman returned with ten incredibly dirty dollar bills.

"Doctor," she said, her accent harsh, and when she smiled Jesse saw that all her top teeth and most of her bottom ones were missing, the gum swollen with what might have been early signs of scurvy.

"Doctor," she said again.

He moved out of the hotel just as the last of his money ran out. The old man's wife, Androula Malakasses, found him a room in somebody else's rambling dilapidated boardinghouse. The house was noisy at all hours, but the room was clean and large. Androula's cousin brought home an old multipositional dentist chair, probably stolen, and Jesse used that for both examining and operating table. Medical substances—antibiotics, chemotherapy,

IV drugs—which he had thought of as the hardest need to fill outside of controlled channels, turned out to be the easiest. On reflection, he realized this shouldn't have surprised him.

In July he delivered his first breech birth, a primapara whose labor was so long and painful and bloody he thought at one point he'd lose both mother and baby. He lost neither, although the new mother cursed him in Spanish and spit at him. She was too weak for the saliva to go far. Holding the warm-assed, nine-pound baby boy, Jesse had heard a camera click. He cursed too, but feebly; the sharp thrill of pleasure that pierced from throat to bowels was too strong.

In August he lost three patients in a row, all to conditions that would have needed elaborate, costly equipment and procedures: renal failure, aortic aneurysm, narcotic overdose. He went to all three funerals. At each one the family and friends cleared a little space for him, in which he stood surrounded by respect and resentment. When a knife fight broke out at the funeral of the aneurysm, the family hustled Jesse away from the danger, but not so far away that he couldn't treat the loser.

In September a Chinese family, recent immigrants, moved into Androula's sprawling boardinghouse. The woman wept all day. The man roamed Boston, looking for work. There was a grandfather who spoke a little English, having learned it in Peking during the brief period of American industrial expansion into the Pacific Rim before the Chinese government convulsed and the American economy collapsed. The grandfather played go. On evenings when no one wanted Jesse, he sat with Lin Shujen and moved the polished white-and-black stones over the grid, seeking to enclose empty spaces without losing any pieces. Mr. Lin took a long time to consider each move.

In October, a week before Jesse's trial, his mother died. Jesse's father sent him money to fly home for the funeral, the first money Jesse had accepted from his family since he'd finally told them he had left the hospital. After the funeral Jesse sat in the living room of his father's Florida house and listened to the elderly mourners recall their youths in the vanished prosperity of the 1950s and '60s.

"Plenty of jobs then for the people who're willing to work."

"Still plenty of jobs. Just nobody's willing anymore."

"Want everything handed to them. If you ask me, this collapse'll prove to be a good thing in the long run. Weed out the weaklings and the lazy."

"It was the sixties we got off on the wrong track, with Lyndon Johnson and all the welfare programs—"

They didn't look at Jesse. He had no idea what his father had said to them about him.

Back in Boston, stinking under Indian summer heat, people thronged his room. Fractures, cancers, allergies, pregnancies, punctures, deficiencies, imbalances. They were resentful that he'd gone away for five days. He should be here; they needed him. He was a doctor.

The first day of his trial, Jesse saw Kenny standing on the courthouse steps. Kenny wore a cheap blue suit with loafers and white socks. Jesse stood very still, then walked over to the other man. Kenny tensed.

"I'm not going to hit you," Jesse said.

Kenny watched him, chin lowered, slight body balanced on the balls of his feet. A fighter's stance.

"I want to ask something," Jesse said. "It won't affect the trial. I just want to know. Why'd you do it? Why did *they*? I know the little girl's true genescan showed 98 percent risk of leukemia death within three years, but even so—how could you?"

Kenny scrutinized him carefully. Jesse saw that Kenny thought Jesse might be wired. Even before Kenny answered, Jesse knew what he'd hear. "I don't know what you're talking about, man."

"You couldn't get inside the system. Any of you. So you brought me out. If Mohammed won't go to the mountain—"

"You don't make no sense," Kenny said.

"Was it worth it? To you? To them? Was it?"

Kenny walked away, up to the courthouse steps. At the top waited the Goceks, who were suing Jesse for $2 million he didn't have and wasn't insured for, and that they knew damn well they wouldn't collect. On the wall of their house, wherever it was, probably hung Rosamund's deathbed picture, a little girl with a plain sallow face and beautiful hair.

Jesse saw his lawyer trudge up the courthouse steps, carrying his briefcase. Another lawyer, with an equally shabby briefcase, climbed in parallel several feet away. Between the two men the courthouse steps made a white empty space.

Jesse climbed, too, hoping to hell this wouldn't take too long.

He had an infected compound femoral fracture, a birth with potential erythroblastosis fetalis, and an elderly phlebitis, all waiting. He was especially concerned about the infected fracture, which needed careful monitoring because the man's genescan showed a tendency toward weak T-cell production. The guy was a day laborer, foulmouthed and ignorant and brave, with a wife and two kids. He'd broken his leg working illegal construction. Jesse was determined to give him at least a fighting chance.

craps

I shall never believe that God plays dice with the world.
—ALBERT EINSTEIN

Gotta have the game or we'll die of shame.
—NATHAN DETROIT

CHARLIE FOSTER was doing lunch with a client at the Burrowing Fern when he choked on a chunk of broccoli al dente in the Fettuccine Primavera. His throat and chest spasmed painfully, but he nonetheless tried to smile reassuringly at the client, Marv

Spanmann of Spanmann Associates, who thought Charlie was having trouble with a partial bridge and so tactfully excused himself to the men's room. With Marv gone, Charlie batted himself on the chest while swallowing hard. When that didn't work he stood up, knocking over an unoccupied chair, clawing at the air and pointing to his throat. "My God," said someone at the next table, "that man's choking!"

The Heimlich maneuver, even as performed by a massive Swedish bartender, didn't help. However, some air must have been getting through the broccoli because Charlie didn't lose complete consciousness. Someone called an ambulance. Charlie staggered forward, knocking over two more chairs and an order of Chicken Greco. Marv Spanmann returned from the men's room and knelt by Charlie, now gasping on the floor, to say, "Don't worry, Chuck, whatever happens, you've definitely got the account!" Women moaned; a siren screamed.

In the ambulance Charlie kept trying to breathe, huge futile gasps that tossed his body from side to side and sent up waves of garlic from the spilled Chicken Greco. The paramedic was still trying to strap him down when the ambulance collided with a silver Mercedes-Benz at the corner of Broad and Exchange. The impact dislodged the broccoli and sent it flying against the back windshield. Charlie sucked in air.

The paramedic, after making sure that normal color had returned to Charlie's fingernails, jumped out of the back of the ambulance. The driver of the Mercedes stood with his fists raised, shouting at the ambulance driver, who shrugged. The passenger door of the Mercedes was folded on itself like sloppy origami. Its owner, still shouting, reached inside for a winged corkscrew and used it to gouge the hood of the ambulance, right above the grille.

Shaky, Charlie stood up and poked at the piece of broccoli, which lay on the ambulance floor just inside the open back door. The broccoli was slimed with saliva flecked with blood. A small boy in a Pepsi cap peered into the ambulance to see if anyone inside happened to be dead; Charlie glared and the small face disappeared.

Leaving the broccoli, Charlie slowly climbed out of the ambulance in time to see the paramedic lunge at the owner of the Mercedes, trying to take the corkscrew away from him. The ambulance driver circled behind the struggling pair, grabbed the Mercedes owner, and pinned his arms against his body. The paramedic yanked away the corkscrew and immediately began asking witnesses for their names and addresses. The Mercedes owner shouted incoherently. Charlie caught a cab and went home.

"Well, that was certainly a freak accident," Charlie's wife Patti said. She didn't sound especially interested, once she had learned that Charlie was all right. Slim and blonde, with the pale polished look of an opal, Patti nonetheless had a growing reputation in the field of subatomic particle physics. Her degrees were from Stanford, she interned at the Fermi Lab, and her IQ was 163. Over the years of their marriage, which had begun when they were both undergraduates, Charlie had grown unadmittedly afraid of her. They had no children.

"Well, I think it was more than a freak," Charlie said. "These things don't just *happen*." He had no idea what he meant.

Patti looked at him a long moment. Then she put her arms around him, cool arms in a sleeveless summer dress. "You didn't get enough attention for your brush with death . . . poor baby!"

"It doesn't matter," Charlie mumbled, heard himself lying, and added with energy, "It's just that these things don't just happen!"

"Only to you," Patti said, smiled, and let him go to return to her notebooks full of precise mathematical symbols the convoluted shapes of broccoli.

Marv Spanmann kept his word and gave the Spanmann account, a quarterly newsletter plus promotion film and four-color brochure, to Charlie's agency. The job would bill at least $125,000, and Charlie's boss, who had been writing a government manual all week, made several hearty jokes about impressing clients with simulated asphyxiation in trendy yuppie restaurants (SATYR). The junior copywriter, art director, and secretary all laughed. Charlie, however, felt that his own laughter was curiously forced, which embarrassed him. He avoided further discussion of his accident.

Three days later, he decided to walk home from work. Patti was in Chicago at a scientific conference. The city summer was in full, hot, rich swing. Women pushed past in sandals and pastel skirts, carrying shopping bags with bright logos. Store window mannequins held tennis rackets perpetually upraised. The air swelled redolent with potted flowers, street-repair machinery, hot pretzels, and hotter pavement. Jackhammers and rock music mingled with the insistent braking of overcrowded buses. Over it all lay the golden dusty light of late afternoon. Charlie, who twenty years before and for no discernible reason had been an anthropology major, thought confusedly of the vital, brawling cities of ancient Sumeria, and tried to remember where Sumeria was.

At the corner of Main and Clark stood the Cathedral of the Holy Name, a vast dark pile of cool stone. The bushes beneath the cathedral windows hadn't been pruned; they straggled over the sills and up the massive walls. Charlie shaded his eyes and leaned back his head to see the place where the top of the cathedral spire pierced the sky. A brick dislodged from the architrave below the spire and fell straight toward him.

The brick seemed to fall too fast for him to dodge, yet slow enough for him to think, "Well—now this is it." But it wasn't. A huge pigeon flew from behind Charlie, crashed into the falling brick, and died instantly. Brick and pigeon deflected from their previous trajectories. The brick missed Charlie by three inches, shattering on the pavement into subbricks that bounded and ricocheted, although not off him. The pigeon hit the sidewalk in a bloody splat and lay there looking at Charlie from black eyes. Fine red brick settled over his shoes.

Charlie lowered himself to sit in the middle of the sidewalk. A woman rushed up to him to ask if he were hurt. A bearded young man carrying a Walkman sprinted up the cathedral steps and began to pound on the wooden door, demanding someone in authority. A man pressed upon Charlie a business card, which said: MARTIN CASSIDY—ATTORNEY AT LAW—LITIGATION SPECIALIST. Charlie put the card in his vest pocket and looked up at the woman. She had a plain middle-aged face furrowed with concern.

He said simply, "That was divine intervention."

Immediately the concern left the woman's face. Her eyes, chin, mouth, and eyebrows all wavered into suspicion: of his sanity, of her own involvement. Charlie saw the change and tried to laugh. The laugh was shaky, but he fortified it with a humorous self-mocking shrug that he often used to good effect with clients who had come up through the manufacturing ranks and so suspected ad agencies of superciliousness. The woman seemed reassured. She helped Charlie to his feet. He looked once more at the cathedral, the particles of brick, the dark unfathomable eyes of the dead pigeon, and over him went a shudder that he did not understand but that, in some way he also did not understand, pleased the part of him that had wondered about Sumeria.

"Books?" Patti said.

"Books," Charlie said. They stood at their kitchen counter, Patti chewing on a strip of leftover take-out sushi, regarding the pile of library books. She wrinkled her nose.

"They smell as if nobody has ever checked them out before."

"The pages on this one aren't even cut," Charlie said. His voice was pleased. He touched the top book on the pile. Thomas Aquinas, Duns Scotus, Francisco Sanchez, Nicolas Malebranche, George Berkeley. Patti sighed.

"Are you really going to read all this philosophy?"

"I certainly am!"

"Why?"

"I need to."

" 'Need to'? Charlie, a good well-written detective novel has more to offer."

"More what?" Charlie said. She didn't answer right away, and Charlie felt a sudden, secret flush of confidence that let him say, "There's a strangeness underlying the universe, Patti. We don't pay enough attention to it!"

Patti stopped chewing. Old resentment rose in her eyes. She said quietly, "I do. I pay attention to what underlies the universe every day of my working life. It's you that's never paid much attention, no matter how important I said it was to me."

"I don't mean subatomic particles," Charlie said, more impatiently than he intended. Something about the way she looked had begun to scare him again.

"That's what there is."

"No," Charlie said. Patti put down her sushi and turned away. Charlie felt a sudden flood of anger, of tenderness, of manic scorn. She didn't understand. She thought the whole world could be verified by equations, reduced to electrons and neutrinos. She thought . . . she only thought. She hadn't choked on a piece of broccoli and been rescued by an ambulance crash, she hadn't been caught in the improbability of a falling brick and witnessed the greater improbability of a dead pigeon, she hadn't glimpsed the underlying strange . . . whatever the hell it was.

"Just remember," Patti said suddenly, viciously, "you work in *advertising*."

Charlie gaped at her. Even Patti seemed abashed by the spiteful energy of this attack. She put on her most remote and polished expression, the one with which she addressed scientific colloquies, and stared at him. Charlie felt a tingling up and down his spine; in some way he didn't understand, he had won. He was free of the rein of her scientific judiciousness; she had freed him herself, by the petty nastiness of her words. No one for whom the probabilities of the world had bent — *twice* — could be touched by something so small. What had happened to him was too powerful, too rich, too important.

He smiled at her with pity.

The books, however, were a disaster. In Berkeley's *Treatise Concerning the Principles of Human Knowledge,* Charlie read:

> It may perhaps be objected, that if extension and figure exist only in the mind, it follows that mind is extended and figured; since extension is a mode or attribute, which is predicated of the subject in which it exists. I answer, those qualities are in the mind only as they are perceived by it, that is, not by way of *mode* or *attribute,* but only by way of *idea.* . . .

Charlie read this twice, three times. He read it after a shower to refresh his mind. He read it after a good night's sleep; after a gin-and-tonic; after a brisk walk. After he had read it for the eleventh time, on a Wednesday evening, Charlie packed up all the books and walked them back to the library.

He slid Berkeley and Duns Scotus into the afterhours book dump with the same sense of rich freedom with which he had faced Patti. The books didn't know. Dry words, intellectual gymnastics, earnest and desperate superiority of just exactly the same type as the broccoli-shaped symbols in Patti's notebook. Just exactly. He was already beyond that. He *knew.* Charlie closed the metal flap on the book dump and began to whistle Beethoven. The night was cold, the sky sullen; Charlie didn't notice. He walked home in his T-shirt, gooseflesh, and Beethoven's Fifth. When a Buick coming around the corner at Canal Street, right after a movie let out, missed him by five inches, he stopped and stared at it with eyes wider than those of the terrified teenage girl driving without the permission of either her father or the state of New York.

"Did I hurt you? Oh, God, did I hurt you?"

Charlie grinned at her. He couldn't stop grinning. She was the most beautiful thing he had ever seen in his life, long blonde hair and tender skin, black leather jacket and obscene T-shirt. "You didn't hurt me."

"Are you sure? I didn't even see you! I just came around the corner and — if you're okay?"

"I'm fine," Charlie said. "I'm wonderful. I'm glad it happened."

The girl stared at him. Her friend in the car, less spectacular except for four pairs of rhinestone earrings dangling from her ears, rolled down the window to listen.

Charlie kept on grinning. "But this was only normal, you know. Not a sign. Only normal."

The girl got back into the car and released the hand brake. Charlie wanted to yell "Thank you," knew he had already said more than enough, knew that the girl had smelled whiskey on his breath, knew she had misunderstood utterly. It didn't matter. He settled for waving after the moving Buick.

"Guy is fucking crazy," the girl muttered, and laid rubber the length of Canal Street.

In the morning, sober, he thought that he had probably behaved like a fool. He was probably thinking like a fool. Brushing his teeth, knotting his tie, he told himself his thinking was bizarre: he was having temporal-lobe electrical spasms, was having a midlife crisis, was having stress manifestations, was having all the pop-psych clichés he could drag up from airport paperback racks and "Phil Donahue." None of it touched him. The feeling of exultation from the night before, of freedom and strangeness in the world, would not leave him. He smiled at people in the lobby at work; he tore into the script of the employee training film for Fullman Foods; he answered eight phone messages and evaded no calls.

"Someone's in a good mood," the secretary said.

Charlie laughed. "Do you believe in chance, Carol?"

"Of course. I buy a lottery ticket every Tuesday."

Charlie laughed again. A lottery ticket! He leaned close to Carol's face, thick with powder and eye shadow, and said, "I'll tell you a secret. *God does play dice with the world.*"

"What?"

"God does play dice with the world. The rules aren't locked in. Everyday reality is only one side of it. Anything could happen, anything at all."

Carol frowned. "You mean, like, I could end up rich?"

"You could end up the queen of Sumeria! All you have to do is *see* it! There is something making its own decisions out there after all, something as real as this fucking desk!"

Her mouth pursed. "I don't really appreciate that sort of language, Mr. Foster."

"Oh, Carol," he said gently. She watched him, frowning, all the way into his office. When he came out two hours later, after having accomplished more work than in any two hours of his life, she watched him again. He walked into the elevator with his boss and the art director. As soon as the elevator door closed, there was a grinding screech. The elevator plummeted six floors to the basement. Both the art director and Charlie's boss were killed. Charlie staggered out of the elevator without a scratch.

Three elevator-company engineers said his survival was a million-to-one interaction of vectors. Two insurance-company doctors said it was an unprecedented medical precedent. Charlie sat in the hospital emergency room after he had been checked over by the incredulous staff, waiting for the dead men's wives and parents to arrive to claim the bodies, and stared at the wall without blinking once.

Patti was patient. She sat close to him on a gurney against one wall of the emergency room, held his hand, and rubbed her thumb in slow circles on his palm. "Listen, Charlie, it happens. They died, darling, and you didn't. We all feel guilty when that happens, there's even a name for it: 'survivors' guilt.' Please don't do this to yourself. . . ."

"You don't understand," Charlie said. "It's all right. I don't feel guilty."

"No?"

"No. I feel ready."

Patti stopped moving her thumb. "Ready for what?"

"I don't know yet."

"Charlie . . ."

"It wouldn't be for nothing. Not after all this trouble. The broccoli, the brick the elevator . . . not for nothing."

"Charlie—"

"I can wait. Now that there's something to wait for. Rolling dice don't have rules, but they have outcomes."

Patti caught her breath. She peered at Charlie, but he caught her at it and smiled, a smile so lucid and tender she was confused all over again. The wife of the dead art director stumbled into the emergency room, her eyes enormous and her face streaked with tears. Charlie walked over to meet her, gait steady and arms outstretched, while Patti sat biting her lip at the edge of the cot from which her husband had just arisen.

In the next few months, Charlie became the mainstay of the agency, and the wonder of the city's advertising grapevine. He took on his boss's work and his own, handling both so efficiently that in October he was made a partner. Every Sunday he and Patti took the widow of the art director and her two small children on an outing: for a walk in a park, to the beach, to a children's matinee of *Aladdin and the Magic Lamp.* The genie rose up to grant Aladdin three wishes, and the younger child burst into terrified tears. Charlie consoled him with a Mars Bar he had thought to bring in his vest pocket, and Patti looked admiringly at his prescience.

People began to comment on Charlie's steadiness, his gentleness, how well he had come through the accident. He took up squash, lost fifteen pounds, and began beating men ten years younger on the court. He was a gracious winner, a better loser.

In November he and Patti celebrated their wedding anniversary in Palermo, where she was giving a paper on muon trajectories. Charlie attended her presentation and was grave and interested. At the reception afterward her colleagues found themselves impressed with her husband, despite his occupation. He avoided so effortlessly all the embarrassments of superfluous spouses at learned gatherings: he neither competed, nor sulked, nor faded into corners. While Patti accepted her congratulations—it was an important paper—he held her hand and smiled. Afterward, he discussed the road system in Sicily with neither condescension nor nervous humor.

"He is a nice man, your husband," Patti was told by a French scientist with whom she had once contemplated an affair, "but he looks always as if he is waiting for something, *n'est-ce pas?* Do you know what it is?"

Patti froze. But she watched Charlie, and he seemed to her happier than ever before, and since she was happy, too, she forgot about it. When the conference ended, they went to Paris. They visited Sainte-Chapelle, gorged themselves at patisseries, bought secondhand prints along the Seine, and made love every night.

In March Patti discovered she was pregnant. She and Charlie held long conversations about commitment and career choices and biological clocks, and decided to have the baby. "You'll make a good father," she told Charlie. "You really will."

The baby was due in December. Patti and Charlie bought a house in a suburb with a good school system, closed in September, and moved. All October, when even the downtown streets swirled with gold-and-yellow leaves, Charlie worked on the house. He pruned arborvitae, sealed the driveway, cleaned the gutters. He grew quieter, but not enough for Patti, absorbed in both pregnancy and pions, to notice.

She was driving home from her lab when one of the sudden electrical storms common to upstate October hit hard. Leaves blew in great rainy gusts against the windshield and were dragged across it by the wipers. Thunder crashed, at first a full minute behind the lightning, but the lag shortened rapidly and then the storm was directly overhead, cacophony and strobe. Saplings seemed bent nearly double by the sheer pressure of sound. Patti drove slowly, turning into her driveway with relief. Jagged cloud-to-ground lightning exploded to her right. She decided to stay in the car until the center of the storm passed.

Through the water streaming across the windshield she saw Charlie open the side door of the house. He walked bent forward against the wind, with the slow portentousness of a man moving underwater. He wore jeans, a red sweatshirt, and canvas loafers. It seemed to take a long time for him to cross the yard, heading toward the only large tree on the Fosters' new property, a forty-foot sycamore whose branches flailed around the trunk like knotted scourges.

Patti put her hand on the inside door handle. Charlie tipped his head back so far it seemed he must lose his balance and slowly put his hand on the trunk of the tree. Lightning flared, followed a nearly imperceptible moment later by thunder, as if the storm had moved on. Charlie lowered his head, and even through the rain Patti could see his eyes, brimming with light. Then a second bolt of lightning seared the sky, the trunk of the sycamore sliced down the center to within fifteen feet of the ground, and Charlie tore through air already rent by deafening sound.

Charlie lay bandaged on his hospital bed. Gauze filmed him like veils. Every time she looked at him, Patti shook with a fury the depth of which scared her so much that her words came out in reasonable calm, as if this were a discussion about library books, about broccoli, about survivor guilt from an elevator crash. Charlie answered with the same tone. To a passing nurse, they might have been discussing tax reform.

"Why, Charlie?"

"I can't explain. I'm sorry."

"You're sorry? For God's sake, Charlie . . . *try*."

He said nothing. Huge dark splotches ringed his eyes, as if he had been in a fistfight. It occurred to Patti that had she passed him on the street like this, she might not have recognized him.

"Charlie . . . I'm scared. The doctor says you're lucky to be alive. At all. I need to understand. Charlie?"

"I thought . . . I wouldn't even care about the pain, the burns, if only. . . ."

"If only what?"

"Lightning hits trees like that all the time. Just like that. In that same way. Seventy-five-thousand forest fires a year start with lightning."

Patti took a deep breath. She laid both hands across her burgeoning stomach, but her voice kept its relentless calm. "Charlie, we've been happy, the last year or so, haven't we? Haven't we been happy?"

"Happier than I've ever been in my life."

"And was it because . . . was it all because of *that*? Because you thought the laws of probability were suspended around you? Because you survived a freak choking and a freak projectile and a freak fall? Because you believed that until now there was some sort of stupid supernatural crapshoot going on and you were the favored player?"

Charlie watched her from his bruised eyes.

"No," Patti went on slowly, "not because you were winning. That's not what turned you on. It was just because you were in the game. Just because you thought there *was* a game. You wouldn't have minded getting maimed by that lightning if it had only left hieroglyphics burned into the sycamore. If it had only spoken to you from a goddamn burning bush. You'd risk . . . you'd have Lem and Ed die in an elevator as long as there was some sign that there was . . . you'd actually rather. . . ."

"No," Charlie said. But his voice was very soft.

Patti looked at him, stood up, and smoothed her maternity jumper free of wrinkles: a fussy gesture, totally unlike her. Never had she looked less like a scientist; never had Charlie been more afraid of her. She groped for her purse where it hung over the back of the stiff hospital chair, fumbled the strap onto her shoulder, and walked out.

Charlie turned his face toward the blank wall.

Three nights later, the burn floor of the east wing of the hospital caught fire. Alarms screamed; the sprinkler system turned on. Charlie awoke to find gentle rain falling on his face. He lay quietly, listening to the running footsteps and shouting voices up and down the corridor beyond his door. The smell of smoke, acrid and tantalizing as a volcano, drifted toward him. He crawled painfully out of bed.

The other two beds in the room were empty; it was a slow week for burns. Charlie groped toward the door, stopping to lean heavily on a utilitarian dresser painted the hideous pink of flayed skin. The fire seemed to be at the far end of the corridor, from which smoke roiled in lazy coils. The temperature rose several degrees within the few steps from his room into the hall.

A stout nurse, jaw clenched in fright, said quietly between her teeth, "Come on, Mr. Foster. This way out. Come on, now." She fastened a hand on Charlie's elbow, just below the loose sleeve of his hospital gown.

Charlie shook off the hand and lurched away from her, toward the elevator. She said sharply, "Elevators are inactive during fires, Mr. Foster, you have to—" The rest drowned in more alarms. The lights went out.

The red EXIT sign still glowed. Charlie stumbled toward the stairs. An orderly carrying an elderly woman so wrapped in bandages that only her bony ancient arm hung free reached the door first and opened it with his foot.

Charlie pushed past them, ignoring the orderly's "Hey!" In the stairwell the lights had not gone out. He lurched down two flights of stairs, followed first by the orderly, then by the stout nurse leading two more bandaged figures, and finally by two men bumping what sounded like a gurney down the metal stairs. Intermittently alarms shrieked, stopped, started again. Between mechanical shrieks Charlie heard the men with the gurney cursing methodically. Each time the door opened above, more smoke drifted into the stairwell.

At the second-floor landing, the fire door burst open and Charlie was engulfed by young women, none of whom looked sick, although they all wore hospital gowns. They jostled against his bandaged burns and he cried out, the sound lost in the din. Borne along in the painful crush of luscious bodies, Charlie reached the first-floor landing and staggered out into the cool night. Away from the building, he collapsed onto a patch of grass ornamented with marigolds in a ring of rocks like a very clean campfire. Sirens screamed as they whipped around the corner to the other side of the building. Someone bent over him, yelled, "This one's okay," and vanished. Charlie wound his hand around a clump of marigolds and held on. He began to tremble.

When the trembling stopped, he raised his head to look at the hospital. It looked solid and intact, each floor except the east-wing third dotted with soft lights from veiled windows. Charlie started to cry.

"Hey," said a young voice beside him. "Don't. It's all right. A fire guy said they got everybody out in time." She put a hand on Charlie's burned arm. He yelled and she jerked back, her pretty uncreased face filled with concern. When she leaned over Charlie, her hair fell in her eyes and her hospital gown slipped off one shoulder. She looked about fifteen.

"Everybody . . . out?" Charlie gasped. It hurt to talk.

"Yeah."

"Not me," Charlie said. The marigolds tore under his hand.

The girl peered at him. "What d'ya mean?"

"I didn't even look. At the fire. I just ran. I didn't even *look*."

The girl inched away from him across the grass. Charlie grabbed her retreating knee. "Was it a normal fire? Was it?"

"A what?"

"A normal fire? Or was there something strange about it, something improbable? Anything at all? Try to remember!"

The girl stopped inching and removed Charlie's hand from her knee. Lips pursed, she scanned his bandaged body, wild eyes, clump of strangled marigolds. Charlie saw that, incredibly, she was chewing gum.

He said eagerly, "Do you always chew gum? Is it that? Do you always chew gum during fires?"

"Do I always—you're whacko, man, you know that?"

Charlie clutched at her. "But do you? *Do* you?"

"Put your hand on my knee again and I'll belt you. An old feeble burned guy like you!"

Charlie groaned. The sound apparently moved the girl from virtue to pity; she sighed and pulled her flannel gown back up on her shoulder. "Look, I don't know if I always chew gum in fires or not. I never *been* in no fires before. I just chew gum since I got pregnant because I stopped smoking, you know? It's bad for kids."

"Pregnant? You're pregnant?"

The girl made a face; suddenly she looked much older. A

floodlight threw abrupt glare onto the hospital. Someone behind the curve of light shouted orders. Charlie saw that the girl's eyes were the same fresh blue as her robe, and her hair a soft brown. In the harsh light there was a firm purity to the line of her jaw.

He choked out, "Did the baby have a . . . bodily father?"

"Ain't no other way to do it, is there?"

"But I need some way to *know!*"

"Know what, for chrissake?"

"*Know,*" Charlie said, but it came out in a whisper.

The girl sighed. "Well, don't freak over it—it was just a guy named Darryl. I met him in a laundromat. Look, man, you need help. Stay here, I'll get somebody."

She wandered off. Charlie lay still, staring at the hospital. The normal paraphernalia of fire fighting came and went: trucks, ladders, streams of water flung into the night.

"All under control," said a male voice somewhere in the darkness to his left. "Everybody out. Fire contained. We should all get goddamn medals."

Someone else laughed. "Just your nice normal textbook fire."

"But is there a *game!*" Charlie cried.

The girl wandered back and sat down. "You okay? I can't find anybody for you, they're all busy with patients. But nobody's hurt. Damn, look at that, I broke a nail." She bent over her hand, then raised blue eyes to Charlie. "It's a wonder nails last at all. I tell you, it's a fucking miracle."

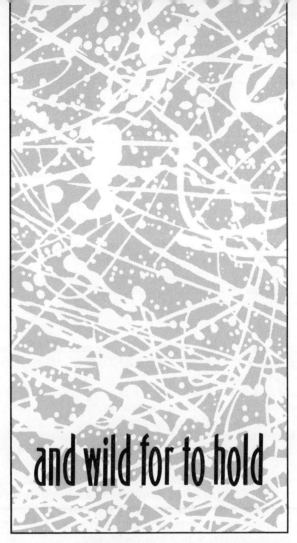

and wild for to hold

THE DEMON CAME to her first in the long gallery at Hever Castle. She had gone there to watch Henry ride away, magnificent on his huge charger, the horse's legs barely visible through the summer dust raised by the king's entourage. But Henry himself was visible. He rose in his stirrups to half-turn his gaze back to the manor house, searching its sun-glazed windows to see if she watched. The spurned lover, riding off, watching over his shoulder the effect he himself made. She knew just how his eyes would look, small blue eyes under the curling red-gold hair. Mournful. Shrewd.

Undeterred.

Anne Boleyn was not moved. Let him ride. She had not wanted him at Hever in the first place.

As she turned from the gallery window a glint of light in the far corner caught her eye, and there for the first time was the demon.

It was made all of light, which did not surprise her. Was not Satan himself called Lucifer? The light was square, a perfectly square box such as no light had ever been before. Anne crossed herself and stepped forward. The box of light brightened, then winked out.

Anne stood perfectly still. She was not afraid; very little made her afraid. But nonetheless she crossed herself again and uttered a prayer. It would be unfortunate if a demon took residence at Hever. Demons could be dangerous.

Like kings.

Lambert half turned from her console toward Culhane, working across the room. "Culhane—they said she was a witch."

"Yes? So?" Culhane said. "In the 1500s they said any powerful woman was a witch."

"No, it was more. They said it before she became powerful." Culhane didn't answer. After a moment Lambert said quietly, "The Rahvoli equations keep flagging her."

Culhane grew very still. Finally he said, "Let me see."

He crossed the bare small room to Lambert's console. She steadied the picture on the central square. At the moment the console appeared in this location as a series of interlocking squares mounting from floor to ceiling. Some of the squares were solid real-time alloys; some were holosimulations; some were not there at all, neither in space nor in time, although they appeared to be. The Project Focus Square, which *was* there, said:

TIME RESCUE PROJECT
UNITED FEDERATION OF UPPER SLIB, EARTH
FOCUS: ANNE BOLEYN
    HEVER CASTLE, KENT, ENGLAND, EUROPE
      1525:645:89:3
CHURCH OF THE HOLY HOSTAGE TEMPORARY PERMIT
#4592

In the time-jump square was framed a young girl, dark hair just

visible below her coif, her hand arrested at her long slender neck in the act of signing the cross.

Lambert said, as if to herself, "She considered herself a good Catholic."

Culhane stared at the image. His head had been freshly shaved, in honor of his promotion to Project Head. He wore, Lambert thought, his new importance as if it were a fragile implant, liable to be rejected. She found that touching.

Lambert said, "The Rahvoli probability is .798. She's a definite key."

Culhane sucked in his cheeks. The dye on them had barely dried. He said, "So is the other. I think we should talk to Brill."

The servingwomen had finally left. The priests had left, the doctors, the courtiers, the nurses, taking with them the baby. Even Henry had left, gone . . . where? To play cards with Harry Norris? To his latest mistress? Never mind—at last they had all left her alone.

A girl.

Anne rolled over in her bed and pounded her fists on the pillow. A girl. Not a prince, not the son that England needed, that *she* needed . . . a girl. And Henry growing colder every day, she could feel it, he no longer desired her, no longer loved her. He would bed with her—oh, that, most certainly, if it would get him his boy, but her power was going. Was gone. That power she had hated, despised, but had used nonetheless because it was there and Henry should feel it, as he had made her feel his power over and over again . . . her power was going. She was Queen of England but her power was slipping away like the Thames at ebb tide, and she just as helpless to stop it as to stop the tide itself. The only thing that could have preserved her power was a son. And she had borne a girl. Strong, lusty, with Henry's own red curling hair . . . but a girl.

Anne rolled over on her back, painfully. Elizabeth was already a month old but everything in Anne hurt. She had contracted white leg, so much less dreaded than childbed fever but still weakening, and for the whole month had not left her bedchamber. Servants and ladies and musicians came and went, while Anne lay feverish, trying to plan. . . . Henry had as yet made no move. He had even seemed to take the baby's sex well: "She seems a lusty wench. I pray God will send her a brother in the same good shape." But Anne knew. She always knew. She had known when Henry's eye first fell upon her. Had known to a shade the exact intensity of his longing during the nine years she had kept him waiting: nine years of celibacy, of denial. She had known the exact moment when that hard mind behind the small blue eyes had decided: *It is worth it. I will divorce Catherine and make her queen.* Anne had known before he did when he decided it had all been a mistake. The price for making her queen had been too high. She was not worth it. Unless she gave him a son.

And if she did not. . . .

In the darkness Anne squeezed her eyes shut. This was but an attack of childbed vapors, it signified nothing. She was never afraid, not she. This was only a night terror, and when she opened her eyes it would pass, because it must. She must go on fighting, must get herself heavy with son, must safeguard her crown. And her daughter. There was no one else to do it for her, and there was no way out.

When she opened her eyes a demon, shaped like a square of light, glowed in the corner of the curtained bedchamber.

Lambert dipped her head respectfully as the High Priest passed.

She was tall, and wore no external augments. Eyes, arms, ears, shaved head, legs under the gray-green ceremonial robe — all were her own, as required by the charter of the Church of the Holy Hostage. Lambert had heard a rumor that before her election to High Priest she had had brilliant violet augmented eyes and gamma-strength arms, but on her election had had both removed and the originals restored. The free representative of all the hostages in the solar system could not walk around enjoying high-maintenance augments. Hostages could, of course, but the person in charge of their spiritual and material welfare must appear human to any hostage she chose to visit. A four-handed Spacer held in a free-fall chamber on Mars must find the High Priest as human as did a genetically altered flyer of Ipsu being held hostage by the New Trien Republic. The only way to do that was to forego external augments.

Internals, of course, were a different thing.

Beside the High Priest walked the Director of the Time Research Institute, Toshio Brill. No ban on externals for *him*: Brill wore gold-plated sensors in his shaved black head, a display Lambert found slightly ostentatious. Also puzzling: Brill was not ordinarily a flamboyant man. Perhaps he was differentiating himself from Her

Holiness. Behind Brill his Project Heads, including Culhane, stood silent, not speaking unless spoken to. Culhane looked nervous: he was ambitious, Lambert knew. She sometimes wondered why she was not.

"So far I am impressed," the High Priest said. "Impeccable hostage conditions on the material side."

Brill murmured, "Of course, the spiritual is difficult. The three hostages are so different from each other, and even for culture specialists and historians . . . the hostages arrive here very upset."

"As would you or I," the High Priest said, not smiling, "in similar circumstances."

"Yes, Your Holiness."

"And now you wish to add a fourth hostage, from a fourth time stream."

"Yes."

The High Priest looked slowly around at the main console; Lambert noticed that she looked right past the time-jump square itself. Not trained in peripheral vision techniques. But she looked a long time at the stasis square. They all did; outsiders were unduly fascinated by the idea that the whole building existed between time streams. Or maybe Her Holiness merely objected to the fact that the Time Research Institute, like some larger but hardly richer institutions, was exempt from the all-world taxation that supported the Church. Real estate outside time was also outside taxation.

The High Priest said, "I cannot give permission for such a political disruption without understanding fully every possible detail. Tell me again."

Lambert hid a grin. The High Priest did not need to hear it again. She knew the whole argument, had pored over it for days, most likely, with her advisers. And she would agree; why wouldn't she? It could only add to her power. Brill knew that. He was being asked to explain only to show that the High Priest could force him to do it, again and again, until she — not he — decided the explanation was sufficient and the Church of the Holy Hostage issued a permanent hostage permit to hold one Anne Boleyn, of England Time Delta, for the altruistic purpose of preventing a demonstrable Class One war.

Brill showed no outward recognition that he was being humbled. "Your Holiness, this woman is a fulcrum. The Rahvoli equations, developed in the last century by—"

"I know the Rahvoli equations," the High Priest said. And smiled sweetly.

"Then Your Holiness knows that any person identified by the equations as a fulcrum is directly responsible for the course of history. Even if he or she seems powerless in local time. Mistress Boleyn was the second wife of Henry VIII of England. In order to marry her, he divorced his first wife, Catherine of Aragon, and in order to do that, he took all of England out of the Catholic Church. Protestantism was—"

"And what again was that?" Her Holiness said, and even Culhane glanced sideways at Lambert, appalled. The High Priest was playing. With a *Research Director*. Lambert hid her smile. Did Culhane know that high seriousness opened one to the charge of pomposity? Probably not.

"Protestantism was another branch of 'Christianity,'" the director said patiently. So far, by refusing to be provoked, he was winning. "It was warlike, as was Catholicism. In 1642 various branches of Protestantism were contending for political power within England, as was a Catholic faction. King Charles was Catholic, in fact. Contention led to civil war. Thousands of people died fighting, starved to death, were hanged as traitors, were tortured as betrayers. . . ."

Lambert saw Her Holiness wince. She must hear this all the time, Lambert thought, what else was her office for? Yet the wince looked genuine.

Brill pressed his point. "Children were reduced to eating rats to survive. In Cornwall, rebels' hands and feet were cut off, gibbets were erected in market squares and men hanged on them alive and—"

"Enough," the High Priest said. "This is why the Church exists. To promote the Holy Hostages that prevent war."

"And that is what we wish to do," Brill said swiftly, "in other time streams, now that our own has been brought to peace. In Stream Delta, which has only reached the sixteenth century—Your Holiness knows that each stream progresses at a different relative rate—"

The High Priest made a gesture of impatience.

"—the woman Anne Boleyn is the fulcrum. If she can be taken hostage after the birth of her daughter Elizabeth, who will act throughout a very long reign to preserve peace, and before Henry declares the Act of Supremacy that opens the door to religious divisiveness in England, we can prevent great loss of life. The Rahvoli equations show a 79.8 percent probability that history will be changed in the direction of greater peace, right up through the following two centuries. Religious wars often—"

"There are other, bloodier religious wars to prevent than the English civil war."

"True, Your Holiness," the director said humbly. At least it looked like humility to Lambert. "But ours is a young science. Identifying other time streams, focusing on one, identifying historical fulcra—it is such a new science. We do what we can, in the name of Peace."

Everyone in the room looked pious. Lambert kept her face blank. In the name of Peace—and of prestigious scientific research, attended by rich financial support and richer academic reputations.

"And it is Peace we seek," Brill pressed, "as much as the Church itself does. With a permanent permit to take Anne Boleyn hostage, we can save countless lives in this other time stream, just as the Church preserves peace in our own."

The High Priest played with the sleeve of her robe. Lambert could not see her face. But when she looked up, she was smiling.

"I'll recommend to the All-World Forum that your hostage permit be granted, Director. I will return in two months to make an official check on the Holy Hostage."

Brill, Lambert saw, didn't quite stop himself in time from frowning. "Two months? But with the entire solar system of hostages to supervise—"

"Two months, Director," Her Holiness said. "The week before the All-World Forum convenes to vote on revenue and taxation."

"I—"

"Now I would like to inspect the three Holy Hostages you already hold for the altruistic prevention of war."

Later, Culhane said to Lambert, "He did not explain it very well. It could have been made so much more urgent . . . it *is* urgent. Those bodies rotting in Cornwall . . ." He shuddered.

Lambert looked at him. "You care. You genuinely do."

He looked back at her, in astonishment. "And you don't? You must, to work on this project!"

"I care," Lambert said. "But not like that."

"Like what?"

She tried to clarify it for him, for herself. "The bodies rotting . . . I see them. But it's not our own history—"

"What does that matter? They're still human!"

He was so earnest. Intensity burned on him like skin tinglers. Did Culhane even use skin tinglers, Lambert wondered? Fellow researchers spoke of him as an ascetic, giving all his energy, all his time, to the project. A woman in his domicile had told Lambert he even lived chaste, doing a Voluntary Celibacy Mission for the entire length of his research grant. Lambert had never met anyone who actually did that. It was intriguing.

She said, "Are you thinking of the priesthood once the project is over, Culhane?"

He flushed. Color mounted from the dyed cheeks, light blue since he had been promoted to Project Head, to pink on the fine skin of his shaved temples.

"I'm thinking of it."

"And doing a Celibacy Mission now?"

"Yes. Why?" His tone was belligerent: a Celibacy Mission was slightly old-fashioned. Lambert studied his body: tall, well-made, strong. Augments? Muscular, maybe. He had beautiful muscles.

"No reason," she said, bending back to her console until she heard him walk away.

The demon advanced. Anne, lying feeble on her curtained bed, tried to call out. But her voice would not come, and who would hear her anyway? The bedclothes were thick, muffling sound; her ladies would all have retired for the night, alone or otherwise; the guards would be drinking the ale Henry had provided all of London to celebrate Elizabeth's christening. And Henry . . . he was not beside her. She had failed him of his son.

"Be gone," she said weakly to the demon. It moved closer.

They had called her a witch. Because of her little sixth finger, because of the dog named Urian, because she had kept Henry under her spell so long without bedding him. But if I were really a witch, she thought, I could send this demon away. More: I could hold Henry, could keep him from watching that whey-faced Jane Seymour, could keep him in my bed. . . . She was not a witch.

Therefore, it followed that there was nothing she could do about this demon. If it was come for her, it was come. If Satan Master of Lies was decided to have her, to punish her for taking the husband of another woman, and for . . . how much could demons know?

"This was all none of my wishing," she said aloud to the demon. "I wanted to marry someone else." The demon continued to advance.

Very well, then, let it take her. She would not scream. She never had—she prided herself on it. Not when they had told her she could not marry Harry Percy. Not when she had been sent home from the Court, peremptorily and without explanation. Not when she had discovered the explanation: Henry wished to have her out of London so he could bed his latest mistress away from Catherine's eyes. She had not screamed when a crowd of whores had burst into the palace where she was supping, demanding Nan Bullen, who they said was one of them. She had escaped across the Thames in a barge, and not a cry had escaped her lips. They had admired her for her courage: Wyatt, Norris, Weston, Henry himself. She would not scream now.

The box of light grew larger as it approached. She had just time to say to it, "I have been God's faithful and true servant, and my husband the king's," before it was upon her.

"The place where a war starts," Lambert said to the faces assembled below her in the Hall of Time, "is long before the first missile, or the first bullet, or the first spear."

She looked down at the faces. It was part of her responsibilities as an intern researcher to teach a class of young, some of whom would become historians. The class was always taught in the Hall of Time. The expense was enormous: keeping the Hall in stasis for nearly an hour, bringing the students in through the force field, activating all the squares at once. Her lecture would be replayed for them later, when they could pay attention to it: Lambert did not blame them for barely glancing at her now. Why should they? The walls of the circular room, which were only there in a virtual sense, were lined with squares, which were not really there at all. The squares showed actual local-time scenes from wars that had been there, were there now, somewhere, in someone's reality.

Men died writhing in the mud, arrows through intestines and necks and groins, at Agincourt.

Women lay flung across the bloody bodies of their children at Cawnpore.

In the hot sun the flies crawled thick upon the split faces of the heroes of Marathon.

Figures staggered, their faces burned off, away from Hiroshima.

Breathing bodies, their perfect faces untouched and their brains turned to mush by spekaline, sat in orderly rows under the ripped dome on Io-One.

Only one face turned toward Lambert, jerked as if on a string,

a boy with wide violet eyes brimming with anguish. Lambert oblig-
ingly began again.

"The place where a war starts is long before the first missile,
or the first bullet, or the first spear. There are always many forces
causing a war: economic, political, religious, cultural. Nonetheless,
it is the great historical discovery of our time that if you trace each
of these back—through the records, through the eyewitness accounts, through the entire burden of data only Rahvoli equations
can handle—you come to a fulcrum. A single event or act or person. It is like a decision tree with a thousand thousand generations
of decisions: somewhere there was one first yes/no. The place
where the war started, and where it could have been prevented.

"The great surprise of time-rescue work has been how often that
place was female.

"Men fought wars, when there were wars. Men controlled the
gold and the weapons and the tariffs and sea rights and religions
that have caused wars, and the men controlled the bodies of other
men that did the actual fighting. But men are men. They acted
at the fulcrum of history, but often what tipped their actions one
way or another was what they loved. A woman. A child. She became
the passive, powerless weight he chose to lift, and the balance
tipped. She, not he, is the branching place, where the decision tree
splits and the war begins."

The boy with the violet eyes was still watching her. Lambert
stayed silent until he turned to watch the squares—which was the
reason he had been brought here. Then she watched him. Anguished, passionate, able to feel what war meant—he might be a
good candidate for the time-rescue team, when his preliminary
studies were done. He reminded her a little of Culhane.

Who right now, as Project Head, was interviewing the new
hostage, not lecturing to children.

Lambert stifled her jealousy. It was unworthy. And shortsighted:
she remembered what this glimpse of human misery had meant
to her three years ago, when she was a historian candidate. She
had had nightmares for weeks. She had thought the event was
pivotal to her life, a dividing point past which she would never be
the same person again. How could she? She had been shown the
depths to which humanity, without the Church of the Holy Hostage
and the All-World Concordance, could descend. Burning eye
sockets, mutilated genitals, a general who stood on a hill and said,
"How I love to see the arms and legs fly!" It had been shattering.

She had been shattered, as the Orientation intended she should be.

The boy with the violet eyes was crying. Lambert wanted to step down from the platform and go to him. She wanted to put her arms around him and hold his head against her shoulder . . . but was that because of compassion, or was that because of his violet eyes?

She said silently to him, without leaving the podium, *You will be all right. Human beings are not as mutable as you think. When this is over, nothing permanent about you will have changed at all.*

Anne opened her eyes. Satan leaned over her.

His head was shaved, and he wore strange garb of an ugly blue-green. His cheeks were stained with dye. In one ear metal glittered and swung. Anne crossed herself.

"Hello," Satan said, and the voice was not human.

She struggled to sit up; if this be damnation, she would not lie prone for it. Her heart hammered in her throat. But the act of sitting brought the Prince of Darkness into focus, and her eyes widened. He looked like a man. Painted, made ugly, hung around with metal boxes that could be tools of evil — but a man.

"My name is Culhane."

A man. And she had faced men. Bishops, nobles, Chancellor Wolsey. She had outfaced Henry, Prince of England and France, Defender of the Faith.

"Don't be frightened, Mistress Boleyn. I will explain to you where you are and how you came to be here."

She saw now that the voice came not from his mouth, although his mouth moved, but from the box hung around his neck. How could that be? Was there then a demon in the box? But then she realized something else, something real to hold on to.

"Do not call me Mistress Boleyn. Address me as Your Grace. I am the queen."

The something that moved behind his eyes convinced her, finally, that he was a mortal man. She was used to reading men's eyes. But why should this one look at her like that — with pity? With admiration?

She struggled to stand, rising off the low pallet. It was carved of good English oak. The room was paneled in dark wood and hung with tapestries of embroidered wool. Small-paned windows shed brilliant light over carved chairs, table, chest. On the table rested a writing desk and a lute. Reassured, Anne pushed down the heavy cloth of her night shift and rose.

The man, seated on a low stool, rose too. He was taller than Henry — she had never seen a man taller than Henry — superbly muscled. A soldier? Fright fluttered again, and she put her hand to her throat. This man, watching her — watching her *throat*. Was he then an executioner? Was she under arrest, drugged and brought by some secret method into the Tower of London? Had someone brought evidence against her — or was Henry that disappointed that she had not borne a son that he was eager already to supplant her?

As steadily as she could, Anne walked to the window.

The Tower bridge did not lay beyond in the sunshine. Nor the river, nor the gabled roofs of Greenwich Palace. Instead there was a sort of yard, with huge beasts of metal growling softly. On the grass naked young men and women jumped up and down, waving their arms, running in place and smiling and sweating as if they did not know either that they were uncovered or crazed.

Anne took firm hold of the windowsill. It was slippery in her hands and she saw that it was not wood at all, but some material made to resemble wood. She closed her eyes, then opened them. She was a queen. She had fought hard to become a queen, defending a virtue nobody believed she still had, against a man who claimed that to destroy that virtue was love. She had won, making the crown the price of her virtue. She had conquered a king, brought down a Chancellor of England, outfaced a pope. She would not show fear to this executioner in this place of the damned, whatever it was.

She turned from the window, her head high. "Please begin your explanation, Master. . . ."

"Culhane."

"Master Culhane. We are eager to hear what you have to say. And we do not like waiting."

She swept aside her long nightdress as if it were Court dress and seated herself in the not-wooden chair carved like a throne.

"I am a hostage," Anne repeated. "In a time that has not yet happened."

From beside the window, Lambert watched. She was fascinated. Anne Boleyn had, according to Culhane's report, listened in silence to the entire explanation of the time rescue, that explanation so carefully drafted and revised a dozen times to fit what the sixteenth-century mind could understand of the twenty-second. Queen Anne had not become hysterical. She had not cried, nor fainted, nor professed disbelief. She had asked no questions. When Culhane had finished, she had requested, calmly and with staggering dignity, to see the ruler of this place, with his ministers. Toshio Brill, watching on monitor because the wisdom was that at first new hostages would find it easier to deal with one consistent researcher, had hastily summoned Lambert and two others. They had all dressed in the floor-length robes used for grand academic ceremonies and never else. And they had marched solemnly into the ersatz sixteenth-century room, bowing their heads.

Only their heads. No curtsies. Anne Boleyn was going to learn that no one curtsied anymore.

Covertly Lambert studied her, their fourth time hostage, so different from the other three. She had not risen from her chair, but even seated she was astonishingly tiny. Thin, delicate bones, great dark eyes, masses of silky black hair loose on her white nightdress. She was not pretty by the standards of this century; she had not even been counted pretty by the standards of her own. But she was compelling. Lambert had to give her that.

"And I am prisoner here," Anne Boleyn said. Lambert turned up her translator; the words were just familiar, but the accent so strange she could not catch them without electronic help.

"Not prisoner," the director said. "Hostage."

"Lord Brill, if I cannot leave, then I am a prisoner. Let us not mince words. I cannot leave this castle?"

"You cannot."

"Please address me as 'Your Grace.' Is there to be a ransom?"

"No, Your Grace. But because of your presence here thousands of men will live who would have otherwise died."

With a shock, Lambert saw Anne shrug; the deaths of thousands of men evidently did not interest her. It was true, then. They really were moral barbarians, even the women. The students should see this. That small shrug said more than all the battles viewed in squares. Lambert felt her sympathy for the abducted woman lessen, a physical sensation like the emptying of a bladder, and was relieved to feel it. It meant she, Lambert, still had her own moral sense.

"How long must I stay here?"

"For life, Your Grace," Brill said bluntly.

Anne made no reaction; her control was awing.

"And how long will that be, Lord Brill?"

"No person knows the length of his or her life, Your Grace."

"But if you can read the future, as you claim, you must know what the length of mine would have been."

Lambert thought: We must not underestimate her. This hostage is not like the last one.

Brill said, with the same bluntness that honored Anne's comprehension—did she realize that?—"If we had not brought you here, you would have died May 19, 1536."

"How?"

"It does not matter. You are no longer part of that future, and so now events there will—"

"*How?*"

Brill didn't answer.

Anne Boleyn rose and walked to the window, absurdly small, Lambert thought, in the trailing nightdress. Over her shoulder she said, "Is this castle in England?"

"No," Brill said. Lambert saw him exchange glances with Culhane.

"In France?"

"It is not in any place on the Earth," Brill said, "although it can be entered from three places on Earth. It is outside of time."

She could not possibly have understood, but she said nothing, only went on staring out the window. Over her shoulder Lambert saw the exercise court, empty now, and the antimatter power generators. Two technicians crawled over them with a robot monitor. What did Anne Boleyn make of them?

"God knows if I had merited death," Anne said. Lambert saw Culhane start.

Brill stepped forward. "Your Grace—"

"Leave me now," she said, without turning.

They did. Of course she would be monitored constantly—everything from brain scans to the output of her bowels. Although she would never know this. But if suicide was in that life-defying mind, it would not be possible. If Her Holiness ever learned of the suicide of a time hostage. . . . Lambert's last glimpse before the door closed was of Anne Boleyn's back, still by the window, straight as a spear as she gazed out at antimatter power generators in a building in permanent stasis.

"Culhane, meeting in ten minutes," Brill said. Lambert guessed the time lapse was to let the director change into working clothes. Toshio Brill had come away from the interview with Anne Boleyn somehow diminished. He even looked shorter, although shouldn't her small stature have instead augmented his?

Culhane stood still in the corridor outside Anne's locked room (would she try the door?). His face was turned away from Lambert's. She said, "Culhane . . . you jumped a moment in there. When she said God alone knew if she had merited death."

"It was what she said at her trial," Culhane said. "When the verdict was announced. Almost the exact words."

He still had not moved so much as a muscle of that magnificent body. Lambert said, probing, "You found her impressive, then. Despite her scrawniness, and beyond the undeniable pathos of her situation."

He looked at her then, his eyes blazing: Culhane, the research engine. "I found her magnificent."

She never smiled. That was one of the things she knew they remarked upon among themselves: she had overheard them in the walled garden. Anne Boleyn never smiles. Alone, they did not call her Queen Anne, or Her Grace, or even the Marquis of Rochford, the title Henry had conferred upon her, the only female peeress in her own right in all of England. No, they called her Anne Boleyn, as if the marriage to Henry had never happened, as if she had never borne Elizabeth. And they said she never smiled.

What cause was there to smile, in this place that was neither life nor death?

Anne stitched deftly at a piece of amber velvet. She was not badly treated. They had given her a servant, cloth to make dresses —she had always been clever with a needle, and the skill had not deserted her when she could afford to order any dresses she chose. They had given her books, the writing Latin but the pictures curiously flat, with no raised ink or painting. They let her go into any unlocked room in the castle, out to the gardens, into the yards. She was a Holy Hostage.

When the amber velvet gown was finished, she put it on. They let her have a mirror. A lute. Writing paper and quills. Whatever she asked for, as generous as Henry had been in the early days of his passion, when he had divided her from her love Harry Percy, and had kept her loving hostage to his own fancy.

Cages came in many sizes. Many shapes. And, if what Master Culhane and the Lady Mary Lambert said was true, in many times.

"I am not a lady," Lady Lambert had protested. She needn't have bothered. Of course she was not a lady—she was a commoner, like the others, and so perverted was this place that the woman sounded insulted to be called a lady. Lambert did not like her, Anne knew, although she had not yet found out why. The woman was unsexed, like all of them, working on her books and machines all day, exercising naked with men, who thus no more looked at their bodies than they would those of fellow soldiers in the roughest camp. So it pleased Anne to call Lambert a lady when she did not want to be one, as Anne was now so many things she had never wanted to be. "Anne Boleyn." Who never smiled.

"I will create you a lady," she said to Lambert. "I confer on you the rank of baroness. Who will gainsay me? I am the queen, and in this place there is no king."

And Mary Lambert had stared at her with the unsexed bad manners of a common drab.

Anne knotted her thread and cut it with silver scissors. The gown was finished. She slipped it over her head and struggled with the buttons in the back, rather than call the stupid girl who was her servant. The girl could not even dress hair. Anne smoothed her hair herself, then looked critically at her reflection in the fine mirror they had brought her.

For a woman a month and a half from childbed, she looked strong. They had put medicines in her food, they said. Her complexion, that creamy dark skin that seldom varied in color, was well set off by the amber velvet. She had often worn amber, or tawny. Her hair, loose, since she had no headdress and did not know how to make one, streamed over her shoulders. Her hands, long and slim despite the tiny extra finger, carried a rose brought to her by Master Culhane. She toyed with the rose, to show off the beautiful hands, and lifted her head high.

She was going to have an audience with Her Holiness, a female pope. And she had a request to make.

"She will ask, Your Holiness, to be told the future. Her future, the one Anne Boleyn experienced in our own time stream, after the point we took her hostage from hers. And the future of England." Brill's face had darkened; Lambert could see that he hated this. To forewarn his political rival that a hostage would complain about her treatment. A *hostage*, that person turned sacred object through the sacrifice of personal freedom to global peace. When Tullio Amaden Koyushi had been hostage from Mars Three to the Republic of China, he had told the Church official in charge of his case that he was not being allowed sufficient exercise. The resulting intersystem furor had lost the Republic of China two trade contracts, both important. There was no other way to maintain the necessary reverence for the hostage political system. The Church of the Holy Hostage was powerful because it must be, if the solar system was to stay at peace. Brill knew that.

So did Her Holiness.

She wore full state robes today, gorgeous with hundreds of tiny mirrors sent to her by the grateful across all worlds. Her head was newly shaved. Perfect synthetic jewels glittered in her ears. Listening to Brill's apology-in-advance, Her Holiness smiled. Lambert saw the smile, and even across the room she felt Brill's polite, concealed frustration.

"Then if this is so," Her Holiness said, "why cannot Lady Anne Boleyn be told her future? Hers and England's?"

Lambert knew that the High Priest already knew the answer. She wanted to make Brill say it.

Brill said, "It is not thought wise, Your Holiness. If you remember, we did that once before."

"Ah, yes, your last hostage. I will see her, too, of course, on this visit. Has Queen Helen's condition improved?"

"No," Brill said shortly.

"And no therapeutic brain drugs or electronic treatments have helped? She still is insane from the shock of finding herself with us?"

"Nothing has helped."

"You understand how reluctant I was to let you proceed with another time rescue at all," Her Holiness said, and even Lambert stifled a gasp. The High Priest did not make those determinations; only the All-World Forum could authorize or disallow a hostage-taking—across space *or* time. The Church of the Holy Hostage was responsible only for the inspection and continuation of permits granted by the Forum. For the High Priest to claim political power she did not possess—

The director's eyes gleamed angrily. But before he could reply, the door opened and Culhane escorted in Anne Boleyn.

Lambert pressed her lips together tightly. The woman had sewn herself a gown, a sweeping ridiculous confection of amber velvet so tight at the breasts and waist she must hardly be able to breathe. How had women conducted their lives in such trappings? The dress narrowed her waist to nearly nothing; above the square neckline her collarbones were delicate as a bird's. Culhane hovered beside her, huge and protective. Anne walked straight to the High Priest, knelt, and raised her face.

She was looking for a ring to kiss.

Lambert didn't bother to hide her smile. A High Priest wore no jewelry except earrings, ever. The pompous little hostage had made a social error, no doubt significant in her own time.

Anne smiled up at Her Holiness, the first time anyone had seen her smile at all. It changed her face, lighting it with mischief, lending luster to the great dark eyes. A phrase came to Lambert, penned by the poet Thomas Wyatt to describe his cousin Anne: *And wild for to hold, though I seem tame.*

Anne said, in that sprightly yet aloof manner that Lambert was coming to associate with her, "It seems, Your Holiness, that we have reached for what is not there. But the lack is ours, not yours, and we hope it will not be repeated in the request we come to make of you."

Direct. Graceful, even through the translator and despite the ludicrous imperial plural. Lambert glanced at Culhane, who was gazing down at Anne as at a rare and fragile flower. How could he? That skinny body, without muscle tone let alone augments, that plain face, the mole on her neck . . . This was not the sixteenth century. Culhane was a fool.

As Thomas Wyatt had been. And Sir Harry Percy. And Henry, King of England. All caught not by beauty but by that strange elusive charm.

Her Holiness laughed. "Stand up, Your Grace. We don't kneel to officials here." *Your Grace.* The High Priest always addressed hostages by the honorifics of their own state, but in this case it could only impede Anne's adjustment.

And what do I care about her adjustment? Lambert jeered at herself. *Nothing. What I care about is Culhane's infatuation, and only because he rejected me first.* Rejection, it seemed, was a great whetter of appetite—in any century.

Anne rose. Her Holiness said, "I'm going to ask you some questions, Your Grace. You are free to answer any way you wish. My function is to ensure that you are well treated, and that the noble science of the prevention of war, which has made you a Holy Hostage, is also well served. Do you understand?"

"We do."

"Have you received everything you need for your material comfort?"

"Yes," Anne said.

"Have you received everything you've requested for your mental comfort? Books, objects of any description, company?"

"No," Anne said. Lambert saw Brill stiffen.

Her Holiness said, "No?"

"It is necessary for the comfort of our mind—and for our material comfort as well—to understand our situation as fully as possible. Any rational creature requires such understanding to reach ease of mind."

Brill said, "You have been told everything related to your situation. What you ask is to know about situations that now, because. you are here, will never happen."

"Situations that *have* happened, Lord Brill, else no one could know of them. You could not."

"In *your* time stream they will not happen," Brill said. Lambert could hear the suppressed anger in his voice, and wondered if the High Priest could. Anne Boleyn couldn't know how serious it was to be charged by Her Holiness with a breach of hostage treatment. If Brill was ambitious—and why wouldn't he be?—such charges could hurt his future.

Anne said swiftly, "Our time is now your time. *You* have made it so. The situation was none of our choosing. And if your time is now ours, then surely we are entitled to the knowledge that accompanies our time." She looked at the High Priest. "For the comfort of our mind."

Brill said, "Your Holiness—"

"No, Queen Anne is correct. Her argument is valid. You will designate a qualified researcher to answer any questions she has—any at all—about the life she might have had, or the course of events England took when the queen did not become a sacred hostage."

Brill nodded stiffly.

"Good-bye, Your Grace," Her Holiness said. "I shall return in two weeks to inspect your situation again."

Two weeks? The High Priest was not due for another inspection for six months. Lambert glanced at Culhane to see his reaction to this blatant political fault-hunting, but he was gazing at the floor, to which Anne Boleyn had sunk in another of her embarrassing curtsies, the amber velvet of her skirts spread around her like gold.

They sent a commoner to explain her life to her, the life she had lost. A commoner. And he had as well the nerve to be besotted with her. Anne always knew. She tolerated such fellows, like that upstart musician Smeaton, when they were useful to her. If this Master Culhane dared to make any sort of declaration, he would receive the same sort of snub Smeaton once had. Inferior persons should not look to be spoken to as noblemen.

He sat on a straight-backed chair in her Tower room, looking humble enough, while Anne sat in the great carved chair with her hands tightly folded to keep them from shaking.

"Tell me how I came to die in 1536." God's blood! Had ever before there been such a sentence uttered?

Culhane said, "You were beheaded. Found guilty of treason." He stopped, and flushed.

She knew, then. In a queen, there was one cause for a charge of treason. "He charged me with adultery. To remove me, so he could marry again."

"Yes."

"To Jane Seymour."

"Yes."

"Had I first given him a son?"

"No," Culhane said.

"Did Jane Seymour give him a son?"

"Yes, Edward VI. But he died at sixteen, a few years after Henry."

There was vindication in that, but not enough to stem the sick feeling in her gut. Treason. And no son . . . There must have been more than desire for the Seymour bitch. Henry must have hated her. Adultery . . .

"With whom?"

Again the oaf flushed. "With five men, Your Grace. Everyone knew the charges were false, created merely to excuse his own adultery—even your enemies admitted such."

"Who were they?"

"Sir Henry Norris. Sir Francis Weston. William Brereton. Mark Smeaton. And . . . and your brother George."

For a moment she thought she would be sick. Each name fell like a blow, and the last like the ax itself. George. Her beloved brother, so talented at music, so high-spirited and witty . . . Henry Norris, the king's friend. Weston and Brereton, young and light-hearted but always, to her, respectful and careful . . . and Mark Smeaton, the oaf made courtier because he could play the virginals.

The long beautiful hands clutched the sides of the chair. But the moment passed, and she could say with dignity, "They denied the charges?"

"Smeaton confessed, but he was tortured into it. The others

denied the charges completely. Henry Norris offered to defend your honor in single combat."

Yes, that was like Harry: so old-fashioned, so principled. She said, "They all died." It was not a question: if she had died for treason, they would have, too. And not alone; no one died alone. "Who else?"

Culhane said, "Maybe we should wait for the rest of this, Your—"

"Who else? My father?"

"No. Sir Thomas More, John Fisher—"

"More? For my . . ." She could not say *adultery*.

"Because he would not swear to the Oath of Supremacy, which made the king and not the pope head of the Church in England. That act opened the door to religious dissension in England."

"It did not. The heretics were already strong in England. History cannot fault that to me!"

"Not as strong as they would become," Culhane said, almost apologetically. "Queen Mary was known as Bloody Mary for burning heretics who used the Act of Supremacy to break from Rome— Your Grace! Are you all right . . . Anne!"

"Do not touch me," she said. Queen Mary. Then her own daughter Elizabeth had been disinherited, or killed. . . . Had Henry become so warped that he would kill a child? His own child? Unless he had come to believe. . . .

She whispered, "Elizabeth?"

Comprehension flooded his eyes. "Oh, no, Anne! No! Mary ruled first, as the elder, but when she died heirless, Elizabeth was only twenty-five. Elizabeth became the greatest ruler England had ever known! She ruled for forty-four years, and under her England became a great power."

The greatest ruler. Her baby Elizabeth. Anne could feel her hands unknotting on the ugly artificial chair. Henry had not repudiated Elizabeth, nor had her killed. She had become the greatest ruler England had ever known.

Culhane said, "This is why we thought it best not to tell you all this."

She said coldly, "I will be the judge of that."

"I'm sorry." He sat stiffly, hands dangling awkwardly between his knees. He looked like a plowman, like that oaf Smeaton. . . . She remembered what Henry had done, and rage returned.

"I stood accused. With five men . . . with George. And the

charges were false." Something in his face changed. Anne faced him steadily. "Unless . . . were they false, Master Culhane? You who know so much of history—does history say—" She could not finish. To beg for history's judgment from a man like this . . . no humiliation had ever been greater. Not even the Spanish ambassador, referring to her as "the Concubine," had ever humiliated her so.

Culhane said carefully, "History is silent on the subject, Your Grace. What your conduct was . . . would have been . . . is known only to you."

"As it should be. It was . . . would have been . . . mine," she said viciously, mocking his tones perfectly. He looked at her like a wounded puppy, like that lout Smeaton when she had snubbed him. "Tell me this, Master Culhane. You have changed history as it would have been, you tell me. Will my daughter Elizabeth still become the greatest ruler England has ever seen—in *my* 'time stream'? Or will that be altered, too, by your quest for peace at any cost?"

"We don't know. I explained to you. . . . We can only watch your time stream now as it unfolds. It had only reached October, 1533, which is why after analyzing our own history we—"

"You have explained all that. It will be sixty years from now before you know if my daughter will still be great. Or if you have changed that as well by abducting me and ruining my life."

"Abducting! You were going to be killed! Accused, beheaded—"

"And you have prevented that." She rose, in a greater fury than ever she had been with Henry, with Wolsey, with anyone. "You have also robbed me of my remaining three years as surely as Henry would have robbed me of my old age. And you have mayhap robbed my daughter as well, as Henry sought to do with his Seymour-get prince. So what is the difference between you, Master Culhane, that you are a saint and Henry a villain? He held me in the Tower until my soul could be commended to God; you hold me here in this castle you say I can never leave where time does not exist, and mayhap God neither. Who has done me the worse injury? Henry gave me the crown. You—all you and my Lord Brill have given me is a living death, and then given my daughter's crown a danger and uncertainty that without you she would not have known! Who has done to Elizabeth and me the worse turn? And in the name of preventing war! *War!* You have made war upon *me!* Get out, get out!"

"Your—"

"Get out! I never want to see you again! If I am in hell, let there be one less demon!"

Lambert slipped from her monitor to run down the corridor. Culhane flew from the room; behind him the sound of something heavy struck the door. Culhane slumped against it, his face pasty around his cheek dye. Almost Lambert could find it in herself to pity him. Almost.

She said softly, "I told you so."

"She's like a wild thing."

"You knew she could be. It's documented enough, Culhane. I've put a suicide watch on her."

"Yes. Good. I . . . she was like a wild thing."

Lambert peered at him. "You still want her! After that!"

That sobered him; he straightened and looked at her coldly. "She is a Holy Hostage, Lambert."

"I remember that. Do you?"

"Don't insult me, Intern."

He moved angrily away; she caught his sleeve. "Culhane—don't be angry. I only meant that the sixteenth century was so different from our own, but s—"

"Do you think I don't know that? I was doing historical research while you were learning to read, Lambert. Don't instruct *me*."

He stalked off. Lambert bit down hard on her own fury and stared at Anne Boleyn's closed door. No sound came from behind it. To the soundless door she finished her sentence: "—but some traps don't change."

The door didn't answer. Lambert shrugged. It had nothing to do with her. She didn't care what happened to Anne Boleyn, in this century or that other one. Or to Culhane, either. Why should she? There were other men. She was no Henry VIII, to bring down her world for passion. What was the good of being a time researcher, if you could not even learn from times past?

She leaned thoughtfully against the door, trying to remember the name of the beautiful boy in her Orientation lecture, the one with the violet eyes.

She was still there, thinking, when Toshio Brill called a staff meeting to announce, his voice stiff with anger, that Her Holiness of the Church of the Holy Hostage had filed a motion with the All-World Forum that the Time Research Institute, because of the essentially reverent nature of the time-rescue program, be removed from administration by the Forum and placed instead under the direct control of the Church.

She had to think. It was important to think, as she had thought through her denial of Henry's ardor, and her actions when that ardor waned. Thought was all.

She could not return to her London, to Elizabeth. They had told her that. But did she know beyond doubt that it was true?

Anne left her apartments. At the top of the stairs she usually took to the garden she instead turned and opened another door. It opened easily. She walked along a different corridor. Apparently even now no one was going to stop her.

And if they did, what could they do to her? They did not use the scaffold or the rack; she had determined this from talking to that oaf Culhane and that huge ungainly woman, Lady Mary Lambert. They did not believe in violence, in punishment, in death. (How could you not believe in death? Even *they* must one day die.) The most they could do to her was shut her up in her rooms, and there the female pope would come to see she was well-treated.

Essentially they were powerless.

The corridor was lined with doors, most set with small windows. She peered in: rooms with desks and machines, rooms without desks and machines, rooms with people seated around a table talking, kitchens, still rooms. No one stopped her. At the end of the corridor she came to a room without a window and tried the door. It was locked, but as she stood there, her hand still on the knob, the door opened from within.

"Lady Anne! Oh!"

Could no one in this accursed place get her name right? The woman who stood there was clearly a servant, although she wore the same ugly gray-green tunic as everyone else. Perhaps, like Lady Mary, she was really an apprentice. She was of no interest, but behind her was the last thing Anne expected to see in this place: a child.

She pushed past the servant and entered the room. It was a little boy, his dress strange but clearly a uniform of some sort. He had dark eyes, curling dark hair, a bright smile. How old? Perhaps four. There was an air about him that was unmistakable; she would have wagered her life this child was royal.

"Who are you, little one?"

He answered her with an outpouring of a language she did not know. The servant scrambled to some device on the wall; in a moment Culhane stood before her.

"You said you didn't want to see me, Your Grace. But I was closest to answer Kiti's summons. . . ."

Anne looked at him. It seemed to her that she looked clear through him, to all that he was: desire, and pride of his pitiful strange learning, and smugness of his holy mission that had brought her life to wreck. Hers, and perhaps Elizabeth's as well. She saw Culhane's conviction, shared by Lord Director Brill and even by such as Lady Mary, that what they did was right because they did it. She knew that look well: it had been Cardinal Wolsey's, Henry's right-hand man and Chancellor of England, the man who had advised Henry to separate Anne from Harry Percy. And advised Henry against marrying her. Until she, Anne Boleyn, upstart Tom Boleyn's powerless daughter, had turned Henry against Wolsey and had the cardinal brought to trial. *She.*

In that minute, she made her decision.

"I was wrong, Master Culhane. I spoke in anger. Forgive me." She smiled, and held out her hand, and she had the satisfaction of watching Culhane turn color.

How old was he? Not in his first youth. But neither had Henry been.

He said, "Of course, Your Grace. Kiti said you talked to the tsarevich."

She made a face, still smiling at him. She had often mocked Henry thus. Even Harry Percy, so long ago, a lifetime ago . . . No. Two lifetimes ago. "The what?"

"The tsarevich." He indicated the child.

Was the dye on his face permanent, or would it wash off?

She said, not asking, "He is another time hostage. He, too, in his small person, prevents a war."

Culhane nodded, clearly unsure of her mood. Anne looked wonderingly at the child, then winningly at Culhane. "I would have you tell me about him. What language does he speak? Who is he?"

"Russian. He is—was—the future emperor. He suffers from a terrible disease: you called it the bleeding sickness. Because his mother the empress was so driven with worry over him, she fell under the influence of a holy man who led her to make some disastrous decisions while she was acting for her husband the emperor, who was away at war."

Anne said, "And the bad decisions brought about another war."

"They made more bloody than necessary a major rebellion."

"You prevent rebellions as well as wars? Rebellions against a monarchy?"

"Yes, it—history did not go in the direction of monarchies."

That made little sense. How could history go other than in the direction of those who were divinely anointed, those who held the power? Royalty won. In the end, they always won.

But there could be many casualties before the end.

She said, with that combination of liquid dark gaze and aloof body that had so intrigued Henry—and Norris, and Wyatt, and even presumptuous Mark Smeaton, God damn his soul—"I find I wish to know more about this child and his country's history. Will you tell me?"

"Yes," Culhane said. She caught the nature of his smile: relieved, still uncertain how far he had been forgiven, eager to find out. Familiar, all so familiar.

She was careful not to let her body touch his as they passed through the doorway. But she went first, so he would catch the smell of her hair.

"Master Culhane—you are listed on the demon machine as 'M. Culhane.'"

"The . . . oh, the computer. I didn't know you ever looked at one."

"I did. Through a window."

"It's not a demon, Your Grace."

She let the words pass; what did she care what it was? But his tone told her something. He liked reassuring her. In this world where women did the same work as men and female bodies were to be seen uncovered in the exercise yard so often that even turning your head to look must become a bore, this oaf nonetheless liked reassuring her.

She said, "What does the 'M' mean?"

He smiled. "Michael. Why?"

As the door closed, the captive royal child began once more to wail.

Anne smiled, too. "An idle fancy. I wondered if it stood for Mark."

"What argument has the Church filed with the All-World Forum?" a senior researcher asked.

Brill said irritably, as if it were an answer, "Where is Mahjoub?" Lambert spoke up promptly. "He is with Helen of Troy, Director, and the doctor. The queen had another seizure last night." Enzio Mahjoub was the unfortunate Project Head for their last time rescue.

Brill ran his hand over the back of his neck. His skull needed shaving, and his cheek dye was sloppily applied. He said, "Then we will begin without Mahjoub. The argument of Her Holiness is that the primary function of this Institute is no longer pure time research, but practical application, and that the primary practical application is time rescue. As such, we exist to take hostages, and thus should come under direct control of the Church of the Holy Hostage. Her secondary argument is that the time hostages are not receiving treatment up to intersystem standards as specified by the All-World Accord of 2154."

Lambert's eyes darted around the room. Cassia Kohambu, Project Head for the Institute's greatest success, sat up straight, looking outraged. "Our hostages aren't—on what are these charges allegedly based?"

Brill said, "No formal charges as yet. Instead, she has requested an investigation. She claims we have hundreds of potential hostages pinpointed by the Rahvoli equations, and the ones we have chosen do not meet standards for either internal psychic stability or benefit accrued to the hostages themselves, as specified in the All-World Accord. We have chosen to please ourselves, with flagrant disregard for the welfare of the hostages."

"Flagrant disregard!" It was Culhane, already on his feet. Beneath the face dye his cheeks flamed. Lambert eyed him carefully. "How can Her Holiness charge flagrant disregard when without us the Tsarevich Alexis would have been in constant pain from hemophiliac episodes, Queen Helen would have been abducted and raped, Herr Hitler blown up in an underground bunker, and Queen Anne Boleyn beheaded!"

Brill said bluntly, "Because the tsarevich cries constantly for his mother, the Lady Helen is mad, and Mistress Boleyn tells the Church she has been made war upon!"

Well, Lambert thought, that still left Herr Hitler. She was just as appalled as anyone at Her Holiness's charges, but Culhane had clearly violated both good manners and good sense. Brill never appreciated being upstaged.

Brill continued, "An investigative committee from the All-World

Forum will arrive here next month. It will be small: Delegates
Soshiru, Vlakhav, and Tullio. In three days the Institute staff will
meet again at 0700, and by that time I want each project group
to have prepared an argument in favor of the hostage you hold.
Use the prepermit justifications, including all the mathematical
models, but go far beyond that in documenting benefits to the
hostages themselves since they arrived here. Are there any questions?"

Only one, Lambert thought. She stood. "Director—were the
three delegates who will investigate us chosen by the All-World
Forum or requested by Her Holiness? To whom do they already
owe their allegiance?"

Brill looked annoyed. He said austerely, "I think we can rely
upon the All-World delegates to file a fair report, Intern Lambert,"
and Lambert lowered her eyes. Evidently she still had much to
learn. The question should not have been asked aloud.

Would Mistress Boleyn have known that?

Anne took the hand of the little boy. "Come, Alexis," she
said. "We walk now."

The prince looked up at her. How handsome he was, with his
thick curling hair and beautiful eyes almost as dark as her own. If
she had given Henry such a child. . . . She pushed the thought away.
She spoke to Alexis in her rudimentary Russian, without using the
translator box hung like a peculiarly ugly pendant around her neck.
He answered with a stream of words she couldn't follow, and she
waited for the box to translate.

"Why should we walk? I like it here in the garden."

"The garden is very beautiful," Anne agreed. "But I have something interesting to show you."

Alexis trotted beside her obediently then. It had not been hard
to win his trust—had no one here ever passed time with children?
Wash off the scary cheek paint, play for him songs on the lute—an
instrument he could understand, not like the terrifying sounds coming without musicians from yet another box—learn a few phrases
of his language. She had always been good at languages.

Anne led the child through the far gate of the walled garden,
into the yard. Machinery hummed; naked men and women "exer-
cised" together on the grass. Alexis watched them curiously, but
Anne ignored them. Servants. Her long full skirts, tawny silk, trailed
on the ground.

At the far end of the yard she started down the short path to that other gate, the one that ended at nothing.

Queen Isabella of Spain, Henry had told Anne once, had sent an expedition of sailors to circumnavigate the globe. They were supposed to find a faster way to India. They had not done so, but neither had they fallen off the edge of the world, which many had prophesied for them. Anne had not shown much interest in the story, because Isabella had after all been Catherine's mother. The edge of the world.

The gate ended with a wall of nothing. Nothing to see, or smell, or taste—Anne had tried. To the touch the wall was solid enough, and faintly tingly. A "force field," Culhane said. Out of time as we experience it; out of space. The gate, one of three, led to a place called Upper Slib, in what had once been Egypt.

Anne lifted Alexis. He was heavier than even a month ago; since she had been attending him every day, he had begun to eat better, play more, cease crying for his mother. Except at night. "Look, Alexis, a gate. Touch it."

The little boy did, then drew back his hand at the tingling. Anne laughed, and after a moment Alexis laughed, too.

The alarms sounded.

"Why, Your Grace?" Culhane said. "Why *again?*"

"I wished to see if the gate was unlocked," Anne said coolly. "We both wished to see." This was a lie. She knew it—did he? Not yet, perhaps.

"I told you, Your Grace, it is not a gate that can be left locked or unlocked, as you understand the terms. It must be activated by the stasis square."

"Then do so; the prince and I wish for an outing."

Culhane's eyes darkened; each time, he was in more anguish. And each time, he came running. However much he might wish to avoid her, commanding his henchmen to talk to her most of the time, he must come when there was an emergency because he was her gaoler, appointed by Lord Brill. So much had Anne discovered in a month of careful trials. He said now, "I told you, Your Grace, you can't move past the force field, no more than I could move into your palace at Greenwich. In the time stream beyond that gate—*my* time stream—you don't exist. The second you crossed the force field you'd disintegrate into nothingness."

Nothingness again. To Alexis she said sadly in Russian, "He will never let us out. Never, never."

The child began to cry. Anne held him closer, looking reproach-fully at Culhane, who was shifting toward anger. She caught him just before the shift was complete, befuddling him with un-looked-for wistfulness: "It is just that there is so little we can do here, in this time where we do not belong. You can understand that, can you not, Master Culhane? Would it not be the same for you, in my Court of England?"

Emotions warred on his face. Anne put her free hand gently on his arm. He looked down: the long slim fingers with their delicate tendons, the tawny silk against his drab uniform. He choked out, "Anything in my power, anything within the rules, Your Grace . . ."

She had not yet gotten him to blurt out "Anne," as he had the day she'd thrown a candlestick after him at the door.

She removed her hand, shifted the sobbing child against her neck, spoke so softly he could not hear her.

He leaned forward, toward her. "What did you say, Your Grace?"

"Would you come again tonight to accompany my lute on your guitar? For Alexis and me?"

Culhane stepped back. His eyes looked trapped.

"Please, Master Culhane?"

Culhane nodded.

Lambert stared at the monitor. It showed the hospital suite, barred windows and low white pallets, where Helen of Troy was housed. The queen sat quiescent on the floor, as she usually did, except for the brief and terrifying periods when she erupted, shriek-ing and tearing at her incredible hair. There had never been a single coherent word in the eruptions, not since the first moment Helen had awoken as hostage and had been told where she was, and why. Since that day Queen Helen had never responded in the slightest to anything said to her. Or maybe that fragile mind, already quiver-ing under the strain of her affair with Paris, had snapped too com-pletely to even hear them. Helen, Lambert thought, was no Anne Boleyn.

Anne sat close to the mad Greek queen, her silk skirts overlap-ping Helen's white tunic, her slender body leaning so far forward that her hair, too, mingled with Helen's, straight black waterfall with masses of springing black curls. Before she could stop herself, Lambert had run her hand over her own shaved head.

What was Mistress Anne trying to say to Helen? The words were too low for the microphones to pick up, and the double curtain of hair hid Anne's lips. Yet Lambert was as certain as death that Anne was talking. And Helen, quiescent—was she nonetheless hearing? What could it matter if she *were*, words in a tongue that from her point of view would not exist for another two millennia?

Yet the Boleyn woman visited her every day, right after she left the tsarevich. How good was Anne, from a time almost as barbaric as Helen's own, at nonverbal coercion of the crazed?

Culhane entered, glanced at the monitor, and winced.

Lambert said levelly, "You're a fool, Culhane."

He didn't answer.

"You go whenever she summons. You—"

He suddenly strode across the room, two strides at a time. Grabbing Lambert, he pulled her from her chair and yanked her to her feet. For an astonished moment she thought he was actually going to hit her—two researchers *hitting* each other. She tensed to slug him back. But abruptly he dropped her, giving a little shove so that she tumbled gracelessly back into her chair.

"You feel like a fat stone."

Lambert stared at him. Indifferently, he activated his own console and began work. Something rose in her, so cold the vertebrae of her back felt fused in ice. Stiffly she rose from the chair, left the room, and walked along the corridor.

A fat stone. Heavy, stolid yet doughy, the flesh yielding like a slug, or a maggot. Bulky, without grace, without beauty, almost without individuality, as stones were all alike. A fat stone.

Anne Boleyn was just leaving Helen's chamber. In the corridor, back to the monitor, Lambert faced her. Her voice was low, like a subterranean growl. "Leave him alone."

Anne looked at her coolly. She did not ask whom Lambert meant.

"Don't you know you are watched every minute? That you can't so much as use your chamber pot without being taped? How do you ever expect to get him to your bed? Or to do anything with poor Helen?"

Anne's eyes widened. She said loudly, "Even when I use the chamber pot? Watched? Have I not even the privacy of the beasts in the field?"

Lambert clenched her fists. Anne was acting. Someone had already told her, or she had guessed, about the surveillance. Lambert could *see* that she was acting—but not *why*.

A part of her mind noted coolly that she had never wanted to kill anyone before. So this, finally, was what it felt like, all those emotions she had researched throughout time: fury and jealousy and the desire to destroy. The emotions that started wars.

Anne cried, even more loudly, "I had been better had you never told me!" and rushed toward her own apartments.

Lambert walked slowly back to her work area, a fat stone.

Anne lay on the grass between the two massive power generators. It was a poor excuse for grass; although green enough, it had no smell. No dew formed on it, not even at night. Culhane had explained that it was bred to withstand disease, and that no dew formed because the air had little moisture. He explained, too, that the night was as man-bred as the grass; there was no natural night here. Henry would have been highly interested in such things; she was not. But she listened carefully, as she listened to everything Michael said.

She lay completely still, waiting. Eventually the head of a researcher thrust around the corner of the towering machinery: a purposeful thrust. "Your Grace? What are you doing?"

Anne did not answer. Getting to her feet, she walked back toward the castle. The place between the generators was no good: the woman had already known where Anne was.

The three delegates from the All-World Forum arrived at the Time Research Institute looking apprehensive. Lambert could understand this; for those who had never left their own time-space continuum, it probably seemed significant to step through a force field to a place that did not exist in any accepted sense of the word. The delegates looked at the ground, and inspected the facilities, and asked the same kinds of questions visitors always asked, before they settled down to actually investigate anything.

They were given an hour's overview of the time-rescue program, presented by the director himself. Lambert, who had not helped write this, listened to the careful sentiments about the prevention of war, the nobility of hostages, the deep understanding the Time Research Institute held of the All-World Accord of 2154, the altruistic extension of the Holy Mission of Peace into other time streams. Brill then moved on to discuss the four time-hostages, dwelling heavily on the first. In the four years since Herr Hitler had become a hostage, the National Socialist Party had all but collapsed in Germany. President Paul von Hindenburg had died on schedule, and the new moderate chancellors were slowly bringing order to Germany. The economy was still very bad and unrest was widespread, but no one was arresting Jews or gypsies or homosexuals or Jehovah's Witnesses or . . . Lambert stopped listening. The delegates knew all this. The entire solar system knew all this. Hitler had been a tremendous popular success as a hostage, the reason the Institute had obtained permits for the next three. Herr Hitler was kept in his locked suite, where he spent his time reading power-fantasy novels whose authors had not been born when the bunker under Berlin was detonated.

"Very impressive, Director," Goro Soshiru said. He was small, thin, elongated, a typical free-fall Spacer, with a sharp mind and a reputation for incorruptibility. "May we now talk to the hostages, one at a time?"

"Without any monitors. That is our instruction," said Anna Vlakhav. She was the senior member of the investigative team, a sleek, gray Chinese who refused all augments. Her left hand, Lambert noticed, trembled constantly. She belonged to the All-World Forum's Inner Council and had once been a hostage herself for three years.

"Please," Soren Tullio smiled. He was young, handsome, very wealthy. Disposable, added by the Forum to fill out the committee, with few recorded views of his own. Insomuch as they existed, however, they were not tinged with any bias toward the Church. Her Holiness had not succeeded in naming the members of the investigative committee—if indeed she had tried.

"Certainly," Brill said. "We've set aside the private conference room for your use. As specified by the Church, it is a sanctuary: there are no monitors of any kind. I would recommend, however, that you allow the bodyguard to remain with Herr Hitler, although of course you will make up your own minds."

Delegate Vlakhav said, "The bodyguard may stay. Herr Hitler is not our concern here."

Surprise, Lambert thought. Guess who *is?*

The delegates kept Hitler only ten minutes, the catatonic Helen only three. They said the queen did not speak. They talked to the little tsarevich a half hour. They kept Anne Boleyn in the sanctuary/conference room four hours and twenty-three minutes.

She came out calm, blank-faced, and proceeded to her own apartments. Behind her the three delegates were tight-lipped and silent. Anna Vlakhav, the former hostage, said to Toshio Brill, "We have no comment at this time. You will be informed."

Brill's eyes narrowed. He said nothing.

The next day, Director Toshio Brill was subpoenaed to appear before the All-World Forum on the gravest of all charges: mistreating Holy Hostages detained to keep Peace. The tribunal would consist of the full Inner Council of the All-World Forum. Since Director Brill had the right to confront those who accused him, the investigation would be held at the Time Research Institute.

How, Lambert wondered? They would not take her unsupported word. How had the woman done it?

She said to Culhane, "The delegates evidently make no distinction between political hostages on our own world and time hostages snatched from shadowy parallel ones."

"Why should they?" coldly said Culhane. The idealist. And where had it brought him?

Lambert was assigned that night to monitor the tsarevich, who was asleep in his crib. She sat in her office, her screen turned to Anne Boleyn's chambers, watching her play on the lute and sing softly to herself the songs written for her by Henry VIII when his passion was new and fresh, six hundred years before.

Anne sat embroidering a sleeve cover of cinnamon velvet. In strands of black silk she worked intertwined H and A: Henry and Anne. Let their spying machines make of that what they would.

The door opened, and without permission, Culhane entered. He stood by her chair and looked down into her face. "Why, Anne? Why?"

She laughed. He had finally called her by her Christian name. Now, when it could not possibly matter.

When he saw that she would not answer, his manner grew formal. "A lawyer has been assigned to you. He arrives tomorrow."

A lawyer. Thomas Cromwell had been a lawyer, and Sir Thomas More. Dead, both of them, at Henry's hand. So had Master Culhane told her, and yet he still believed that protection was afforded by the law.

"The lawyer will review all the monitor records. What you did, what you said, every minute."

She smiled at him mockingly. "Why tell me this now?"

"It is your right to know."

"And you are concerned with rights. Almost as much as with death." She knotted the end of her thread and cut it. "How is it that you command so many machines and yet do not command the knowledge that every man must die?"

"We know that," Culhane said evenly. His desire for her had at last been killed; she could feel its absence, like an empty well. The use of her name had been but the last drop of living water. "But we try to prevent death when we can."

"Ah, but you *can't*. 'Prevent death'—as if it were a fever! You can only postpone it, Master Culhane, and you never even ask if that is worth doing."

"I only came to tell you about the lawyer," Culhane said stiffly. "Good night, Mistress Boleyn."

"Good night, Michael," she said, and started to laugh. She was still laughing when the door closed behind him.

The Hall of Time, designed to hold three hundred, was packed.

Lambert remembered the day she had given the Orientation lecture to the history candidates, among them what's-his-name of the violet eyes. Twenty young people huddled together against horror in the middle of squares, virtual and simulated, but not really present. Today the squares were absent and the middle of the floor was empty, while all four sides were lined ten-deep with All-World Inner Council members on high polished benches, archbishops and lamas and shamans of the Church of the Holy Hostage, and reporters from every major newsgrid in the solar system. Her Holiness the High Priest sat among her followers, pretending she wanted to be inconspicuous. Toshio Brill sat in a chair alone, facing the current Premier of the All-World Council, Dagar Krenya of Mars.

Anne Boleyn was led to a seat. She walked with her head high, her long black skirts sweeping the floor.

Lambert remembered that Anne had worn black to her trial for treason, in 1536.

"This investigation will begin," Premier Krenya said. He wore his hair to his shoulders; fashions must have changed again on Mars. Lambert looked at the shaved heads of her colleagues, at the long loose black hair of Anne Boleyn. To Culhane, seated beside her, she whispered, "We'll be growing our hair again soon." He looked at her as if she were crazy.

It *was* a kind of crazy, to live everything twice: once in research, once in the flesh. Did it seem so to Anne Boleyn? Lambert knew her frivolity was misplaced, and she thought of the frivolity of Anne in the Tower, awaiting execution: "They will have no trouble finding a name for me. I shall be Queen Anne Lackhead." At the memory, Lambert's hatred burst out fresh. She had the memory, and now Anne never would. But in bequeathing it forward in time to Lambert, the memory had become secondhand. That was Anne Boleyn's real crime, for which she would never be tried: She had made this whole proceeding, so important to Lambert and Brill and Culhane, a mere reenactment. Prescripted. Secondhand. She had robbed them of their own, unused time.

Krenya said, "The charges are as follows: That the Time Research Institute has mistreated the Holy Hostage Anne Boleyn, held hostage against war. Three counts of mistreatment are under consideration this day: First, that researchers willfully increased a hostage's mental anguish by dwelling on the pain of those left behind by the hostage's confinement, and on those aspects of confinement that cause emotional unease. Second, that researchers failed to choose a hostage that would truly prevent war. Third, that researchers willfully used a hostage for sexual gratification."

Lambert felt herself go very still. Beside her, Culhane rose to his feet, then sat down again slowly, his face rigid. Was it possible he had . . . no. He had been infatuated, but not to the extent of throwing away his career. He was not Henry, any more than she had been over *him*.

The spectators buzzed, an uneven sound like malfunctioning equipment. Krenya rapped for order. "Director Brill — how do you answer these charges?"

"False, Premier. Every one."

"Then let us hear the evidence against the Institute."

Anne Boleyn was called. She took the chair in which Brill had been sitting. "*She made an entry as though she were going to a great triumph and sat down with elegance*" . . . but that was the other time, the *first* time. Lambert groped for Culhane's hand. It felt limp.

"Mistress Boleyn," Krenya said — he had evidently not been told that she insisted on being addressed as a queen, and the omission gave Lambert a mean pleasure — "In what ways was your anguish willfully increased by researchers at this Institute?"

Anne held out her hand. To Lambert's astonishment, her lawyer put into it a lute. At an official All-World Forum investigation — a *lute*. Anne began to play, the tune high and plaintive. Her unbound

black hair fell forward; her slight body made a poignant contrast
to the torment in the words:

> *Defiled is my name, full sore,*
> *Through cruel spite and false report,*
> *That I may say forever more,*
> *Farewell to joy, adieu comfort.*
>
> *O death, rock me asleep,*
> *Bring on my quiet rest,*
> *Let pass my very guiltless ghost*
> *Out of my careful breast.*
>
> *Ring out the doleful knell,*
> *Let its sound my death tell,*
> *For I must die,*
> *There is no remedy,*
> *For now I die!*

The last notes faded. Anne looked directly at Krenya. "I wrote that,
my Lords, in my other life. Master Culhane of this place played
it for me, along with death songs written by my . . . my brother. . . ."

"Mistress Boleyn . . ."

"No, I recover myself. George's death tune was hard for me to
hear, my Lords. Accused and condemned because of *me*, who
always loved him well."

Krenya said to the lawyer whose staff had spent a month review-
ing every moment of monitor records, "Culhane made her listen
to these?"

"Yes," the lawyer said. Beside Lambert, Culhane sat unmoving.

"Go on," Krenya said to Anne.

"He told me that I was made to suffer watching the men accused with me die. How I was led to a window overlooking the
block, how my brother George knelt, putting his head on the block,
how the ax was raised—" She stopped, shuddering. A murmur ran
over the room. It sounded like cruelty, Lambert thought—but
whose?

"Worst of all, my Lords," Anne said, "was that I was told I had
bastardized my own child. I chose to sign a paper declaring no valid
marriage had ever existed because I had been precontracted to Sir
Henry Percy, so my daughter Elizabeth was illegitimate and thus
barred from her throne. I was taunted with the fact that I had done

this, ruining the prospects of my own child. He said it over and over, Master Culhane did. . . ."

Krenya said to the lawyer, "Is this in the visuals?"

"Yes."

Krenya turned back to Anne. "But, Mistress Boleyn—these are things that, because of your time rescue, did *not* happen. *Will* not happen, in your time stream. How can they thus increase your anguish for relatives left behind?"

Anne stood. She took one step forward, then stopped. Her voice was low and passionate. "My good Lord—do you not understand? It is because you took me here that these things did not happen. Left to my own time, I *would have been responsible for them all.* For my brother's death, for the other four brave men, for my daughter's bastardization, for the torment in my own music . . . I have escaped them only because of *you.* To tell me them in such detail, not the mere provision of facts that I myself requested but agonizing detail of mind and heart—is to tell me that *I* alone, in my own character, am evil, giving pain to those I love most. And that in this time stream you have brought me to, I *did* these things, felt them, feel them still. You have made me guilty of them. My Lord Premier, have you ever been a hostage yourself? Do you know, or can you imagine, the torment that comes from imagining the grief of those who love you? And to know you have *caused* this grief, not merely loss but death, blood, the pain of disinheritance— that you have caused it, and are now being told of the anguish you cause? Told over and over? In words, in song even—can you imagine what that feels like to one such as I, who cannot return at will and comfort those hurt by my actions?"

The room was silent. Who, Lambert wondered, had told Anne Boleyn that Premier Krenya had once served as Holy Hostage?

"Forgive me, my Lords," Anne said dully, "I forget myself."

"Your testimony may take whatever form you choose," Krenya said, and it seemed to Lambert that there were shades and depths in his voice.

The questioning continued. A researcher, said Anne, had taunted her with being spied on even at her chamber pot—Lambert leaned slowly forward—which had made Anne cry out, "I had been better had you never told me!" Since then, modesty had made her reluctant to even answer nature, "so that there is every hour a most wretched twisting and churning in my bowels."

Asked why she thought the Institute had chosen the wrong hostage, Anne said she had been told so by my Lord Brill. The room exploded into sound, and Krenya rapped for quiet. "That visual now, please." On a square created in the center of the room, the visuals replayed on three sides:

"*My Lord Brill . . . Was there no other person you could take but I to prevent this war you say is a hundred years off? This civil war in England?*"

"*The mathematics identified you as the best hostage, Your Grace.*"

"*The best? Best for what, my Lord? If you had taken Henry himself, then he could not have issued the Act of Supremacy. His supposed death would have served the purpose as well as mine.*"

"*Yes. But for Henry VIII to disappear from history while his heir is but a month old. . . . We did not know if that might not have started a civil war in itself. Between the factions supporting Elizabeth and those for Queen Catherine, who was still alive.*"

"*What did your mathematical learning tell you?*"

"*That it probably would not,*" Brill said.

"*And yet choosing me instead of Henry left him free to behead yet another wife, as you yourself have told me, my cousin Catherine Howard!*"

Brill shifted on his chair. "*That is true, Your Grace.*"

"*Then why not Henry instead of me?*"

"*I'm afraid Your Grace does not have sufficient grasp of the science of probabilities for me to explain, Your Grace.*"

Anne was silent. Finally she said, "*I think that the probability is that you would find it easier to deal with a deposed woman than with Henry of England, whom no man can withstand in either a passion or a temper.*"

Brill did not answer. The visual rolled—ten seconds, fifteen—and he did not answer.

"Mr. Premier," Brill said in a choked voice, "Mr. Premier—"

"You will have time to address these issues soon, Mr. Director," Krenya said. "Mistress Boleyn, this third charge—sexual abuse—"

The term had not existed in the sixteenth century, thought Lambert. Yet Anne understood it. She said, "I was frightened, my Lord, by the strangeness of this place. I was afraid for my life. I didn't know then that a woman may refuse those in power, may—"

"That is why sexual contact with hostages is universally forbidden," Krenya said. "Tell us what you think happened."

Not what did happen—what you *think* happened. Lambert took heart.

Anne said, "Master Culhane bade me meet him at a place . . . it is a small alcove beside a short flight of stairs near the kitchens. . . . He bade me meet him there at night. Frightened, I went."

"Visuals," Krenya said in a tight voice.

The virtual square reappeared. Anne, in the same white nightdress in which she had been taken hostage, crept from her chamber, along the corridor, her body heat registering in infrared. Down the stairs, around to the kitchens, into the cubbyhole formed by the flight of steps, themselves oddly angled as if they had been added, or altered, after the main structure was built, after the monitoring system installed . . . Anne dropped to her knees and crept forward beside the isolated stairs. And disappeared.

Lambert gasped. A time hostage was under constant surveillance, that was a basic condition of their permit, there was no way the Boleyn bitch could escape constant monitoring. But she had.

"Master Culhane was already there," Anne said in a dull voice. "He . . . he used me ill there."

The room was awash with sound. Krenya said over it, "Mistress Boleyn—there is no visual evidence that Master Culhane was there. He has sworn he was not. Can you offer any proof that he met you there? Anything at all?"

"Yes. Two arguments, my Lord. First: How would I know there were not spying devices in but this one hidden alcove? I did not design this castle; it is not mine."

Krenya's face showed nothing. "And the other argument?"

"I am pregnant with Master Culhane's child."

Pandemonium. Krenya rapped for order. When it was finally restored, he said to Brill, "Did you know of this?"

"No, I . . . it is a hostage's right by the Accord to refuse intrusive medical treatment . . . she has been healthy. . . ."

"Mistress Boleyn, you will be examined by a doctor immediately."

She nodded assent. Watching her, Lambert knew it was true. Anne Boleyn was pregnant, and had defeated herself thereby. But she did not know it yet.

Lambert fingered the knowledge, seeing it as a tangible thing, cold as steel.

"How do we know," Krenya said, "that you were not pregnant before you were taken hostage?"

"It was but a month after my daughter Elizabeth's birth, and I had the white leg. Ask one of your doctors if a woman would bed a man then. Ask a woman expert in the women of my time. Ask

Lady Mary Lambert."

Heads in the room turned; ask whom? Krenya said, "Ask whom?" An aide leaned toward him and whispered something. He said, "We will have her put on the witness list."

Anne said, "I carry Michael Culhane's child. I, who could not carry a prince for the king."

Krenya said, almost powerlessly, "That last has nothing to do with this investigation, Mistress Boleyn."

She only looked at him.

They called Brill to testify, and he threw up clouds of probability equations that did nothing to clarify the choice of Anne over Henry as Holy Hostage. Was the woman right? Had there been a staff meeting to choose between the candidates identified by the Rahvoli applications, and had someone said of two very close candidates, "We should think about the effect on the Institute as well as on history. . . ." Had someone been developing a master theory based on a percentage of women influencing history? Had someone had an infatuation with the period, and chosen by that what should be altered? Lambert would never know. She was an intern.

Had been an intern.

Culhane was called. He denied seducing Anne Boleyn. The songs on the lute, the descriptions of her brother's death, the bastardization of Elizabeth—all done to convince her that what she had been saved from was worse than where she had been saved to. Culhane felt so much that he made a poor witness, stumbling over his words, protesting too much.

Lambert was called. As neutrally as possible she said, "Yes, Mr. Premier, historical accounts show that Queen Anne was taken with white leg after Elizabeth's birth. It is a childbed illness. The legs swell up and ache painfully. It can last from a few weeks to months. We don't know how long it lasted—would have lasted—for Mistress Boleyn."

"And would a woman with this disease be inclined to sexual activity?"

" 'Inclined'—no."

"Thank you, Researcher Lambert."

Lambert returned to her seat. The committee next looked at visuals, hours of visuals—Culhane, flushed and tender, making a fool of himself with Anne. Anne with the little tsarevich, an exile trying to comfort a child torn from his mother. Helen of Troy, mad and pathetic. Brill, telling newsgrids around the solar system that the time-rescue program, savior of countless lives, was run strictly in conformance with the All-World Accord of 2154. And all the time, through all the visuals, Lambert waited for what was known to everyone in that room except Anne Boleyn: that she could not pull off in this century what she might have in Henry's. That the paternity of a child could be genotyped in the womb.

Who? Mark Smeaton, after all? Another miscarriage from Henry, precipitately gotten and unrecorded by history? Thomas Wyatt, her most faithful cousin and cavalier?

After the committee had satisfied itself that it had heard enough, everyone but Forum delegates was dismissed. Anne, Lambert saw, was led away by a doctor. Lambert smiled to herself. It was already over. The Boleyn was defeated.

The All-World Forum investigative committee deliberated for less than a day. Then it issued a statement: The child carried by Holy Hostage Anne Boleyn had not been sired by Researcher Michael Culhane. Its genotypes matched no one's at the Time Research Institute. The Institute, however, was guilty of two counts of hostage mistreatment. The Institute charter as an independent tax-exempt organization was revoked. Toshio Brill was released from his position, as were Project Head Michael Culhane and intern Mary Lambert. The Institute stewardship was reassigned to the Church of the Holy Hostage under the direct care of Her Holiness the High Priest.

Lambert slipped through the outside door to the walled garden. It was dusk. On a seat at the far end a figure sat, skirts spread wide, a darker shape against the dark wall. As Lambert approached, Anne looked up without surprise.

"Culhane's gone. I leave tomorrow. Neither of us will ever work in time research again."

Anne went on gazing upward. Those great dark eyes, that slim neck, so vulnerable . . . Lambert clasped her hands together hard.

"Why?" Lambert said. "Why do it all again? Last time use a king to bring down the power of the Church, this time use a Church to—before, at least you gained a crown. Why do it here, when you gain nothing?"

"You could have taken Henry. He deserved it; I did not."

"But we didn't take Henry!" Lambert shouted. "So why?"

Anne did not answer. She put out one hand to point behind her. Her sleeve fell away, and Lambert saw clearly the small sixth finger that had marked her as a witch. A tech came running across the half-lit garden. "Researcher Lambert—"

"What is it?"

"They want you inside. Everybody. The queen—the other one, Helen—she's killed herself."

The garden blurred, straightened. "How?"

"Stabbed with a silver sewing scissors hidden in her tunic. It was so quick, the researchers saw it on the monitor but couldn't get there in time."

"Tell them I'm coming."

Lambert looked at Anne Boleyn. "You did this."

Anne laughed. *This lady*, wrote the Tower constable, *hath much joy in death*. Anne said, "Lady Mary—every birth is a sentence of death. Your age has forgotten that."

"Helen didn't need to die yet. And the Time Research Institute didn't need to be dismantled—it *will* be dismantled. Completely. But somewhere, sometime, you *will* be punished for this. I'll see to that!"

"Punished, Lady Mary? And mayhap beheaded?"

Lambert looked at Anne: the magnificent black eyes, the sixth finger, the slim neck. Lambert said slowly, "You *want* your own death. As you had it before."

"What else did you leave me?" Anne Boleyn said. "Except the power to live the life that is mine?"

"You will never get it. We don't kill, here!"

Anne smiled. "Then how will you 'punish' me—'sometime, somehow'?"

Lambert didn't answer. She walked back across the walled garden, toward the looming walls gray in the dusk, toward the chamber where lay the other dead queen.

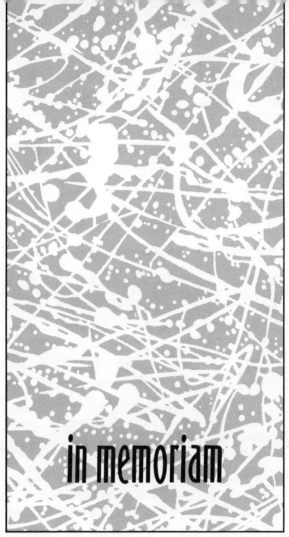

in memoriam

AS SOON AS Aaron followed me into the garden, I knew
he was angry. He pursed his mouth, that sweet exaggerated fullness
of lips that hadn't changed since he was two years old and that
looked silly on the middle-aged man he had become. But he said
nothing — in itself a sign of trouble. Oh, I knew him through and
through. As well as I knew his father, as well as his father had known
me.

Aaron closed the door behind us and walked to the lawn chairs,
skirting the tiny shrine as if it weren't there. He lowered himself

gingerly into a chair.

"Be careful," I said, pointlessly. "Your back again?"

He waved this remark away; even as a little boy he had hated to have attention called to any physical problem. A skinned knee, a stiff neck, a broken wrist. I remembered. I remembered everything.

"Coffee? A splash?"

"Coffee. Come closer, I don't want to shout. You don't have your hearing field on, do you?"

I didn't. I poured him his coffee from the lawn bar and floated my chair close enough to hand it to him. Next door, Todd came out of his house, dressed in shorts and carrying a trowel. He waved cheerfully.

"I know you don't want to hear this," Aaron began—he had never been one for small talk, never one for subtlety—"but I have to say it one more time. Listen to Dr. Lorsky about the operation."

"Sugar?"

"Black. Mom—"

"Be quiet," I said, and he looked startled enough, but his surprise wasn't followed by a scowl. Aaron, who always reacted to a direct order as if to assault. I sat up straighter and peered at him. No scowl.

He took a long, deliberate sip of coffee, which was too hot for long sips. "Is there a reason you won't listen to Dr. Lorsky? A real, rational reason?" He didn't look at the shrine.

"You know the reason," I said. Thirty feet away in his side yard, Todd began to weed his flower beds, digging out the most stubborn weeds with the trowel, pulling the rest by hand. He never used a power hoe. The flowers, snapdragons and yarrow and azaleas and lemondrop marigolds, crowded together in the brief hot riot of midsummer.

Aaron waggled his fingers at the shrine he still wouldn't see. "That's not a reason!"

He was right, of course—the shrine was effect, not cause. I smiled at his perceptiveness, unable to help the sly, silly glow of a maternal pride thirty years out of date. But Aaron took the smile for something else: acquiescence, perhaps, or weakening. He put his cup on the grass and leaned forward. Earnestly—he had been such an earnest little boy, unsmiling in the face of jokes he didn't understand, putting his toys away in the exact same spots each night, presenting his teenage demands in carefully numbered lists, lecturing the other boys on their routine childish brutality.

A prig, actually.

"Mom, listen to me. I'm asking you to reconsider. That's all. For three reasons. First, because it's getting dangerous for you to live out here all alone. Despite the electronic surveillance. What if you were robbed?"

"Robbed," I said dryly. Aaron didn't catch it; I didn't really expect him to. He knew why I had bought this house, why I stayed in it. I said gently, "Your coffee's getting cold." He ignored me, pressing doggedly on, his hands gripping the arms of his chair. On the back of the left hand were two liver spots. When had that happened?

"*Second*, this business of ancestor worship or whatever it's supposed to be. This shrine. You never believed in this nonsense before. You raised me to think rationally, without superstition, and here you are planting flowers to your dead forebears unto the nth generation and meditating to them like you were some teenaged wirehead split-brain."

"We used to meditate a lot when I was a girl, before wireheads were invented," I said, to annoy him. His intensity was scaring me. "But Aaron, darling, that's not what I do here."

"What *do* you do?" he said, and immediately, I could see, regretted it. The shrine shone lustrous in the sunlight. It was a triptych of black slabs two feet high. In the late afternoon heat, the black neo-nitonol had softened into featurelessness, but when night fell, the names would again spring into hard-etched clarity. Hundreds of tiny names, engraved close together in meticulous script, linked with the lines of generation. At the base of the triptych bloomed low flowers: violets and forget-me-nots and rosemary.

"'There's rosemary, that's for remembrance,'" I said, but Aaron, being Aaron, didn't recognize Ophelia's line. Not a reader, my Aaron. Bytes, not books. Oh, I remembered.

In the other yard, Todd's trowel clunked as it hit a buried stone.

"It isn't healthy," Aaron said. "Shrines. Ancestor worship! And in the third place, time is running out for you to have the operation. I spoke to Dr. Lorsky yesterday—"

"You spoke to my doctor without my permission—"

"—and he said your temporal lobes still scan well, but he can't say how much longer that will be true. There's that cutoff point where the body just can't handle it anymore. And then the brain wipe wouldn't do you any good. It would be too late. Mom — you *know*."

I knew. The sheer weight of memory reached some critical mass. All those memories: the shade of blue of a dress worn fifty years ago, the tilt of the head of someone long dead, the sudden sharp smell of a grandmother's cabbage soup mingled with the dusty scent of an apartment razed for two decades. And each memory bringing on others, a rush of them, till the grandmother was there before you, whole. The burden and bulk of all those minute sensations over days and years and decades, triggering chemical changes in the brain, which in turn trigger cellular changes, until the body cannot bear any more and breakdown accelerates. The cutoff point. It is our memories that kill us.

Aaron groped with one hand for his coffee cup, beside his chair on the grass. The crow's-feet at the corners of his eyes were still tentative, like lines scratched in soft sand. He ducked his head and mumbled. "I just . . . I just don't want you to die, Mom."

I looked away. It is always, somehow, a surprise to find that an adult child still loves you.

Next door, Todd straightened from one flower bed and moved to the next. He pulled his shirt over his head and tossed it to the ground. Sweat gleamed on the muscles of his back, still hard and taut in his midthirties body. The shirt made a dark patch on the bright grass.

A bee buzzed up from the flowers around the black triptych and circled by my ear. Glad of the distraction, I waved it away.

"Aaron . . . I *can't*. I just can't. Be wiped."

"Even if you die for it? What point is there to that?"

I stayed silent. We had discussed it before, all of it, the whole dreary topic. But Aaron had never before looked like that. And he had never begged.

"Please, Mom. Please. You already get confused. Last week you thought that woman in the park was your dead sister. I know you're going to say it was just for a second, but that's the way it starts. Just for a second, then more and more, and then it's too late for the wipe. You say you wouldn't be 'you' anymore with a wipe — but if your memory goes and the body follows it, are you 'you' anyway? Feeble and senile? Are you still 'you' if you're dead?"

"That isn't the point," I began, but he must have seen on my face something that he thought was a softening, a wavering. He reached for my hand. His fingers were dry and hot.

"It *is* the point! Death is the point! Your body can't be made any younger, but it doesn't have to become any older. You *don't*. And you have the bodily strength, still, you have the money — Christ, it isn't as if you would be a vegetable. You'd still remember language, routines — and you'd make new memories, start over. A new life. *Life,* not death!"

I said nothing to that. Aaron could see the years of my life stretching behind me, years he wanted me to cut off as casually as paring a fingernail. He could not see the other, greater loss.

"You're wrong," I said, as gently as I could, and took my fingers from his. "I'm not refusing the wipe because I want death. I'm refusing it because too much of me has already died."

He stared at me with incomprehension. The bee I had waved away buzzed around his left ear. I saw his blue eyes flick to it and then back to me, refusing to be distracted. Linear thinking, always: was it growing up with all those computers? Such blue eyes, such a handsome man, still.

Next door Todd began to whistle. Aaron stiffened and half turned to look for the first time over his shoulder; he had not realized Todd was there. He looked back at me. His eyes shadowed and dropped, and in that tiny sideways slide — not at all linear — I knew. I suddenly knew.

He saw it. "Mom . . . Mother . . ."

"You're going to have the wipe."

He raised the coffee cup to his mouth and drank: an automatic covering gesture, the coffee must have been cold. Repulsive. Cold coffee is repulsive.

I folded my arms across my belly and leaned forward.

He said quietly, "My back is getting worse. The migraines are back, once or twice every week. Lorsky says I'm an old forty-two, you know how much people vary. I'm not the easy-living type who forgets easily. I take things hard, I don't forget, and I don't want to die."

I said nothing.

"Mom?"

I said nothing.

"Please understand . . . please." It came out in a whisper. I said nothing. Aaron put his cup on the table and eased himself from the chair, leaning heavily on its arm and webbed back. The movement attracted Todd's attention. I saw, past the bulk of Aaron's body, the moment Todd decided to walk over and be neighborly.

"Hello, Mrs. Kinnian. Aaron."

I watched Aaron's face clench. He turned slowly.

Todd said, "Hot, isn't it? I was away for a week and my weeds just ambushed everything."

"Sailing," Aaron said carefully.

"Yes, sailing," Todd said, faintly surprised. He wiped the sweat from his eyes. "Do you sail?"

"I did. Once. When I was a kid. My father used to take me."

"You should have kept it up. Great sport. Mrs. Kinnian, can I weed those flowers for you?"

He pointed to the black triptych. I said, "No, thank you, Todd. The gardener will be around tomorrow."

"Well, if you . . . all right. Take care."

He smiled at us: a handsome blue-eyed man in his prime, ruddy with health and exercise, his face as open and clear as a child's. Beside him, Aaron looked puffy, stiff, out of shape. The skin at the back of Aaron's neck formed ridges that worked up and down above his collar.

"Take care," I said to Todd. He walked back to his weeding. Aaron turned to me. I saw his eyes.

"I'm sorry, Mom. I am . . . sorry. But I'm going to have the wipe. I'm going to do it."

"To me."

"For me."

After that there was nothing else to say. I watched Aaron walk around the flowered shrine, open the door to the house, disappear in the cool interior. There was a brief hum from the air conditioner, cut off the moment the door closed. A second door slammed; Todd, too, had gone inside his house.

I realized that I had not asked Aaron when Dr. Lorsky would do the wipe. He might not have told me. He had already been stretched as far as he would go, pulled off center by emotion and imagination, neither of which he wanted. He had never been an imaginative child, only a practical one. Coming to me in the garden with his math homework, worried about fractions, unconcerned with the flowers blooming and dying around him. I remembered.

But *he* would not.

Todd came back outside, carrying a cold drink, and returned to weeding. I watched him awhile. I watched him an hour, two. I watched him after he had left and dusk began to fall over the garden. Then I struggled out of my chair—everything ached, I had been sitting too long—and picked some snapdragons. Purple, deepened by the shadows. I laid them in front of the black triptych.

When Todd and I had been married, I had carried roses: white with pink undertones at the tips of the petals, deep pink at the heart. I hadn't seen such roses in years. Maybe the strain wasn't grown anymore.

The script on the shrine had sprung out clear and hard. I touched it with one finger, tracing the names. Then I went into the house to watch TV. A brain-wipe clinic had been bombed. Elderly activists crowded in front of the camera, yelling and waving gnarled fists. They were led away by police, strong youthful men and women trying to get the old people to *behave* like old people. The unlined faces beneath their helmets looked bewildered. They *were* bewildered. Misunderstanding everything; believing that remembrance is death; getting it all backward. Trying to make us go away as if we didn't exist. As if we never had.